A Perfect Scandal

Also by Tina Gabrielle

Lady of Scandal

Published by Kensington Publishing Corporation

A Perfect Scandal

TINA GABRIELLE

ZEBRA BOOKS
KENSINGTON PUBLISHING CORP.
http://www.kensingtonbooks.com

ZEBRA BOOKS are published by

Kensington Publishing Corp.
119 West 40th Street
New York, NY 10018

All Kensington titles, imprints, and distributed lines are available at special quantity discounts for bulk purchases for sales promotion, premiums, fund-raising, educational, or institutional use.

Special book excerpts or customized printings can also be created to fit specific needs. For details, write or phone the office of the Kensington Special Sales Manager: Attn. Special Sales Department. Kensington Publishing Corp., 119 West 40th Street, New York, NY 10018. Phone: 1-800-221-2647.

ISBN-13: 978-1-4201-0849-1
ISBN-10: 1-4201-0849-2

First Printing: October 2010
10 9 8 7 6 5 4 3 2 1

Printed in the United States of America

Chapter 1

London, May 1814

"I've heard Lord Walling has depraved appetites in the bedroom."

Isabel Cameron's lips twitched at the words whispered into her ear by her close friend and fellow debutante, Charlotte Benning.

Isabel scanned the glittering ballroom, noting the magnificent chandeliers, the priceless artwork, and the crush of well-dressed people all vying amongst themselves for attention.

At Isabel's silence, Charlotte touched her arm. "What? Do not tell me that you of all people find such talk shocking?"

Isabel pushed a wayward dark curl off her shoulder and turned to Charlotte. "It's not the information that shocks me, but the thought of where you learned such private concerns regarding Lord Walling's bedroom antics. Have you been eavesdropping on your mother and her friends again?"

Charlotte chewed on her lower lip. "I cannot help myself. Those gossipers are an endless source of education."

Isabel glanced at Charlotte as her friend vigorously

fanned her red cheeks. Charlotte was a petite, slender girl with a wealth of frizzy blond hair and round blue eyes.

Charlotte leaned close, covered her lips with her fan, and lowered her voice. "They even said Lord Walling pays a woman in Cheapside to indulge his fancy."

Isabel couldn't control her burst of laugher. "I pity the woman forced to endure his attentions, paid or not."

"Speaking of the man," Charlotte said. "Your soon-to-be betrothed waddles toward you as we speak."

Waddles.

Isabel's humor vanished, and she frowned. Lord Walling was indeed waddling. A portly man with fleshy jowls and a sagging stomach, he had strands of thinning hair, which he parted on the side and combed over a growing patch of shiny scalp. At fifty-three years of age, he was thirty-three years her senior.

"Can you imagine him intimate with a woman?" Charlotte asked.

Isabel's gut clenched tight.

Charlotte reached out and grasped her hand. "Dear Lord, what will you do if you cannot persuade your father against the match?"

Bloody hell! Isabel thought. *What will I do?*

"I've tried speaking with my father," Isabel whispered urgently. "He's unrelenting on the subject and insists that at my age I should be suitably settled. I've even attempted to dissuade Lord Walling of the notion that I would make a good wife, but to no avail. It's clear he is keenly interested in my family's reputation, title, and wealth. I'm afraid I have to take matters into my own hands."

"Oh dear," Charlotte said. "Not again, Isabel."

Lord Walling walked forward, directly toward her, nodding when she met his stare. His beady brown eyes reminded her of a ferret she had once seen at a country fair.

Walling bowed stiffly as he stood before Isabel and

Charlotte. "Good evening, ladies. I trust you are enjoying Lady Holloway's ball."

"The evening is most entertaining, Lord Walling," Charlotte said.

He turned his attention to Isabel. "May I have the honor of the next dance, Lady Isabel?"

"I'm afraid I'm not feeling well tonight, Lord Walling, and would not be a suitable dance partner."

He looked at her in utter disbelief. "Oh? Your father told me that you had attended an exhibition at the Royal Academy of Arts just yesterday and that you were positively blooming."

"I found the art inspiring and must not have felt the effects of my illness until I arrived home."

"You shouldn't bother yourself with such artistic nonsense. A true lady, especially one of your age, should focus on domestic matters."

Charlotte took a quick sharp breath.

Isabel opened her mouth, then snapped it shut, stunned by his bluntness.

"My apologies, Lord Walling," Isabel said, finding her voice. "Perhaps another partner would be more willing."

"Should I tell your father to take you home, then?" he asked.

"No need to trouble yourself. My father is aware of my condition."

Lord Walling's lips thinned with irritation. "Nonsense. It is no trouble at all. I see the earl across the room, and we have much to discuss. I shall call upon you tomorrow then, Lady Isabel. I believe I have the earl's full approval on the matter," he said, a critical tone to his voice.

He bowed again and walked away.

"My goodness, Isabel. He's as persistent as a bloodhound during hunting season," Charlotte said.

"I fear he needs to marry for money. It's public knowledge

that his country estate cannot sustain his spending habits. Even knowing this, my father is insisting upon the match."

At twenty, both Isabel and Charlotte were fourth-year debutantes on the marriage mart. One more season to go and they would be official spinsters of unmarriageable age. While Charlotte sought a love match, Isabel wanted nothing more than to escape the marital web and return to Paris to live with her eccentric aunt and study her only true love—painting watercolors.

"I must be more creative in my efforts to dissuade him."

"As your best friend, Isabel, I implore you, please exercise more discretion than the last time," Charlotte pled.

Isabel looked away, uncomfortable with her friend's beseeching gaze.

It was then that she saw him. Two gentlemen had just set foot in the ballroom; both stood tall and straight and were dark-haired. Both were meticulously dressed in breeches and form-fitting double-breasted jackets. But whereas one carried himself with a commanding air of self-importance associated with the nobility, the other was shrouded in an air of isolation and aloofness.

It was the second man who captured her attention, the only one she knew—Marcus Hawksley. A childhood memory brought a wry, twisted smile to her face.

His profile was rugged, somber, and vaguely familiar. He was far from delicately handsome and effeminate as many of the dandies of the ton. His face was granitelike and striking, and his strong features held a raw sensuality, a smoldering dangerousness, which captivated her attention, and which she suspected women would secretly find deliciously appealing.

Hawksley's face was bronzed and his eyes sinfully dark. His black curling hair was cut short and gleamed in the candlelight from the chandeliers above. He was tall and muscularly built. Even from across the room, Isabel could see the rich outline of his shoulders straining against the fabric of his jacket.

There was a restless energy about his movements as if he did not want to be in the ballroom with these people and wanted to depart as soon as his obligations of attendance were satisfied.

"Marcus Hawksley is here," Isabel blurted out. "I haven't seen him in years."

Charlotte shrugged. "That's because he hasn't been to a public event in years. He was quite the rogue in his youth. But then came the *horrific* scandal when he reformed and entered trade by becoming a stockbroker in the London Stock Exchange. Mother insists that trade is considered worse than the plague amongst the upper classes. Even his father, the Earl of Ardmore, and his older brother and heir, want nothing to do with him."

Isabel's lips puckered with disgust. It was just like the *beau monde* to overlook a gentleman's roguish behavior—his drinking, gambling, and womanizing—but consider it unforgivable when the same man reformed himself by becoming a successful businessman. Isabel had never paid much attention to the scandals, but Charlotte, whose mother was a close friend of Lady Jersey, one of the powerful patronesses of Almack's, was obsessed with gossip.

"Who is he with?" Isabel asked.

"Lord Ravenspear, the handsome earl whose wife, Victoria, is increasing with child."

"I wonder why Marcus is here tonight," Isabel said.

"Lady Holloway is his godmother. I suspect he has attended out of respect for her."

As if on cue, their hostess, Lady Holloway, approached the two gentlemen. Marcus bowed, and an easy smile played at the corners of his mouth. The smile was boyishly affectionate, softening his features, and it was clear he held Lady Holloway in high regard. He had the same look years ago when he had caught Isabel, an infatuated impetuous girl, filling his best riding boots with sand.

A sudden thought struck Isabel. "He caused a *horrific* scandal, you say? You are a genius, Charlotte!"

Charlotte's brows drew together. "Whatever do you mean?"

"I mean to gain my freedom."

Ignoring Charlotte's confused look, Isabel gathered her skirts and wove her way through the crowd.

The music from the orchestra grew louder as she walked, and couples whirled by in a colorful blur on the dance floor. Several older ladies glanced at her as she hurried past with a purpose—straight for Marcus Hawksley himself.

She came up to Marcus and Lord Ravenspear as Lady Holloway walked away to greet her other guests.

"Good evening, Mr. Hawksley. It has been quite some time since we have seen each other. Do you remember me?" Isabel asked.

Two pairs of eyes snapped to her face—Ravenspear's were deep blue; Marcus Hawksley's were dark and unfathomable.

One corner of Marcus's mouth twisted upward. "Lady Isabel Cameron. Of course I remember you. How many years has it been? Ten or more?"

Eight to be exact, she thought.

As an infatuated adolescent of twelve, she remembered him clearly. He had been a reckless rogue, a sworn bachelor at the age of twenty-two, and had been the object of her schoolgirl fantasies. Looking into his face now, there were no traces of the pleasure-seeking scoundrel.

Marcus Hawksley appeared severe and serious, and quite simply her savior if she played her cards right.

"It has been a while," she said.

"May I introduce Lord Ravenspear?" Marcus turned toward the earl.

"It is a pleasure to meet you, Lady Isabel," Ravenspear said.

Isabel raised her gaze to find Ravenspear watching her. His cobalt eyes sparkled with humor. Isabel could imagine what the earl was thinking—that a debutante approaching a bachelor without a chaperone or her father in a crowded ballroom was quite forward.

Good, Isabel thought. *May all of the upper crust watch, especially Lord Walling.*

"If you will excuse me, I see friends I'd like to speak with," Ravenspear said.

To Isabel's surprise, the earl gave a sly wink before departing.

She was left alone with Marcus. "Mr. Hawksley," she said, reaching out to touch his sleeve. "I'm afraid my request may sound forward, but I have not had a gentleman ask me to dance this evening. I cannot bear to be the talk of all the other debutantes here. Will you save me from such a fate?"

Marcus Hawksley's expression stilled and grew hard. His mercurial black eyes sharpened and blazed down into hers.

Her hand froze on his velvet jacket, and his muscles tensed under her fingertips. Heat emanated from his body, and he appeared as tightly coiled as a spring.

Suddenly, she was unsure of herself, of her outrageous behavior.

What if she had made a grave mistake? Had underestimated his reformation from rogue to serious businessman?

She took an abrupt step back, away from his tense, hard body, and made to turn on her heel. "Forgive me. I—"

He reached out and grasped her wrist.

"For old times' sake then," he murmured as he led her to the dance floor, leaving her no choice but to follow.

The orchestra had begun the waltz, and he swept her

into his arms. It was the perfect dance for Isabel's intent. Known as the "forbidden" waltz because of the close contact of the dancers, she had a heightened awareness of their audience. As they started to dance, she wondered if he knew the steps since he hadn't been to any society functions in quite some time. But she needn't have worried for his tall frame moved with easy grace.

He looked down at her. "You realize that by dancing with me you may cause more gossip than by not dancing with any man the entire evening?"

She feigned innocence. "Whatever do you mean?"

"Don't pretend you don't know. There's a black mark on my name, Isabel."

A shiver of excitement ran down her spine. *I'm counting on it, Marcus!*

She was conscious of his hand touching hers, of his powerful body moving beside her, grazing her skirts. Her skin became increasingly warm, her breath short.

As they whirled across the floor, she glanced in the direction of her father and Lord Walling.

Her father appeared confused and agitated, and wiped at his brow with a handkerchief.

Walling looked furious, his fleshy face and neck mottled red.

Encouraged, she leaned lightly into Marcus, tilting her face toward his. "A black mark does not scare me, Mr. Hawksley. I'm old enough to know that society can be harsh, can be too judgmental, and rarely is correct when it comes to a person's true character."

He looked at her in astonishment, and then grinned. "Not only have you grown into a beautiful woman with your raven hair and clear blue eyes, but an astute one as well. A true surprise you have become, Lady Isabel."

She didn't know whether it was the attractive smile that had transformed his face or his flattering words, but her pulse leapt to life, and her feet seemed to drift along on a cloud over the dance floor.

The bold passage of his jet eyes over her face and the curve of her neck heightened her senses. She found herself extremely attuned to his strength, his overwhelming masculinity. He was unlike any other male she had ever known. Here was no fop, no dandy that the young debutantes swooned over. Here was a powerful man whose dangerous nature was disguised by a thin veneer of respectability.

Reason told her to flee, to abandon her impulsiveness, but instead a thrill tingled along her nerves.

Their eyes locked, and his dark brows slanted in a slight frown.

He senses it, too! she thought.

As the dance neared its end, she realized with bewilderment that she was no longer acting the awed female entirely for the benefit of her father and Lord Walling, but that she indeed felt an undeniable attraction to Marcus Hawksley.

Chapter 2

"I'm furious!" stated Edward Cameron. "For the third time, I've arranged a perfectly good match for you and how do you reward me? You turn down Lord Walling only to dance with Marcus Hawksley instead. He's nothing more than the impoverished younger son of an earl, a mere stockbroker."

Isabel watched her father pace back and forth on the thick Aubusson carpet in his library. Edward Cameron, the fourth Earl of Malvern, was short and stocky with round spectacles and a brow perpetually creased with worry. Tufts of sparse gray hair stood on end as he ran his fingers over his scalp in agitation. His mouth was tight and grim, his eyes flashing in a familiar display of impatience.

Isabel stiffly sat in a leather chair, her fingers curling around the nail head armrest. Her father had ushered her into the library as soon as they had returned home from Lady Holloway's ball. She immediately knew it was going to be a lengthy night. Last time, he had taken her to the drawing room, and the lecture had been brief. He hadn't been concerned with possible interruptions by the servants. But to demand her presence in his library—well, that meant the lecture would be severe enough to warrant complete privacy. No servant would dare interrupt the earl here.

Straightening her spine, she took a deep breath. "I apologize for having upset you by dancing with Mr. Hawksley, Father. But I'm not sorry that Lord Walling no longer wants the engagement to proceed."

Edward stopped his pacing to stare at her. He reached up to rip his spectacles from his face, only to snag one of the wires behind his ear. It twisted and bowed as he tugged it free.

"Who said anything about Lord Walling not pursuing an engagement? It took considerable effort on my part, but I managed to assuage Walling's doubts regarding your poor discretion."

Isabel tossed her head. "Poor discretion! I do not wish to wed Lord Walling."

"Why not?"

"He's positively ancient. He has no interest in my art. And . . . and . . . he"—she struggled for the words—"he has depraved appetites in the bedroom," she blurted out, not knowing how else to persuade her father.

"What?" Edward's jaw dropped.

Her face grew hot. "That's the latest gossip."

He blew out his cheeks like a blowfish before releasing a burst of air. "Of all the nonsense, please stop listening to your friend, Charlotte Benning."

His anger slightly abated, he took a seat in a chair next to hers and reached out to take her hand.

"My Isabel," he said. "I will not live forever, and I need to see you well settled before I die. Your mother, bless her soul, would have wanted you respectably married."

Isabel's heart lurched, and a stab of guilt pierced her heart. Despite everything, she loved her father dearly. She squeezed his hand. "What would make me happy is to live with Auntie Lil in Paris. I could study my watercolors, just as she did. Ever since my visit two summers ago, she has regularly written asking for me to stay with her."

Edward shook his head. "Your mother's sister is an eccentric who never married. That's what happens to women who never have a man's guidance and who never bear children."

"I don't believe that."

"Either way, you are a few months shy of your twenty-first birthday. You have already destroyed two previously good matches, now must you destroy a third?"

"I didn't destroy anything."

"Ah, you merely told Lord Darby that you were unable to bear children, and you merely let Lord Shelton's controlling mother believe that insanity runs in the family, by using your Auntie Lil as an example. Both men ran as fast as their legs would carry them."

"I won't apologize for either man. Darby only sought a brooding mare to produce heirs, and Shelton wanted the country estate in Herefordshire that you had promised him. Don't you see, Father, I want *more*."

"It's unspeakable. Forget returning to Auntie Lil. Letting you travel to Paris was an unfortunate mistake. As for Lord Walling, I gave him permission to pay a visit tomorrow afternoon. You had best be a perfect lady. The engagement will go forward."

Edward rose and patted her shoulder. "As the eldest child, think of the twins. You will be setting a good example for them."

Isabel often did think of her younger twin siblings, Anthony and Amber, and believed that setting a good example meant passionately pursuing one's dreams.

At her silence, her father smiled. "Good girl, Isabel. I know you will stop carrying on about this artistic nonsense. I've allowed your watercolors as a pastime fancy, but now it is time for you to put art out of your mind and secure your future as a wife."

Head bent low, Isabel nodded in what she hoped was a demure manner. From a sideways glance, she watched him turn and leave.

As soon as the library door clicked closed, she jumped to her feet and rushed to her father's desk. Yanking open a heavy file drawer, she began to rummage through mounds of paper.

If Walling was coming tomorrow afternoon, there was no time to waste.

Marcus Hawksley took the front steps to the Westley mansion two at a time in his haste. He did not like to lose, and there was a Gainsborough at stake.

The London Stock Exchange had been particularly busy this morning. When Marcus had heard about the estate sale in which the 1781 painting by Thomas Gainsborough, *Seashore with Fishermen*, would be auctioned off to the highest bidder, his secretary had scrambled to reschedule several important appointments.

Marcus reached the mansion's top steps, and before he could knock, a dour-faced butler swung the door open. People were already milling about inside, attesting to his lateness.

A muscle flicked at his jaw. He refused to be outbid.

He stepped into a grand vestibule lavishly appointed with marble floors, high ceilings hung with sparkling crystal chandeliers, and quality paintings on the walls.

A tall, reed-thin man approached. He was dressed in striped trousers that made his long legs appear as if he walked on stilts. He was strikingly bald with pale blue eyes in a narrow face.

"Good afternoon, Mr. Hawksley," the man said. "I anticipated I would see you today."

Marcus greeted Dante Black, the former Bonham's auctioneer, with a curt nod. "Where is it, Dante?"

"The late Lord Westley had several intimate drawing rooms to showcase his art throughout his home. Gainsborough's *Seashore with Fishermen* is located on the upper floor, at the end of the hall, past the library. There are other notable pieces exhibited there as well that may interest you. All the items are rare and exquisite." Dante Black withdrew a gold pocket watch from his waistcoat. "Only fifteen minutes remain for prospective buyers to view the art before the auction takes place in the parlor."

Marcus nodded. "That's all the time I need, Dante."

Wondering what other art the auctioneer had in mind, Marcus bounded up the staircase. He was always open to adding new quality works to his vast collection.

He nodded at passersby as he strode down the hall, recognizing other wealthy collectors, museum curators, and titled nobility with a taste for fine art. Even Lord Yarmouth, the Regent's personal art agent, who was an influential and informed art collector in his own right, was present. His robust wife, Lady Yarmouth, was by his side. Marcus was well aware that Prinny was an avid collector of Thomas Gainsborough's work, and he suspected Yarmouth was present to bid on the same piece.

Pulse pounding in anticipation, Marcus opened the door and rushed into the first room past the library.

His gaze swept the room's dimly lit interior.

He stopped short, shocked.

Seconds passed, then he burst out laughing.

Row after row of erotic statues crammed the vast room. Naked nymphs with huge breasts, fierce warriors, and boys on the brink of manhood—all with enormously oversized penises—were arrayed in splendid decadence throughout the space. Couples in various sexual positions, some with amazingly flexible and contorted limbs; others in the throes of ecstasy, heads thrown back, mouths open simulating pleasure. Erotic frescoes and paintings lined the walls as well, depicting orgies in Roman togas and marble pools.

In the back of the room was an immense, round bed, big enough to hold at least four people. Red satin sheets adorned the mattress and a canopy of fine red gauze shrouded the perimeter of the bed. A fabric swing, two people wide, hung from the ceiling beside the bed. Marcus's fertile imagination pictured lovers in the swing, swaying back and forth, culminating their passion.

Who would have thought the late Lord Westley, a respectable member of society and the House of Lords, had such wild tastes?

Marcus turned in a full circle, absorbing the erotic scene before him.

He became instantly aroused.

He was, after all, a flesh-and-blood man.

"Mr. Hawksley."

Marcus spun around at the sound of a soft, feminine voice. He saw nothing save a gaudy statue of Diana, the Roman goddess of the hunt, one hand cradling a large breast, and the other hand cupping the V between her legs.

"Who's there?" he called out.

"It's me, Mr. Hawksley."

Sunlight from a small, overhead window cast a shadow on the Diana statue. A slender woman appeared from behind, her hand grazing the statue's white hip as she glided to stand before it.

Marcus blinked, wondering if his imagination had conjured her forth. "Isabel?"

She smiled and met his gaze.

She looked ethereal, unreal in the dim light, dressed in a flowing white dress with a low embroidered bodice. The gown was an arousing concoction, modest enough not to be daring, yet sufficiently tantalizing to reveal a narrow waist, slender hips, and the curve of a full breast.

Her striking sable hair was loose, unlike at the Holloways' ball, and hung in thick waves down her back. Her only jewelry was two mother-of-pearl combs, sweeping the hair from her face, revealing blue eyes and delicately boned features.

He had thought her a beautiful woman last night, but here . . . now . . . amongst the backdrop of eroticism, dressed as she was, she was exquisite.

Immediately, his guard came up. "What are you doing here?"

"I need you, Mr. Hawksley."

It was the last thing he had expected to hear, and the most damaging thing she could have said to his already overstimulated senses.

"What are you talking about?" His voice sounded harsh to his own ears.

She stepped closer, and her perfume—a subtle scent of lilacs—wafted toward him.

"I need your help, Marcus."

Marcus. At the sound of his Christian name on her lips, his heart pounded an erratic rythm.

He realized he was staring, gawking at her. "Help you?" he asked, coming to his senses. "Do you realize what will happen if we are found alone like this, especially here, in this room?"

He shifted to the side, looking behind her. "Where is your chaperone? Your father?"

"I'm alone, of course."

"But why?"

She stepped even closer, her ripe body swaying like that of a skilled courtesan, yet surrounded by an aura of innocence. The contradiction was fascinating and alluring all at once. She looked, quite simply, like a sacrificial virgin in one of the frescoes on the wall.

Looking him straight in the eye, she said, "I need to have a liaison, and I want it to be with you."

He stood absolutely still and wondered if he had heard her correctly. After a moment, realization dawned on him, and he chuckled. "Is this some kind of joke?"

"Why would you think that?"

"After not seeing you for all these years, you approach me at Lady Holloway's ball and very forwardly ask me to dance. Then the next day you show up here"—he spread his arm toward the debauchery in the room—"and ask me to become your lover. If this is not a joke, then what else can it be?"

A thoughtful smile curved her mouth. "I assure you, Marcus, this isn't a joke."

"However did you find me?"

"I rummaged through my father's files to find your business address. Father is a member of the Stock Exchange, you see. When I arrived at your place of business, your secretary, James Smith, was leaving the building and told me where you had gone. So this is no joke. I'm quite serious about my offer."

He shook his head. "I spent a summer at your father's country manor when you were twelve years old. You were an adorable child, creating mischief, exasperating your elders, and training your younger twin siblings to follow your example. I was fond of you and your father and that's why I feel obligated to speak some sense into you."

She held up a slender hand and rolled her eyes. "Not another lecture. I've received one too many lately."

"Not enough, judging by your behavior. Respectable young women who are unmarried debutantes don't wander around unchaperoned propositioning men to have affairs. Especially a man with a black cloud hovering over his head."

"Exactly," she said. "That's why you are perfect. My father has arranged a match for me, you see. A much older, domineering lord."

"He sounds quite acceptable. Your father has your best interests at heart."

She pouted, showing full, red lips . . . very kissable lips.

"I don't love Lord Walling. He's thirty-three years my senior, has no interest in who I am, and he waddles."

Marcus had to drag his gaze from her mouth to her flashing blue eyes. "He sounds even better. What do you need me for?"

"I need to create a scandal, ruin my reputation. It's the only way to get out of Lord Walling's trap and to stop my father's relentless matchmaking. Only then will I be free to return to Auntie Lil in Paris. She's waiting for me with open arms."

He felt a stab of anger that she sought only to use him, and a sudden round of deep-seated memories assailed him.

Just like Bridget, he mused.

Before her death, Bridget had used him and then had betrayed him. Isabel sought to make use of his infamous social reputation, but would she also seek to betray him?

"Again, madam, your plan is unsound and irrational. You should obey your father," he said in a harsh voice.

She reached out and touched his chest. "You may say such things, but your eyes tell another story. I know you felt something for me when we danced last night. I could feel it, and I'm guessing you did as well."

Marcus's throat tightened at her touch. Despite his reservations, his common sense, he was by no means blind to her face and form. His gaze dropped from her blue eyes to her full, bottom lip, and a trickle of sweat formed on his brow.

It's this room, he told himself. *Any man would be stiff as*

a board if he were propositioned by a beautiful woman in
such an erotic environment.

He placed his big hand over her smaller one and moved
it away. "You're wrong. How would an innocent girl like
you know how I felt last night?"

She stepped forward; he stepped back.

"I'm not a girl and you know it. I'm past the age of
schoolgirl fantasies. I'm a real woman with interests and
desires, and being married off to a dominating, old lord is
not one of them."

He continued retreating until he realized with dismay
that they were closer to the round, satin-encased bed.

Damnation.

If she were an experienced lady looking for sport, he
would oblige her and happily. But this was Isabel Cameron,
an innocent lady whose influential father was an earl and a
friend of Marcus's father. Memories of her childhood antics
were still pure and clear in his mind.

"Isabel," he warned, his tone low and rough.

"I'm very persistent when I want something. Remember
how I was as a young girl, Marcus? As a grown woman,
I'm even more tenacious when I desire something." Her
voice was a velvet murmur.

She was so close he could see her irises grow in the dim
light. She stared at him with longing, and he was completely taken by surprise. No one had looked at him that
way in a long time, especially not a lady. He was an out-
sider, an outcast, whose own family looked down upon
him. Here was a remarkably beautiful woman who gazed
at him as if he were her *savior*, and a spark of unfamiliar
need flared inside him so great he struggled to deal with
the ravaging emotion.

His gaze fell to the creamy expanse of her neck, then
lower still, to the rounded tops of her full breasts. When his
eyes returned to hers, there was no maidenly innocence in

the sky blue depths, only physical awareness of him as a man. Her invitation was a passionate challenge, impossible to resist. He had an overwhelming desire to hold her, taste her, trace her full bottom lip with his tongue . . .

His body grew hot; his heart hammered in his chest.

How much could a man resist?

After all, what harm could one kiss do?

He moved toward her, impelled involuntarily by his own lust. She glided into his arms and wrapped her arms around his neck.

Still, he held himself back and looked into her eyes. "Isabel, this is madness."

"That's what makes it perfect," she whispered, and then drew his face to hers.

Chapter 3

He was solid like a mountain. Isabel felt every hard muscle of his chest pressing into her body. His arms tightened around her, and she could feel the heat of his hands through the thin fabric of her gown. His mouth hovered above hers, his hot breath fanning her lips. A wild look flashed in his eyes, but he hesitated.

"For someone who claims to want a lover, I think you're ignorant of men," he said.

"That's not true," she protested.

"Have you ever been kissed before?"

"Of course. Three times to be exact." When he looked at her with disbelief, she rushed to add, "On the mouth."

"By whom?"

"Is that important? All I can say is that I'm a fourth-year debutante. I've had my fair share of spins around the dance floor and private walks in the garden."

"Is that where it happened?"

"Where what happened?"

"The kisses. In the garden."

She looked at him quizzically. "I don't recall."

"That's odd. I would think you would remember every detail of those kisses, especially your first. Perhaps you're overestimating your experience. You shouldn't seek a lover after all. A husband sounds more appropriate," he said, his tone harsh.

"That's a falsehood conjured up by men. Auntie Lil says a woman must experience at least two lovers to be happy, neither of which should be her husband."

"Does she now? Your aunt sounds quite unconventional."

"Oh yes, she is. She's wonderful in her forward way of thinking and behaving. She's an artist, like me, only she tends to work with oils while I prefer watercolors. Either way, she lives a full and exciting life which includes many male artists and models, but no husband. I visited her last summer in Paris and can't wait to return. Father doesn't understand Auntie Lil's progressive ideas. He thinks there is no alternative for me except to be suitably settled."

"He's right. As a child who thrived on mischief, you needed a strong hand. Nothing has changed."

She met his gaze without flinching. "Why refuse me? I thought all men, married and bachelors, had affairs."

"Wherever did you hear that?"

She shrugged. "Women talk, Marcus."

"Well, it is not true. Some men have respect for the sanctity of marriage, and as a rule, gentlemen don't have liaisons with titled debutantes."

He dropped his arms from around her, and she felt a sudden inexplicable sense of loss.

For the first time since arriving at the Westley mansion, a flicker of apprehension coursed through her. She had been certain that Marcus would be a willing participant in her scheme. From what she had heard about men, their base needs always overrode their reason.

A sudden unbidden image of Lord Walling seared her brain. Depraved appetites in bed, Charlotte had said.

No, she could never imagine a life of wifely servitude to Walling. Isabel's spine stiffened with resolve. No matter how crazy her plan sounded to Marcus, she had to find a way to convince him.

Wasn't freedom worth the price? What was a scandal, a ruined reputation, compared to a lifetime of unhappiness?

She rested her hand against his jacket, and felt the strong beat of his heart through the fine material. "I'm not asking for a permanent relationship. A fleeting affair would be perfect."

"No, Isabel—"

"We don't have to disclose it to all of society as I had initially desired, just my father and Lord Walling." She licked her lips.

His dark gaze fell to her mouth, and she sensed a vulnerability in him. Stepping close, pressing herself against his chest, she tipped her head to his.

"Are you certain?" she asked.

He pushed back a long lock of dark hair that brushed her shoulder, and his arms again closed around her. "God help me. You've talked nothing but complete insanity since you've walked in here, yet I can't seem to come to my senses and leave this room."

"Perhaps you will reconsider."

Firm lips brushed her forehead, her temple. "No, Isabel. You deserve far better than me. I'm damaged, not worthy." His mouth lowered to within an inch of hers.

Her lashes fluttered closed, and she awaited the touch of his lips.

The door burst open, crashing against the opposite wall.

Marcus stiffened and thrust her behind him.

Isabel stumbled back and fell onto the satin-encased bed.

"There he is," a voice boomed.

A long-limbed man strode into view. Hairless, with pencil-thin brows and a pointed nose, he projected an air of haughtiness. He was flanked by two big, brawny men dressed entirely in black, their menacing expressions masks of stone.

"Where is it, Mr. Hawksley?" the lanky man who appeared to be in charge asked.

Marcus's brow furrowed. "Where's what, Dante?"

The man named Dante walked forward, eye to eye with Marcus. The pair of intimidating lackeys who looked like overgrown guard dogs followed in Dante's wake.

"You know precisely what I'm speaking about," Dante snapped. "The Thomas Gainsborough painting, what did you do with it?"

Marcus's expression grew hard. "I have no idea what you're talking about. As for the Gainsborough painting, I haven't seen it since I walked into the Westley mansion."

Dante snorted. His bald head glistened as if he had polished his scalp to add to his air of superiority. "Lying will not help your case. The auction was scheduled to take place over half an hour ago. I sent my guards"—he jerked a hand in the direction of the two men beside him—"to search the mansion when they discovered the painting was missing."

"So? What does that have to do with me?" Marcus asked.

"You were the last person to view the painting. I'm aware of your fascination—your obsession—with Gainsborough's work."

"You're mistaken," Marcus said. "I never laid eyes on it. You gave me directions to this room, and as far as I can tell, there is no Gainsborough painting here."

Dante shook his head. "I never led you here. I gave you specific directions to the room at the end of the hall past the library where *Seashore with Fishermen* was hanging in prominent display."

"This is the only room I've been in, and I resent your accusatory tone that I'm the one responsible for the missing painting. Anyone in this mansion could have taken it," Marcus said.

"I'm fully aware of the interests and tastes of every one of the prospective clients that I allow in my auctions. The only other that was interested in the Gainsborough painting was Lord Yarmouth, on behalf of the Regent himself. It would have sold for a hefty price. I realize that, as a working stockbroker, you may not have sufficient funds to bid on so valuable a piece of artwork. Perhaps your obsession clouded your brain, and you stole the painting. That is what a justice of the peace will call motive, Mr. Hawksley."

Marcus's face set in a vicious expression. "Listen here, Dante, because I'm only going to say this once. I never set eyes on the Gainsborough painting."

"You can tell that to the constable."

A muscle leapt at Marcus's jaw. Fists clenched at his sides, he stepped toward the auctioneer.

The gargantuan guards blocked his path.

"Wait!" Isabel cried out.

Four pairs of eyes turned to her, Dante and the two guards seeing her for the first time. Sitting on the round bed, gripping the satin sheets, she had been concealed by Marcus's large frame. But now that she had called attention to herself, she sensed the tension from each man in the room pierce her like a dagger.

She struggled to find her voice, her throat suddenly as dry as old parchment. "Marcus didn't take the painting. I can attest to this fact."

Dante's stare drilled into her. "Who are you?"

Isabel felt her face grow hot. "Marcus did not steal anything."

Marcus scowled at her. "Not another word—"

"Who are you?" Dante repeated.

Marcus stepped toward her. "Don't say anything—"

"My name is Lady Isabel Cameron." She shimmied off the bed, the slippery sheets sliding beneath her. It seemed a long way off the round bed with the attention of four intimidating men focused on her, but her feet finally touched the floor. She stood and, with damp palms, smoothed imaginary wrinkles from her skirts.

With confidence she did not feel, she directed her attention to Dante. "As I said, I'm Lady Isabel Cameron, daughter of Lord Cameron, the Earl of Malvern." Her tone insinuated that any auctioneer worthy of his salt would be familiar with the titled nobility.

Dante blinked. "I must ask, Lady Isabel, how do you know Mr. Hawksley was not involved in the disappearance of the painting at issue."

"I'm sure you can surmise the truth."

Dante's bold gaze raked over her figure, noting the low-cut bodice of her gown, the dark disheveled hair brushing her shoulders and flowing down her back. He smirked.

"No, Lady Isabel," Dante said, "I dare not surmise anything without proof. But perhaps you're mistaken. After all, the painting was insured by Lloyd's of London, and the company will promptly send an insurance investigator who will want to take your statement, to question you. Your father, the earl, will undoubtedly be notified. Everyone will know, especially Lord Yarmouth, the Regent's own art agent who wanted the painting for Carlton House. Even Lady Yarmouth, whom I understand is firmly entrenched in the ton, accompanied him today. Is that what you want, Lady Isabel?"

He's trying to intimidate me! she thought.

The implication was clear. Dante was threatening her with social ruin if she continued to act as Marcus's alibi. But what the arrogant auctioneer didn't know was that Isabel had planned and failed to achieve such a fate only moments ago.

Tossing her head, she eyed Dante with cold challenge. "Mr. Hawksley was with me the entire time. We are lovers, you see."

"Isabel," Marcus growled. He spun to face Dante. "She's lying."

"I am not."

Dante's cold eyes clawed her like talons, and his narrow, pinched face twisted in anger. She was taken aback at the auctioneer's fury.

Shouldn't he be relieved to know that one suspect was cleared and to start searching for another?

Alarm rippled along her spine. It was as if he *wanted* Marcus to be guilty of the theft.

"I see," Dante said, an icy edge to his voice. "Since you are so eager to vouch for Mr. Hawskley despite the consequences to yourself, I must insist that you give a full accounting of what time you arrived and what transpired."

"I have no objection," she said.

"I do," Marcus snapped.

"An informal statement will eliminate the need to call the constable. I'm certain the Lloyd's investigator will find the information useful to eliminate Mr. Hawksley as a suspect. Unless of course, Lady Isabel has changed her mind."

"I have not," she said.

Dante's eyes narrowed, and again she was struck by his anger. "Please follow me then, Lady Isabel," he said, turning to leave.

It was a demand more than a request. The two burly guards escorted Marcus as they followed Dante out of the room.

Isabel averted her gaze from the erotic art as she hurried past. It seemed odd that the obscene nature of the statues hadn't disturbed her when she had been alone with Marcus, but now that she was in the presence of Dante and his men, the artwork made her skin crawl.

They were led to the parlor of the Westley mansion, which was now empty after the auction.

Marcus gave her a penetrating look. "Don't do anything until I get back."

He then turned on his heel and followed Dante and the guards out of the room, leaving her alone.

She looked about the parlor. Remaining pieces of artwork that had not sold were sprawled around the perimeter of the room. Canvases rested against the wall, a copy of a Greek bust sat in a corner, and bronze bowls and crystal figurines were spread out on a table. Dust mites swirled in a stream of light from a nearby window. Isabel sneezed and rubbed her arms, suddenly chilled.

She sat in an armchair by the empty fireplace and waited for what seemed like a long time. A majestic longcase clock in a dark corner ticked by the seconds, and the sound echoed throughout the room. Her anxiety built with the passage of time, and she experienced a sudden, inexplicable urge to flee. It was as if the solitude in the strange room exposed the impulsiveness in her plan. To escape a loveless match by sullying her reputation now felt recklessly foolish. There had to be another way to ensure her freedom, to convince her father that Lord Walling was ill suited for her, and most importantly, that her fascination with art was not a woman's passing hobby.

She stood, ready to flee the room, the mansion, and return home.

Footsteps echoed down the hall.

The door swung open, and Isabel lurched in surprise. Not only did Lord and Lady Yarmouth enter, but so did her father and Lord Walling.

Chapter 4

Face ruddy and eyes wide behind round spectacles, Edward Cameron rushed to Isabel's side and clasped her upper arms.

"Isabel, we have been fraught with worry. The entire household has been looking for you."

Isabel looked at her father in surprise and said the first thing that came to mind. "How did you find me?"

Edward frowned. "Lord Walling arrived for you this afternoon, and when you were nowhere to be found, we started to worry. Mr. Dante Black"—her father jerked his head to the door—"came to the house and informed us that you were at the estate sale of the late Lord Westley, and that you needed my aid."

Isabel looked behind her father to see that Dante had entered the room to stand beside Lord and Lady Yarmouth.

Marcus Hawksley was nowhere in sight.

"What would possess you to come here, Isabel?" Edward asked.

"I, ah—"

Dante Black stepped forward. "Perhaps if everyone will be seated, I will attempt to explain matters."

Isabel's heart hammered as the occupants in the parlor

followed Dante's directions. The Yarmouths took the only settee in the room, and everyone else chose chairs.

Isabel glanced at the Yarmouths. Lord Yarmouth was quite ordinary looking, a middle-aged man of average height with a receding hairline. Lady Yarmouth, the illegitimate daughter of the fourth Duke of Queensbury, was rotund with an ample bosom and shrewd brown eyes. After receiving a sizable inheritance from the deceased duke, she spent most of her time in Paris, but was currently visiting England. Isabel was well aware that Lady Yarmouth was a close acquaintance of Charlotte's mother and a vicious gossipmonger. Anything that was said today would be speedily spread to all the female members of the ton by sunset.

Dante spoke first. "I've summoned you here today because we all have one thing in common. The missing Gainsborough painting."

"Whatever are you speaking about?" Isabel's father asked.

"The Thomas Gainsborough painting is missing?" Lord Yarmouth sat forward, an intense look replacing his previously drab expression.

Dante held up a hand. "The painting was scheduled to be auctioned off early this afternoon. When I sent my man to bring the painting to this parlor, he was attacked and the painting stolen."

"Attacked?" Isabel cried out. Dante had previously failed to mention an attack. "Is your man dead?"

"No," Dante said. "He sustained a nasty knock on the head, but he will survive. But as for the painting, it is worth a small fortune and is missing. The only man that had expressed interest in the painting, other than Lord Yarmouth on behalf of the Prince Regent, was Mr. Marcus Hawksley."

"Marcus Hawksley?" Lord Walling spoke up, the nostrils in his bulbous nose flaring in his florid face.

"Yes." Dante nodded. "As I was saying, Mr. Hawksley

was the only other person that had viewed the work"—
Dante stopped to look at Isabel—"or so I had believed.
When I found Mr. Hawksley to question him, Lady Isabel
came to his defense and said that he could not have taken
the painting. Isn't that correct, Lady Isabel?"

"Isabel?" her father asked, a look of confusion on
his face.

All eyes turned to her, and she felt light-headed.

Here is the moment of my ruin, she thought. *The price I
have to pay for my freedom.*

Her prior misgivings increased a hundredfold. Her
breathing became ragged; her blood rushed through her
ears like an avalanche.

Save yourself! Her inner voice cried out.

She looked at Dante Black, and was taken aback by the
cold, calculating glint on his pinched face. She could
almost hear his sinister thoughts: *This is what I told you
would happen if you defended Marcus Hawksley, but
there's still time to change your story.*

Perhaps she should seize the opportunity Dante offered.
Cry confusion. Female hysterics. Loss of memory. Claim
she had attended the auction to view quality watercolors.
Knowing her interest in the arts, *that* was a story her father
would believe. After all, there was even more at stake than
a stolen painting; a man had been assaulted.

She glanced again at Dante, and her blood chilled at
the victorious gleam in his eye. A thought struck her, and
she froze.

What about Marcus?

He needed her as an alibi. For whatever reason, Dante
wanted to prove Marcus guilty for crimes that she knew for
a fact he did not commit.

Could she abandon an innocent man? A good man?

And Marcus was a good man, she was certain, despite
the "black cloud," as he had called it, which hovered over

his head. He had refused her blatant offer when she was certain most men would not have. Others would have taken her virtue without a second thought, knowing that society would smear the woman's reputation all the while praising the man for his sexual prowess.

But not Marcus. He had thought of her father, had even said she deserved better than him. No, she had to stay. She couldn't throw an innocent man to a bloodthirsty wolf like Dante Black.

She looked her father straight in the eye. "I'm sorry for disappointing you, Father. But Mr. Hawksley didn't steal the painting or attack Dante's man."

Edward stiffened. "Isabel?"

"Mr. Hawksley was with me, you see. We were . . . together the entire time."

Isabel heard Lady Yarmouth's quick intake of breath followed by Lord Walling's low curse.

"I see." Edward stood, his expression tight with strain. "And just where might I find Mr. Hawksley?"

In the library of the Westley mansion, Marcus clenched his fists in futile frustration as the two guards eyed him warily. Both had pulled out pistols from their coat pockets and aimed them at his chest as soon as the library door was secured.

Marcus's jaw hardened. Dante Black knew his business. If the crooked auctioneer had left Marcus alone with one armed guard, it would have been a hell of a fight. But with two? And more critically, with Isabel Cameron somewhere in this house alone, Marcus couldn't risk starting a battle.

An image of Isabel flashed through his mind as he had last seen her. Long, sable hair, the clearest blue eyes he had ever looked into, and the body of a temptress robed in virginal white. With the feel of all that soft, womanly flesh pressed against him, he had come dangerously close to taking what she had eagerly offered.

If it wasn't for Dante's untimely interruption . . .

Marcus strode to a window behind a dusty oak desk, all the while aware of the guard's eyes on his every move. Leaning on the window sill, Marcus surveyed the gardens below.

None of this made any sense. Dante Black wanted to blame the theft of the Gainsborough work as well as the assault of one of his men on him. But why?

Marcus knew little of the auctioneer. Dante had worked for the prestigious Bonham's Auction House. Bonham's opened its doors in 1793, twenty-one years ago. Thomas Dodd, a well-known print dealer, and Walter Bonham, a book specialist, founded the firm, and its reputation was unsullied. Dante Black had been the head auctioneer at Bonham's until it was rumored that he had a falling out with Thomas Dodd himself. Since then, Dante had resorted to estate sales of deceased wealthy art patrons. Marcus had attended numerous auctions conducted by Dante over the past year in his quest for quality artwork.

So why would Dante Black want so desperately to accuse Marcus?

They had never exchanged a cross word. To the contrary, Dante had made a lucrative profit from the art Marcus had acquired from him.

Dante's current hostile behavior was illogical. Unless he was working for someone else, someone who despised Marcus, a rival who wanted him destroyed . . .

A low knock sounded on the door. One of the guards pocketed his pistol and cracked open the door. He spoke in a low voice as he motioned behind his back for the other guard to put away his pistol.

The door was opened wide, and Edward Cameron, the Earl of Malvern, entered the library.

To Marcus's surprise, the guards slipped out and closed the door behind them.

"Lord Malvern," Marcus greeted Isabel's father, wary of the older man's stiff posture.

Edward strode forward, his corpulent features twisted in anger. "Well, Mr. Hawksley. You look as if you were expecting me."

"To be truthful, I was, just not this soon."

"Your arrogance knows no bounds. My daughter is downstairs as we speak having her reputation torn to shreds and her future destroyed—all in your defense. What do you have to say for yourself?"

"Lord Malvern, nothing happened between Lady Isabel and myself. On my honor—"

"Your honor!" Edward roared. "From what I understand, Mr. Hawksley, you haven't had honor in over ten years. I showed you nothing but kindness and respect those many years ago. I was aware of your roguish behavior, but I had foolishly believed you would outgrow it. Instead, you lost whatever morals you had possessed when you entered trade and have reduced yourself to ruining the lives of innocent young women."

"I haven't ruined anything. We were never together."

"Do you confess to stealing the painting then?" Edward asked.

"Absolutely not."

"Then you admit to being alone with Isabel at the time of the theft?"

"Yes, but nothing transpired between us."

Edward hesitated, and a brief look of uncertainty flashed across his face, but as quickly as it had appeared, it vanished. "Whether I believe you or not, Mr. Hawksley, it's too late. Isabel stood in the parlor just moments ago and confessed to being caught in a highly compromising position with you in the presence of both Lord and Lady

Yarmouth and Lord Walling. Needless to say, Lord Walling will not have Isabel now at any price."

"Then Walling is a fool."

Edward looked startled, and then said through gritted teeth, "It doesn't matter. There is no longer an option. You must marry at once."

Marcus felt an imaginary noose cinch around his neck. "I was wondering when the subject would arise." He reached up and loosened his tightly knotted cravat with a forefinger. It felt as if the fabric was closing off his air supply.

"Now that you have your alibi, will you do right by her?"

Ah, and there is the rub, Marcus thought.

Isabel had saved him with her galloping tongue and her crazy scheming. No matter how much he did not want to be forced into marriage, he needed an alibi. He was all too aware that he would have been the primary suspect for the theft of the Gainsborough painting if it were not for Isabel's testimony. Dante had gone to great pains to ensure it. Marcus was grudgingly grateful that Isabel had followed through with her mad plan and told all that they were together during the critical time in question.

But at the same time, he was irked that she had lied about them having a salacious affair.

The hard truth was it would have mattered naught in the eyes of society. She was an unmarried woman caught alone with a bachelor of dreadful character in a room with enough erotic art to tempt a bishop. She was ruined either way. The least he could do in return was salvage her tattered reputation, even though marriage to him was not nearly as desirable, in her father's eyes, as a union with the titled Lord Walling.

"I'll agree to whatever terms you set forth," Marcus said dryly.

"Before I tell Isabel," Edward said, "I wanted to confront

you first—man to man. It's no secret that I had hoped for Lord Walling as a match for my daughter. He is a titled widower from an established family line. But since that is no longer possible, I hope to save her from the cruelties of society."

Marcus thought of Isabel's reaction to the news. Life was ironic indeed. By conniving to get herself out of one unwanted marriage, she had unwittingly trapped herself into another.

Chapter 5

It was dark outside by the time Isabel and her father returned home from the Westley mansion. Her head throbbed, and her back ached between her shoulder blades. Her father hadn't spoken a word in the carriage the entire journey home. He had stared out the window in stony silence, his whole demeanor severe and angry. She had bitten her lip to stop from asking what had transpired between him and Marcus Hawksley.

By the time the carriage pulled up to their town house on Park Lane, a cold drizzle fell, washing out the May evening in a dreary blur that matched her mood. Isabel trudged behind her father up the front steps and entered the marble vestibule.

The delicious aroma of roast lamb wafted to her, and her stomach growled. She realized she had missed not only luncheon, but dinner as well. She wanted nothing more than to change out of the low-cut silk gown, have her maid deliver a dinner tray to her room, and seek the solace of her watercolors.

The butler took her cloak, and she turned to the winding staircase. Hand clutching the banister, she was halfway up the stairs when she glanced down.

Her father stood at the bottom of the stairs, staring up at her, and as their eyes met, a flash of fury crossed his face. Several heartbeats later, he pivoted on his heel and disappeared, his footsteps echoing down the marble hall like a general leading his troops into war.

She bit her lip and rushed to her room. Shutting the door, she threw her reticule on the four-poster. Her eyes were immediately drawn to the corner of the bedchamber, beneath a window, where an easel with a half-completed landscape beckoned. Beside the painting was a small table which held a jar crammed with brushes, several water bowls, and a dozen tiny, hard cakes of soluble watercolor.

Not permitted a room in the house for a designated studio, she had made use of the corner of her bedroom. Since she was the daughter of an earl, her father had initially paid for basic art lessons to contribute to a well-rounded education befitting a debutante of her station. But when she had expressed an interest in furthering her studies, he had adamantly refused, stating that "a young woman should focus her energies on Almack's marriage mart."

She strode to the easel, picked up a cake of pale blue watercolor, dipped it in water, and rubbed it on an oyster shell with her Asiatic martin brush. The landscape was of a section of Hyde Park she most enjoyed, showing the Serpentine River at springtime. She had been putting the finishing touches on the sky this morning, but this time, with each stroke of her brush, instead of finding a familiar sense of inner calm, her nerves remained tense and brittle. Her brush strokes were jerky rather than flowing, and the clouds formed a distorted shape on the paper.

Dear Lord, not even painting could soothe her anxiety tonight. A soft knock on the door stopped her in midstroke. "Yes."

The door opened and her maid, Kate, entered. A plain-looking woman, Kate had thin brown hair, brown eyes, and a wagging tongue. Her inquisitive nature was the last thing Isabel desired tonight.

"Your father is asking for you, Lady Isabel."

"Where?"

"In his library."

Not the library! she thought. She had never seen him as furious as she had tonight, and she dreaded the confrontation to come.

She reassured herself that all would work out as planned. Walling would never have her now. What suitable man in England would? No doubt Lady Yarmouth was already flapping her overzealous lips to every influential society matron within a ten-mile radius of London. Isabel would be free to leave for Paris.

She should be happy, thrilled, relieved—yet all she felt was an unexpected void.

Her thoughts wandered to Marcus Hawksley. She experienced a strange curiosity—an unfamiliar pang of longing. What would become of him? What was he doing now? And most surprisingly, what did he think of her? She was disturbed to realize that she cared about his opinion. He must think her a conniving jade, a spoiled tart.

An odd twinge of disappointment settled in her stomach. She'd likely never see him again. He was not a regular attendee of ton functions, and she would no longer be one after tonight. She would be in Paris, where scandalous behavior was prized rather than ostracized.

Still, questions raced through her mind like quicksilver. Why would Dante Black seek so urgently to blame Marcus Hawksley for the art theft? Would Marcus attempt to learn the identity of the true thief? But would a working stockbroker be able to afford a private investigator? From what everyone had said, Marcus's funds were limited.

She shook her head at her thoughts. She must think

about the future, *her future*. Even though she had used Marcus, she had helped him by giving him an alibi.

She shouldn't feel guilty.

With firm resolve, Isabel raised her chin. "If I must meet my father, then please help me change, Kate." She wanted to get past her father's haranguing speech and plan for tomorrow.

She chose a modest gown of gray muslin, with a high collar and long sleeves. She opened her bedroom door and again the aroma of lamb and roasted vegetables from the dining room made her mouth water. If her watercolors could not ease her tension, then perhaps food would. She prayed the lecture wouldn't take long.

Straightening her spine, she hurried down the hall and entered the library.

Her father was sitting behind his massive desk. At her entrance, he looked up and adjusted his spectacles on his nose.

"Sit, Isabel."

She took a chair by the fire and folded her hands in her lap. A movement from the corner of the room drew her attention, and she started.

Marcus Hawksley stood rigid, his obsidian eyes boring into her. He strode forward, into the firelight, and her breath caught. He dominated the room with his attitude of self-command and rugged masculinity. There was a firm resolve in him, a hardness in his features that made him look like a predator studying his prey, and she was completely alarmed by his presence.

What was he doing in her father's library?

"Good evening, Lady Isabel." He chose a chair beside hers and crossed his long legs in front of him.

"Good evening, Mr. Hawksley." She had trouble meeting his gaze, and she ended up studying her hands.

"Well, Isabel," her father said. "Is there anything you want to say?"

She looked up, suddenly flooded with a sense of shame. "I'm sorry for any trouble I caused you, Mr. Hawksley. I can only hope that I helped you with my testimony." She turned to her father. "I'll pack my bags first thing tomorrow morning."

"Your bags? For what?" Edward asked.

"For Auntie Lil's, of course."

"Auntie Lil's? You think I would allow you to go there?" His expression was incredulous.

"Why not? Lord Walling won't have me now."

A muscle twitched near her father's right eye. He appeared even more furious than when she had sat beside him in the carriage on the journey home.

"I think I understand," Edward said, his lips a thin line. "Mr. Hawksley was telling the truth, wasn't he? Your impetuous nature has finally ruined you. You are recklessly impulsive and never think things through. No doubt dreams of Paris, Auntie Lil, and male models were flashing through your mind when you plotted this catastrophe. As my eldest child, I've indulged you, Isabel. I've let you twist me about your finger, but no longer. I'll not speak around the subject. You and Mr. Hawksley must marry."

"Marry!" She felt the blood drain from her face.

Edward turned his attention to Marcus. "I'm uncertain what part you played in all of this, Mr. Hawksley. Whether you were a willing participant in my daughter's foolish plan or not, I still hold you partly responsible. You are older and worldlier than Isabel, and I would expect a *gentleman* to exhibit more restraint than to be found alone with an innocent woman in a room surrounded by inflammatory artifacts. Notwithstanding my beliefs, however, I do hope you will follow through on your word and do the honorable thing."

"I gave my word, Lord Malvern. And despite what you said earlier, I'm good for it."

"Isabel has a dowry, and although I feel it is my right under the circumstances, I'll not withhold it."

"There's no need. I'll not take a shilling," Marcus said, his voice firm.

Isabel came to her senses and sprang to her feet. "Do not speak as if I were not present. I will not marry Mr. Hawksley, or anyone for that matter."

Her father's eyes narrowed. "You have no choice in the matter, Isabel. You sealed your fate when you failed to consider the full consequences of your foolish actions. Thank goodness you and Lord Walling were not yet engaged. A scandal will result, no doubt, when Lady Yarmouth blabs to her influential friends. But after you and Mr. Hawksley are married, the scandal will blow over and will become lessened over time. Had you been engaged to Walling, the outcome would have been too horrendous to fathom. The twins, Amber and Anthony, would never have been accepted by society, and their futures would have been tainted by your actions."

"I still refuse." She looked to Marcus, her eyes pleading. "You can stop this, please, before it goes any further."

"I'm afraid it's past my doing. I have my sense of honor."

"Honor!" Her voice was shrill to her own ears. "This is a lifetime we're speaking of."

"No doubt."

"Then speak up!"

"Your father is right. It's the only reasonable course of action."

She scowled at him, speechless.

Edward rose from behind his desk. "Perhaps Mr. Hawksley can convince you better than I, Isabel. I'll leave you in private for a few minutes to talk things through." He left the library without a backward glance.

As soon as the door closed, Marcus stood and went to

the liquor cabinet. He pulled out two glasses and a bottle of her father's favorite port. Pouring two fingers' worth in both glasses, he picked up one, downed the glass, refilled it, and then turned to her.

"A celebratory toast, Lady Isabel?" he said, holding out the second glass of amber-colored liquor. "I do believe the occasion warrants one. It's not every day I *propose* marriage to a young, titled lady."

Isabel eyed him warily. His arm rested on the back of an armchair, his long, muscular frame, leaning to the side in an insolent manner. Broad shoulders strained against his tailored navy jacket—shoulders that she knew from first-hand experience were not padded like those of other men of her acquaintance. She vividly recalled the powerful muscles in his arms as he had held her and she had eagerly waited for his lips to touch hers . . .

Except they never did . . .

She frowned. Something about his resigned acceptance of her father's demands disturbed her. He was not the type of man to easily relinquish control. To the contrary, he was a man who was used to following his own rules, not the dictates of society.

Hadn't he left behind the lazy world of privilege to become a stockbroker in the London Stock Exchange?

A sudden realization dawned upon her. "You feel guilty, don't you?"

Dark eyes narrowed, and he lowered the offered glass. "What?"

She forced her lips to part in a curved, stiff smile. "You feel a crushing sense of guilt because without my admission as to our 'scandalous relationship,' you would not have had an alibi for the Gainsborough theft. You feel as if you owe me. And your twisted sense of honor is telling you that the only way to repay me is to marry me and salvage my reputation, despite my firm and repeated objections."

Marcus sauntered forward, hand clutching the glass, powerful body coiled. "You have me all figured out, don't you?"

She stood and lifted her chin a notch. "Am I correct, Mr. Hawksley?"

"It's Marcus."

"Don't evade my question. Am I correct?"

"Yes, I suppose you're correct," he ground out. "Contrary to what the gossips whisper about me behind my back, I do have a strong moral code . . . a sense of honor. Just so you understand, I do not condone the lies you told at the Westley mansion. I detest being manipulated in business or in personal matters. What you did was selfish and immature, and yet if you had not been where you were, if you had not plotted this 'catastrophe,' as your father called it, I would be at Bow Street as we speak being questioned by an underpaid and overly zealous constable. So, yes, Lady Isabel, I do feel guilty and somewhat responsible for your predicament. I am fully aware that by marrying the younger son of an earl and a working stockbroker to boot, you are stepping down in the eyes of society, but it will spare you from complete scandal. It is the least I can do for your father and your family since you do not seem overly concerned for them."

Her mind fluttered away in anxiety at his determination to follow through with her father's marital notions. "But I have plans, and marriage to you is not one of them."

"I had plans as well, and although marriage was not in my imminent future, a relationship was."

Her heart skipped a beat. "There's another woman? Charlotte had assured me you were a sworn bachelor, and she knows everything."

A mocking smile invaded his stare. "Whoever Charlotte is, she does not know everything."

She shook her head regretfully. "I apologize. I never

intended to cause trouble between a love match." She felt a strange twinge of foreign emotion. Jealousy that Marcus Hawksley had a lover?

Ridiculous! she mused. *You hardly know him.*

He stepped forward and touched her hand. His fingers, warm and strong on her sensitive skin, sent a tingle of awareness up her arm.

She met his gaze, and the intense look in his eyes startled her.

"What's done is done," he said. "I'll not change my mind. Your plans of Paris and Auntie Lil will have to be delayed."

"Yes," she murmured, her mind spinning. "Delayed . . . perhaps not all is lost." She reached out to take the glass of port from him. "Perhaps we can agree to postpone our plans and not dismiss them forever. I'd drink a toast to that."

"What are you scheming?"

"A marriage of convenience, Mr. Hawksley. A *temporary* marriage of convenience."

"I'm listening, but I don't think I like it—"

"It's perfect. We agree to marry for six months until the scandal has passed and my twin siblings are not tarnished. Thereafter, we can go our separate ways. Me to Paris and you back to your lady friend. Many married couples among the *beau monde* lead separate lives, some on separate continents. Since neither of us desires to be shackled by marriage, it's the perfect solution."

"And what about intimate relations during those six months?"

She gave an anxious little cough. "I hadn't thought of that."

"Really?" he drawled. "Just a few hours ago that is all you had thought about."

She ignored his sarcastic tone. "It must be a passionless

relationship. It should be easy to maintain. Separate bedrooms are commonplace after all."

"Ah, what do I get out of this fraudulent marriage?"

"It will assuage your guilt. Whatever your honor is telling you to do, then it should be satisfied."

"My honor can be salvaged by a real marriage."

At his firm resolve, she switched tactics. "But what of your previous life? Your lady friend? Your work? Everything will change if you marry me. As my husband, Father will expect you to limit, maybe even cease, your work at the Exchange."

"I see."

"If we agree to a temporary marriage, then you need only comply for six months. Surely that short amount of time is endurable." Leaning forward, she eyed him with a calculating expression. "Most importantly, you would be assured access to the inner circle of the ton."

"What makes you think I would want that?" he asked softly, mockingly.

"I presume you plan to seek out the true culprit of the theft of the Thomas Gainsborough painting? No one is more convinced than I that you are not the thief. Whoever the criminal is, he is most assuredly working for a member of the *beau monde*, someone who can afford expensive art, or at the least, someone who has the financial means to hire a crooked auctioneer such as Dante Black to frame you. As my husband, you would be on the guest list of every ball, party, masque, and soiree. You could move freely amongst them, listen to their conversations, and even search their houses for information. No one would be the wiser."

"Lady Isabel, you never cease to amaze me. You're correct in presuming that I *will* learn the identity of the true thief," he said, his black eyes glowing with a savage inner fire. "I'm not convinced it's Dante Black either, but another more influential and wealthy mastermind behind the ill deed."

"We are in agreement then?" she asked.

"Ah, but you're forgetting one thing."

"What?"

"You may now believe you will never want to marry, but what if circumstances change?"

She tilted her head at him and smiled. "I don't believe a woman must marry to find fulfillment or happiness. Auntie Lil never married and she is quite content, joyous really. But in the unlikely event that circumstances should change, then we could seek a divorce."

Marcus shook his head. "Divorce is near impossible and requires a Private Act of Parliament. Only rare cases involving a wife's adultery have been sufficient grounds of late. Legal separation is more available."

She didn't miss a beat, desperate to convince him. "Since we will not have children, and I truly have no desire to marry, separation suits us perfectly."

"I commend your swift thinking, Lady Isabel. If half of the stockbrokers at the Exchange thought as quickly on their feet as you, I would have no clients left."

She quickly raised her glass, lest he change his mind. "A toast to us then?"

"I have a better way to seal our bargain." He plucked the glass from her limp hand and pulled her into his arms. "If I am going to embark on a passionless marriage of convenience, then I want to sample what I am giving up."

Chapter 6

Isabel's eyes widened and her lips parted in surprise. A thrill of frightened anticipation touched her spine a moment before Marcus's mouth lowered to hers.

The touch of his lips was a delicious sensation, and his firm mouth coaxed and demanded her response. Her arms rose of their own volition, her fingers digging into his arms, as the heat of the kiss sizzled like molten fire through her veins. Her breasts, pressed against his hard chest, tingled from the contact. His tongue traced the soft fullness of her bottom lip, and she shivered.

His nearness was overwhelming. Nothing in her childhood fantasies had prepared her for the reality of the man. He was so much bigger, bolder . . . so much more *masculine.*

He pulled her closer still, and she gasped. He slipped in between her parted lips to explore the recesses of her mouth. She tightened her arms around his neck, ten fingers sinking into the dark curls on his head. His hair was not rough, as she had thought, but felt like silk as it glided between her fingers. He did not wear cloying cologne like most gentlemen, but instead he smelled clean, fresh, as if he spent much of his time outdoors.

Her eyes slid closed; her skin grew hot. Her heart beat like a drum, and her breathing became ragged. Or was that his breathing? She couldn't tell. All she knew was that her trembling limbs clung to him.

She had kissed other men. But never had those rushed interludes felt like this. Those kisses had been wet and sloppy—the partners rushed and overeager as if the kissing was just an inconvenience to do what they really sought to do—grope her thigh, her buttocks, or her breast.

Here was a man who enjoyed kissing, took his time and thoroughly enjoyed holding her, exploring her lips, her mouth, her . . .

His lips moved to her ear, then the curve of her neck. She gasped again—the sensations overwhelming.

"Oh, my," she whispered. "I hadn't expected it to be quite so . . . enjoyable."

He raised his head, and then dropped his arms from around her. "Neither did I," he said, his voice harsh.

She was confused by his sudden withdrawal, the tensing of his body. Perhaps he wasn't as affected by their shared embrace as she? She knew there had been lovers in his roguish days.

What could a mere kiss mean to a former rake?

Then she met his gaze and changed her opinion. There was a wild look in his dark eyes, a smoldering promise of more to come. The tensing of his powerful body was not from cold disinterest, but from measured restraint.

"I used to dream about you when I was a girl," she blurted out, then was immediately embarrassed by the admission.

"I know."

She frowned. "A little humility would suit you."

"Perhaps. But if we are to *act* the loving couple, then we must be completely honest with each other. Do you agree?"

"Of course. Then if I may ask, why did you kiss me?"

"Because I wanted to. Because I've thought of little else since you propositioned me in Lord Westley's erotic gallery."

Her heartbeat throbbed in her ears at his words. "I see," she said, raising a forefinger to her swollen bottom lip.

Footsteps echoed down the hall, and the library door swung open. Edward Cameron stood in the doorway.

"Well, Mr. Hawksley? Is everything settled between the two of you then?"

Marcus nodded. "We are in agreement, Lord Malvern."

"Good. We shall announce the engagement immediately to stem the tide of forthcoming gossip. The sooner the marriage takes place, the better. I'll attempt to acquire a Special License, but if my connections are unsuccessful, then we shall have to arrange for the reading of the banns. Shall I contact Lord Ardmore, or will you?"

Marcus straightened. "There's no need. I'll speak with my father and older brother."

Isabel recalled Charlotte's bit of gossip at Lady Holloway's ball. Marcus Hawksley had become estranged from his family after entering trade as a stockbroker. It had seemed like such a harsh course of action by the Earl of Ardmore. Had the old man no feelings for his younger son? And what of Marcus's brother, the heir to the earldom? How could he fault his younger sibling for seeking to earn a living rather than begging for every shilling from his father as all younger sons had to do?

It made no sense. She wondered what else was behind the rift. Glancing at Marcus's strong profile, she decided then and there that she would find out not just the truth about his family, but about who was trying to frame him for thievery.

"You did what?"

Isabel poured Charlotte a cup of tea and took a seat

across from her friend. They were in the parlor of Isabel's home, where Isabel had invited Charlotte for afternoon tea to update her on yesterday's shocking course of events.

"I don't know what to think myself," Isabel said. "I was trying to get out of one engagement only to find myself forced into another."

Charlotte sat still, her color alarmingly pale. Isabelle reached across an end table, past the sterling silver tray, to touch her friend's hand. "Charlotte?"

Charlotte blinked, her eyes focusing on Isabel's face. "Engaged to Marcus Hawksley? You lucky devil, Isabel."

"Lucky?"

"Of course!"

"Whatever do you mean? As my closest friend, you know that I don't want to marry."

"But that was to Lord Walling," Charlotte said. "The *waddling* Lord Walling. Not to the young, devilishly masculine Marcus Hawksley. The man you used to incessantly talk about after your father's summer house party when you were twelve."

"That was a long time ago."

"So? Look me in the eye and tell me you are not attracted to him now."

Isabel fidgeted in her seat. "That's not the point. I must tell you that Marcus and I have come to an agreement, an understanding that no one is to know about. No one but you. But you must promise not to whisper our secret to another soul. I know how you love to gossip, Charlotte, but you must swear to keep your flapping lips sealed."

Charlotte's blue eyes widened. "You have raised my curiosity, Isabel. I promise on our lifelong friendship."

Isabel glanced at the closed parlor door to ensure no servants were about, and then turned to look at Charlotte. "We are to be together in name only," Isabel whispered.

Charlotte blinked. "Whatever do you mean?"

"Our relationship shall remain passionless until the gossip has subsided, and Marcus can discover the true thief of the Thomas Gainsborough painting. Then we will be free to live our separate lives. I can travel to live with Auntie Lil in Paris, and Marcus can return to his . . . his former life."

For some reason, Isabel could not bring herself to divulge—even to Charlotte—that Marcus Hawksley had a lady friend waiting for him.

Charlotte set her teacup on a saucer with a loud *clink* and sat forward. "Have you lost your wits, Isabel? How in the name of Hades do you plan on remaining *passionless* around Marcus Hawksley—a man you used to pine after and secretly watch? Did you not sneak into his guest room at your father's country manor, rummage through his wardrobe, and wear his shirts?"

Isabel's face grew warm at the memory. "I told you that was years ago."

Charlotte dismissed Isabel's argument with a wave of her hand. "I don't believe you. Perhaps you should give *true* marriage a try."

"No! You know what I have planned, what I have looked forward to for years. Marriage will ruin everything. Married women must forgo all their freedom to the dictates and whims of their husbands. My own mother was no different. Even though she loved my father, she sacrificed her dreams of writing because it was not socially acceptable for a countess to pen love stories. She always had regrets that even my loving father was aware of and dismissed as a woman's unimportant fancy. I'll not follow in her footsteps."

Charlotte sighed. "All right, Isabel. I'll support you in this as in everything. I can only hope to be as *unlucky* as you are and find myself engaged to a man as ruggedly attractive as Marcus Hawksley."

Isabel cracked a smile. "Thank you, Charlotte."

Charlotte leaned close. "Now tell me about the auctioneer who was after Marcus. What if he tries to accuse Marcus again?"

"Marcus plans to find the true thief, or at the least, determine who hired the thief to frame him. He believes the culprit has wealth and status."

"Oh, I do love a good mystery," Charlotte said, licking her lips. "I shall help you investigate the members of the *beau monde*. They are all hypocrites as far as I am concerned. You should hear Mother's friends. Their vicious tongues are nothing less than shocking in their attempts to discredit others behind their backs."

Isabel gave a grudging nod. "I told Marcus that I would help him infiltrate high society in order to find the evildoer. But what I failed to mention was that my involvement would be more than as a titled lady on his arm at every social event of the Season, and that I would take on more of an active role."

"Ah, it seems Marcus Hawksley has yet to learn the true constitution of his betrothed."

"Everyone will soon learn what has occurred at the Westley mansion," Isabel said. "Lady Yarmouth happened to be visiting from Paris and had accompanied Lord Yarmouth to the auction. Your mother is a friend of hers, is she not?"

"Of course. My mother and stepfather are having a ball next Saturday, and Lord and Lady Yarmouth will be in attendance."

"With my mother gone, do you think your mother would officially announce my engagement?" Isabel asked.

Charlotte's face creased into a sudden smile. "What a wonderful idea! My stepfather, even more than my mother, loves attracting attention to their events, and what would attract more attention than the engagement of Lady Isabel Cameron to the Earl of Ardmore's youngest son?"

"You mean the Earl of Ardmore's damaged son."

"No matter. It will add fuel to the fire. My stepfather will be in his glory." Charlotte licked her pink lips and lifted her teacup. "Now tell me about Lord Westley's room of erotic art and don't miss a detail."

Chapter 7

The artist's studio was like all the others Dante Black had frequented over the years. Dilapidated and drafty, it stank of paint, turpentine, and the desperation that oozed out of the pores of every struggling artist in London. Bottles of paint in every color of the rainbow crowded wooden shelves on the walls. Canvases and wood frames were scattered around the perimeter of the room. Brushes and dirty rags soaked in jars of cloudy water, waiting to be cleaned.

The only difference today was a package wrapped in plain brown paper—slightly larger than three feet by four feet—which rested in the corner of the room. None would suspect the nondescript wrapping held the valuable 1791 painting by Thomas Gainsborough, *Seashore with Fishermen*.

Dante turned away from the hidden painting and paced the small space. He had arrived before his contact, and his stomach churned with anxiety. Sweat trickled down his bald head and ran into his eyes. Every five paces, he swiped at his forehead with an impatient hand.

"Damn," Dante spat out loud. "The bitch ruined everything."

He viciously kicked at a can of turpentine on the floor, splattering the contents across the paint-stained hardwood and onto his polished Hessians. He cursed again, and the strong stench of the spilled turpentine burned his nostrils.

"We expected better from ye, Dante."

Dante whirled around at the sound of the raspy male voice.

Robby Bones, the criminal who had recruited Dante, slithered into the center of the studio. Although he was near the same impressive height as Dante, the physical similarities between the two men stopped there. Whereas Dante was thin, Robby Bones was a testament to his name—gaunt, cadaverous, near-emaciated in appearance. Black hair hung in greasy strands to his shoulders, hiding sunken cheekbones and deep eye sockets. His fingertips, as well as his teeth, were tobacco stained to an uncomely brown. His trademark, which he boasted about, was a chipped front tooth that had sheared in half during a bar brawl, and that he now used to hold a cheap cigar in place without having to clamp his lips together. It was rumored that Bones worked as a grave digger when his illicit activities were not sufficiently profitable.

Disgust, comingled with disquiet, infused Dante. He considered himself a gentleman and the riffraff before him was insulting. "The girl's presence was unforeseeable. Her testimony was beyond my control."

"'Is lordship paid ye good blunt fer yer services. If ye 'ad used yer men like ye should 'ave, ye would 'ave known that Hawksley wasna alone in that room, an' ye could 'ave seen to the chit."

At the mention of "his lordship," the anonymous employer who'd hired both Dante and Robby Bones to do his bidding, Dante's curiosity rose again. Dante had no idea as to the true identity of "his lordship," but he suspected three things: First, the man was part of high society, whether he held a title or not; second, he was sufficiently wealthy to pay the exorbitant price Dante had required; and third, he *hated* Marcus Hawksley with a vengeance.

Dante's temper rose to his defense. "The *chit* turned out to be Isabel Cameron, the daughter of the very influential and wealthy Earl of Malvern. She wasn't a common whore whom no one would notice had gone missing. The disappearance of a titled lady would have invited unwanted attention, to say the least."

Robby Bones stepped forward, his dishwater brown eyes hard and filled with dislike. "Ye failed at a simple task. Hawksley is a free man, an' 'e's not the type to sit back an' do nothin'. 'E'll search fer ye to get the truth."

Dante's nerves tensed immediately at the mere notion that Marcus Hawksley would hunt him down. He felt as if the temperature of the room rose twenty degrees, and he wiped at the increased perspiration on his brow. "What shall I tell him?"

"That's yer problem, Dante. But keep yer mouth shut about me. One word from 'is lordship, an' ye'll be ruined. Yer days of sellin' fancy art to the stinkin' rich will be over. Lucky fer ye, 'is lordship 'as more plans fer Hawksley that require yer services."

Robby Bones turned his back on Dante and walked to the corner of the room. He picked up the wrapped Gainsborough painting and made to leave.

"Where are you taking that?" Dante asked. Despite everything, Dante was a true art lover, and the mere thought of what a rancid criminal like Robby Bones would do with such a masterpiece disturbed him.

Bones stopped and shrugged dismissively. "'Is lordship knows Hawksley wanted it and that's why 'e'll keep it. Ye can hide from Hawksley, but don't leave London, Dante. Next time, if the chit gets in the way, *I'll* take care of 'er."

Chapter 8

Marcus went up the steps of the impressive mansion on Berkeley Square with the foreboding enthusiasm of a front line foot soldier marching into battle. He had wanted to put off the visit for another day, but duty prevailed. Gritting his teeth, he banged the solid brass knocker.

The door swung open to reveal a heavyset, glum-faced butler. The servant's mouth pulled into a sour grin as he stared at Marcus.

"Mr. Hawksley, sir. Lord Ardmore was not expecting you."

"I'm certain my father will want to speak to me today, Bentley." Marcus stepped past the butler and into the hall. "Where is he?"

Bentley blinked and hurried to close the door, his formal demeanor abandoned as he rushed to catch up with Marcus. "Perhaps you should wait in the parlor while I advise Lord Ardmore of your visit."

"Good idea," Marcus replied. "If you would be so kind as to advise my brother of my presence as well."

Marcus walked down the hall and paused in the parlor doorway, watching Bentley rush off in the opposite direction. As soon as the butler was out of sight, Marcus spun on his heel and headed for the library.

Wait in the parlor like hell, Marcus thought.

He suspected Bentley was under strict orders not to summon the master of the house if his younger son was to pay an unannounced visit. No doubt Bentley would return advising Lord Ardmore was indisposed, but would send a note when he was available. Marcus refused to wait around like a secondhand guest only to be turned out.

This was, after all, his childhood home—no matter what his father's current attitude was toward him.

He found his father sitting behind a massive desk, reading the latest issue of *The Regal Hound*. The library, with its rich mahogany furnishings and bookshelves lined with priceless volumes, was as opulent as the rest of the home.

"Good morning, Father."

Randall Hawksley, the Earl of Ardmore, stiffened, and his eyes snapped to the doorway. His mouth thinned with displeasure as he spotted Marcus. Although the earl was close to sixty, he appeared younger with a full head of dark hair, just graying at the temples. Shrewd brown eyes beneath thick brows glared at his younger son.

"What are you doing here?" Ardmore said tersely.

Marcus stepped into the room. "It's always a pleasure to see you, too, Father."

Footsteps echoed down the marble hall and Bentley appeared at the door. "I requested he stay in the parlor, my lord, until I could find you and advise you of his presence, but—"

"No matter, Bentley," Ardmore said with a wave of his hand. "Marcus was never good at following instructions."

"Not true, Father," Marcus said as he took a seat. "Just your instructions."

Bentley, discreet as always, disappeared from the doorway.

Ardmore slapped down the hunting paper in his hand, irritation written on every line of his face. "Have you come to torment me in front of the hired help or is there another reason for this untimely visit?"

"I apologize if I've disturbed your reading," Marcus said, a bitter edge of cynicism in his voice, "but I've come to give you good news. I'm to marry."

Ardmore looked at him in surprise. "To whom?"

"Lady Isabel Cameron, the daughter of Edward Cameron, the Earl of Malvern."

"You're jesting."

"No. Why would you think that?"

"I heard about the scandal at the Westley mansion. It explains everything," Ardmore said.

"What do you mean?"

"Why else would a titled heiress marry *you*?"

Despite anticipating his father's response, Marcus's temper flared. "What? No toast to celebrate your son's impending nuptials?"

Ardmore ignored Marcus's hard tone. "I always said you would bring shame upon the family name, and I was right. First you became a reckless gambler, a drunk, and a womanizer. Then there was that distasteful incident with that girl, that commoner, who killed herself rather than spend a lifetime with you, after which you completely lost whatever breeding was instilled in you by entering trade. Now you blackmail a titled lady into marriage just to clear your name from stealing a—"

"That's enough, Father."

At the sound of an authoritative voice, both Marcus and Ardmore turned to the door of the library. Roman Hawksley, heir to the earldom and Marcus's older brother, eyed the occupants of the room. Tall, dark, and broad-shouldered, there was an inherent strength in his face. Where Marcus had jet eyes, Roman had deep green eyes, which seemed to blaze in his bronzed face. Women had always flocked to him, and Marcus had suspected it was due to his physical appearance even more than his status as the heir.

Roman walked forward and extended his hand to Marcus. "I overheard. I believe congratulations are in order."

Marcus met his brother's green gaze. A silent battle of wills raged between them, before Marcus stood and reluctantly extended his own hand. "Thank you, Roman."

Roman strode to the liquor cabinet. "Let's drink to the lovely Lady Isabel Cameron, shall we?" He poured three glasses and handed the first one to their father.

"Yes," Ardmore said. "I can use a strong drink right now."

"There's no need for hostility, Father," Roman said. "It's not every day one of your sons gets engaged."

Randall Hawksley's glare moved from Marcus to Roman. "I had expected it to be you. Perhaps Marcus can give you a few pointers on how to ensnare an heiress."

Ah, Marcus mused. *Isn't that just like Father to pit brother against brother to serve his needs.*

A sudden anger lit Roman's eyes. "No lady has appealed to me of late. Perhaps I find myself yearning for the type of marriage you and Mother had," Roman said, his tongue heavy with sarcasm.

Good one! Marcus thought. *That should put the old dog in his place.*

Their parents had despised each other. Their deceased mother, who had been passive by nature and had hated conflict, had been dominated by their father. The only matter in which their mother had prevailed was in choosing her sons' Latin names. She had loved mythology and had chosen both—Marcus, the Roman God of fertility, and Roman, a man of Rome.

Ardmore downed his glass and slammed it on the desk. "I've had enough of my offspring for one afternoon." He rose and strode to the door. Turning back, he glared at Marcus. "I await the wedding invitation, Marcus. I admire Edward Cameron and thus approve of the match, however it came about." The door slammed behind him.

"Well, that's as close to a compliment as I have received from him in my adult memory," Marcus said dryly.

"Be glad of it," Roman said. "He's been ruthless in his quest for me to marry this past year. He's quite pleased by your choice and will incessantly throw it in my face, you know."

"You deserve it."

Roman shrugged. "I suppose I do. Another drink then? We can toast my anticipated misery if you like."

Marcus waved his brother off and rose from his seat. "Sit. I'll get the liquor. We may polish it off." Marcus brought over a crystal decanter, and the two brothers pulled up chairs across from each other.

"I heard about the Thomas Gainsborough painting," Roman said.

"It never ceases to amaze me how fast gossip travels in this town. It has only been a day."

"Do you know who stole it?" Roman asked.

"No."

"Do you have any idea why the auctioneer claimed you did?"

"No."

"Have you questioned the man?"

"Dante Black is missing. No one knows his whereabouts," Marcus said, his frustration evident in his voice. He had tried to locate Dante, but the auctioneer had not appeared at his place of business or his residence since yesterday's auction.

"Do you need help investigating?" Roman asked. "I have resources—"

"No. I can handle the matter."

"Just as you handled Bridget?"

Marcus's head snapped up. "Ah, your true feelings always surface, don't they, Roman?"

The tragedy and treachery of Bridget always came up between them. It had destroyed their bond as brothers. And here it was again, like water when it freezes between a tiny crack in a rock, splitting the rock in two, separating it forever.

Marcus was the first to admit he had been a reckless fool in his early twenties. For years, Marcus's father had told him he was worthless. Marcus had grown to believe his father's prophecy and had become a rogue and a womanizer.

And then Marcus had met Bridget Turner, the flirtatious daughter of a prosperous London merchant whose family was not included in the tedious workings of the *beau monde* that he had grown to resent. At first Marcus had avoided her like he did all self-professed virgins. Messy business, he had thought. But *she* had been relentless in her pursuit of *him*, and despite Roman's warnings to end the liaison, Marcus and Bridget had continued their affair.

When she had become pregnant, he had at first been alarmed. But the more Marcus had thought about it, about having a child of his own, he became thrilled. Here was a chance to raise a child with love, unlike how he and his brother had been brought up. Marcus secretly proposed to Bridget, and on the morning of their anticipated elopement, he had shown up an eager groom.

But Bridget had tricked and betrayed him; she had not been the innocent, loving girl he had believed her to be. She had aspirations above her station, and unbeknownst to Marcus, she had mistakenly thought him the heir to the earldom. Once his status as the younger son was revealed to her, she had cruelly rejected him as valueless. When Bridget's double-crossing had failed, her father had threatened to toss her into the streets. She had retaliated by doing the unthinkable: She had taken her life and that of their unborn babe.

Marcus had been devastated, not just from the murder of his child, but from Bridget's shocking deception.

When Roman learned of the girl's death, they had a fierce fight. Roman was angry that Marcus had not ended the affair as he had advised, and he hadn't believed the story of Bridget's duplicity. Whereas Bridget's chicanery had failed during her lifetime, it created a bitter rift between the once-close brothers after her death.

Marcus had felt betrayed by everyone he had ever trusted. Bridget had killed herself and his child. Roman had rejected him. His father thought him a useless spendthrift. Marcus had left home and had begun to drink himself into oblivion when, by the grace of God, he met Blake Mallorey. The newly returned Earl of Ravenspear had fled his own past demons and had introduced Marcus to the Stock Exchange.

Roman leaned forward, his expression serious. "I didn't mean to bring up old wounds, Marcus. I only offer aid if you need help finding the real culprit," he said, his tone apologetic.

Roman had recently tried to make amends with Marcus, and as a result, their relationship had gone from frigid to irritably tolerant.

"I appreciate your offer," Marcus said, "but I am not the same man as in my youth. I don't need my older brother to fix my problems. I'll find the man responsible and it will be on my terms."

Chapter 9

Two unpleasant visits in one day could turn a focused stockbroker into a bitter businessman. Only this time, as Marcus lifted the brass knocker to bang on the door, a smiling housekeeper greeted him and immediately ushered him inside.

Simone Winston glided down the staircase to greet him. "Marcus, darling. What a wonderful surprise."

A wealthy widow in her early forties, Simone was twelve years older than Marcus. With a crown of auburn hair, a porcelain complexion, and a voluptuous figure, Simone was sought after as a lover by many males of the *beau monde*. That she had been having an affair with the dark and dangerous Marcus Hawksley added an air of mystery to her widowed status.

How irrational and ironic was society, Marcus thought, for if a widow entered into a salacious relationship with him, it would enhance her reputation, but if an innocent such as Isabel Cameron was even suspected of being alone in a room with him, it would destroy hers beyond repair.

Dressed in a green silk concoction that set her hair aflame, Simone wrapped slender arms around Marcus's neck and kissed him full on the mouth. Her familiar expensive perfume enveloped him.

"I'm so glad you came to see me, Marcus. I felt horrible after our argument last week, and I've missed you terribly."

She pressed her full breasts against his chest, but this time, he was slow to respond to her feminine allure.

He pulled back. "It's good to see you, too, Simone, but there's something I must tell you."

"There's no need to apologize, darling. I understand you have been under pressure at the Stock Exchange, and that you truly did not mean what you had said last week about us never marrying."

His mouth set in annoyance. "May we talk elsewhere, Simone, other than in the front hall?"

She licked a full bottom lip. "Of course, darling. Let's go upstairs." She took his hand and turned.

Marcus didn't budge. "Your bedroom is not what I had in mind. Perhaps one of the sitting rooms."

She froze. She appeared stunned that any man would turn down her bedroom. "The sitting room?" Her gaze slid downward, noting his tailored suit. "You're coming from the Exchange. I don't understand your obsession with working really. You don't need to—"

"Not now, Simone." His tone was impatient and finally gained her full attention.

"How impolite of me. You must need refreshment." She led him to the first room on the right, a lavishly decorated sitting room for receiving formal guests. She went to a sideboard and made to pour him a drink.

"That's not necessary. I don't want a drink. I want to talk."

She turned, arching a well-plucked eyebrow.

Unsure how to break the news to her, he chose a straightforward approach. "I'm afraid we can no longer see each other. I'm to be married."

All animation left her face. "Married! To whom?"

"Lady Isabel Cameron."

"How could you? Not less than one week ago, you stood before me and said you would not marry—me or *anyone*. We had a terrible fight over it. And now you are telling me you want to end our affair because you are to marry?"

"I'm sorry for misleading you."

Cold eyes sniped at him. "You're sorry! What changed your mind?"

"The gossip has been all over London. I'm surprised that you haven't heard."

"I've been out of town visiting my sister and returned just this morning. What on earth have I missed?"

For the second time that day, Marcus had to explain himself, a task that he did not relish and that he had sworn never to do again since Bridget's suicide.

At Simone's thunderous expression, Marcus took a deep breath. In as few words as possible, he explained what had occurred at the Westley auction. He was careful to leave out the bargain he had struck with Isabel to remain married for only six months' time. No one need know until the art thief was found and Isabel was in Paris with her unconventional Auntie Lil.

At first he had initially contemplated continuing his liaison with Simone while he was married to Isabel, but the idea quickly vanished as it held little appeal. Simone Winston never could keep her mouth shut, and she would talk about her continued relationship with Marcus Hawksley to anyone with an open ear.

An unnerving thought floated into his mind and took root, that after meeting Isabel, Simone's feminine wiles seemed overtly contrived and jaded.

He mentally shook himself. No, he would not put his marriage to Isabel—sham or not—at risk.

At his staunch silence, Simone's expression softened

from fury to disappointment with the calculated efficiency
of a chameleon.

"So you are marrying this girl simply because her testimony makes you feel compelled to do the right thing?" Her
full lips formed a pout, and she reached out to stroke his
chest, her long fingers playing with the buttons of his waistcoat. "You don't have to do this, Marcus. Marry me instead."

"And what of Isabel Cameron?"

"The girl chose her own fate. Your defense is solid now.
Let her suffer for her rash behavior."

Even knowing Simone's selfish nature, he was struck by
her coldness. "No, Simone. I gave my word."

He turned, but her hand shot out to clutch his arm.

"Then nothing has to change between us. We can continue to be lovers. A man like you needs a real woman beneath him, an experienced lover who knows how to
pleasure you. A blue-blooded virgin will never be anything
but frigid in your bed."

An unbidden image of Isabel Cameron surrounded by
erotic art flashed through Marcus's mind. He had held
Isabel in his arms, had kissed her, and knew firsthand she
was anything but frigid.

His gaze returned to Simone's upturned face. Marcus
knew that where Simone was as well practiced as any courtesan, Isabel would be innocent, yes, but as recklessly impulsive in bed as she was out of it.

But you will never know Isabel Cameron intimately,
Marcus thought. *You made a bargain not to touch her, no
matter how much you desire her.*

Marcus shook his head. "Nevertheless, Simone, I've come
today to tell you of my decision to end our relationship."

Simone's face twisted into a cruel mask. "You'll be
back," she spat, "and you'll beg me for scraps of affection."

"No. I won't, Simone."

"Get out!"

He was more than happy to oblige her, relieved really. He had never liked female entanglements and was well aware that Simone had wanted to marry. The problem was Marcus had never intended to marry after Bridget.

Life had taught him a cruel, but valuable lesson: People could not be trusted; lovers and family were no exception. But Marcus did pay his debts. And he owed Isabel Cameron . . .

If six months together would salvage her family from disgrace and give Isabel the freedom she so desired, then he would do it.

He turned and walked to the door. Unladylike curses spewed from Simone behind him. He glanced back just in time to see Simone pick up an expensive crystal vase and dump the flowers and water onto the thick Aubusson carpet.

Anticipating her intent, he deftly dodged the vase, and it shattered against the wall on his way out.

Chapter 10

"I'm not certain about this," Marcus said as he sat opposite Blake and Victoria Mallorey, the Earl and Countess of Ravenspear, in their crested carriage. They were stuck in a row of carriages that lined the drive to the Bennings' mansion in Grosvenor Square, and Marcus's dread increased with each passing moment.

"The Bennings are to officially announce your engagement at their ball tonight. You must attend," Blake said.

"You're enjoying my discomfort, aren't you?" Marcus asked.

Blake grinned. "Shouldn't I? As a well-sought-after broker, you are seen everywhere at the Stock Exchange, the coffeehouses, and the clubs, but as for the social events of the season, you are a hermit. This is good for you."

Marcus glared at Blake. He had known Blake Mallorey for years and quite simply owed the earl his life. After Bridget's death, Marcus had wandered about, bingeing on alcohol and reckless behavior as a form of self-punishment. One afternoon, he had sauntered into Gentleman Jackson's and had arrogantly challenged the famous boxing Champion, Tom Cribb—known as "Killer Cribb"—to a match. Thankfully, Blake had been present in the ring and saw through Marcus's cocky bravado. Blake, who had been good friends with Cribb, had intervened, soothing the boxer's pride and calming his temper.

Blake had befriended Marcus that day. As an avid investor, Blake had introduced Marcus to the London Stock Exchange and later hired him as his own stockbroker. Without a doubt, Blake Mallorey had saved him, and in return, Marcus had made the already-rich earl one of the wealthiest men in England.

Blake had always understood Marcus better than anyone, and was never intimidated by the foul gossip that surrounded him. Of course, it helped that Blake had himself been an outcast, a menace intent on revenge upon his return to England almost three years ago.

But that was before Victoria. His wife and savior.

"Never mind my husband's rude manners," Victoria said, touching Blake's hand. "We are excited for you. I can think of no other that deserves to be happy. That's why when I had first learned the good news a week ago, I insisted you travel with us tonight."

Marcus smiled at Victoria. She was a beautiful woman with dark hair and emerald eyes that shone with intelligence and wit. Like Blake and Marcus, she had past secrets as well.

Marcus had been stunned to discover Victoria was an anonymous investor in the male-dominated London Stock Exchange.

Almost three years had passed since she had "tamed" Blake and they had married. Now she was in the later stages of pregnancy. She had delayed her confinement for the sole purpose of attending the ball tonight to celebrate Marcus's engagement.

Their vehicle lurched forward as the crush of carriages made their way up the long drive. Marcus frowned; a rush of restlessness arose within him as the well-lit mansion came into view.

He detested social events, was never comfortable attending them. In his experience, the women would smile politely, then whisper behind their fans as soon as he turned his back. No doubt, the Earl of Ardmore's estranged younger son was excellent fodder for gossip. The ridiculousness of overprotective mamas ushering their virginal daughters away from him had always irked him. Then there were the men who dared not ignore him for fear of his power at the Stock Exchange. Some were his clients, others clamored to be, and all were aware of his ruthless success in the market. And at every social event there was always one overly judgmental matron who considered trade well beneath her station, who would give him "the cut direct" by looking him straight in the eye only to turn away without acknowledging him.

The stuffy matron, whoever it might be, would reaffirm his philosophy on life: *Art and money don't betray you, only people do.*

The Ravenspear carriage reached the front steps of the mansion. The doors were opened by a liveried footman and they descended. Blake carefully held Victoria's hand as though she were a fragile porcelain doll.

They joined the crowd of well-dressed people on the front steps. Muted strains of the orchestra drifted from the house. It was a warm May evening, and the ladies vigorously fanned themselves while the men perspired in full evening attire. Marcus's silk cravat felt like a wool scarf.

As they neared the ballroom, their attention was captured by two gargantuan statues of Chinese emperors on both sides of the doorway. Fifteen feet high, and what appeared to be half as wide, the statues stood guard at the entrance of the ballroom. Dressed in traditional *shenyis*, full-length robes that wrapped around their robust bodies, they had slanted eyes and long, jet hair. The stony-faced pair looked down upon the guests with haughty rebuke. Granite signs at their sandaled feet identified them as "Ming" and "Chang."

Blake grimaced in distaste. "Good Lord! Who would want those two monstrosities in their home?"

"*Chinoiserie* décor is highly desirable, darling," Victoria said. "The Regent himself has hired decorators to copy the Chinese style."

Marcus laughed. "With the Port of Canton closed to foreigners and traders, I wonder how authentic the decorators' designs truly are."

"It doesn't matter," Victoria said. "It's all the rage and makes a hostess look sophisticated."

Marcus glanced inside the ballroom, where the scene was no better. The wallpaper was covered with a bamboo pattern. Exotic birds and panda bears, with their distinctive black and white markings, wove their way around the walls. Smaller statues of Chinese women draped in gold robes were positioned in the four corners of the room.

The décor must have cost a small fortune, but it was garish and gaudy. Everything was ostentatious, designed to openly display the wealth of the owners, but only succeeded in showing their lack of culture and taste.

As they waited their turn to enter the ballroom, a servant with a red vest, embroidered with what Marcus assumed were Chinese symbols, formally announced them.

"The Earl and Countess of Ravenspear and Mr. Marcus Hawksley," the servant boomed out.

All eyes turned to them. Marcus stood straight and proud. After a few tense moments in which he knew he was being critically observed, the feeling passed. No doubt accompanying Blake and Victoria aided his cause.

Their hostess approached them at the bottom of the stairs. Leticia Benning had a heavily painted face, and wore a gown of blinding-gold tissue with a plunging bodice. Her enormous breasts were stuffed inside the low-cut gown like mounds of soft dough. Piles of blond curls, reaching a foot high, topped her head in what could only have been false hair.

She smiled as she touched Marcus's sleeve, her kohl-lined eyes devouring him.

"I'm glad you could join us, Mr. Hawksley," she drawled. "My daughter, Charlotte, and Isabel are inseparable friends, and it is a pleasure to officially announce your engagement tonight."

Marcus bowed. "Thank you, Mrs. Benning. I understand your events are the talk of the town."

"What a charmer you are, Mr. Hawksley." Leticia giggled, and tips of rosy nipples peeped from her bodice.

Just then a man came up beside Leticia. Marcus's first instinct was shock, and he couldn't stop staring.

Leticia smiled up at the man. "May I present my husband, Mr. Harold Benning."

Christ! Marcus thought. *He's more effeminate than his wife.*

Harold Benning wore a purple velvet suit with a snowy cravat so intricately folded that Marcus would not have been surprised if it took his manservant an hour to tie. His violet shoes had a heel which angled his portly body forward, accentuating his large paunch. A quizzing glass hung from his waistcoat with a matching purple ribbon. His face was powdered; his watery blue eyes glazed over as if he had made one too many trips to the punch bowl.

"Good evening, Mr. Hawksley. It's not every day a gentleman sweeps our dear Isabel off her feet. Love is so romantic, is it not, my dear," Benning said, glancing at his wife.

It didn't take Marcus long to size up the Bennings. Flamboyant attention seekers, they had the money to carry out their every whim, no matter how ridiculous. Yet they were as transparent in their insincerity as polished glass. No wonder the ton adored them. Marcus wondered what their daughter, Charlotte Benning, was like.

If she was as disingenuous as her parents, how could Isabel befriend her?

After the proper pleasantries were exchanged, Marcus and Blake strolled away, leaving the ladies and Harold Benning to socialize.

"Harold Benning is more of a dandy than Beau Brummel," Blake murmured.

Marcus laughed as he reached for two glasses of champagne from a passing servant's tray and handed one to Blake.

Marcus's gaze roamed the rest of the room, and stopped short when he spotted Isabel Cameron. Escorted by her father, she stood at the top of the stairs leading to the ballroom.

His reaction was swift. The thudding of his heart drowned out the roar of conversation in the crowded room. He couldn't tear his gaze away from her.

She was stunning in a blue silk gown, which enhanced the vivid blue of her eyes. A lace-trimmed train flowed at her feet. The gown's neckline was fashionably low, and a pearl clasp between her breasts drew the eye to the creamy skin rounded enticingly above her bodice. Matching pearl combs held her sable hair up and away from the sides of her face, and loose curls fell down her back.

"Easy, Marcus," Blake said. "You look like a starving wolf spotting its prey. You don't want to scare the girl."

Isabel met his gaze across the room and smiled.

Marcus's heart hammered, and his gut tightened like a fist.

For the first time, Marcus noticed two youths, a male and a female, standing beside Isabel, and he surmised they must be her twin siblings, Amber and Anthony.

They were attractive adolescents, and he guessed their ages to be close to thirteen years. They were both blond and their blue eyes were wide as disks as they surveyed the Bennings' ballroom. This was most likely their first ball, and without the younger sister's coming out in society, they were permitted to attend tonight in honor of their elder sister's engagement.

The Cameron family wove their way through the crowd and came up to them.

"Good evening," Edward said, addressing Marcus and Blake.

Marcus had to force his eyes from Isabel to her father. "Lord Malvern."

"All should go as planned. Charlotte Benning is Isabel's close friend, and as I'm certain you have surmised, Harold Benning loves attention," Edward said, a note of mockery in his voice.

The earl's tone spoke volumes about his feelings toward Benning.

He doesn't like the dandy, Marcus mused.

Isabel introduced Amber and Anthony, and the twins politely greeted him. Amber bit her lip as she looked around; Anthony's spine was stiff as he stood to his full height of five and a half feet. The pair appeared as uncomfortable and anxious as goldfish dumped out of their bowls onto a Persian carpet.

Marcus could commiserate.

Leaning down, Marcus met the twins' wide-eyed gazes. "Did you know that there is a Chinese-style pagoda outside in the gardens? I've heard it's four stories tall and replicated to look quite authentic. The Chinese use their pagodas as temples or memorials."

Anthony's eyes lit up. "Can we go outside and see it, Izzy?"

Amber chimed in. "Yes, please, Izzy."

"What a wonderful idea," Isabel said. "Go ahead and explore."

The twins smiled at Marcus for the first time, their relief almost palpable. They bounded off to the nearest French doors that led outside to the gardens.

"You've won them over quite easily, Mr. Hawksley," Isabel said.

"That's because I understand their need for fresh air."

She smiled. "How odd. Does that need strike you often?"

"I love nothing more than a hard ride in the park or the country."

She cocked her head to the side, accentuating the long line of her slender throat. "Yes, I can picture you riding fast."

He swallowed at her words, certain she had no idea the erotic picture they evoked in his mind. "Would you like a glass of champagne?" he asked, changing the subject.

"Yes, Mr. Hawksley." She turned away with him, leaving her father and Blake conversing behind.

"It's Marcus, remember?"

"Not here. We don't want to be overheard," she whispered.

"For a woman who desperately sought to ruin her reputation, I find it surprising that you care if others overhear our familiarity."

She lowered thick black lashes. "Things have changed. We must act the part of a proper couple."

Ah, he thought. He didn't miss her words "act the part." He kept having to remind himself she wanted nothing to do with him as a flesh-and-blood man, just as a facade to dupe society.

The refreshment table was at the far end of the ballroom. As they walked past, couples watched them, some whispering behind their fans. No doubt, gossip about what had occurred at the Westley mansion was the topic as well as word of their impending engagement. Marcus ignored them, his gaze staying on Isabel's delicate profile. She had a natural grace about her, but he sensed that beneath the surface simmered her true volatile nature.

They reached the table, and Marcus tore his eyes from her face. He looked up and froze.

Splotches of brilliant color, lines, and forms covered the walls. Row after row of awe-inspiring paintings hung in splendid display. He spotted works by British portrait painters Sir Joshua Reynolds and John Hoppner. There were paintings by sporting artists James Ward and George Stubbs. Even Dutch and Flemish masterpieces were in the collection as well as quality watercolors of famous landscapes. When he had first entered the ballroom, he had not been able to see the far wall, and thus had missed the most impressive part of the room.

Good Lord, the artwork did not fit the distasteful Chinese décor, and Marcus guessed that was why Leticia and Harold Benning had hung them in the far end of the ballroom. Still, the works were stunning, and Marcus's mind reeled at the sight.

Isabel must have noticed his fascination. "I see you admire Mr. Benning's collection."

His gaze remained riveted to the wall. "I would not peg him the art lover."

"That's because he's not. Charlotte told me he buys art only to enhance his status as a premier host. That is the extent of his interest. That's why the paintings are displayed in the ballroom and not in his study or bedroom for private enjoyment. He wants others to envy his possessions."

"How wasteful. They should be prized and shared with others in a museum, not a stuffy ballroom."

She arched a brow. "Don't you acquire art and keep it squirreled away for your pleasure?"

He turned away from the wall. "Yes and no. I frequently loan my treasures to the museums. I find just as much fulfillment in sharing what I have obtained with those that otherwise would never have an opportunity to view a true masterpiece."

Clear blue eyes studied him. "You surprise me, Mr. Hawksley. As an artist myself, I spend quite a lot of my time frequenting the museums. I suppose I owe my enjoyment to generous collectors such as you."

Marcus's pulse throbbed at her words. "Tell me about Charlotte. Is she like her father?"

"Oh, no. Harold Benning is her stepfather. Her mother was widowed for the third time four years ago when Charlotte was just sixteen. Each elderly deceased husband left Leticia a small fortune, and she is free to spend her money however she desires. Harold Benning was a perfect match for her flamboyant lifestyle. He actually enjoys being a spendthrift more than his wife. But Charlotte is not like either her mother or stepfather. She finds her stepfather — how shall I say it?—irritating, but endures his nature for her mother. You shall meet Charlotte and see."

"I look forward to it."

"I sympathize with her," Isabel said. "Mr. Benning's mannerisms can be most annoying. But I must admit there is no one more knowledgeable to accompany a woman to the dressmaker's. He has a knack for finding what colors and styles most flatter a woman."

Marcus rolled his eyes and handed her a glass from the table. "Leticia Benning approaches as we speak. I believe our time to become 'formally announced' as a couple has arrived."

Isabel touched his forearm. "Don't look so tense. This is your entry into society in order to find the true mastermind behind the theft of the Thomas Gainsborough painting. Mr. Benning's collection is small compared to others. After tonight, you will be on the guest list of every avid art collector in London."

"I'm counting on it," Marcus said dryly.

Chapter 11

"Absolutely not, madam. You will stay out of this, do you understand?" Marcus said.

Isabel looked up into Marcus's hard face. Every line of his powerful body was tense, his dark eyes narrowed, and despite herself, she felt a shiver of apprehension course down her spine.

But damned if she would back down.

"You are making no sense, Mr. Hawksley," she said.

"No. I make perfect sense. It's you who has temporarily lost your mind."

She glowered up at him. They were in the Bennings' gardens, standing behind a stone statue and a big evergreen, a secluded spot perfect for an assignation between lovers or—as in their case—for a private conversation away from prying eyes and straining ears. The moon was hidden behind thick clouds, and the area was dim, save for a single torch which half-illuminated Marcus's face.

They had been formally announced less than an hour ago by Leticia Benning, with a preening Harold Benning by her side, in the center of the ballroom. The guests, after overcoming an awkward silence at learning that the Earl of Malvern's daughter was to wed the estranged Earl of

Ardmore's younger son, had toasted to their future happiness. Almost immediately, a horde of the socially elite had descended upon them and had freely conversed about balls, masques, and garden parties they planned to host during the remaining Season and in which they desired their attendance.

Marcus had slipped into the role of sought-after-gentleman-guest easily, despite his prior reservations.

She had waited until the overeager mass of well-wishers had subsided before requesting a garden walk for fresh air. Her true motives had been not only to escape the ballroom and clear her head, but also to persuade Marcus of her plans to aid him with his investigation.

But never had she anticipated his adamant and angry refusal.

"All I suggest is that I assist with your investigation," she said. "To help find the true criminal behind the theft of the Thomas Gainsborough painting. As a respectable member of society as well as a fourth-year debutante, I believe I know better than you where to start. I can easily determine those art collectors with impressive—"

"I said no."

"Why not?"

"Because that was never part of our bargain."

"And what was?"

"I save you from scandal, which in turn preserves your twin siblings' futures. You get to go to your Auntie Lil and do whatever you think you want to do in Paris. In return, I get my alibi unencumbered by guilt. And we are both free after a six-month marriage devoid of sins of the flesh."

She felt an instant's squeezing hurt. His matter-of-fact tone and his direct, unwavering gaze took her off guard. He made their engagement and upcoming nuptials sound formulaic.

But isn't that what I had planned from the beginning? she thought. *Then why is his businesslike tone so disturbing?*

Isabel inhaled deeply in an attempt to calm herself, the scent of roses from the nearby bushes wafting to her. She looked away, playing for time. Her gaze skimmed the gardens, noting that here, as well as inside, no attention to detail had been overlooked. The shrubbery and rosebushes were meticulously trimmed, an intricate maze lay before them, a water fountain with a seminude mermaid tipping a jug poured water from its spout, and lights blazed distantly from each of the four stories of the Chinese pagoda. The faint outline of a horticultural conservatory could be seen behind the pagoda.

She turned back to face him, only to find him watching her. Masking her inner turmoil with a deceptive calmness, she said, "So you have it all thought out, then?"

There was a slight hesitation in his predatory eyes. "May I point out that it was *you* who contrived our temporary relationship."

"I suppose you are correct, but it was never my intention to be pushed aside and to assume a completely passive role."

"Whatever role would a proper wife play except passive?"

At his careless words, she lost her fight to control her swirling emotions. Her temper flared; she tossed her head and met his black eyes without flinching.

"That might be acceptable to some ladies," she snapped, "but not to me. The Bow Street authorities may believe you innocent of the theft because of my alibi, but that does not mean the ton does as well. You of all people should be aware that malicious gossip is commonplace and thrives among them. If there is even the slightest suspicion upon your name as a thief, then as your betrothed, it affects my family as well. Once the painting is found, society will have nothing to gossip about. I'm not accustomed to having matters decided for me, especially when I know full well that action on my part can change the outcome. And I don't intend to alter my nature just because of a 'bargain' you think we made and your rigid beliefs of how a wife should behave."

He moved with a quickness that made her gasp and pulled her into his arms. "I wondered how long it would take for your fireworks to explode. You do not disappoint, Isabel. I hadn't long to wait."

Heat burst through her body both from his outrageous words and his touch. Even though they were both fully clothed, she was conscious of where his sinewy frame touched hers, and a sliver of heat rushed through her breasts and belly. His fingers caressed her arms through the silk fabric of her sleeves, and her heart lurched madly.

He was so disturbing to her in every way, and her physical response to him alarmed her.

Be careful! an inner voice warned. *Such an attraction is perilous.*

She pulled back. "Let me go."

"Not a chance. If you change our bargain from the beginning, then you tempt me to alter my end as well."

"Whatever do you mean?"

"Our 'passionless' arrangement, as you had called it."

"I haven't changed my part of our agreement, sir, so you must stick to yours." Her voice sounded high-pitched to her own ears.

"It's Marcus."

She scowled and once again tried to step away. His arms were like steel bands. "Fine. Marcus. Now let me go."

"You agree to stay out of my business then?"

She shot him a withering glance. "I still don't understand why—"

"Has your safety ever entered your stubborn brain?"

He pulled her closer, and the heat that had been simmering

in her veins burst into flame, setting her blood afire. Every part of her body that was pressed against his hard length was highly sensitive. She was aware, more than ever before, of the physical differences between them. Her soft curves molded traitorously to the contours of his muscular body.

"Well, well. What have we here?"

At the sound of an intruding male voice, Marcus immediately released her. Isabel stumbled back and would have fallen if not for Marcus's steady hand that shot out to grasp her arm.

She turned to find Lord Walling step forward, his fleshy face illuminated by the torch. Strands of thinning hair were slicked back, revealing a shiny, perspiring scalp.

"Are the two love birds arguing? I've heard that betrothals and marriage have an uncanny ability to bring out the worst in a couple, but you have only been promised to each other for"—he reached into his waistcoat and pulled out a pocket watch with a flourish—"only an hour."

Walling took a step closer to Isabel, and the overpowering stench of alcohol assailed her nostrils.

Realizing Walling was drunk, Isabel chose her words carefully. "I never had an opportunity to apologize, Lord Walling. The past few days have been a whirlwind."

He waved her off with a jeweled hand. "No need for apologies now. I do believe that your behavior at the Westley auction was for my benefit as much as for Hawksley's. There I was thinking you were innocent and perfect marriage material for a man of my station. It's a good thing my interest never became public knowledge. A woman of your loose morals would be more suitable as my mistress, not my wife."

Isabel gasped.

With one stride, Marcus grasped Walling around the throat. The older man's eyes bulged from their sockets, his round face turning an alarming shade of red.

She stared, tongue-tied. For a man of his size, Marcus had moved remarkably fast.

"You will watch your tongue around Lady Isabel, understand?" Marcus growled in Walling's face.

Walling nodded, an unnatural gurgling sound coming from his throat, and he reached up to pry Marcus's fingers loose.

Marcus released his grasp. Walling stumbled sideways, clawing at his cravat to rub his bruised throat.

Marcus smoothed his double-breasted jacket with steady hands. "Next time you are honored by Lady Isabel's presence, you will distinctly recall that she is my betrothed—soon to be my wife—and that any insult you make to her will be taken as if you spoke it to my face. Now as a *gentleman*, I do believe apologies to the lady should be forthcoming."

Marcus's voice bordered on boring, as if he was discussing the mundane mathematical calculations behind the rise and fall of shares in the Stock Exchange. Yet an air of deadly efficiency surrounded him.

Silence loomed like a heavy mist as Lord Walling struggled to find his voice.

"Please pardon my earlier behavior, Lady Isabel," Walling said, his blood-shot eyes focusing on her. "I do believe I've overindulged in Benning's spirits and have spoken inappropriately this evening."

"Apology accepted, of course," Isabel whispered.

Lord Walling turned on his heel and scurried back down the gravel path toward the terrace leading into the ballroom.

Isabel whirled on Marcus. "Do you realize what you have done?"

Marcus shrugged. "Stood up for my future wife."

"Lord Walling is quite influential. You made an enemy of him tonight."

"No, Isabel. *You* made him one when you stood in the

parlor of the Westley mansion and declared to be my lover, knowing full well that Lord Walling was in negotiations with your father for your hand in marriage."

"You blame me for what just occurred?"

"Not entirely. But you must recognize the consequences of your impulsive actions."

She blinked, knowing full well the truth behind his words. She had desperately sought to dissuade Lord Walling from his marital pursuit. But to physically attack him at a ball?

Marcus's behavior was outrageous. Reckless. Arrogant.

And worst of all, utterly fascinating.

Chapter 12

Isabel Cameron rarely took "no" for an answer when she truly wanted something. Her friends and family knew this, but as her future husband, Marcus Hawksley had yet to be enlightened.

Isabel had strolled down Threadneedle Street before, its bustling shops and throngs of pedestrians a familiar sight. But this time, instead of entering the dressmaker's, she rounded a corner and stopped in front of the Bank of England. She turned east and caught sight of her destination—the London Stock Exchange. A striking building of stone and white brick, it occupied a substantial triangular area in the city. The imposing structure was where Marcus spent much of his time, and with luck, where he was today.

As she gazed up at the building, a sudden memory came to her, and she vividly recalled her father's excitement when he had gained official membership to the Stock Exchange years ago. Since that time, she had never had the opportunity to step inside. As a woman, she had never been welcome or had reason to visit.

Until today.

You cannot ignore me, Marcus Hawksley. I refuse to be pushed aside.

Taking a deep breath, she gathered her courage, clutched her reticule to her side, and wove her way through the crowd toward the main entrance of the Exchange—known as "Capel Court" in Bartholomew Lane. Here businessmen rushed about, coats billowing in the early morning breeze.

Isabel walked brusquely across the cobblestone courtyard toward a grand set of double doors which loomed ahead. A doorman, dressed in a red uniform with a black top hat and gloves, nodded and opened the doors as she approached.

Hoping to hide her nervousness, she smiled and swept past him, entering a long, rectangular-shaped lobby. With a marble floor and stone walls, the lobby was bare and lacked the opulence she had anticipated. A row of chairs lined a wall and several men were seated together. Heads bent low, they were in deep conversation. She heard the words "bad Baltic trade," "oil," and "tallow" and suspected a group of investors were meeting. They paid her little heed. Cigar smoke wafted to her and swirled like fog in the rafters of the ceiling.

She walked across the lobby, unsure of her destination. She spotted a pair of double doors near the end of the room and wondered if Marcus was inside.

She headed for the doors just as they swung open, and a cacophony of noise blasted her from inside.

Her eyes widened at the scene.

The room was packed with bodies; businessmen scurried about on the trading floor, their expressions animated and anxious at the same time. Some wore hats and coats as if they did not have time to take them off before engaging in business matters. Others had their sleeves rolled back as if they had been present since the crack of dawn. They yelled and gestured wildly at one another to be heard above the din. Strips of paper littered every square inch of the floor, and she marveled how not one person slipped on the mess.

The trading floor itself was a mammoth, elongated hall. A gilt dome and arched glass roof drew her eye upward. It appeared as if the roof was suspended in midair, but then she noticed impressive granite columns supporting the structure. Her father had once told her the dome was dazzling, yet she suspected its beauty was lost on the packs of men who were too busy running back and forth, scrambling about, to look at the brilliant work of art above their heads.

She stood in stunned silence, absorbing the chaos.

The overpowering masculinity in the hall was like a throbbing, thriving beast. She could smell the intensity, the power, and the fanaticism emanating in waves. Her mind spun, and she wished she had a pencil and paper to sketch the scene.

Don't be foolish! It would take a master artist to capture the feverish zeal spread out before you on canvas.

The noise level rose as the doors opened wide, and then faded as a group of men exited the floor and the doors closed behind them.

"May I be of assistance?"

At the sound of a deep, masculine voice, Isabel whirled around.

A handsome man with sandy-colored hair and piercing green eyes stared at her with interest. He was young, she noticed, close to Marcus's age, and dressed in a moss-colored waistcoat and jacket that matched the exact shade of his eyes. He smiled, revealing straight, white teeth.

"I, ah . . . I'm looking for someone," she said.

"Then perhaps I can be of assistance. My name is Ralph Hodge and although I do not pretend to know everyone here," he said, motioning to the double doors that led to the exchange floor, "I am a well-known stockbroker."

He smiled again, and she was aware of his eyes roaming her features like a potential investor considering a commodity he intended to purchase. Handsome, charming, and arrogant, she suspected he was quite successful with the ladies.

"I'm looking for a broker as well," Isabel said. "I had foolishly thought I could have found him here easily enough, but that was before I laid eyes upon the floor for the first time."

"A fellow broker, you say. Who?"

"Mr. Marcus Hawksley."

"Hawksley?" There was a sudden narrowing of Ralph Hodge's green eyes, a pinched look to his lips, but then the trademark smile was back in place.

"If you are seeking a broker for investment advice, I am more than avail—"

"No, Mr. Hodge. You misunderstand. Mr. Hawksley is my betrothed."

A blond eyebrow arched. "I see, Miss—"

"Lady Isabel Cameron."

Hodge's green gaze grew more intense, a feat Isabel would have thought impossible.

"Please excuse my ignorance, *Lady* Isabel," he said. "But if I may be so bold as to ask, however did Hawksley acquire the good fortune to find you?"

"Luck."

"Luck?" he repeated dumbly, his smile cracking. He was clearly perturbed, and her curiosity rose a notch.

He reached out to cup her elbow. "I suppose Hawksley has had a lucky streak in the market of late. And you are also fortunate today, for I do indeed know Mr. Hawksley and can locate—"

Just then, the swinging doors opened, and Marcus strode out.

He stopped short as he spotted her. Jet eyes took in the

scene, missing no detail, narrowing on Ralph Hodge's hand on Isabel's sleeve.

"Isabel," Marcus said. "What are you doing here? With him?"

Marcus looked overbearing and commanding, and like a gladiator in his own arena, he radiated confidence and power. He held a sheath of papers at his side, his long, dark fingers contrasting with the whiteness of the paper.

"I came to see you," Isabel said.

Marcus shot her a penetrating look. "Why?"

"We never finished our discussion last night, and I have new information." She was conscious of Ralph Hodge's hand on her sleeve as well as his keen interest in their conversation.

"You never mentioned you were engaged, Hawksley," Ralph interrupted. "Why would you keep the lovely Lady Isabel a secret?"

"Mind your own business, Hodge. And remove your hand from the lady," Marcus ground out. He reached out, pulled Isabel out of Hodge's grasp, and nearly dragged her away by her arm.

She hurried to keep up with Marcus as he strode across the lobby. She could feel Hodge's sharp eyes boring into her back with each rushed step.

"What in the world was that about?" she gasped.

"Stay away from Ralph Hodge."

"You dislike each other. Why?"

"It's complicated."

They reached the front of the lobby, and Isabel panicked, thinking he was going to escort her out of the building, but instead of heading for the outside, Marcus swung right and opened a door she hadn't noticed before. He led her into a small room lined with file cabinets and a desk littered with stacks of paper.

"We can talk privately here."

"Where are we?"

"An antechamber the jobbers use as a temporary office."

"Jobbers?"

"Jobbers buy and sell shares for the stockbrokers. They earn money for their services by inflating the price they offer the broker." He leaned against the desk and folded his arms across his chest. "Educating you on the workings of the Exchange is not the reason you came today. So tell me what is."

She took a deep breath and tried to relax. She had been certain of her bold actions earlier by coming here, but as was customary of late, she now doubted the wisdom of her impulsiveness.

"Things between us were not settled last night," she said. "After the incident with Lord Walling, you left the Bennings' ball."

He shook his head. "No, Isabel. I was quite clear on the subject, and as I recall, you had agreed with me as well."

"I most certainly did not. I never agreed to be the 'passive wife' you expect, and I fully intend to be involved in your investigation."

"Why? I want to know why you are so adamant about this."

"I told you last night," she said matter-of-factly. "It does not take much for people to gossip, and if there is the slightest implication that you were the thief of the painting, then as your future wife, it will adversely affect my father and the twins. If my involvement can aid the situation, then it is impossible for me to sit back and do nothing. Now, when I tell you what I have learned, you will undoubtedly see that I am an indispensable ally and change your stubborn mind."

He cocked his head to the side. "Oh, please enlighten me."

She reached into her reticule and pulled out a piece of paper. "I have compiled a list of wealthy art collectors who have dealt with the auctioneer Dante Black within the last year. I have also learned who amongst the ton owns Thomas Gainsborough paintings and who collects portraits similar to Gainsborough's style."

Marcus pushed away from the desk, eyes blazing. "Dante Black has gone missing. He has not showed at his place of business or his private residence since the Westley auction. Have you perchance learned of his location?"

"No, but perhaps one of these collectors knows. Dante was a well-respected auctioneer who catered to his rich clients. I assume some of them would know how to reach him."

"How did you learn all this?"

"I tried to tell you last night, but you wouldn't listen. I have been attending society functions for years, and as an aspiring artist, I take an interest in the artwork I see. Plus, Charlotte Benning is my best friend, and her mother knows everyone."

"I regret leaving the ball last night without meeting your friend. Perhaps I should have hired her rather than the investigator I obtained," he said dryly.

"You hired an investigator?" She wanted to ask how he could afford such an expense, but held her tongue. No sense insulting the man when she was trying to get on his good side.

"There's more," she rushed. "A masque is being hosted this week by a couple who happen to be the only collectors that have both utilized Dante Black's services *and* own several Thomas Gainsborough paintings. I have heard that they are avid collectors, have a private gallery in their mansion, and that they pay outrageous sums for quality works. We can attend the masque and discreetly search for the mysterious gallery to see if they have possession of the *Seashore with Fishermen*."

"Who's hosting the masque?"

He reached for the paper in her hand, but she pulled it out of his grasp.

"Not until you agree we are partners."

His eyes narrowed. "Partners in an illegal search of a wealthy and powerful couple's house? Do you have no fear for yourself? I'll not be responsible for your neck."

"We won't get caught." She waved the paper at him. "Partners then?"

"You are the most outrageous, stubborn woman I have ever met."

She gifted him with a smile. "Thank you. I'll take your compliment as a yes."

"I seem to have no choice."

She handed him the paper. "The masque is being hosted by Lord and Lady Gavinport."

A low knock on the door echoed through the small room. They both whirled around when the door opened, and Ralph Hodge stood in the doorway.

A blond lock fell over Hodge's forehead, and he flashed a pearly white smile. "The lady said she was looking for a broker. I came to see if she changed her mind as to which one."

"Out. Now," Marcus growled.

At the thunderous expression on Marcus's face, Hodge grinned, then turned and shut the door.

Isabel reached for the paper in Marcus's hand.

His mouth twisted wryly. "What are you doing?"

"It appears I need to add Mr. Hodge to my list of possible suspects."

Chapter 13

"It must be on the second floor. I can't imagine Gavinport housing his private gallery on the same floor as the ballroom," Isabel whispered.

Charlotte gripped Isabel's arm. "Don't be foolish! You must wait for Marcus."

Isabel gave Charlotte a sideways glance and adjusted her black velvet half-mask. She scanned the Gavinports' ballroom, but was disappointed to find no signs of Marcus.

She had dressed with care, wearing an exquisite white satin evening gown with a low bodice trimmed with small lilies. Her dark hair fell in loose curls down the back of her neck, and a pearl necklace rested between the swell of her breasts. The black half-mask matched her ebony hair and contrasted with the white satin, inviting lustful looks from several gentlemen.

She knew she looked attractive, and the thought froze in her brain that she wanted Marcus to see her this way, wanted him to think she was beautiful.

Don't flirt with danger, her inner voice warned.

But the truth was his dangerous, predatory nature was part of the attraction. He was his own man, and his air of isolation, his nonchalance, as if he hadn't a care of what anyone in the world thought of him, drew her like a moth to a flame. After spending four years on the marriage mart overwhelmed by strutting peacocks, he was a breath of fresh air. The men she had known had never earned a shilling their entire lives, relying instead on their families' fortunes. They were fat, lazy, and completely uninteresting.

But Hawksley . . .

"How will you ever find Marcus amongst all the masked guests?" Charlotte asked.

The guests would normally be announced by a Gavinport servant, but tonight was a masque, and the formalities were overlooked. A mysterious charge of excitement pervaded the room. Champagne flowed freely, and the masked guests mingled about—many with licentious anticipation— seeking fellow revelers who desired to indulge their own guilty pleasures without revealing their identities.

"Marcus is so much taller than most of the men present, I should be able to spot him in the crowd, masked or not," Isabel said.

"Are you two lovely ladies looking for me?" a deep masculine voice asked.

Both Isabel and Charlotte jumped and whirled around.

Marcus grinned, standing behind them. He was dressed entirely in black from his mask to his formal evening wear. Tall and well-muscled, he looked devastatingly handsome, every inch the conquering pirate.

He held out two bubbling flutes of champagne. "For you both."

"Marcus!" Isabel said. "You near scared us to death. I have been looking for you all evening. However did you sneak by?"

"My apologies for keeping you waiting, my dear." His eyes roamed over her face then down her satin-clad figure, and he grinned again.

There was a spark of some indefinable emotion in his dark eyes, and her pulse quickened in response.

He turned his attention to Charlotte. "Miss Benning, I presume. I've heard wonderful things about you from Isabel."

Charlotte looked up at Marcus with wide blue eyes and giggled. "No doubt, Mr. Hawksley, but please know Isabel has a gift for exaggeration."

"Ah," Marcus sighed, "I see you truly do know our Isabel then."

Charlotte flushed prettily and smiled.

An unexpected spark of jealousy flared in Isabel's chest. She bit down hard on her lower lip.

Ridiculous. Charlotte was her best friend, and she wasn't flirting with Marcus.

Or was she?

"I thought you would have arrived earlier, Mr. Hawksley," Isabel snapped.

At her sharp tone, both Charlotte's and Marcus's eyes turned to her.

One corner of his mouth twisted upward. "If you must know, I was exploring the layout of our host's mansion."

"Without me?" Again Isabel failed miserably to control her annoyance.

A gleam of mockery invaded his stare. "I did not know I needed permission."

Charlotte coughed, breaking the tension. "I believe I shall leave you two to your business." With a swish of her skirts, she walked away, leaving Marcus and Isabel alone.

The noise of the party dimmed to a low roar in her ears. She felt like a fool, standing before Marcus, unable to control her wayward tongue.

Marcus broke the awkward silence. "Gavinport approaches."

Isabel turned to see Frederick Perrin, the Marquess of

Gavinport, weave his way through the crowd. He was unmasked, greeting his guests as he passed by. Their host was slim, remarkably short, and had a full head of dark hair that was cropped tight to his scalp. His face was dominated by a round nose that resembled a ripe tomato.

Isabel smiled as Lord Gavinport came up to them.

"Good evening," Gavinport said. "I dare not guess as to my guests' identities tonight, but I trust you are enjoying yourselves?"

Marcus nodded and raised his glass. "Excellent champagne, Gavinport."

Isabel blinked, surprised to see that up close Lord Gavinport was a solid inch shorter than she was. He had to crane his neck to look up at Marcus. Yet Gavinport had a military manner about him, a shrewdness to his gaze, and his cropped black hair and small stature reminded her of pictures she had seen of Napoleon.

"Your home is lovely," Isabel said. "The new Lady Gavinport has exquisite taste."

At the mention of his young wife, Gavinport's sharp gaze scanned the ballroom. A cold, critical expression settled on his face, and a shiver ran down Isabel's spine. "Excuse me then," he said and ventured off.

"Meeting the marquess has not changed my impression," Marcus said.

She knew he was referring to Lord Gavinport's possible involvement in the theft of the painting. "Mine either."

"From what I've seen," Marcus said, "Gavinport's private gallery is most likely on the second floor. I suggest we go up the back staircase separately so as not to draw untoward attention."

"Yes, that sounds like a fine plan."

"Can you meet me at the top of the servants' stairs in ten minutes?" he asked.

She nodded without meeting his stare, still feeling foolish and awkward after her earlier jealous outburst.

He reached out and caught her gloved hand.

She raised her eyes to find him studying her with a curious intensity. Heat spread from his fingers through her satin glove, and her skin prickled pleasurably.

"Try to control your impulsiveness, my dear." He flashed a devastating grin, then was gone.

She stood awkwardly, watching him walk through the crowd. He was so disturbing to her senses, and her feelings toward him were becoming confused. For the first time, she wondered as to the sanity of the bargain she had made with him. She had insisted he agree to a sterile engagement and marriage, and here she was unable to control her own wayward thoughts and jealousy.

Sipping her champagne, she smiled at acquaintances and depicted an ease she didn't feel. She waited precisely nine minutes then headed for the servants' staircase.

At the sight of Isabel sneaking up the stairs, Marcus's breath hitched. From the top of the landing, he had a perfect view of the fat pearl resting between the swell of her breasts, and he imagined licking the jewel before burying his face between her enticing flesh. Then her foot landed on the top stair, and her clear blue eyes flashed through her mask like glittering sapphires. A surge of excitement passed through him.

Madness.

He was struck by the sudden thought that he was going to have to exercise a lion's share of self-control over the next six months. The realization cooled his blood like an ice bath.

"The floor is empty, but we must hurry," he said.

Taking her hand, he ushered her down the hall. Portraits

of deceased male Gavinports mounted on their horses with hunting dogs beside them hung on the flocked walls. The second-floor corridor was long with many doors, but Marcus strode to the last one.

"I checked all the others. This is the only one that is locked," he said.

Her eyes widened. "Locked? But how can we—"

He withdrew a black pouch from the inside pocket of his coat. Taking out the lock picks, he inserted the longest pick into the lock.

Her eyes widened. "Wherever did you learn this skill?"

"I once had a locksmith as a client. He taught me."

She smiled up at him, and his heart pounded erratically in his chest.

He turned his attention back to the lock until he felt a slight click in the mechanism. Reaching for the handle, he opened the door a crack and pressed his ear to the doorjamb. When he heard nothing to suggest another's presence, he ushered her inside and closed the door behind them.

Isabel took off her half-mask and whirled around. "Oh, my," she whispered in awe. "This is what wealth can buy."

She walked past him, her eyes feasting on the walls where oils, engravings, watercolors, frescos, and charcoals hung in splendid display.

Stopping in front of an engraving, her gaze was riveted. "Look here! It's William Hogarth's *The Marriage Contract*, the first of the three scenes comprising *Marriage à la Mode*. I love his work."

Marcus walked up to the engraving. The artist showed a poor nobleman marrying his son to the daughter of a rich commoner. As the fathers negotiate the marriage contract, the engaged couple, obviously not a love match, ignore each other as the future bride flirts with the solicitor, her soon-to-be lover. It was common knowledge that Hogarth had made engraved copies of his paintings and had sold them cheaply in large quantities for money. But it appeared by the single digit in the corner of the piece, that the engraving in Gavinport's collection was one of the first, and thus, quite valuable.

He turned to Isabel. "Do you admire it because Hogarth mocks marriage in the series?"

She looked at him in surprise. "You must admit Hogarth's satire is refreshingly honest."

He thought of his own parents' disastrous union. "Yes, I suppose most marriages are far from blissful matches."

She looked away and pointed to a painting. "Here's a self-portrait of the Flemish master Peter Paul Rubens. His art is tremendously popular with the Regent, who owns several of his works." Turning to a group of others, she said, "and there are oils from English portrait painters, Joshua Reynolds, John Hoppner, and Thomas Lawrence, all favorites of Prinny's."

She spotted another piece and took a quick sharp breath, her eyes brimming with excitement. "Oh! Just look at this breathtaking watercolor by Joseph Mallord William Turner!" She read the inscription on the frame, "*Warkworth Castle, Northumberland—Thunder Storm Approaching at Sun-Set*. What a stunning landscape, a vision of vapor and nimbus clouds. I can only dream to paint a watercolor with half the talent some—"

"Over here, Isabel." Marcus strode to a large oil well hidden in the back of the room. "It's a Gainsborough."

Isabel rushed to his side. "*The Mall in St. James's Park*," she read the title out loud.

Close to four feet tall and nearly six feet wide, the 1783 painting was enormous, showing numerous well-dressed figures promenading through the park. The women's shimmering dresses perfectly captured the light against the landscape that surrounded them. In the painting the artist had cleverly included himself poised behind a copse of trees, holding his palette. Marcus had read that Gainsborough had used dolls as models, but as he studied the painting closely, it was difficult for him to fathom what he'd read, as the figures in the painting looked very much like breathing models.

"It's beautiful, but it's not the *Seashore with Fishermen*," Isabel stated the obvious.

"I know it's not the stolen painting, but look at this." He pointed to a small business card attached to the bottom-right-hand side of the frame. In bold block letter script it read: DANTE BLACK AUCTIONS.

Isabel gasped. "My sources said Lord Gavinport owned a Thomas Gainsborough painting and that he had dealt with Dante Black in the past, but I never suspected that he acquired a Gainsborough work *through* Dante Black."

"Gavinport must have paid Dante Black a tidy sum for this picture. From what I see in this private gallery, Gavinport has expensive taste in art and is willing to pay a hefty price to acquire it. I would not be surprised if he has previously purchased work on the black market, or more importantly, that he would hire a crooked auctioneer like Dante Black to fake the theft of another Gainsborough painting to add to his collection. It would not matter to Gavinport if the painting was stolen since he would house it in his private gallery. No one would be the wiser."

"But if that were true, where is the stolen painting?" Isabel asked.

"Perhaps Dante hasn't had a chance to deliver it yet. Knowing Dante, he is probably keeping a low profile to avoid attention from Bow Street until he can turn over the painting."

"But how will we know when he does deliver it?"

"I don't know yet, but we have spent too much time in this room. We should leave before we are discovered," Marcus said.

She blinked as if coming to her senses. "You're right, of course."

They went to the door, and Marcus opened it slightly to see if anyone was about. When he was satisfied they were alone, he drew her into the hallway and closed the door behind them, stopping only to ensure the lock was once again engaged.

Halfway down the hall, he heard footsteps coming up the stairs. Just as a woman's voluminous skirts and a man's trouser leg came into view around the corner, Marcus opened the nearest door and thrust Isabel inside.

Stepping inside, he quietly shut the door.

The first thing he registered was that it was a dim, windowless room. A small sliver of light flowed in from a crack in the doorjamb, slicing a pie wedge out of the darkness. Several seconds passed before he realized they were in a linen closet.

Shelving on both sides was piled with linens and towels engraved with the Gavinport crest. Sizable sachets, hanging from ceiling hooks, were full with what smelled like dried lilacs and roses and filled the small space with the scent of spring flowers.

He turned to Isabel and put a finger to his lips to signal her to be quiet. Her blue eyes were as round as saucers. The closet was small and cramped, and Isabel was pressed close to him.

Footsteps came closer and the couple stopped somewhere near the closet. There was the rustle of skirts and a soft moan.

Marcus froze, straining to hear.

"This is so dangerous, Olivia," a male voice said.

"That's why it's so exciting," a female responded. "There's nothing to worry about really, darling. Gavinport and his guests have all indulged in plenty of alcohol tonight. No one will notice we've gone missing. Besides we have done this many times before under Gavinport's nose, he'll not suspect me now. I am the perfect wife and hostess at his parties."

"But if he ever finds out—"

"*Hush*, darling. Watching you all evening and pretending you are a mere formal acquaintance has been torture. I promise, the monster shall never know. He is obsessed with his wretched art collection. He'd rather look at his droll paintings than at me. All he's talked about lately was buying another obscenely expensive piece from his auctioneer."

"How could he prefer to look at a painting over his own wife's exquisite beauty?"

"Oh, darling. Don't make me wait a second longer. Kiss me."

The crinkle of clothing and groans could be heard.

Heat rose in the small space of the closet and beads of perspiration formed on Marcus's brow. He was highly aware of Isabel's soft curves pressed against him, of her own delicate perfume mingling with the fragrance in the closet, and of the uneven rhythm of her breathing.

Isabel must also have sensed the ripple of excitement between them for she made to step back an inch and bumped her head on the wood shelf beside her.

She grunted.

"What was that?" the male outside the closet snapped.

Reacting instinctively, Marcus pulled Isabel into his arms and kissed her hard.

A split second later, the closet door was thrust open.

Chapter 14

Isabel stiffened and her eyes opened wide in shock, but Marcus held her tightly and deepened the kiss.

"What are ye two doing here?" a man demanded.

Marcus was slow to respond, dragging his lips from Isabel's. He did not have to act the highly aroused and irritated male, for the mere touch of their lips, however brief, had sent his blood pounding. It must be the danger and the excitement that had aroused him so swiftly, he rationalized.

He raised his head and found a red-haired man glowering at him. Behind the man, Lady Gavinport's blond hair and diamond necklace flashed. A second wife to Frederick Perrin, the Marquess of Gavinport, she was more than a decade younger than her wealthy husband. She was deathly pale at the moment, and panic, stark and vivid, glittered in her eyes.

Marcus stepped out of the closet and held the door for Isabel. "It appears we've been found, my dear."

Isabel blinked, her eyes unfocused; her chest rose and fell with agitated breaths.

"What are ye doing here?" the red-haired man repeated.

"I suppose it is obvious, isn't it? The lady and I sought a few moments of privacy."

"Who are—"

"Good heavens, Donald." Lady Gavinport stepped forward. "This is Lady Isabel Cameron and Mr. Marcus Hawksley, my guests for the evening. Their engagement was recently announced at the Bennings' ball."

Donald looked taken aback at the mention of Marcus's name, and Marcus immediately linked the man's name to his face. Donald MacKinnon. Son of the Scotsman Keith MacKinnon, who was one of Marcus's oldest clients at the Stock Exchange. Marcus wondered what Donald's strict and wealthy father would do if he knew of his son's affair with the married Lady Gavinport.

Donald's expression was tight with strain. "They could have heard—"

Isabel stepped toward Olivia Gavinport. "Our deepest apologies, Lady Gavinport. We were so consumed with each other that we did not hear you approach until after you opened the door and came upon us."

Marcus didn't miss the flash of relief on Lady Gavinport's face or the tense lines that relaxed on Donald MacKinnon's face.

He had to give Isabel credit. She didn't miss a beat. He knew she was unnerved, but she had disguised her discomfort as that of an embarrassed lady caught in a compromising position.

"We are constantly chaperoned, you see." Isabel's face flushed, and she cast her eyes downward. "And we wanted to be alone just once before the wedding."

"I must say you are fortunate to want to be together," Lady Gavinport said. "Most betrothed couples have little if any interest in each other. But nonetheless, you should not be up here. Lord Gavinport would not approve."

Isabel's eyes clung to the woman's. "You won't tell of our indiscretion?"

Olivia Gavinport looked so relieved she swayed on her

feet. "We are ladies first. I'll keep your secret." The woman's unspoken words were as clear as day: *If you keep mine.*

Bravo, Marcus thought. Isabel had managed to entrust Lady Gavinport and Donald MacKinnon's silence. Both couples had secrets, only Marcus hoped theirs appeared to be that of two lovers wanting intimacy rather than two spies breaking into a private art gallery.

"Guests aren't allowed to roam about the second floor. I'll escort ye down," Donald said.

Marcus nodded, and they followed behind. When they were once again amongst the masked guests in the ballroom, Isabel turned to him, a glint of mischief behind her velvet mask.

"I told you I would make a most useful ally," she said, her full lips curving into a secretive smile.

His heart took a perilous leap. "Yes, my dear. You continue to amaze me."

Isabel's breath caught in her lungs as a bolt of blue velvet was unrolled at her feet. She reached out to touch the material, awed by its softness.

"It's perfect. The exact shade of your eyes," Charlotte said.

"But there are so many others, I can't choose," Isabel protested.

They were in the Bennings' Grosvenor Square mansion, and Isabel was attempting to select the color, fabric, and style of the gown for her wedding breakfast. Thankfully, she had previously decided that she would wear her mother's wedding gown, which saved her from having to make another choice. Kneeling on an Aubusson carpet, she gazed in wide-eyed wonder at dozens of swatches—satins, silks, velvets, brocades, and crepes in every color of an

artist's pallet—scattered around her. Selected rare bolts of
fabric spilled onto the floor like shimmering pools of color.

Madame Antoinette, a renowned French dressmaker,
had agreed to leave her busy London shop as a personal
favor to Mr. and Mrs. Benning, who were her best cus-
tomers. Isabel had been stunned when two hackney cabs
had pulled up the drive, one transporting the couturière herself and the other her materials, patterns, and drawings.
Two well-built French assistants had carried everything
inside. Madame Antoinette's face was flushed with eager-
ness, knowing custom-made outfits were sought not only
for the bride, but also for Charlotte, Leticia Benning, and
Isabel's twin siblings, who were all present.

The dressmaker picked up a swatch of material and held
it up to Isabel's cheek. "Perhaps Mademoiselle would like
this emerald satin. It goes perfectly with her flawless skin
and dark hair."

Amber nodded her head, her blond curls bouncing. "Oh
yes, Izzy. It's so beautiful."

Anthony stood in the corner. With his arms crossed over
his chest and the corner of his mouth twisted with exasperation, he appeared completely irritated by the overly feminine environment.

"Let Izzy decide for herself, Amber," Anthony said
tersely. "If you favor the green so much, then order it for
yourself."

Amber turned and glowered at her twin.

Isabel's lips twitched at Anthony's brooding mood. She
had to insist upon his presence today. Her younger brother,
who had sprouted in height and breadth within the last six
months, no longer fit into many of his clothes and was in
dire need of formal attire for the wedding.

"Which will you choose, Isabel?" Charlotte asked,
drawing Isabel's attention back to the material in the dressmaker's hands.

Isabel sighed. "I'm completely overwhelmed."

Leticia touched Isabel's arm. "Nonsense. A lady can never have too many choices or too many gowns in her wardrobe."

Just then, Harold Benning walked into the room. His watery blue eyes widened with pleasure at the scene before him. Clasping his hands to his chest, he sighed at the sight.

Isabel stared agog at his flamboyant clothing. He wore a matching waistcoat and trousers of purple and pink checked fabric and a ruffled shirt with Brussels lace cascading down the front and at his shirt cuffs. Clutching a jewel-encrusted snuff box in one hand, he held the ever-present quizzing glass with matching purple ribbon in the other.

Benning turned to Isabel. "What's this I hear? You are having trouble selecting a gown for your wedding breakfast? Why did you not ask for me? Everyone knows I'm gifted when it comes to women's fashions."

He went to the swatches, and with an efficiency that was startling, sorted through the staggering pile until he found one to his liking, a diaphanous blue silk. Next he picked up a stack of sketches, and with repeated flicks of his wrist, discarded unwanted sketches of gowns on the floor. He stopped short, and then nodded. He held up the chosen sketch, and his fleshy face melted into a buttery smile.

He placed the swatch and sketch before Isabel. "This is what I call perfection. There are shoes, fan, gloves, reticule, cloak, and other trimmings to select, of course, but I'm certain Madame Antoinette has wonderful accessories to complement this glorious confection."

Isabel stared at Benning's selection in her lap.

Stunning.

The sketch showed a rich blue silk robe over a slip of satin. Long full sleeves, a fitted round bodice, and a low back trimmed with small roses at the bosom and hem completed the ensemble.

She had to give Harold Benning credit. He was amazing when it came to female fashion. The women in the room—Charlotte, Leticia, Amber, and the dressmaker—were all enthralled by Harold's selection.

"Will you chose my fabric and style as well, Mr. Benning?" Amber asked, adoration written on her young face.

Anthony smirked in the corner, clearly uncomfortable with Harold Benning's effeminate side.

Harold Benning nodded at Amber, and then his eyes lit up as he spotted a bolt of canary yellow velvet. Stroking the material with reverence, he said, "It's superb. I simply must have a jacket made with a matching waistcoat."

Charlotte exchanged a subtle look of amusement with Isabel at her stepfather's choice.

Isabel couldn't imagine a male wearing such a shade, but held her tongue. What would Marcus think?

As if sensing her thoughts, Charlotte asked, "Isabel, how have you and Mr. Hawskley been faring since the announcement of your engagement?"

Charlotte was the only one that knew about her temporary marriage of convenience with Marcus, and as far as Isabel knew, her friend had kept her secret.

"Since Father was unable to obtain a special license from the Bishop, the reading of the banns has begun," Isabel said.

Charlotte's eyes grew openly amused. "I know. I was at church this past Sunday and heard the priest read the banns from the pulpit, Isabel. But what we all want to know is how you two are getting along?"

Isabel was aware of every eye in the room upon her, especially the twins. "We are getting along quite well, better than I had expected. Marcus's good friends, the Earl and Countess of Ravenspear, have invited us to their home this week for a private dinner to celebrate our engagement, and we are both looking forward to the evening."

A mischievous smile curved Charlotte's mouth. "Really? We have noticed Mr. Hawksley looking happier of late. Perhaps marriage will suit him despite the fact that everyone, including his friends, had believed him to be a sworn bachelor."

A sudden unbidden memory of Marcus's urgent kiss in the Gavinports' linen closet rushed through her mind. He had kissed her out of fear of discovery, but there had also been a smoldering passion in his lips that had thrilled her, had made her blood soar. Despite her firm resolve not to get physically involved with Marcus, their shared embrace was an awakening experience that had left her reeling. It had also aroused her curiosity as to what a dark, dominant male like Marcus Hawksley would be like intimately . . .

Suddenly aware of Amber and Anthony's inquisitive stares, Isabel pushed her wayward thoughts aside. She felt flushed as if the sun which flowed through the windows had radiated directly upon her for hours.

"I doubt his pleasant state is from our impending nuptials," Isabel blurted out.

Harold Benning dropped the yellow velvet. "Maybe he is falling in love with you, Isabel." He looked to Leticia. "Would that not be utterly romantic, darling?"

Leticia Benning's lips twitched with amusement. "It's more likely he is relieved to put the ugly business of the Westley auction behind him."

Benning waved a dismissive hand. "I never believed the nonsense that Mr. Hawksley is somehow responsible for the theft of a valuable piece of artwork. There has been gossip, of course, but if Bow Street does not suspect him, then neither do I." A probing query came into Benning's eyes. "I did not want to bring up the subject, but whatever has transpired with that auctioneer?"

"He has disappeared," Isabel said.

"Has Mr. Hawksley tried to locate him?"

"Yes, but he has had no success to date. I suspect Dante Black won't show his face for some time. At least not until the missing painting is found by the constable."

Benning nodded. "Yes, of course. I'm sure that will be soon. Dreadful inconvenience, I say."

Charlotte stood. "It is all in the past. I, for one, am certain that Mr. Hawksley is quite enamored of our Isabel and growing more so each day. I suspect that soon he will be more attached to her than to his own art collection."

Harold Benning clapped. "Bravo! We must toast to love." He directed a servant to bring glasses and a bottle of champagne.

"But it's two o'clock in the afternoon," Leticia protested.

"So?" Benning shrugged. "We are celebrating Mr. Hawksley's blooming affection for our Isabel. Whatever else could be more important?"

Chapter 15

Isabel leaned her head against the side of her father's padded carriage. She was on the way home from the Bennings', and her mind was spinning. Even after Harold Benning's selection of material and style of a gown, there had been a whirl of accessories to choose from. Then there had been Amber and Anthony's clothes to select. Thankfully, the twins had stayed behind to pick their own accessories.

Isabel sighed and shut her eyes, longing for a strong cup of tea and the soothing solitude of her watercolors.

The ride was blessedly short, and the carriage soon came to a stop before her father's town house. There was a squeak of springs as the driver jumped down and opened the door. Lowering the step, he held out his hand to assist her.

Isabel smiled at her father's driver. "Thank you, Jarvis." Her foot touched the first step.

"Lady Isabel?" a feminine voice called out.

Isabel turned to see a stunning red-haired woman descend from a carriage parked on the street. She was dressed in an exquisite jade walking dress that accentuated her jewel green eyes and creamy complexion. She was older than Isabel, but exotically beautiful.

"Do I know you?" Isabel asked, facing the woman.

"My name is Simone Winston. We have never met before, but you should know of me," the woman said.

It was a fact, not a question, and the hair on the nape of Isabel's neck rose on end. The woman's demeanor was not friendly, but neither was it overly hostile.

"Is there a place where we may speak privately?" Simone asked.

"I'm not—"

"It is of interest to you, I assure you."

When Isabel still hesitated, the woman said, "It's regarding Marcus."

Alarm bells went off in Isabel's head. Although she didn't recognize the woman's name, she had said *Marcus*, not Mr. Hawksley.

A sudden sickening thought made bile rise up in Isabel's throat.

"We can talk privately inside." Isabel escorted the woman into the town house to a drawing room. Shutting the doors, Isabel turned to face her. Not waiting for a servant, Simone had stripped off her cloak and had laid it on a nearby settee. Isabel was struck by her voluptuous figure.

"I am Marcus's lover and have been for the past year."

The discomfort that had been simmering in Isabel's stomach threatened to turn to full-blown nausea.

So this was the love interest Marcus had mentioned. Meeting the woman face-to-face was like a blow to her solar plexus, much worse than merely knowing of her existence.

Isabel forced herself to take a deep breath, to act and think rationally. After all, *she* was the one that had intruded in Marcus's life, had assumed he had not been involved in a relationship when she had brazenly propositioned him in Lord Westley's room of inflammatory art. She had all but forced Marcus's hand into an engagement. She should feel guilty and selfish for her reckless actions.

So why did despair and bitter jealousy stir inside her?

You agreed to a six-month farce. Thereafter, Marcus will be free to return to Simone Winston. What warm-blooded male wouldn't?

At Isabel's silence, Simone continued. "I have inquired about your engagement. It seems you had a ludicrously short courtship if one at all."

At a loss for words, Isabel shook her head.

Simone cocked her head to one side. "I don't believe the rumors that you and Marcus were having an affair. The only bed he was sharing was mine."

At the woman's icy tone, Isabel's anger came to her defense, and she found her voice. "You sound so certain."

Simone snorted an unladylike sound. "Even if you two had dallied once or twice before the Westley auction, I know for a fact that Marcus never intended to marry. I can only surmise that he agreed to marry you for your family's wealth and title."

Isabel stiffened. "Perhaps it was just *you* he never intended to marry."

Simone gasped, her eyes narrowing. "If you manage to trap him in your deceitful web, he won't stay with you for long. It will be a lonely marriage in name only. A virile man like Marcus Hawksley has certain needs and appetites that a girl like you wouldn't dream of satisfying. I suspect your bed will be cold as ice the morning after your wedding day."

Isabel's shock yielded quickly to a scalding fury. She clenched her fists at her sides, leaving crescent-shaped marks in her palms. She forgot how she had sought a sterile marriage, exactly what Simone Winston now threatened her with.

She lashed out with the one insult she knew would cut a self-absorbed woman like Simone Winston to the bone. "Men often get bored with their conquests. It appears as if

Marcus has had his fill of you and is looking elsewhere for excitement."

Simone's features contorted with anger. "Bitch! We shall see who Marcus chooses."

With a swish of jade-colored skirts, Simone pivoted on her heel, grabbed her cloak, and stormed out of the room. The front door slammed on her way out.

Isabel collapsed in a chair. The day had taken its toll; she felt drained and listless. There had been the endless sorting through voluminous swatches and sketches while being questioned by her family and friends regarding her relationship with Marcus. And now the horrid confrontation with Marcus's beautiful, but spiteful mistress . . .

You are a fool, Isabel! her inner voice cried out.

She had allowed herself to be drawn to Marcus Hawksley, had forgotten her senses and her goals after a quick, urgent interlude in a linen closet. She had no real claim on him. A disturbing pain squeezed her heart at the thought that after half a year she would watch him walk away and into the eager arms of his exotic, experienced mistress.

She knew now, more than ever before, that she must stay focused on her goal of returning to Paris. Her lifelong dream was real, not the temporary revival of schoolgirl fantasies.

She shook her head and rose from the chair. She climbed the grand staircase up to the second floor, entered her bedroom, and strode to the easel in the corner.

Picking up her paintbrush, she went to work.

Chapter 16

"Are you feeling well, my dear?" Marcus asked. "We can always make our excuses and plan for another evening. Blake and Victoria will not mind."

Isabel avoided Marcus's concerned gaze and studied the elegant drawing room. They had arrived at the Ravenspears' London home a short while ago, and the butler had led them here to await their host and hostess.

Isabel picked at an imaginary piece of lint on her skirt as she sat across from Marcus on a velvet settee.

"I feel perfectly fine," she insisted. "We are here now, and I wouldn't dream of disappointing the earl and countess. It was extremely kind of them to invite us to celebrate our engagement." It had been three days since she had announced to her twin siblings and the Bennings that she and Marcus were to dine with the Ravenspears, and Isabel had been nervous ever since.

Marcus sat forward. "You did not seem fine in the carriage. Even your maid looked worried."

Isabel rolled her eyes. Her father had insisted her maid, Kate, act as her chaperone and accompany them to the Ravenspears' home tonight. After they had arrived, Kate had immediately departed to share a meal with the other servants. Isabel had thought the charade ludicrous since she and Marcus were officially betrothed, and all of society knew they had been caught together in a highly compromising position at the Westley auction. Yet her father insisted that the appearance of propriety still be upheld.

As for her uncharacteristic behavior on their journey here, she had purposely been withdrawn for fear of gazing upon Marcus in the close confines of the carriage and unwittingly reminiscing about her youthful infatuation—or worse—his kiss. She was still surprised at her own eager response to the touch of his lips.

Then thoughts of his mistress's visit would intrude, and Isabel's gut twisted.

"I apologize if I was quiet during our journey. I was deep in thought," she said.

"Over what?"

She took a breath and then blurted out, "Over the unexpected visit of your mistress at my home three days ago."

He stared, complete surprise on his face. "Simone Winston came to your house?"

"The woman was quite honest about her prurient relationship with you over the past year and her intent to continue it."

"Damnation! My relationship with Simone was all but officially over before I set eyes on you at Lady Holloway's ball."

"She believes you two should marry. I can't blame her really. I did intrude into your life at the Westley auction even though I had believed Charlotte when she had said that you were not involved with any particular lady. If it were not for my father's insistence and your odd sense of honor, you would be free to marry her."

"I never intended to marry Simone. I had told her so weeks ago."

"She has yet to believe it."

"Then she's lying."

Displaying an ease she didn't necessarily feel, she said, "You owe me no explanations. After all, we had agreed to certain terms. It's unreasonable to expect you to alter every aspect of your life based on a mere temporary arrangement."

His gaze was so galvanizing it sent a tremor down her spine. "Are you always going to be so maddening?"

She sat back, baffled by his words.

He sighed. "I apologize for Simone's unpleasant visit. Had I suspected she would be so bold as to seek you out, I would have warned her to stay away when I ended my relationship with her."

Isabel looked away, careful to sheath her inner feelings. "No one can control the actions of others."

He reached out to touch her hand, his fingers warm and strong. "Look at me, Isabel."

She raised her eyes to his and was surprised by the smoldering intensity in the dark depths.

"Simone Winston is in my past. I have no intention of ever resuming relations with her."

She was saved from having to respond by the sound of footsteps in the hallway. The drawing room doors opened, and Blake and Victoria entered.

Victoria, heavy with child, moved slowly across the room. Blake was by her side, a steady hand on her elbow.

Isabel was struck by the countess's beauty. Her dark hair was piled in loose ringlets atop her head, and a few loose tendrils brushed the graceful curve of her neck. Her wide emerald eyes were slanted like a Persian cat's and shone with intelligence.

"Welcome," Victoria said. "We have been looking forward to a quiet evening with good friends."

Victoria's friendly nature and sincere smile put Isabel at ease, and she took an instant liking to the countess. "Thank you for inviting us, Lady Ravenspear. Your home is lovely," Isabel said.

Blake smiled politely at Isabel, and then turned his attention to Marcus. "I've made inquiries regarding Lord Gavinport. We can speak over dinner."

Isabel knew Marcus confided in Blake, but she had no idea as to what extent. It seemed the earl was assisting Marcus with his investigative efforts.

"I'm anxious to know what you've learned," Marcus said. "Gavinport is my top suspect."

Marcus and Blake stepped out of the drawing room, leaving Isabel alone with Victoria.

Victoria appeared amused by the men's behavior. "Men are more comfortable speaking business, whereas women prefer more personal conversation."

Curiosity rose in Isabel, and she boldly asked, "You know Marcus well?"

Victoria smiled and reached out to squeeze Isabel's hand. "Very. After dinner, Blake and Marcus will remain to drink their port, and we can leave to speak privately. You can ask me questions about him, and if I know the answers, I'll promise to tell you the truth."

Isabel was surprised by the countess's openness, and her earlier interest blossomed. She would love to learn more about Marcus Hawksley, starting with why he never married, and why he left his family to become a working stockbroker.

They left the drawing room and found the men waiting outside the doors. Marcus offered Isabel his arm, and as they followed behind their hosts, Isabel was stunned by the beauty of the Ravenspear home. Whereas Blake and Victoria were not art collectors, they had exquisite and expensive taste. Rich mahogany furniture, exotic rugs, and costly vases and crystal decorated their home.

On the way to the dining room, they passed numerous

rooms—a music conservatory, a lower-level library, and a ballroom with a parquet floor agleam from a recent polish.

The dining room was massive, with a long table capable of comfortably seating fifty guests. But for tonight, the table was set for two couples on one end. A snowy white tablecloth and fine china bearing the Ravenspear crest gleamed beneath the candlelight.

Victoria and Blake took their seats.

Marcus held Isabel's chair, and his long fingers brushed her shoulders. She shivered despite the warmth from the fireplace.

Two liveried footmen entered the dining room, carrying steaming platters of food. The fare was excellent, beginning with turtle soup, followed by a saddle of mutton, fowl, and salmon drizzled with a delicate lemon sauce, accompanied by fresh vegetables. Isabel learned Blake and Victoria had recruited their French chef on their honeymoon in Paris.

Expensive sherry flowed freely, and Isabel drank as much as she ate in part to soothe her nerves. She hated to admit how much Marcus's admission—that Simone Winston was in his past and would remain so—had thrilled her. So she imbibed to numb her uncomfortable feelings.

Marcus sipped his glass and looked at Blake. "Tell me what you have learned of Lord Gavinport."

"He is an obsessive art collector and has no qualms about bidding outrageous sums of money to obtain any piece of work that catches his eye. He has purchased works from his peers which he believes he must own. He has also dealt with auctioneers and gallery owners of questionable character," Blake said.

"You mean Dante Black?" Marcus asked.

Blake shook his head. "He has dealt with Dante, but from what I've heard, Dante Black was one of the more respectable auctioneers. Gavinport has dealt with others, and it is rumored that he has a private gallery that rivals a museum."

"He does," Marcus said.

"You've seen it?"

"Not by invitation."

Blake's mouth twitched with amusement. "My man of affairs, Justin Woodward, has let it be known that I am willing to pay an exorbitant sum for an original Thomas Gainsborough painting. We have yet to hear anything from disreputable or official sources."

"That reaffirms my belief that the thief stole for an individual's private collection," Marcus said.

"Other than Lord Gavinport, do you know of any others who would want to see you accused of a crime?" Victoria asked.

Isabel, emboldened by the sherry, chimed in. "Oh yes, Marcus has enemies. I've already met a few."

Silence descended, and Victoria and Blake turned to her.

"Since we've only recently become involved, what could you know of my enemies?" Marcus asked dryly.

The couple's head swung toward Marcus.

Isabel placed her silver fork down on the edge of her plate. "Well, there's a handsome stockbroker I met at the Exchange just last week by the name of Ralph Hodge whom you were quite rude to. Then there's Lord Walling, whom you attacked in the Bennings' gardens during a ball. And lastly, there's the embittered woman—whom I will not mention by name—you have spurned. All have motive."

Marcus's eyes darkened dangerously. "Lord Walling did not know me prior to the Westley auction, and therefore, he can be dismissed as a suspect."

Isabel raised her chin and met his glare. "What of the other two?"

"She's right," Blake said. "Both have motive. Hodge has been your rival at the Exchange for years and has reason to want to see your privileges as a broker revoked. As for Simone . . . ah . . . the female Isabel has mentioned, a scorned woman can be dangerous. Both deserve looking into."

"It seems to me you are all overlooking the obvious," Victoria said.

Marcus looked at the countess. "Such as?"

Victoria drew her lips in thoughtfully. "What about Lord Gavinport's second home? I assume that you had searched his private gallery during his recent masque, but he does own another residence in London. It is a town house, not as grand as the mansion you had visited, but legally his property upon his marriage to his second wife, Olivia Gavinport."

"I had no idea," Isabel said.

Victoria shrugged. "It is a simple town house and was part of Olivia's dowry and included in their marriage contract. The Gavinports would never entertain there. The only reason I know about it is because my brother, Spencer, was looking to buy a London home close by and had inquired about the property."

"It's possible that Gavinport stored the stolen painting there for safety during the masque," Blake said. "Or that he plans to keep it there until the investigation by Bow Street and the insurance company ceases."

"I must search his town house." Marcus said.

"Spencer is currently in Italy on business for Blake. I'm afraid I do not know the property's address," Victoria said.

"It doesn't matter," Marcus said. "My investigator can check the property records to determine its location. I intend to search it."

"How will you get inside if he does not entertain there?" Isabel asked.

"He doesn't have to. I'll find a way," Marcus said, his tone cold and exact.

"You mean to break in?" Isabel asked, incredulous. "What if you are caught, or worse, injured?"

She was horrified that Marcus would even entertain the thought. If Frederick Gavinport was hiding the *Seashore with Fishermen* in his town house, he would post a guard to watch over the priceless painting. It was highly probable that it would be an *armed* guard.

A flash of humor crossed Marcus's face. "Are you concerned for my safety, my dear?"

"Of course. I would not like for any man to suffer injury in an attempt to prove his innocence."

"Ah, but what about *this* innocent man?"

She was irritated by his mocking tone. The sherry had loosened her tongue, and she was upset with herself for unwittingly mentioning Marcus's former lover in front of the earl and countess. It appeared that Marcus now sought retaliation by forcing her to publicly acknowledge her feelings for him despite their agreement to stay emotionally and physically uninvolved.

Isabel twisted her napkin in her lap, aware of everyone's eyes upon her, and her annoyance increased. She raised her chin and met his stare. "We are to marry in less than two weeks, and the scandal we had created at the Westley auction will pale in comparison if my groom is arrested and thrown into Newgate."

Marcus shot her a penetrating look. "If appearances are all you are concerned with, my dear, never fear. I don't plan on being imprisoned anytime soon."

Chapter 17

Dinner was finally over. Isabel marched out of the dining room like an irate general—head held high, chest thrust forward, and back ramrod stiff. The battle of wills between her and Marcus, combined with too much liquor, had inflamed her senses. She itched to confront him, to continue sparring. But manners prevailed, and she found herself following Victoria into the parlor while the men stayed behind to drink their port.

Isabel chose a seat opposite the countess in a comfortable leather chair. It was a chilly May evening, and a bright fire blazed in the grate of an overlarge fireplace, warming the room.

Victoria leaned back in her chair, hands splayed over her swollen abdomen, and smiled casually at Isabel. "We have much in common."

Puzzled, Isabel looked up. "In common with what?"

"You're attracted to him despite yourself."

Isabel blinked in surprise. "Whatever do you mean?"

"I realize we have just met, but Marcus is like a brother to my husband. May I speak plainly with you?"

Isabel nodded, her ire dissipating beneath the countess's green gaze.

"You find Marcus Hawksley attractive, and he in turn clearly desires you, but for reasons I have yet to learn, you are fighting your feelings," Victoria said.

"Why would you believe that?"

"Because it is precisely how I felt before the earl and I were married."

Isabel looked at Victoria with utter disbelief. "But Ravenspear adores you! His admiration is written all over his face whenever he looks at you. And you appear to love him. Any woman would be envious of your marriage."

Victoria shook her head. "It wasn't always so. There was a time that I had despised Blake as much as I had desired him. My emotions were so confused, I regarded my attraction for him a weakness, and I loathed myself for it."

"Why?"

"Because Blake forced me to become his mistress."

Isabel gasped, momentarily speechless in her surprise.

"I don't speak of it," Victoria said, "but since you are to marry Marcus, I feel you should know the truth."

"Why would Ravenspear do such an awful thing?"

Victoria threaded her fingers over her distended stomach. "Blake hated my father for past unspeakable sins, and he sought to ruin him socially as well as financially. Blake purchased my father's outstanding notes and called in the loans. When my father could not make the interest payments, Blake offered to extend the loans only if I lived with him as his mistress for one year."

"How ghastly! How did you ever forgive him?"

Victoria sighed. "I did not at first. I was infatuated with him in my youth, and despite his unspeakable actions, I fought daily not to succumb to his seductive efforts. But Blake was fighting his own personal demons—a festering need for revenge, hatred for my father, and his desire for me. He never once forced me to bed him, and he even swore not to touch me until I willingly came to him. As you can surmise from my current condition, I eventually did."

Isabel held her breath, her mind racing. Blake's promise not to touch Victoria reminded Isabel of the arrangement she and Marcus had made. Only *she* had insisted Marcus agree to the farce, and *she*—unlike Victoria—had no intention of ever breaking their agreement.

"Now that I have told you my secrets, will you tell me what is going on between you and Marcus?" Victoria asked.

Isabel experienced a sudden desperate urge to confess all to the countess and seek her advice. Victoria, unlike Charlotte, had experienced the frustrations of a perilous attraction.

Isabel sat in her chair, her fingers tense in her lap. "You are correct in your observations, Lady Ravenspear. I do not want to marry Marcus Hawksley or any man for that matter. What I want, what I have always wanted, is to move to Paris for formal art studies."

"I see. And after the ludicrous scandal at Lord Westley's estate sale where your testimony saved Marcus, your father insisted upon you two marrying."

"Yes, and Marcus stubbornly agreed with my father," Isabel said.

"You feel that by marrying Marcus, you are forced to sacrifice your dreams?" Victoria asked.

Isabel shook her head. "I refuse to. I still plan on going to Paris." She left out the pertinent fact that she and Marcus would never consummate their marriage.

A twinkle of mischief shone in Victoria's eye, as if the older, more experienced woman suspected the truth. "Ah, you seek to hold yourself apart to protect yourself. It may be harder than you think. You adored Marcus Hawksley as a girl, just as I did my Blake."

"That was over eight years ago."

"Yes, but I suspect you are battling old feelings now."

Isabel shifted in her seat. She was uncomfortable with Victoria's uncanny ability to read her mind. "It matters naught. I am no longer a child and can control my base emotions."

Liar! she thought. *You still think about him, only now it is as a grown woman fantasizing about a man, not a twelve-year-old girl doting over a rogue.*

Victoria looked at her with understanding. "I will not pry deeper, Isabel, but I want you to know you can speak to me without fear of my revealing our discussions to Blake or Marcus."

"If I may be so bold, why would you do that?"

"I had a woman—a worldly baroness—befriend me when I first came to reside with Blake at Rosewood, his country estate. I was scared, confused, and in desperate need of wise feminine advice. Although our personalities differ—you are impulsive, bold, and blessedly unconcerned with what society thinks, whereas I was reserved and feared scandal—I sense that you could use a friend. You see, I believe you are exactly what Marcus needs in his life."

Isabel chose her words with care. "Marcus does not need anyone, most certainly not a wife thrust upon him."

A thoughtful smile curved Victoria's mouth. "You are an intelligent and independent woman who gives naught for society's rigid expectations. You seek freedom, and Marcus's reputation amongst the haut ton doesn't give you the slightest hesitation as it has many other flighty debutantes. You are not intimidated by his fierce countenance and stand up to him. He will find you irresistible."

Isabel felt a thrill at the woman's words. What would it feel like to have a man like Hawksley find her "irresistible"?

"What of his past? Why has he never married?" Isabel asked.

"There were dark years that I know had to do with a

woman's betrayal, but as to the details, only he knows. Marcus has never spoken of it."

"Is that why he became a stockbroker?"

"Blake befriended Marcus at a critical time in his life and introduced him to the Stock Exchange. Marcus has an instinctive shrewdness for business and is very good at what he does. Blake considers his talents irreplaceable, and Marcus takes great pride in his work. That is why it is so important to Marcus to determine the true identity of the man who attempted to frame him for the theft of the painting. Marcus wants to maintain his stellar business reputation at the Stock Exchange," Victoria explained.

Leaning forward, Isabel lowered her voice an octave. "He says he has hired a private investigator. I understand they can charge exorbitant fees, yet Marcus declined my dowry. How can a working broker afford such an expense?"

Victoria threw her head back and laughed. "You think Marcus Hawksley is impoverished?"

Isabel was taken aback. "Perhaps not impoverished, but certainly not wealthy."

"Have you seen his home? Where you will live after you marry?"

"No. Why do you ask?"

"Because, darling, once you visit him, you will see with your own eyes that he is filthy rich."

Shock flew through her. "What?"

Victoria reached for a pencil and paper on an end table and began scribbling. "This is his address. He purchased Blake's former town house on St. James's Street after Blake and I married. Go see him tomorrow."

Isabel took the paper and stared down at it with a dumbfounded expression on her face. "Are you sure?"

"Marcus Hawksley has more money than many of the members of the ton. He is a virtuoso when it comes to investing and it is not only his clients whom he has made fabulously wealthy. As an experienced investor myself, I am awed by his talent. He is a highly sought after broker who can choose his own clients."

Isabel looked at Victoria with renewed interest. "Marcus had mentioned that you were a successful anonymous investor in the London Stock Exchange. When I visited the place, I did not see a female face. How bold of you to fool the men and work in their world."

"I do have investing savvy, Isabel, but I am the first to admit that Marcus Hawksley's talent puts mine in the shade. He is obsessive about his work."

"And I am just as passionate about studying art."

Victoria chuckled. "I've witnessed the sparks fly between you two. I soon predict that both of your obsessions will turn sharply in a different direction."

Chapter 18

The artists' district was vacant at the crack of dawn. It was a Sunday, and most artists—who were, by nature, free sprits—were recovering from a night of indulgence, drinking cheap ale with their fellow creative comrades.

Dante Black pulled the collar of his frock coat about his neck and the curled brim of his hat down to shield his face. It had rained last night, and puddles had collected in the depressions between the cobblestones. He walked swiftly, scanning the street for signs of life. The old boots he was forced to wear had cracks in the leather, and rainwater penetrated the openings and saturated his threadbare stockings.

He swore beneath his breath.

The run-down studio came into view. Dante took the rickety wooden steps to the second floor two at a time. Using a key, he opened the door, which creaked on its hinges as it slowly opened.

Vacant.

He exhaled in relief. Lord, how he hated this place. It was where he met his criminal contact, Robby Bones. Where he received "his lordship's" orders.

And what good had come of the bloody mess?

Dante had been in hiding since the debacle at the Westley

auction. It didn't matter that his lordship had paid Dante a hefty fee for his underhanded services. Dante could not spend a farthing of the money.

He was a hunted man.

Damn Marcus Hawksley.

Dante shut the door behind him and walked into the room. He took a seat by a crate of dried paint cans. The filth and stink of the room made his skin crawl. He had once been used to fine clothing, food, and wine. Now he scurried about London in hiding like a common street rat and had given up his previous luxuries.

I must stay calm, Dante thought. *When this ugly business with Hawksley is settled, I will be able to resume my previous lifestyle.*

The door creaked once again, and Dante's head snapped to attention.

Robby Bones entered the room. Lanky and gaunt with greasy black hair shielding his eyes, he walked with a slight limp, and his right boot scraped across the dirty wood floor.

Dante stared beneath lowered lids. The injury was new, and he wondered if it was due to Bones's criminal activities or from his part-time occupation as a gravedigger.

Robby Bones spotted Dante seated in the corner. He shot Dante a twisted smile, which revealed his tobacco-stained teeth, the front tooth sheared clean in half.

"I 'ave new marchin' orders for ye, Dante," Bones said.

Dante stood, his spine stiff. "I've done everything asked of me, and I'm in hiding because of it. What else could the man want of me?"

Bones pulled out a cheap cigar from the inside pocket of his coat, bit off the tip, and spit it at Dante's feet. "Yer in hidin' because ye failed to 'ave Marcus Hawksley arrested. 'Tis no fault of 'is lordship." Bones struck a match against a splintered easel and lit the cigar. He blew smoke in Dante's face.

Dante stood stock still, hatred twisting his innards. "I told you before, the circumstances were beyond my control. The Cameron girl vouched for Hawksley."

"Ye can fix yer mistake. Get rid of Hawksley fer good. 'Is lordship is willin' to pay ye more fer yer services."

A fissure of interest pierced Dante's wall of reluctance. Despite everything, the prospect of more money appealed to him. "What do I have to do?"

"Move the painting."

"The Gainsborough painting? To where?"

"To Hawksley's office."

"Is he mad?" Dante's voice rose in surprise. "The *Seashore with Fishermen* is large—over three feet tall and four feet wide. How on earth does he expect me to sneak it into Hawksley's office unnoticed?"

"Ye 'ave delivered paintings to places of business before. Ye can do it again."

"Yes, but never one that was stolen, and never when I have been hiding from Hawksley and his hired investigator," he argued, his voice sounding shrill to his own ears.

Smoke curled around Bones's face. "'Is lordship 'as faith in ye."

"Say I do manage to move the painting to Hawksley's place of business. What purpose will that serve?"

"I'll make certain Bow Street searches there. When they find the painting, Hawksley will be arrested fer the theft."

Dante had to give Robby Bones credit. He was a creative criminal.

"But the painting is no longer here," Dante pointed out. "The last time we met, you said his lordship wanted it and planned to move it."

"'E did, but it will be returned 'ere. Ye are to wait fer the package to be delivered tomorrow. 'Is lordship wants ye 'ere when it arrives so that 'tis never left alone. Understand?"

With effort, Dante kept his features cool and composed.

"This is no easy task. I have to find a way to get the painting inside Hawksley's office unnoticed. How much will he pay?"

"Ye have already been paid a 'efty fee—"

"How much?"

"Two hundred pounds."

Two hundred pounds!

Dante licked his lips in anticipation. "Tomorrow then."

Chapter 19

Isabel paid the driver of the hackney cab and alighted without waiting for assistance. She lifted her chin a notch at the stares she received walking alone down St. James's Street. She had lied about her whereabouts this afternoon, saying she was shopping with Charlotte, and had evaded Kate's hovering presence.

This was not the type of visit in which a chaperone was desired.

She spotted the popular male establishments, Brooks's, Boodle's, and White's. Despite the early afternoon hour, men were in the bay window of White's, liquor glasses in hand.

Isabel recalled her conversation the prior evening with Lady Ravenspear, which had been both surprising and enlightening. Victoria had said the earl had sold the town house on St. James's Street—a prestigious and popular address for a wealthy bachelor's home—to Marcus.

Victoria had also claimed Marcus Hawksley was not only well-to-do, but "filthy rich."

Could it be true?

It would explain Marcus's unusual behavior: He had rejected her dowry; he had hired an investigator; he had never, at least to Charlotte's knowledge, asked his family for money; and he was an avid art collector.

Isabel's curiosity was piqued, and she felt compelled to learn the truth. She spotted the town house, and her inquisitiveness grew with each step she took.

She reached the porch and lifted the heavy brass knocker.

The door swung open, and a butler with a somber expression opened the door and looked down at her.

"Lady Isabel Cameron to see my betrothed, Mr. Hawksley."

The butler's face immediately softened at the sight of the future mistress standing on the porch. "My lady, what a pleasure." He stepped back and opened the door wide. "I will inform Mr. Hawksley at once."

Isabel stepped inside. Her eyes were immediately drawn to the black and white marble floor, elegant chandelier, and grand long-case clock in the corner. She handed her cloak to the butler, her eyes never leaving the well-appointed vestibule.

"Would you like refreshment while you wait, my lady?"

"No thank you Mr. . . ."

"Jenkins, my lady. Mr. Hawksley calls me Jenkins."

She smiled. "Then Jenkins it is."

She turned to follow Jenkins to a formal receiving room, when Marcus strode into the vestibule. He was carrying a sheath of papers, and stopped short when he spotted her.

"Isabel! What a surprise."

She couldn't discern by his tone whether he was pleased or not, but she smiled at him just the same.

"Good afternoon, Mr. Hawksley."

Marcus walked forward with a grin of amusement. "Welcome to *your* future home."

He took her elbow and looked back at the butler. "Jenkins, please have Mrs. McLaughlin bring tea for the lady."

Taking her elbow, Marcus led her not to the receiving room, but to the library instead.

It was a large room, and from the stacks of papers piled high on a massive desk, it was clearly his office as well.

Row after row of books bound in supple leather lined the walls. Massive mahogany shelves on one side of the room held art history and picture books, only some of which she recognized. Matching shelves on the opposite wall held books pertaining to the London Stock Exchange and economics in general. Two wheeled ladders hung on runners so they could be wheeled back and forth, ensuring access to the top shelves. The desk and a leather hammer-head chair sat in front of a wide bay window, and she assumed Marcus spent many hours here conducting business. A pair of smaller leather chairs were situated before a fireplace.

Isabel knew books were costly, and the furnishings in the room combined with the content on the shelves clearly pronounced that it was an affluent man's library office.

But affluent did not mean "filthy rich."

Marcus tossed the sheath of papers in his hand onto a stack on the desk. He then led her to one of the chairs before the hearth and sat beside her.

"I'm glad you came," he said. "I want to thank you for accompanying me to the Ravenspears' home last evening. Blake is like a brother to me, more so than my own."

She tilted her head, looking at him uncertainly. "I thought you would be upset with my loose tongue at dinner."

"You mean when you brought up a list of my enemies?" he said, a faint glint of humor in his eyes. "You had reason to be upset."

Isabel knew he was referring to Simone Winston's dreadful visit.

"I also realize the sherry was partly responsible for your haranguing speech," Marcus said.

She grimaced and rubbed her temple. "You may be happy to learn I woke with a pounding headache."

He gave her a smile that sent her pulses racing. "I had wondered about your physical state this morning."

She smiled back. "A truce then?"

"How could a man refuse?"

He raised her fingers to his lips and kissed the back of her hand. His lips were whisper soft, his kiss chaste, and yet she inhaled sharply at the contact. His clean and manly scent wafted to her, and her heartbeat skyrocketed.

He raised his head, his dark, unfathomable eyes meeting hers. Something passed between them, a vaguely sensuous light . . . a thread of attraction that was as mesmerizing as it was dangerous.

The door opened suddenly and an older, matronly woman entered carrying a tray laden with a silver teapot and china. A crisp uniform strained against her ample bosom, and her steel gray hair was pulled back in a tight bun. Walking into the library, she placed the heavy tray on an end table beside Marcus. At the sight of Isabel, her wrinkled face creased into a friendly smile.

Marcus cleared his throat and made the introduction. "This is my devoted housekeeper, Mrs. McLaughlin."

Isabel stood. "It is a pleasure to meet you. Your services will be invaluable to me after we marry. I hope you do not mind when I look to you for all manner of advice."

Mrs. McLaughlin beamed. "I would be honored, my lady. I speak on behalf of the entire staff, and we all look forward to your arrival as mistress."

The housekeeper departed, and Marcus chuckled. "You seem to have charmed both Jenkins and Mrs. McLaughlin easily enough."

"You may find it surprising, but most people like me."

"I never doubted you, my dear." He picked up a gleaming silver teapot from the tray and made to pour her a cup.

Isabel shook her head. "Perhaps later. I would much rather first see your home, especially your art collection."

Marcus set the teapot down. "That is a splendid idea. It is rare that I have the opportunity for an artist to view my collection."

She followed him out of the library and three doors down into a spacious room that had been converted into his private gallery. He opened the door, and she strained to see behind him. She glimpsed an array of canvases on the walls and stone pedestals that held busts and sculptures in the center of the room. Bright sunlight streamed in from the windows. The only furnishings, a chaise and a dainty cherry wood table, sat in a corner.

Isabel pictured Marcus sitting on the chaise, his brow furrowed in deep concentration, admiring his collection.

They walked farther into the room, and as the canvases came into focus, she started, instantly awed by the beautiful artwork he had acquired. There were oils, charcoals, watercolors, and artifacts, each piece obviously chosen with care. There were works by sporting artists, showing the fine lines and majestic breeding of stallions. Others were landscapes of glorious faraway places and exotic beaches. But to her surprise, there were no portraits.

"I thought you were a connoisseur of Thomas Gainsborough's work."

He met her eyes and nodded. "I am."

"But I don't see any portraits here, and Thomas Gainsborough was known as a portrait painter."

"True, but his real love was painting landscapes. Painting the nobility was merely a way to support himself. That's why I wanted to acquire the *Seashore with Fishermen*. It was one of a set of coastal scenes he had displayed at the Royal Academy in 1781 which had been painted from sketches made in Ipswich, the seaport town where he and his young wife had resided. The painting is said to be so realistic that you can almost feel the spray of the ocean on your face as you gaze upon it."

She sighed. "I heartily wish I had a chance to view it before it was stolen."

"So do I," he said with light bitterness.

"May I keep looking?"

He motioned with his hand. "Of course."

An imposing oil on the far wall caught her eye. "This is an exquisite replica of Rembrandt's *Shipbuilder and His Wife.*"

"How did you know it was a copy?"

"I know because the Regent himself bought the original three years ago, in 1811, at an auction for five thousand guineas. Prinny hung it in the Blue Velvet Room of Carlton House."

Marcus laughed. "Bravo! You truly are more knowledgeable than most. Lord Stafford saw my copy and believed it to be the original, despite my protests, until he viewed the real painting at Carlton House himself."

"It is a remarkable reproduction."

"What do you think of my watercolors?"

She turned to study another wall in which Marcus's watercolors were grouped together. Most were landscapes and still-life paintings, but a few were of country folk conducting activities of daily life. "They are breathtaking."

He moved to stand beside her, his body mere inches from her. A ripple of awareness passed through her, and she realized how much she was drawn to him . . . how much she enjoyed talking with him about their common love of art.

His eyes caught and held hers. "Tell me why you prefer watercolors," he said.

"I am only an amateur in need of further instruction,"

she said, "but I fell in love with watercolors over oils because they can be carried out with complete freedom. Watercolors blur the boundary between painting and drawing. When I paint, my brush flows onto the paper swiftly and inspires me to capture the moment with fierce spontaneity."

"Free, spontaneous, impulsive, and beautiful . . . that does describe you perfectly."

Heat throbbed in her cheeks. He was not the type of man to flatter a woman. Compliments did not roll off his tongue like the popinjays of the ton. He meant every word, and his admission stirred her. The thought crossed her mind that, as a mischievous and impish twelve-year-old girl, she would have given her front teeth to hear such praise from him.

His appeal was devastating, and it was too easy to get lost in her emotions and forget their agreement. Uncomfortable with her feelings, she said the first thing that came to mind. "Lady Ravenspear told me you were 'filthy rich,' but I doubted her word."

"What?"

"Seeing your home, your collection, for the first time, tells me she was right."

"You thought I was poor?" he asked.

"You never led me to believe otherwise."

His lips twitched with amusement. "I didn't think my financial status was of concern to you when you had first propositioned me for a salacious affair, or afterward when we agreed to a marriage of convenience."

"Nonetheless, you could have informed me."

He grinned. "I'm not accustomed to discussing my wealth, and unlike the Bennings, I do not feel the need to openly display it to inflate my ego."

She rolled her eyes. "Thank goodness for small blessings."

He threw his head back and laughed. "I am glad you

came today. I have something for you, my dear." He moved
to the table beside the chaise. Opening a slender drawer, he
pulled out a cigar-sized box.

He came up to her and handed it to her. "Please open it."

Curiosity swelled in her breast. She glanced at him, then
reached for the lid. She opened the box, and gasped.

A radiant ruby ring the size of a pigeon's egg surrounded by brilliant diamonds lay nestled in folds of black
velvet. Beside the ring sat a miniature artists' palette of
handcrafted silver. Precious jewels of opal, ruby, emerald,
sapphire, onyx, and a yellow diamond represented the
colors in the palette.

She looked up at him, at a loss for words.

"I realize that you did not seek to get married, but I
wanted to give you a betrothal ring, and at the same time,
the artist's pallet is to remind you of your life-long dream."

A vibrant chord hummed throughout her body at his
words. The ruby was as extravagant as it was stunning, but
it was the symbolic thoughtfulness behind the miniature
artist's pallet that brought tears to her eyes.

"Oh, Marcus. They are both lovely. Thank you."

She threw her arms around his neck, the box clutched in
her right hand behind him. Standing on tiptoe, she pressed
her lips to his in a brief kiss.

She felt him stiffen and thought he would move back,
but instead his arms swiftly encircled her, one hand in the
small of her back, holding her tight against him.

She looked up, and a compelling eager look flashed in
his eyes. In that instant, the undeniable magnetism that had
been building between them seemed to intensify a hundredfold, and she felt the blood surge from her fingertips
to her toes.

"Sweet Lord, Isabel. What have you done to me?"

His mouth swooped down to capture hers. His kiss was
urgent and hungry at once, like the soldering heat that joins

metals. In wicked remembrance, she parted her lips in eager anticipation of his ravishment. He took full advantage, eagerly exploring her mouth. Her tongue touched his, tentatively at first, until a delicious shudder heated her body, and she boldly returned his kiss. The box slipped from her fingers and fell to the floor with a loud thump.

She jerked back. "The jewels—"

"Forget them," he growled. Holding her head captive with firm fingers, he reclaimed her lips.

She grasped his shoulders, his muscles hard slabs beneath his shirt. Succumbing to an overwhelming impulse to touch him elsewhere, her fingers grazed over his arms, and she was exhilarated by his tightly coiled power. Her roaming hands moved to his chest, and she reveled in the strength and warmth of his flesh and the pounding of his heart through the thin cotton fabric.

He groaned low in his throat at her touch. His lips left her mouth and traced a sensuous path down her neck. He nipped at her ear, then sucked the sensitive lobe full into his mouth.

Isabel nearly jumped out of her skin at the heady sensations that coursed through her. She grasped fistfuls of his shirt, afraid she would fall to the floor.

Marcus's hands tightened about her waist and pulled her closer still. His lips lowered to the modest neckline of her walking gown. Holding her tight with one hand, he used the other to unfasten the tiny buttons behind her back and tugged the material of her bodice and thin chemise down with his teeth. Her breasts sprang free, and her nipples firmed from the cool air in the room.

"Isabel," he breathed. "You're so beautiful, like a priceless piece of fine art ripe for the taking." His moist breath caressed her exposed breast a moment before he lowered his dark head to tease a taut nipple.

The pleasure was pure and explosive, and a hot ache

surged between her legs. Her prior reservations flew from her mind with each slick stroke of his tongue. Her head, suddenly too heavy to hold up, fell back. Her fingers thrust into his thick hair as she pulled him closer and arched her spine forward at the same time in wanton abandon.

Through her half-closed eyes, the radiant watercolors on the wall blended with her heightened senses until each stroke of his tongue on her heated flesh felt like brush-strokes on a canvas. He was the master painter and she his fervent masterpiece.

"You are so eager, Isabel. I'll go mad." His voice, harsh with longing, served to fuel her passion.

"Yessss. I feel it, too. Please don't stop, Marcus."

His head stiffened beneath her fingers, and it took her several seconds before she realized he had stopped kissing her heated flesh.

He raised his head, his breathing labored. His eyes burned with unmistakable desire. "We cannot go forward like this, Isabel. *I* cannot."

Her vision spun. Her mind was sluggish, swimming through a haze of newfound desire. She tried to catch her breath, tried to force her confused emotions into order and focus on his fierce expression.

"What do you mean?"

He straightened, pulling her with him. With jerky movements, he tugged the chemise and bodice of her dress over her breasts, spun her around, and struggled with the tiny pearl buttons.

Her lips, still warm and moist from his kisses, trembled at the touch of his fingers on her skin. She turned to face him when he finished.

"A man has certain base needs, Isabel. If I am to hold to our bargain, then there have to be rules about touching. The way you embraced me and kissed me—"

"I merely meant to thank you for your gift," she responded sharply.

"I am a flesh-and-blood man."

"So you keep saying. Do you intend to blame me for what just occurred?

"Of course not."

A vulnerable thought struck her, and she asked, "Do you regret kissing me?"

"Surprisingly, no. But you should. You deserve better than to lose your innocence with a tarnished soul like me. I am not worthy of such a gift."

She felt the color drain from her face. His reputation did not bother her, but the truthfulness of his words regarding her virginity did. All that had kept her from lying with him on the floor of his glorious gallery was *his* self-control in recalling the bargain they had struck. She should feel shame or immense relief to have had her innocence spared, but the truth was, she felt nothing but an acute sense of loss.

Marcus Hawksley was an ever-changing mystery, a rare type of male. Despite her initial determination not to get physically involved with him, he sparked her passionate nature. Much like her watercolors, he was becoming an obsession.

"Is that why you never married and instead turned to trade? Because you believe you are not good, not worthy?" she asked.

His expression darkened. "No. Work, money, and art don't betray a man; only people do."

"Lady Ravenspear had said you were betrayed by a woman."

"Victoria should mind her own business."

"Why don't you get along with your family?"

He sighed. "I don't wish to discuss my past, Isabel. I only want to discuss how we are to maintain our charade."

She reached out to touch his arm. "I don't believe any of it, Marcus. I *know* you are a good man."

The hunger in his eyes had nothing to do with lust, but rather everything to do with her trust and faith in him.

His gaze dropped to her lips.

He looks like he is going to kiss me again. Lord, let him kiss me, her mind raced.

A low knock sounded on the door.

Marcus sighed and straightened. "Enter."

Jenkins stood in the doorway. "Your brother, Lord Ardmore, is here to see you. He says it is regarding urgent business."

A frown creased Marcus's brow. "See him in, Jenkins."

The butler nodded, and a moment later, a startlingly handsome man strode into the gallery.

His green gaze shifted from Isabel to Marcus. "I know where Dante Black is hiding. But we must move quickly before he leaves."

Chapter 20

Isabel had met Roman Hawksley before. Their fathers, both influential earls, were social acquaintances, and as the heir to the Ardmore earldom, Roman had dutifully attended his fair share of balls and social soirees. But it was the first time she had seen him since her engagement to his brother.

"Lady Isabel," Roman Hawksley said, bowing gallantly. "Forgive my untimely intrusion."

"Nonsense. You have valuable information that needs to be immediately addressed. Whatever are we waiting for?"

A gleam of surprise crossed Roman's face before it was replaced with gratitude. "My brother chose well despite himself," he said, grinning mischievously.

Minutes later, they were seated inside the lavish Ardmore crested carriage, traveling at a brisk pace. Isabel studied Marcus beneath lowered lashes. He was withdrawn, every line in his body tense in anticipation of the confrontation with his nemesis, Dante Black . . .

Marcus and Roman sat across from Isabel on the padded bench. The two brothers were remarkably similar in appearance, both dark-haired and powerfully built. But whereas Marcus had eyes the color of liquid chocolate, Roman's were a brilliant green. Roman's aquiline nose and straight forehead gave him a handsome appearance that she suspected drew many feminine glances.

But she grudgingly admitted it was Marcus's ruggedly masculine face that drew her like a lodestone.

She nervously smoothed her hands over her skirts. The tension between Marcus and his older brother was palpable.

"How did you learn of Dante Black's location?" Marcus's voice cut the silence.

"I hired a man to look into things after you came to the house."

"I told you not to interfere."

Roman shrugged. "Yes, but it's a good thing I did, isn't it?"

"I hired my own investigator," Marcus said tersely.

"Then he's clearly not as efficient as mine."

"Damn, Roman. Do you enjoy baiting me?"

Roman's expression sobered. "No. I don't. I thought to help."

"You mean to make amends for the past."

"Does it matter now?"

A heated glance passed between the brothers. She was certain her presence prevented them from divulging what grievance they referred to. She was startled to realize that she desperately wanted to know. She was nearly overcome with the need to learn about Marcus's past, to find out what had damaged him to the point that he thought his very soul tarnished.

Roman pulled up the tasseled shade and looked out the window. "We're almost there." He banged on the roof of the carriage with his walking stick and instructed the driver. "Stop out of view across the street. We don't want to be seen in the Ardmore vehicle."

Staring out the window, Isabel didn't recognize the part of town. The dwellings were small, dilapidated, and huddled close together. Shabbily dressed people sat on doorsteps; a baby wailed in the distance; a stray dog stopped to make a quick meal out of a pile of unrecognizable debris in the street. It was the part of London that a well-bred lady dared not step foot in.

Despite the warmth of three bodies inside the carriage, gooseflesh rose on her arms.

She studied the house in which Dante Black had been hiding. A gray two-story structure, it had broken and missing shutters, an unkempt garden choked with weeds, and a loose door knocker that hung askew. She wondered wildly what an affluent, influential art auctioneer like Dante Black would be doing hiding out in such a hovel.

The answer rang loud as a bell in her head.

Marcus Hawksley.

Dante was hiding out of fear of Marcus.

"What are you thinking?" Marcus asked Roman.

"That we question Dante about his employer."

"We suspect Gavinport," Marcus said.

Roman's brows drew together. "Frederick Perrin, the Marquess of Gavinport? I suppose he has the resources to hire criminals to steal a Gainsborough painting, but it's improbable that Dante Black will confess to working for a man as influential as Gavinport. It would mean the end of Dante's career."

"Then we'll have to persuade him to speak, won't we?"

Roman met Marcus's hard stare. "I stand behind you, Marcus. I'll not allow history to repeat itself."

Surprise flashed in Marcus's eyes, but the emotion dissipated as quickly as it had appeared and was replaced by a familiar mask of indifference.

"How do you plan to get inside?" Isabel interrupted.

"We could force the door," Roman said.

Marcus shook his head. "No. Dante would just run out the back door. Lucky for us, I grabbed my lock picks before leaving my home."

Roman grinned. "Your locksmith client?"

"Of course. Other than money, I occasionally do gain useful skills from my clients."

Marcus's eyes snapped to Isabel. "Stay in the carriage. This should not take long."

"I want to come," she protested.

"No," both men said in unison.

"I may be able to help," she insisted.

"I agreed to allow you to accompany us on the condition that you stay in the carriage," Marcus said.

"But—"

"No." Marcus's eyes were like chips of stone.

She sighed, knowing this was one argument she would never win. She had eagerly capitulated to Marcus's demands at his home in order to be able to accompany them.

Roman reached for the door handle, and the brothers jumped down and headed for Dante's hideout.

Scooting to the window, she watched as Marcus picked the lock and the brothers snuck inside. The door closed behind them.

Time passed slowly. Her eyes never wavered from the front door. The temperature inside the carriage rose as the afternoon sun streamed in through the window and heated her face.

What were they up to?

Had they found Dante Black? Were they interrogating him at this moment? Was Dante confessing to Lord Gavinport's involvement?

Her fingers grazed the silver door handle and itched to fling the door wide open so she could run across the street. She had never had much patience. Thankfully, her father's wealth and status had ensured that she never had to wait overly long for anything.

After fifteen more minutes, her nerves were tight with tension.

To hell with waiting!

She reached for the handle, then froze, remembering the driver. No doubt, the Ardmore servant had been given strict instructions to keep her barricaded inside the carriage.

Her overwrought mind whirled with ideas for escape, but then she stilled, hearing footsteps outside. The distinct high-pitched sound of feminine laughter followed. Looking out the window, she spotted two women waving to the driver. Bright yellow- and peacock-colored dresses with obscenely low bodices and heavily painted faces pronounced that they were working prostitutes.

"What a fancy carriage, sir. 'Ow about we come up and join ye?" The harlot with the yellow dress called up to the driver.

A booming male laugh. "I'm working, ladies."

"So are we."

"How about I come down for a minute."

Isabel heard the squeaking of springs as the driver jumped down. Taking full advantage of the diversion, she quietly opened the door on the opposite side and slipped out. She sprinted across the street, stopping before Dante's hideout to catch her breath, and then pressed an ear to the front door.

Silence.

She pushed against the door, careful not to dislodge the broken knocker. It opened easily, and she stepped inside a tiny vestibule.

Faded brown wallpaper peeled off the walls and a moldy smell permeated the space. The stairs leading to the second floor had a worn green carpet runner, bare to the wood in spots. She peered into a tiny sitting room and found it empty. A narrow hallway before her led to the rest of the living space on the main floor.

Tiptoeing down the hall, she heard male voices.

Yelling. The sound of booted feet scuffling across a wooden floor, and then a loud groan.

The hair rose on her nape. Whoever was inside, they were fighting, or more likely beating someone to a bloody pulp.

Hugging the wall, she crept forward. Her sleeve snagged on a peeling seam of wallpaper, and a puff of old plaster smote the air.

Her nose itched, and she smothered a sneeze.

She came to the bottom of the staircase and was about to pass by when a shadow caught the corner of her eye. She looked up, and her eyes widened at the sight of a menacing figure poised at the landing.

A looming, cadaverously thin man, with long black hair and soulless eyes leered down at her. A heartbeat passed, and he raised his arm, an ominous pistol in his hand.

She let out a bloodcurdling scream.

The demon flew down the stairs like a bat and pinned her against the wall with a fierce, wiry strength.

Pitch eyes bore into hers. "Damn meddling bitch. Ye keep poppin' up at the wrong time. Stay away if ye know what's good fer ye," he snarled, specks of foul spittle spraying her face.

Footsteps pounded down the hall.

He released her, and fled through the front door just as Marcus and Roman rounded the corner.

"Go after him, Roman!" Marcus yelled.

Roman sprinted out the door; Marcus rushed to her side.

"Isabel! Are you all right?" His face was tense, his lips pursed. Without waiting for her reply, his frantic hands ran up and down her arms, checking for signs of injury.

"Yess . . . I'm fine," she stammered, touching his sleeve.

He cradled her face in his big hands and looked into her eyes. "You're shaking like a leaf. Tell me what happened? Did he touch you?"

Her words came out in a great rush. "Nothing happened, really. The front door was unlocked. I heard noises so I followed the sounds down the hall when I spotted . . . when I saw someone." *A demon*. She shivered despite her firm resolve to appear brave. "He had a pistol, you see, so I screamed and he rushed down the stairs. He must have heard you coming because he ran."

Marcus's hands dropped to his side. His expression turned thunderous. "Little fool! I told you to wait in the carriage. You had agreed to do so."

"Marcus, I—"

He shook his head vehemently. "You could have been gravely hurt!"

His eyes blazed in his bronzed face, and despite her common sense, Marcus's anger and concern thrilled and frightened her at the same time.

Roman burst into the vestibule, his breathing labored. He looked at Isabel, then Marcus. "Is she all right?"

"By the Grace of God," Marcus said.

"I lost the man. I gave him a good chase, but he was familiar with the neighborhood and vanished into thin air," Roman said.

"A dangerous street criminal, no doubt," Marcus said. "Isabel said he had a pistol."

Roman's voice rose in surprise. "What's his connection to Dante?"

Isabel spoke up. "He said that I kept interfering at the wrong time. The only other incident that I was involved in was at the Westley auction when I acted as Marcus's alibi. He must be Dante's contact or accomplice."

"She's right, Marcus," Roman said. "Most likely he was the hired criminal that stole the painting at the auction. Maybe he feared Dante would confess the names of everyone involved, and he sought to kill you today. If Dante had outlived his usefulness, then he may have planned to eliminate Dante as well."

"Then my presence stopped him," Isabel said in a small voice.

Marcus stood there, towering and angry. "No, Isabel. He would have killed you, too, had you not screamed and alerted us."

She felt the blood drain from her face. "Good Lord, Marcus. I never thought the theft of one painting could lead to murder."

"A criminal like the one you just encountered would not hesitate to shoot a woman—lady or not."

Roman looked to Marcus, as if a thought had suddenly struck him. "What about Dante?"

"Forget him," Marcus snapped. "I heard the back door slam shut when we left to rush to Isabel's side. He's long gone by now."

Isabel bit her lip, realizing that her interference had led to Dante Black's escape after Marcus and Roman had exerted such efforts to locate him. With an experienced criminal accomplice, the slippery auctioneer could successfully hide for months.

"Did Dante confess as to Lord Gavinport's involvement?" she asked.

Marcus shook his head. "His lips were sealed tight. We did not have enough time to cajole him to loosen his tongue."

Roman stepped forward and held her hand. "Do not worry, Lady Isabel. Dante would not have spoken. He is more afraid of his employer than of physical harm. Your safety is of utmost importance. After meeting you, I for one am convinced that you are the perfect lady for my ill-mannered brother."

Marcus glared at Roman, and took Isabel's hand from him. He tucked it possessively under his arm. "Pay no mind to my charming brother. There's a reason he remains a bachelor. Now let's get you home before your father starts to worry."

Chapter 21

After Isabel was safely dropped off on her doorstep and Roman departed in the Ardmore carriage, Marcus strode into his town house and slammed the door. He waved Jenkins off with an impatient hand.

"I'll be in my library office working. I'm not to be disturbed."

Ever the perceptive butler, Jenkins nodded. "Yes, sir."

Marcus sat behind his desk, intending to immerse himself in the piles of paper before him. His blood was still pounding in his veins, and he sought the numbing solace of his work. It was the one constant in his life since his father's emotional abandonment and Bridget's death.

He reached for a particularly imposing stack and rummaged through the pages. When he found the sheet he was looking for, a company's annual business report, he tried to study the narrow columns listing profit margins, losses, and estimated future earnings. He blinked, his eyes focusing on the figures, but his mind failed to register its content. A pair of clear blue eyes and inky hair clouded his vision instead.

He shook his head, his elbow accidently jostling one of

the piles. Sheets of paper fell to the floor like New Year's confetti.

Bloody hell.

Isabel's brush with danger had affected him to the point of distraction. He vividly recalled her scream; the sound rivaled his worst nightmares. He had experienced instantaneous panic and a crazed need to go to her, to ensure she was not harmed.

Fresh in his mind was the taste and feel of her in his arms. A mere hour before she was attacked, she had stood in the center of his art gallery, kissing, touching, and eagerly responding to his caress. Just the thought of her strawberry-tipped breasts made his mouth water.

He was a lustful, besotted fool.

And in her innocence, Isabel had called him *good* . . .

He had never been good. To the contrary, his youthful, roguish days had been spent gambling, drinking to excess, and chasing women, habits which had led him straight into Bridget's trap. The only honorable thing he had done was propose to Bridget and show up on the day of their wedding. But his good intentions—however late—had led to carnage, as he had been ignorant of her ultimate devious plans. Like everyone else in his past, she had betrayed him, and even in death, she had managed to mercilessly wound him through the murder of their unborn child. Years later the memory was a dull ache, but the sordid experience had tainted him, turning him into an obsessed, overworking stockbroker and fanatic art collector.

As for Isabel, he had capitulated to Lord Malvern's insistence that they marry as a way to ease his conscience. He always paid his debts, and he did owe Isabel for her testimony which had spared him from Dante Black's well-planned trap.

But what had started out as a way to save her and her

twin siblings from complete disgrace had turned into a foolish bargain on his part.

How was he to refrain from touching her for six months when her mere presence inflamed his lust? Worse still—her instinctive and passionate response served as a powerful aphrodisiac. All he wanted to do was mount her on the chaise in his private gallery, spread her silky hair over the cushions, and pose her naked body like a piece of priceless art for his viewing pleasure.

But where would that get them?

From the beginning, she had been open and honest about her desire to travel to Paris to further her art studies. She had no desire to marry, or to remain shackled to one man. To truly repay her as his alibi, he must respect their arrangement. It was the only honorable course of action.

And then there was the ugly business of the stolen painting. He was no closer to finding the *Seashore with Fishermen* or the master conspirator behind the theft. The interrogation of Dante Black had been too brief. Unlike Roman, he was not convinced that Dante would not have revealed whom he was working for—most likely Lord Gavinport. Marcus was confident that he could have persuaded the former Bonham's auctioneer to speak, and it would not have taken a beating.

Greedy men like Dante always capitulated for money.

The appearance of Dante's criminal accomplice had complicated matters. Marcus had caught a glimpse of the bastard as he had fled—long-bodied, skeleton-thin, dirty hair, and an overall menacing appearance.

If Isabel had been harmed . . .

His jaw clenched like a lump of granite.

The wedding was within two weeks' time. He would smother his lust; do right by her, even if it took every ounce of his willpower. He owed her a great debt, and a woman like Lady Isabel Cameron deserved better than the darkly damaged man he had become.

"I want out. I escaped Marcus Hawksley and his brother by chance, and I'll not again put myself at risk," Dante said in a choked voice.

"Calm yerself," Robby Bones hissed.

They were in a dark London alley that smelled of rubbish, cat piss, and human squalor. Past midnight, the gas lamps from the street did not illuminate the alley, and the orange glow from Bones's cigar cast an eerie shadow over the grave digger's face. Smoke curled around his head like an opaque snake.

Dante, who had grown to detest the smell of Bones's cheap cigars, moved aside. "I'm not crazy," he snapped. "Hawksley had every intention of beating me until I confessed to the information he sought."

"It wouldn't 'ave come to that. I was goin' to take care of 'em, but the Cameron woman showed up."

"Lady Isabel?" Dante laughed, and the hysterical sound was shrill to his own ears. "I told you that the lady has a bad habit of interfering. Now you know how it feels."

Bones snarled, spraying spittle and showing his broken half-tooth.

Dante quieted and took a step back.

"She needs to be put in 'er place. Next time, she won't be so lucky," Bones said.

Dante shook his head. "There won't be a next time, at least not for me. Tell his lordship that I'm leaving London. He can hire another lackey to move the Gainsborough painting to Marcus Hawksley's place of business."

"I wouldn't do that if I were ye."

"Why not?"

With lightning reflexes, Bones stepped forward and

pressed the tip of his cigar into Dante's chest. Dante yelped and jumped back, but not before the cigar burned through his threadbare cotton shirt and singed his flesh.

Robby Bones's lips curled into a gruesome mask. "'Is lordship can find ye. 'E has money enough to hire men to do it, men not as nice as me."

Dante clutched his wound, bile rising up his throat. *The crazy bastard thinks he's nice!*

"Do yer job, Dante, and move the painting as planned." Bones turned to leave the alley, blending into the shadows like a wraith.

Chapter 22

The following two weeks passed by in a blur for Isabel, and it was mid-June when the parish priest read the final banns from the pulpit.

On the morning of her wedding, Isabel sat at her dressing table as Kate styled her hair.

"It's a perfect day for a wedding, my lady. Not a cloud in the sky," Kate said.

"Thank you, Kate," Isabel said woodenly. Feeling a mix of anxiety and apprehension that the day had finally arrived, she had awakened with a knot in her neck, and her shoulders were tight with tension. She leaned her head to the side, hoping to ease her cramped muscles.

A sharp pain stung her scalp as Kate pulled on a tress.

"Be still, my lady. I'm not finished with your hair," Kate admonished.

Isabel mumbled an apology and smoothed damp palms on the skirt of her chemise. She gazed in the mirror as the last curl was pinned atop her head. Kate was indeed talented with styling hair, and Isabel could not help but admire the maid's work. Her loose curls were arranged in the latest fashion and held in place by a crown of tiny white rosebuds.

Isabel stood, and Kate helped her into an ivory satin

wedding gown. It had been her mother's and hugged her curves, flared at her waist, and brushed the tips of her matching slippers. A long veil was pinned to her hair and cascaded over her shoulders and down her back like a waterfall.

Isabel turned before a pedestal mirror, her heart drumming in her ears.

Is this truly me? Will Marcus be pleased?

Her thoughts startled her. When had his opinion become so important to her?

"You look lovely," Kate sighed. "I'm honored to be accompanying you to your new home, but I know for a fact that the entire household here will miss you sorely."

Isabel felt a pang at the maid's words, and her stomach churned with uneasiness. She had been raised by many of the servants under her father's roof, and the realization that she would be leaving to embark on a new chapter of her life, even a temporary one with Marcus Hawksley, was nerve-wracking. She knew she would never return to live here.

Am I doing the right thing? she wondered. *I never wanted to marry, but rather only to pursue my art studies.*

A knock on her bedroom door interrupted her thoughts.

Amber rushed inside, blond curls bouncing. Her eyes widened when she saw Isabel.

"Oh, Izzy! I hope to look half as beautiful as you on my wedding day."

Isabel embraced her younger sister. "Amber, you will be a ravishing bride. Someday your prince will come, sweep you off your feet, and capture your heart forever."

Amber looked up at her adoringly. "Is that what Marcus has done to you, Izzy?"

For a heart-stopping moment, the question was a stab in Isabel's heart, but then a surprisingly easy smile came to her lips. "Of course, darling. Why else would I be marrying him?"

* * *

The wedding breakfast took place at the Ravenspear mansion. It was a small, but elegant affair, with fifty well-attired guests. An orchestra played country reels and waltzes in the ballroom, and the French doors were wide open as guests mingled outside on the terrace. Champagne flowed freely, and Blake's prized French chef outdid himself with buffet tables laden with delicacies to suit every palate.

Marcus and Roman conversed in a corner of the ballroom. The incident with Dante Black had served to draw the brothers closer, and although their youthful bond was not completely healed, they were more amicable and tolerant of each other.

Blake came over and handed each of them a dram of whiskey. "Although most of the guests prefer champagne and wine, I thought to celebrate with stronger spirits."

"You always were a good host, Ravenspear," Roman said, tipping the glass to his lips.

"How have you escaped the marital web so far?" Blake asked Roman.

"By the skin on my teeth," Roman said, looking across the ballroom to where his father, Lord Randall Ardmore, stood.

"I always thought it was overzealous mamas that pushed matrimony on their sons," Blake said.

"Not in Roman's case," Marcus said. "Now that the black sheep of the family has married, the pressure on Roman is even greater to produce an heir."

Roman gave Marcus a black-layered look. "Don't act so pleased."

Marcus laughed. "Why not? I find Father's harassing amusing, especially since it is not directed at me."

"Not all marriages are bad ones," Blake said, his eyes

resting on Victoria, who, late in her pregnancy, was seated on an overstuffed chair brought into the ballroom for her. She had insisted on hosting the wedding breakfast for Marcus and Isabel, despite her condition. She thought of Marcus as Blake's brother and had grown fond of Isabel.

"You are the exception to the rule," Roman said. "Most marriages are as amicable as a battlefront. Our parents had a disastrous union."

"Marcus is a fortunate soul. Lady Isabel is aglow today," Blake said.

Roman nodded. "Yes, my brother is damned lucky. Lady Isabel is as beautiful as she is courageous. She slipped through my fingers. But Marcus better watch her like a hawk. She may be off the marriage mart, but now she's up for grabs as a lover by the many bucks and dandies who pursue married women like sport."

Marcus frowned at his brother's crude remark. His fists tightened at his sides as he exercised iron determination not to punch Roman square in the mouth.

Marcus's sharp gaze searched out Isabel. She had changed from her wedding dress into less formal attire, and she looked radiant in her blue silk gown, which deepened the color of her eyes and displayed her soft curves to perfection. Her dark hair was artfully swept up, and a few loose curls brushed her neck and collarbone. She was surrounded by well-wishers, and looked the dazzling bride, conversing with her guests with grace and ease.

As if sensing his scrutiny, she turned and met his heated gaze, gifting him with a secret smile.

A fierce wave of possessiveness cut through him like a sharp blade. Roman's words echoed in his head: *Now she's up for grabs as a lover by the many bucks and dandies who pursue married women like sport.*

Like hell.

But the troublesome truth was that their marriage was in name only and for six months at that.

His thoughts went to the marriage ceremony. She had been a vision in white satin walking down the aisle and had stolen his breath. The priest's words had been quick, their vows exchanged, and a brief kiss given before their guests. Isabel had smiled up at him the entire time, an innocent, trustful expression on her lovely face. Not a doubt that he would uphold his part of the bargain had been reflected in her blue eyes. Thoughts of Paris, Auntie Lil, and her future two lovers were probably whirling through her head.

His stomach twisted in a tight knot.

"What's the matter, Marcus? You're scowling. You're sure to scare the bride on her wedding night," Roman said.

No, I won't. Especially since the bride will be safely tucked away in her own chamber.

Marcus raised his glass and took a good quaff of whiskey before answering. "I spotted Father talking to Lord Malvern," he said, changing the subject from Isabel.

Roman shrugged. "It means nothing. Ardmore and Malvern have been acquainted for years and belong to the same clubs. They are probably not talking about your marriage, but are most likely discussing which club they will attend afterward."

"I should only be so lucky, but fortune has never been on my side when it comes to our father," Marcus said dryly.

"Ah, here comes the lovely bride," Blake said.

Isabel glided over, a charming smile on her face. "I've come to see what the three most handsome men in the room are discussing with such serious expressions on their faces."

Blake kissed her hand. "You are quite a flatterer, Lady Isabel. If you must know, we were debating marriage."

Isabel looked to Roman. "Since only Lord Ardmore remains a bachelor, what is your opinion on the subject?"

A devilish look came into Roman's green eyes. "Please call me Roman. After all, you are now my sister-in-law."

"Indeed, I am," Isabel said. "But don't change the subject."

"Alas, it seems the best lady was taken today," Roman said.

Isabel motioned across the room with her fan. "Nonsense! My lovely friend, Miss Charlotte Benning, is quite a jewel, and she is right over there with Lady Ravenspear as we speak."

"She has you cornered, Roman," Marcus said with a smirk.

Roman turned to where Isabel motioned. A slight gleam of interest lit his eyes, but when his gaze returned to his friends, the familiar mask of noble aloofness was back in place. "I shall introduce myself to Miss Benning," Roman said, "after I have a dance with the bride."

"You will have to wait. I promised my husband the next dance," Isabel said with a smile.

Marcus stepped forward to take her hand as the musicians began a waltz. She glided into his arms with ease and they whirled around the dance floor.

She looked up at him. "Do you remember the last time we danced the waltz?"

"I'll never forget Lady Holloway's ball. You came right up to me and forwardly asked me to dance. A saucy piece of baggage you were, Isabel."

"Saucy! You were quite intimidating, I almost turned and ran."

"You run from a challenge? I find that hard to believe. I should have known you were trouble," he said with mock severity.

Her smile was as intimate as a caress. "I hardly think I'm trouble. I believe our relationship will serve both our interests perfectly."

He felt an instant's disappointment at her words, and his fingers tensed slightly around her waist.

"Our fathers have been speaking. It seems they both want to pay a visit to your town house after the celebrations," she said.

"Today?"

She nodded. "I thought it unusual as well."

"Aren't newly married couples expected to go to their home alone after the festivities to celebrate in private?"

A blush stained her cheeks. "Yes, that is tradition."

"Isabel, I didn't mean it to sound that way. I only meant—"

"I understand. I think my father wants to make certain that I will be properly cared for. Our marriage came about abruptly, and after talking with Lord Ardmore, he became concerned," she said.

"I see. I can imagine what my parent told yours. No doubt your father wants to ensure I am not a complete derelict and that I can afford a wife," he said, his tone laced with cynicism. "We will have to put on a good show for their benefit."

"How long do you suppose they will stay?" Isabel asked.

Marcus's lips thinned with irritation. "If I have a say, then as short as possible."

Chapter 23

If Marcus ever had doubts as to his father's true feelings toward him, then his wedding night clarified any misconceptions.

Isabel and Marcus arrived at the town house on St. James's Street ahead of their parents. Jenkins, Mrs. McLaughlin, and the entire staff were gathered in the vestibule to congratulate the couple and welcome their new mistress.

"The master's chamber has been prepared for you and your trunks taken up. You must want to change before the evening meal," Mrs. McLaughlin said.

Isabel looked to Marcus.

"Isabel shall occupy the chambers across from mine," Marcus told the housekeeper.

Mrs. McLaughlin blinked, but quickly recovered at the news that the new mistress would not sleep in the same bedroom as her husband. It was common practice, but by the plump housekeeper's surprised expression, it was obviously not what she had expected.

"Of course, Mr. Hawksley. My lady's belongings shall be moved at once."

Marcus then turned to address the entire staff. "Both Lord Malvern and Lord Ardmore will arrive shortly. I know this is last-minute news, but they are expected to dine with us."

"I shall speak with Cook," Mrs. McLaughlin said. She made to leave, then stopped in midstride and looked at Isabel. "As the new mistress, would you prefer to speak with Cook about the menu?"

Isabel shook her head. "I'll leave it in your capable hands."

With a bob of her capped head, the housekeeper departed.

No sooner had Marcus handed Isabel's cloak to Jenkins, than Edward Cameron and Randall Hawksley knocked on the door.

"Isabel." Edward stepped into the vestibule and hugged his daughter. "I've come to see with my own eyes where you are to live." Concern for his daughter's well-being was etched all over his plump face.

Isabel embraced her father. "Marcus's home is lovely, Father, especially his art collection, which you must see for yourself someday."

Randall Hawksley strode inside. "Marcus," he said as he spotted his younger son. "It's been years since my last visit. I've also come to see how you are living."

"You were welcome any time, Father. I find it curious as to why you chose my wedding day to visit," Marcus said, his voice heavy with sarcasm.

"Ah, but you had the audacity to enter trade against my advice. You were hardly worth a father's trouble." Randall's loud voice echoed across the marble floors.

"What has changed?" Marcus asked, his tone chilly.

Randall slapped Edward on the back. "Why, now that you have married an earl's daughter, I find it hard to ignore you."

Edward Cameron's eyes widened behind his round spectacles.

Marcus bit back an angry retort. "Is your newfound interest why Lord Malvern is here?"

"No," Randall said. "We were reminiscing about the past, and I must have alluded to your youthful years as a drunk and wastrel. As a responsible father, Edward seeks to ensure his daughter's welfare."

"How considerate of you." Marcus's tone was velvet, yet edged with steel.

The rest of the visit went no better. Throughout the evening meal, Randall ate and drank with gusto and bickered with and tried to insult Marcus at every opportunity. Edward sat rigid, his mouth a tight line, his brow furrowed. His eyes darted between Marcus and Randall like a trapped animal. An anxious Isabel tried to interrupt the father-son pair with nervous chattering about upcoming art shows and exhibitions. When that failed, she stopped all pretense of eating and repeatedly reached for her wineglass. Before long, her cheeks flamed red and her eyes glazed over.

Marcus drank heavily, hoping to quench his anger and drown out his father's grating voice.

Randall had laughed and boomed, "Old habits die hard, son."

Before the last course was served, Isabel looked ready to lay her head in her dessert.

Marcus rose. "It's been a long day. My bride needs sleep."

Edward pushed back his chair and assisted Isabel to her feet. "Of course. I shall visit again soon, Isabel. Please send a note if you need anything before then."

With a firm grip on her elbow, Marcus helped Isabel climb the staircase. They were silent as they walked down the long hall until they reached the door of her assigned rooms, and he pushed it open. She stumbled inside, and his hand tightened on her arm, steadying her.

Her eyes slanted up at him. "I'm sorry about dinner."

"Why? It wasn't your fault."

"But your father—"

"Is an arrogant ass."

She reached up to touch his cheek. "Oh, Marcus. How can you stand it? He is so wrong about you. You are nothing like he says. You are hardworking and good and—"

"You're drunk, Isabel."

She shrugged as if her inebriated state had nothing to do with her words. "I always imagined a woman's wedding night to be full of romance, laughter, and a delicious dose of passion."

"That's not reality. Most couples are not even physically attracted to each other."

She stepped close and looked up at him through thick, black lashes. "Do you find me attractive?"

His gaze dropped to the wildly fluttering pulse at the base of her neck. "Isabel—"

"When I was a twelve-year-old girl and you were staying at our country manor, I would sneak into your room and wear your shirts. I loved the smell and imagined you were embracing me."

He blinked, stunned and flattered by her admission. "Isabel, I—"

She moved closer still and turned around, her back facing him, her silk skirts brushing his trousers. "Please help me with my buttons."

"I'll call Mrs. McLaughlin."

"No. I don't want to wait. Can't you help me?"

He brushed aside loose curls that had fallen down her neck. The tendrils were like rich black silk against his rough palm. A bead of perspiration formed on his brow as he reached for the row of tiny buttons. The top three opened, and warm, smooth flesh touched his fingers.

With helpless frustration, he felt his arousal grow hot and heavy.

When all the buttons were undone, she turned in his arms and held the dress to her breasts.

"I should leave," he said, but his feet stayed rooted to the carpet.

She swayed forward, and pressed her lips to his throat. "Don't go," she whispered.

He was blasted by lust. He had a hard time recalling their agreement, or anything beyond the feel of her wet lips on his overheated skin.

"Isabel," he hissed. Touching her bare shoulders, he pushed her back and held her.

She cocked her head to the side, her glassy blue eyes studying his features. "I had planned to remain virtuous, but truth be told, what's wrong with experiencing passion? Perhaps I was wrong. Marriage doesn't have to change anything between us. We can still part as planned—me to Paris and you to your . . . to your lady friend. Auntie Lil insists on at least two lovers. Why can't you be one of them?"

Yes, why can't I? he thought.

The basest part of him seriously considered her offer, but bitter truth permeated his lust. Just because she desired him in her inebriated state did not mean that she would not regret her actions tomorrow. Their agreement would be damned—along with her dreams of Paris should she become pregnant. She would most likely grow to resent him, and he wouldn't blame her.

What kind of man was he to take advantage of an intoxicated virgin—his bride no less?

She licked her full lower lip and whispered, "Marcus?"

He took a deep breath, closed his eyes, and willed his aroused body to calm.

"Let's get you in bed," his said, his voice rough.

"Yes . . . bed," she breathed.

She had misunderstood his intentions but he did not

seek to correct her. The sooner she was safely tucked under the covers, the sooner he could drag himself from her side.

She made it to the side of the bed, then released her grasp on her gown. The entire ensemble slid down her body in a seductive whoosh. Contained in her corset, her breasts rose and fell enticingly with each breath, and her slim waist flared into rounded hips. She stepped out of the pool of blue silk, sat on the edge of the bed, and patted the mattress beside her.

"Come, Marcus. I don't pretend to have as much experience as you so you will have to teach me everything."

Every ounce of blood drained from his head and flooded his loins. His trousers grew unbearably snug, and his heart hammered in his ears. The muscles in his body tensed, like a volcano on the verge of erupting, and he knew he needed to leave the room, needed to leave her presence before he succumbed to her feminine lure.

He knelt by the bed, and coaxed her into a lying position.

As soon as her head touched the pillow, she yawned, showing a mouthful of pearly, even teeth. She slid a hand around his neck and urged his head down. Brushing her lips against his once, then again, she went limp beneath him.

He pulled back just as her eyelids slid closed. She snored and then breathed deeply, lost in a blissful drunken slumber.

He smoothed her hair back from her brow, and straightened slowly, painfully. Gazing down at her profile, he whispered, "Good night, sweetheart," and then turned and left the room.

Chapter 24

Isabel rolled over and groaned. Bright sunlight flowed into the room through the lace curtains and cut across the bed. Disoriented, she struggled to sit up, and then immediately regretted the movement. Her head throbbed as if an elephant sat upon it; her mouth felt like she had sucked on dry cotton. She held up a hand to shield her sensitive pupils from the invasive light reflecting off the white walls.

Trying to gain a sense of awareness, she looked about her—mauve carpet, a chest of drawers, an oversized wardrobe, and a padded chair situated by a fireplace.

Her eyes flew back to the chair and the blue silk gown thrown across its cushions.

A terrifying realization washed over her. Memories of her wedding day focused in her mind—the church ceremony, the wedding breakfast at the Ravenspears' mansion, and afterward . . .

Her face burned as she remembered bits and pieces of the night. The dinner debacle between Marcus and his father, and the vast quantity of wine she had drunk to ease her nerves. Then there was later, much later, when Marcus had helped her up the stairs, had shown her to her rooms, had helped her undress . . .

No, she had all but demanded that he assist with her buttons. She had acted a wanton, a woman of very loose morals, and had propositioned him when *she* was the one that had insisted on a marriage in name only. She couldn't recall the precise words she had said to him, but she knew that she had all but begged him to make love to her.

Had he taken her up on her offer?

She touched her breasts, and then lowered her hand between her legs. She was not sore and did not feel any different.

No, Marcus Hawksley was a true gentleman, a *good* man, and he would never take advantage of a drunken woman, even one who urged him to do so.

A quick and disturbing thought flew through her. She realized that she was not dismayed at the notion of losing her innocence to Marcus, but rather that she would have no memory of the experience. If she slept with Marcus, then she wanted to recall every vivid detail, memorize the feel of his flesh against hers, the scent of their passion, and cherish those memories for the rest of her life. For she was certain that such a virile, masculine male like Hawksley would be a once-in-a-lifetime experience that a woman would never forget.

She shook her head, forcing her thoughts back to the present. How was she to face Marcus today? And what about the staff? The entire household must know that their new mistress had been foxed—or rather, stinking drunk—on her first night here. She felt a shudder of humiliation.

She slid off the bed, gripped the bedside table, and forced herself to stand straight. "No sense fretting about what you cannot control," she spoke out loud.

She spotted her trunks in the corner of the room. No doubt, the ever-efficient Mrs. McLaughlin had ordered her belongings brought up before Isabel had even stepped foot through the doorway of her new rooms. Her dresses were probably pressed and hanging in the wardrobe.

Good. She would summon the housekeeper, get dressed, and immediately request a strong cup of tea. She was never one to dwell on the past or her mistakes, but rather looked to the future.

She walked slowly across the room, aware of her throbbing temples, until she reached the first trunk. She opened the lid and cracked a smile when she spotted the package wrapped in bright red paper and tied with a matching ribbon. Beside the package rested the cigar-shaped box containing the miniature artists' palette of handcrafted silver that Marcus had given her.

She wouldn't wait for Marcus to come to her this morning to see how she fared after last night. She would bravely seek him out instead and give him the gift she had worked on over the past weeks with such diligence.

Washed, dressed, and three cups of tea later, Isabel felt like a new woman. If Jenkins or Mrs. McLaughlin had known of her sodden condition on her wedding night, then neither of them had let on.

During a breakfast of steaming eggs, bacon, and biscuits in the dining room, she had learned that Marcus had gone to his office on Threadneedle Street as was his customary routine for a Monday morning. Mrs. McLaughlin had pursed her lips in disapproval, saying the master of the house should have taken a few days off to give his wife a proper honeymoon before returning to business so quickly, but Jenkins had assured Isabel that an urgent matter had arisen.

Finding herself ravenous, Isabel ate every morsel on her plate and knew her appetite was due to a late night of imbibing too much wine and not eating enough food.

As soon as she left the dining room, she immediately sought out Jenkins.

"Jenkins, will you summon a hackney cab for me? I'd like to visit Marcus at his office today."

Jenkins looked at her with a blank expression. "If you seek to go out, you are free to use Mr. Hawksley's carriage."

"I wasn't aware he had his own carriage."

Jenkins nodded. "He has a phaeton as well that he chose to utilize this morning."

Isabel kept forgetting her new husband was a man of substantial means. "I see. Then please summon the carriage."

"Of course, my lady."

The ride from St. James's Street to Threadneedle Street passed quickly, and as she stepped from the carriage, she looked up at a three-story brick building overlooking the Bank of England and the London Stock Exchange on Bartholomew Lane.

"Shall I wait for you, Lady Hawksley?" the driver asked.

Isabel shook her head. "There's no need. Mr. Hawksley shall see me home." Tucking the wrapped package under her arm, she made her way to the building's entrance.

The first floor was a well-appointed business space, with costly yet functional furnishings. There were unoccupied chairs on one wall and a receiving desk at the end of the vestibule, directly across from the doors. A staunch, serious-looking man sat behind the desk and glared at her beneath thick spectacles as she stepped inside.

With a confident step, she approached the man. "Lady Isabel Hawksley to see Mr. Marcus Hawksley."

The man blinked, obviously surprised that Marcus had taken a wife. "The stairs are behind me to the right. Mr. Hawksley is currently in his office, on the third floor."

She spotted the spiral staircase, and her heart fluttered in her breast as she climbed the steps. She was nervous to confront him after her embarrassing behavior last night, but at the same time, she looked forward to observing him in his work environment. She wanted to see firsthand his reaction when she gave him her present.

She reached the top of the stairs on the third floor, and started down a long hall. Closed doors on both sides ran the length of the hall, and brass plates with their occupants' names were mounted on each door.

Halfway down the hall, a door opened and a man rushed out. He stopped when he spotted her.

"Lady Isabel? Is it really you?" the man asked, coming up to her.

Isabel looked up and was surprised to see Ralph Hodge standing before her. He was as attractive as she remembered with his green eyes, sandy-colored hair, and charming smile. He wore a frock coat and a high-crowned hat with a curled brim and held a walking cane.

"Mr. Hodge, I did not expect to see you here today."

"I can say the same for you. Many stockbrokers have offices here since it is a stone's throw from the Stock Exchange. I pray you have come to your senses and have decided to pay me a visit." He winked at her before continuing, "My services are always available to you."

She smiled at him. His outrageously flirtatious behavior was amusing and flattering. "But you appear to be on your way out."

He took off his hat with a sweeping motion, and gave her body a raking gaze. "I will change my plans for such a beautiful woman."

"I suspect your bold tongue has gotten you into trouble in the past, Mr. Hodge."

His green eyes glittered at her unintended sexual remark. "The ladies have never complained."

He reached for her, but she stepped away, clutching the package in front of her.

"Mr. Hodge—"

"Tell me you're not here to see Hawksley and that you have had second thoughts about marrying him."

"It's too late for that. We were married last night."

He shrugged and then grinned. "It's no matter, my offices are across from his, and I would not turn you away if you decided to pay me a social visit."

"Why would I do that?"

"Your husband is known for spending long hours working, and as his new beautiful wife, should you feel neglected, it is no fault of yours if you seek companionship elsewhere. Hawksley quite deserves it, you see."

She laughed, despite his lecherous manners. "I doubt you will be in sore need of female company anytime soon."

He reached for her hand, leaving her to hold her package with her other arm, and his lips lingered on her skin.

A door opened down the hall and the sound of approaching footsteps echoed off the walls. Isabel leaned to the side to see behind Ralph Hodge's shoulders.

"Marcus!" she called out.

"Isabel?"

Ralph Hodge reluctantly released her hand and turned.

Marcus strode down the hall, a scowl on his dark face as he took in the scene before him.

He reached their side, and spoke to Hodge. "This reminds me of another time when I found you with the lady, only now she is my wife."

"I've heard, Hawksley," Ralph said. "I was merely congratulating her on her nuptials."

"Good. Now get lost."

"Marcus!" Isabel was shocked at his rude behavior.

Ralph flashed Marcus a look of disdain. "Careful, Hawksley, lest she see the true barbarian beneath your crumbling facade of diligent stockbroker and devoted husband. You don't want her to discover your surly disposition and lack of ethics so soon."

Marcus grabbed the smaller man by the collar of his frock coat and pushed Hodge toward the spiral staircase. "Go. Now. Before the barbarian in me breaks your neck."

Ralph turned to address Isabel. "My offer still stands, Isabel," he said, then descended the stairs.

"What offer?" Marcus snapped.

"Never mind that. Why do you two hate each other?" Isabel asked.

"We have a long history."

"I have all afternoon."

"It hardly matters."

"I beg to differ. From what I just witnessed, Ralph Hodge has more motive than Lord Gavinport to want to frame you for theft and see you rot in prison."

Chapter 25

The corner of Marcus's mouth twisted with exasperation, and he glared at her. She wondered if he would dismiss her outright, but then he sighed and raised his hand to motion her down the hall.

"Let's go inside my office, where we can talk privately and you can tell me what brought you here today," he said.

She followed him down the hall and into his office. It was a substantial space, and she counted ten cabinets for filing and five overflowing bookshelves. Stacks of paper littered the floor in what appeared a random pattern, and additional piles covered a massive desk.

Isabel wildly wondered how on earth he ever made sense of the volume of information or if there was a methodology to his filing system. It was a completely masculine domain, obviously never intended for a woman's eyes, and she found it fascinating and overwhelming at the same time.

He shut the door and studied her reaction. "I apologize for the disorder. My secretary, James Smith, who is in charge of my filing, has been recuperating from a cold. I wasn't expecting a visit."

"It's fine. I wanted to see how you worked. What your days are like."

She strode to a wide window behind the desk and was delighted to find an excellent view of Threadneedle Street. From this height, she had a bird's-eye view of one of the entrances to the Stock Exchange. Serious businessmen rushed about like busy ants to and from their hill, oblivious to everything but their immediate destination. She knew the principal entrance of the Exchange was from Bartholomew Lane through Capel Court, and that there were three other entrances from Throgmorton Street. She wondered how much traffic passed through them each day.

She turned around, and Marcus's gaze dropped to the package she was holding.

"What's that?"

She walked over and handed the package to him. "This is my wedding present to you."

He looked down, surprise written on his face. "This is for me?"

She gave him a mischievous smile. "I had intended to give it to you last night, but I believe I drank a little too much."

A glint of humor lit his eyes. "That would be an understatement. What do you recall of last night?"

Her face grew hot. "Enough."

His grin was irresistibly devastating, and it sent her spirits soaring. Her flesh tingled as memories of his touch lingered in the recesses of her mind.

"Let's put it behind us, shall we?" he said. "If we are to spend the next six months together, there's no sense being uncomfortable in each other's presence."

"Yes, thank you," she whispered.

He turned his attention back to her gift. "I'm anxious to see what my new wife has brought me. He pulled the string and tore open the bright paper to reveal a watercolor painting of the trading floor of the London Stock Exchange.

His eyes widened in amazement. "Did you paint this?"

"I've been working on it for over two weeks now. It's the Exchange as I saw it that day when I first came to visit you. I was fascinated by the mass pandemonium, the chaos. The place seemed like a powerful living beast with a pulse of its own, and I knew I had to somehow try to capture the activity on canvas."

His fingers caressed the golden frame, his eyes devouring her work, and like an anxious child, she realized she desperately wanted his approval.

"It's stunning," he said. "You included everything down to the smallest detail. The mammoth elongated hall, the gilt dome, and arched glass roof supported by its sturdy stone columns. There's even the cherry wood hat rack that runs its perimeter, the high rostrum, and of course, the brokers and jobbers in heated negotiations. The painting captures the energy of the tumultuous arena perfectly."

He looked at her, his eyes studying her with a curious intensity. "Thank you. I've never received such a special gift."

She swallowed. She felt a curious sweeping pull at her innards, and she found herself entranced by his compelling masculinity, his lean, dark visage. She knew her feelings for him had nothing to do with reason.

"I am a novice at my watercolors," she said. "There was so much activity on the trading floor that day that I feared only a master could capture the essence of the scene."

"Nonsense. You are quite talented, Isabel."

"My father believes it a woman's passing fancy."

"Didn't he pay for your painting lessons?"

"Yes, but only as many as to make me a desirable debutante. Many ladies of my station have lessons in either the pianoforte, singing, or painting. But further instruction is considered unnecessary, a waste even. Young titled women are expected to focus their energies on the Season and Almack's marriage mart."

He drew his lips in thoughtfully. "I am most grateful for your talent, Isabel, and I will treasure my wedding present. I plan to hang it in a prominent place in my library office at home so that I may view it for inspiration when I am working."

She felt a bubbling joy at his sincere praise. "Now will you tell me about the animosity between you and Ralph Hodge?"

"Ah, I see I was unable to distract you."

"I enjoyed your compliments, but I am most tenacious when I want something."

His eyes darkened. "I know."

She laughed at the barb. "I know you believe Lord Gavinport is our leading suspect, but you cannot dismiss Ralph Hodge either. From what I've seen, he dislikes you immensely."

"More like hates me."

She cocked her head to the side, contemplating his words. "It's not beyond Hodge to use me to hurt you. I received the distinct impression that it would thrill him to induce me into becoming his mistress just to cuckold you."

"Just like the swine," Marcus said bitterly. "He is no different in business. He started out as a jobber before becoming a stockbroker, an unusual jump in professions."

She held up a hand. "Forgive me. You once told me what a jobber was, but I have forgotten."

"You should sit." He picked up a stack of papers from a chair, dropped them on a corner of the desk, and motioned for her to sit. He took a chair across from hers and folded his long legs in front of him.

"Only the stockbrokers have contact with the public. It is the jobbers who buy and sell shares for the stockbrokers behind the scenes," Marcus said. "Jobbers earn money for their services by inflating the price they offer the brokers; the difference is called their 'turn.' Jobbers deal in certain markets, and the markets have their own designated spots on the trading floor. That way brokers won't waste time soliciting the wrong jobbers. Hodge was a jobber that specialized in the West Indies trade—namely companies that deal with sugar, rum, and coffee.

"When I had started out as a broker, I had a client request to buy shares in the West India Trading Company. I went to the vicinity on the floor where those jobbers specializing in West India companies gathered. I was immediately approached by Ralph Hodge, who was a jobber at the time, and we made a deal as to the buying price. No formal documents were required; a gentleman's agreement is still sufficient.

"The next morning, my secretary, James Smith, went to confirm the agreement at the Exchange Clearing House and to ensure that the appropriate transfer deeds were drawn up. Everything seemed in order, but on settlement day, a fortnight later, I went to pay for the shares and discovered Hodge had somehow inflated the buying price, listing an extraordinarily high value. He must have bribed a clerk at the Exchange Clearing House to alter the figures. All stockbrokers must pay for the shares on settlement day or their reputations are destroyed and they are expelled from the Stock Exchange. I had no choice but to pay the exorbitant price in order to receive the deed. Later, when the shares were signed and I was to be paid by my client, I gave the client the price we had originally agreed on and swallowed the enormous loss. As a new broker, Hodge almost bankrupted me."

"How horrible. So that's why you hate each other?" she said.

Marcus shook his head. "No. There's more. Once a jobber always a jobber, but Hodge saw an opportunity to rise. His uncle was a well-respected broker, and Hodge convinced the man to take him under his wing. His uncle died soon after, and as his only living relative, Hodge inherited his uncle's brokerage as well as his clients. Two of those clients, his wealthiest investors, chose to fire Hodge and hire me. Hodge was furious and accused me of soliciting and bribing the wealthy men, a lie, of course."

"Has he retaliated?" she asked.

"He's tried by bribing one of the six Lords Commissioners of the Treasury for confidential information concerning companies listed on the Stock Exchange. Hodge then used that information in an illegal manner to invest and turn a profit. It was the only way he was able to keep his uncle's clients, for Hodge's knowledge of the market was limited to his field of expertise in the West Indies, where he specialized as a jobber. A good broker must be knowledgeable in all investing areas in order to successfully sustain a full client list."

Isabel looked at him in surprise. "How do you know he bribed such a high-ranking official?"

"The official who sold out to Hodge was Junior Lord Commissioner Charles Ashton, Lady Ravenspear's father," Marcus said.

Shock flew through her. "Victoria's father, Blake's wife?"

Marcus nodded. "Blake hated Charles Ashton. The corrupt Commissioner was responsible for Blake's father's suicide, his mother and sister's demise, as well as Blake's years in the poorhouse. But because of Blake's love for Victoria, he had arranged a deal with Robert Banks Jenkinson, Second Earl of Liverpool and First Lord of the Treasury, to have Charles Ashton discretely leave England. Last I've heard the man is in France with his wife."

She didn't know whose audacity was worse—Hodge's to approach a Junior Lord Commissioner of the Treasury or Charles Ashton's to accept the bribe. "How did Ralph Hodge escape unscathed?"

"There was no direct evidence linking Hodge to the

bribes, but Charles Ashton confessed to Victoria. She, in turn, told Blake and me."

Isabel sat forward in her seat. "If Ralph Hodge suspects you know the truth, he would hate *and* fear you. Don't you think he would want you imprisoned for the theft of the Gainsborough painting? It would ensure his prior illegal activities would remain secret."

"Yes, but I don't think he's knowledgeable enough in the art world to hire a man like Dante Black or to know that I collect Gainsborough's works and, therefore, to arrange to have one stolen. My money is still on Gavinport."

"But what motive would Lord Gavinport have to frame you?"

"None, but if he desired a Gainsborough painting, then as an avid art collector who had worked with Dante Black in the past, he would be aware of what I collect and would in turn know to frame me for the theft of the *Seashore with Fishermen*."

Her brow creased with worry. "You trust no one, do you? Not even your father or your own brother?"

"Trust has to be earned, and the past is difficult to change," he said dryly.

"Your father—"

"Never wanted a younger son and always treated me as a useless wastrel. It was a self-fulfilling prophecy. I became what he had expected."

"And your brother?"

"I don't like to speak of it. Needless to say, I had been involved in a disastrous relationship that had ended badly, and Roman had suspected the worst of me, just like our father."

"From what I have seen, Roman is trying to make amends," she said.

"Yes, but the past has a bad habit of repeating itself."

Chapter 26

Isabel awoke to a low knock on her bedroom door. She yawned as Kate entered the room with a smile and proceeded to open the curtains to let in the morning sunlight.

Isabel stretched and rose from the bed. She was grateful that her father had allowed the maid to accompany her to Marcus's town house. Kate talked too much and loved to gossip, but she had a good heart and had been with Isabel for over five years. In her new home, Kate was a comforting presence whom Isabel could rely upon.

Isabel dressed quickly and grabbed her sketch book and charcoals. Closing her bedroom door, she rushed down the hall. Over the course of the past week, she had fallen into a pleasant routine of eating a small breakfast followed by a leisurely walk in Hyde Park. The park was beautiful in June with its rosebushes and colorful, flowering shrubs in full bloom, and she looked forward to the artistic inspiration.

She turned a corner, reached the grand staircase, and froze.

Marcus stood at the bottom of the stairs and smiled when he spotted her.

"Good morning, Isabel," he called out.

She hesitated, her foot on the top step, her hand resting

on the banister. As was his routine, she had expected him to be off early to his office on Threadneedle Street.

His dark eyes bathed her in admiration, and she was glad she had chosen one of her prettier gowns. Her pink walking dress of French muslin, trimmed at the bodice and hem with an intricate ivy pattern, complemented her sable hair and complexion.

"Good morning to you, too," she answered. "I thought you had left for the day."

"I normally would have, but I wanted to show you something."

"You must know I love surprises."

His laugh was deep and warm. "Don't all women?"

She made it to the bottom of the stairs, and he tucked her hand beneath his arm. He wore fawn-colored trousers with a pleated shirt. Without his jacket, his broad shoulders appeared a mile wide. His cravat was loosely tied, as if he'd been in a hurry when he dressed, and she had a maddening urge to reach up and fix it. Looking up at the clear-cut lines of his profile, her pulse quickened.

He led her down the hall, in the opposite direction of the dining room. Her curiosity grew when he stopped at a closed door across from his library office. He reached for the door handle, and said, "This is what I've wanted to show you."

He opened the door and ushered her inside.

She stopped short at the sight of an empty room. Gleaming hardwood floors and the pleasant smell of lemon polish wafted to her. Four wide windows facing east captured the full light of the morning sun. There wasn't a stick of furniture in the entire space.

She turned to him and blinked with bafflement. "It's empty."

"Of course. It's your art studio. After you have your paints and supplies moved here, I thought you would like to furnish it yourself."

She took a quick sharp breath. "My own studio?"

He grinned. "Yes, all yours."

Her heart sang with delight. "I've never had a room of my own to paint. Father never thought it necessary, and my supplies were always crammed in the corner of my bedroom. But this," she said as she walked farther into the room, "this is such a spacious room, and the windows provide optimum lighting." In her mind, she could picture her easels in front of the windows, her paints in the corner, and her canvases hanging on the walls.

She looked back at him, still unsure. "Are you certain you want to sacrifice this room?"

"Absolutely. Your enthusiasm is my reward. I want you to be happy here."

A warm glow flowed through her, and she rushed to his side. "I shall endeavor to paint you."

He laughed. "That's not necessary. I thought you painted landscapes."

"I do, but only because I have never found any other subject to interest me. Until now."

"Careful, Isabel," he said, a teasing light in his eyes. "I've heard of artists who become entranced with their subjects."

She stiffened as if receiving a blow to her gut. *Damnation! He's right! Except I'm already entranced by him.*

A low knock on the door made her jump.

Jenkins entered. "Sorry to interrupt. You have a visitor, Mr. Hawksley."

"Who is it?" Marcus asked, a thread of irritation in his voice.

"A Mr. Benjamin Harrison to see you. I put him in the receiving room."

"I'll be right there. See that the man is offered refreshment," Marcus said.

Jenkins nodded and departed.

Marcus looked at her. "It's Roman's hired investigator. The man must have discovered the address of Lord Gavinport's town house property," he explained.

"I thought you had your own investigator," Isabel said.

"I did, but when Roman's man first learned the location of Dante Black, I fired mine. No sense supporting incompetency." He offered her his arm. "Shall we?"

"You want me present?"

"Quite shockingly, yes. I have found your insight and your resources to be invaluable."

She knew by insight he meant her knowledge of the art lovers of the ton and by resources he meant her relationship with Charlotte. She gloried briefly that he valued her opinion.

She walked beside Marcus as they entered the receiving room. A heavyset man with steel gray hair rose from a leather chair. He was short, thick around the waist, and his brown eyes were level under one continuous eyebrow. There was a watchful fixity in his face that she suspected made him excel in his profession.

"I have the information you requested, Mr. Hawksley." Harrison's eyes briefly glanced at Isabel. "Would you prefer to speak in private?"

"This is my wife, Lady Isabel Hawksley. You may speak freely in her presence."

Harrison handed Marcus a paper. "Frederick Perrin, the Marquess of Gavinport's town house is located on Lombard Street."

"That's a stone's throw from the Royal Exchange in Cornhill," Marcus said.

"Yes. I've watched the property for three days now, and as far as I can tell, it's vacant. No guards have come and gone, and Gavinport has not set foot inside. The only activity was a maid who entered with a bucket and mop to clean the place."

"Thank you, Mr. Harrison. Please send the bill for your services to me and not my brother."

As soon as the investigator left, Isabel looked to Marcus. "If the place is not being guarded, then surely the stolen painting is not being kept there."

"Not necessarily. Gavinport may be arrogant enough to think no one would suspect him. He may also believe the presence of guards would attract unwanted attention from the neighbors."

"What are you planning?" she asked.

"To search the place. If I find the painting, then I shall alert the appropriate authorities at Bow Street. Once they have the painting in their possession, then they will have sufficient evidence to arrest Gavinport."

"Then I want to come with you when you search it."

Marcus looked at her questionably. "Isabel—"

She raised a hand to stop his anticipated refusal. "You tried to stop me before, remember? If the place is vacant, then there is no risk. Whether or not you give me permission, short of tying me to the bedpost, I'll follow you anyway."

"Don't tempt me," he drawled.

"You said you valued my help," she countered.

"I meant from a safe distance. But since I plan to search the house in the middle of the day, then having you beside me is safer than wondering if you are sneaking in through an unlatched window." He eyed her pink walking dress with the delicate French muslin. "Change into something more suitable."

Puzzled, she glanced down at her outfit. "Such as?"

"Do you have anything darker, less likely to draw the eye?"

"I attended a distant relative's funeral last year. I wore a black gown and black net veil, but I lost the gloves. I can carry a muff."

"Forget the muff. The veil sounds perfect as it will conceal your face. Get dressed. There's no sense waiting to learn the truth."

Chapter 27

The town house on Lombard Street was in a well-to-do neighborhood a brisk walk away from the Royal Exchange. Isabel and Marcus arrived by hackney cab rather than his carriage so as not to draw attention to themselves.

Isabel studied the area through the window of the cab. It was the middle of the afternoon, and only a few people were about. Isabel guessed the lack of pedestrians and traffic was due to the fact that many of the residents were traders that could be found at the Royal Exchange in Cornhill. Marcus's decision to search the property during the day seemed to be a good one.

Marcus donned a hat and pulled the collar of his coat up. As they alighted from the cab, he tossed a coin up to the driver. "Wait for us and there will be more for you."

"Yes, sir." The driver caught the coin in midair and slid it in his pocket.

Marcus took her arm and whispered in her ear, "Act as if you own the place and walk straight to the porch."

Isabel adjusted her veil to fully conceal her features. "I'll follow your lead."

They approached the front door, and Marcus pulled out a lock pick he had hidden beneath his sleeve. He inserted the pick into the lock, and in less than thirty seconds, they were inside.

Shadows enveloped them. They stood still as their eyes adjusted from the bright sunlight outside to the dimness in the vestibule. Heavy draperies covered the windows, and a musky smell permeated the space.

"See if you can find a lamp," Marcus said.

She stepped forward, hands in front of her, and a solid object jabbed into her right hip. "Ouch!"

"What is it?"

"Nothing serious," she said, rubbing her bruised flesh. "There's an end table here that I did not see."

"There's a lamp on it." Marcus struck a match and lit the lamp, casting the room in a low, yellow glow.

"Let's search upstairs first. I suspect he would store anything of value on the second floor rather than the ground floor." He picked up the lamp and headed up the stairs. "Stay behind me."

She didn't argue with him. The place was eerie, and gooseflesh rose on her arms. What had seemed like an exciting adventure in the comfort of Marcus's home now felt like a tour of a haunted house. She stuck close to him, and the stairs creaked as they climbed to the second floor. A long corridor branched off into different sections.

"Which way?" she asked.

"We'll search the bedrooms first, starting with the master chamber."

Halfway down the corridor, they made a right turn toward what they anticipated was the master bedroom. Light from the lamp caused shadows to flicker like ghosts on the striped wallpaper as they crept past. Isabel's stomach twisted in a tight knot; her heart beat fast in her chest.

Pushing open the bedroom door, Marcus stepped inside. She followed behind, then stumbled over an object.

Marcus raised the lamp high. "The room has been ransacked."

Debris was scattered across the floor. Clothes, books, and personal belongings were haphazardly strewn about. She glanced down and saw that she had tripped over a leather boot. Judging by its size, it was a man's.

"I thought the house was vacant," she whispered. "If there's no bed or furniture in the room, then why is there clothing?"

"Turn around," he said, an edge to his voice.

"Why?"

"We have to leave. It's not safe."

"But we haven't found the painting," she protested.

He gripped her arm. "We go. Now."

He pushed her toward the door.

She sensed the newfound urgency in him, and it heightened her own fear.

Dear Lord, what had gone on here?

She rushed down the dim corridor, Marcus on her heels. In her haste, she took a wrong turn.

"No, Isabel! This way."

She pivoted at Marcus's voice, and made to move back when she tripped over a large object. Her hands flailed in the air, but she failed to catch her balance and she fell.

She did not hit the ground as she had expected, but landed on something soft. Confused and disoriented, she crawled off, her ungloved fingers dragging through a sticky substance.

"Are you all right?" Marcus asked, concern in his voice.

He squatted down and lowered the lamp to reveal a horrid sight.

Dante Black lay in a pool of blood, his head pitched back, his throat slashed.

Isabel scurried back, stifling a cry with a hand. As soon

as her palm touched her mouth, she realized the viscous matter on her fingers was blood, and she screamed.

Marcus hauled her up by her arm. "Isabel!"

She buried her face in his chest, horrified at the gory scene. She tasted blood—Dante's blood—and bile rose up in her throat.

Marcus set the lamp down, reached inside his jacket, and pulled out a handkerchief. He wiped the blood from her mouth and fingers.

Please don't let me vomit! she thought.

She gagged and would have wretched if he did not roughly shake her and force her to meet his intense gaze.

"Listen to me very carefully, Isabel. I know you are in shock, but he's dead and can do you no harm. We need to leave and it is imperative that we not draw attention to ourselves. No one must identify us later when the body is discovered. Do you understand?"

She looked into his jet-black eyes and shivered. She knew she would never forget the grotesque image at her feet.

She repeatedly swallowed, forcing the bitter bile back down her throat by sheer will. "I understand."

This time, he led the way down the stairs and out the front door. The hackney cab was waiting for them, and he helped her inside and shut the door.

"Are you going to faint?"

She leaned back on the bench and struggled to gain her composure. "No. I've never fainted. I'll be fine."

"I'm sorry you had to witness that. Have you ever seen a dead man before?"

"Dead, yes. Murdered, no."

Blood . . . there had been so much blood. Would she ever forget Dante's soulless eyes, his gaunt face, or his slashed throat?

What type of man could mutilate another human being so ruthlessly?

She looked down at the splotches of blood on her gown. Thank goodness Marcus had insisted she change. The dark fabric hid the stains, but she knew that as soon as they returned home, she would strip, bathe, and have the dress burned.

"When was he killed?" she asked, trying to keep her voice level.

"Judging by the warmth of the body and the lack of putrid smell, Dante Black was very recently murdered. Whoever did this must have just left the house. By the Grace of God, we did not run into the killer."

She felt the blood drain from her face. "Do you think it was the rancid man I previously encountered?"

"It's a safe assumption. A wealthy man like Gavinport would never dirty his hands or put himself at risk by committing murder on his own property. He has the means to hire any criminal to do the dastardly deed for him."

A wave of apprehension swept through her that she may have had close contact with the killer. "What are we going to do? Should we report the murder?"

"No. The housekeeper will find the body in a few days' time. With any luck, no one witnessed us coming and going. And if they did, they would not be able to identify us."

"We never searched the entire property. Maybe the painting is inside."

"Possibly. Although it's just as likely the murderer took it with him. I'll find out more when I return tonight under cover of darkness."

"You're going back?" she asked, alarmed.

"I must. Judging by the men's clothes and personal belongings strewn about, Dante Black was hiding out there. If he did manage to successfully hide the painting, it may still be inside. And if it was removed, then clues may have been left behind regarding its whereabouts."

Icy fear twisted around Isabel's heart. "What if the killer returns?"

"I doubt it. The criminal chose to slit Dante's throat rather than shoot him. It's a more personal method, but much quieter as well. A loud gunshot would have alerted the neighbors. Whoever it was, he took a great risk when he came here to kill Dante. He'll not want to jeopardize himself by returning to the scene."

"Still, I don't think it is a good idea—"

Marcus leaned forward on the bench opposite her, and taking her limp hand in his, he kissed the back of her hand. "Your concern is touching, but I promise to take every precaution."

His long legs brushed her skirts, and the heat of his lips felt like a brand on her flesh. Her emotions were raw, and looking into his compelling eyes, she had a maddening urge to throw herself into his arms and lean on his strength.

"I'll be back in time to escort you to Lady Carrington's ball tonight," he said.

She blinked. "I had forgotten about the ball. I'm not up to attending any festivities. It seems inappropriate after what we just encountered."

"We must attend. All of society will be there, including the Gavinports. It is the perfect opportunity for me to return to Lombard Street. We do not want to act differently, especially in front of the ton. You once said you would make a most useful ally, remember?"

Yes, she remembered. But that was before she had stumbled over a bloody corpse. The stakes were higher now—much higher.

What had started out as the theft of a valuable piece of art had now evolved into a man's gruesome murder.

Chapter 28

The waiting was hell.

Isabel paced back and forth in her new art studio, her nerves tense, her fingers curled into tight fists. It had started raining sometime after they had returned to the town house, and a pattering of drops cascaded down the windows, creating a gloomy, humid atmosphere that matched her mood.

Where was Marcus?

He had left for Lombard Street over two hours ago. She was fully dressed in a violet gown trimmed with lace and seed pearls with matching satin slippers. Attending the Carrington ball seemed abhorrent to her after discovering Dante's body, but she recognized the wisdom of Marcus's decision to attend.

That is, if she ever saw her husband again . . .

Fear clawed at her innards, and her pacing increased. She widened her path around trunks scattered about on the hardwood floor. Jenkins, exercising his usual competency, had arranged to have her art supplies delivered from her father's house within hours after Marcus had gifted her with the room.

She kicked the leg of a wooden easel in frustration as

she passed. Not even her precious paints and canvases offered her the slightest bit of comfort.

She couldn't stop thinking: What if the fearsome, ghoulish criminal she had encountered face-to-face was Dante Black's murderer? Worse still, what if he returned to Lombard Street and had a run-in with Marcus?

The truth was she was in a state of near panic over Marcus's prolonged absence. She hadn't realized how much his well-being meant to her until it was threatened. It was a startling thought, considering she would leave him to his own devices in little less than half a year.

She heard the front door open, followed by low voices. She rushed to the vestibule.

At the sight of Marcus handing Jenkins a soaked cloak, she ran to his side. "Marcus! Thank goodness you're home."

Dressed entirely in black, he looked imposing, ominous—and most importantly—in perfect health.

A grin softened his rugged features, and he reached out to touch her cheek. "Thank you for the warm welcome, Isabel. If I had anticipated such an enthusiastic reception from a wife, I would have married years ago."

She eyed him warily and stepped back. "Bah! I was overwrought for your welfare, but now that I know you are in one piece, I demand to know what took you so long."

He laughed and looked to Jenkins. "Was my lady wife truly *overwrought*?"

The butler's eyes traveled from mistress to master, clearly uncomfortable. "Lady Isabel was concerned by your clandestine activities."

The humor left Marcus's eyes. "I'm truly sorry that I was delayed, but it was due entirely to the weather and not any danger." He eyed her violet evening gown. "I must change so that we are not more than fashionably late to Lady Carrington's ball. I shall tell you everything in the carriage on the way."

* * *

"So you found nothing?" Isabel asked.

"I wasn't surprised," Marcus responded. "The murderer would have removed the painting if it happened to be there. Otherwise, when Dante Black's body is discovered, Bow Street will make a connection between Dante, Lord Gavinport, and the theft of the Gainsborough painting at Lord Westley's estate sale."

Isabel sipped from the glass of wine in her hand and studied the crowd in the Carringtons' ballroom. The scene was one of melted elegance, as the glittering ballroom and the warm June evening resulted in a crush of lavishly dressed people overheated and vigorously fanning themselves in the humid air. The French doors were open, but the steady rain prohibited the guests from venturing outdoors onto the terrace.

Hoping to catch a breeze, a group of people stood by the open doors overlooking the moonlit gardens.

Isabel handed her near-full glass to a passing footman. Neither food, wine, nor music had succeeded in taking the edge off her nerves tonight. She was as tightly wound as a top; the strain of pasting on a stiff smile and acting as if she were having a wonderful evening as a newlywed was exhausting. She wanted nothing more than to return to the town house on St. James's Street.

She glanced at Marcus to determine how he was faring. He looked strikingly handsome in his black formal attire. His jet hair gleamed beneath the candlelight of the chandeliers, his profile spoke of raw power and masculine grace, and his dark eyes held a sheen of purpose. If he felt uncomfortable or anxious at what they had earlier discovered, he showed no outward signs.

"How long must we stay?" she asked as the orchestra struck up another tune.

"A little while longer. We need to mingle before we leave. I see Lady Jersey and Lady Castlereagh speaking with Lady Carrington."

The last thing Isabel wanted was to make polite conversation with their hostess and two powerful patronesses of Almack's. Before she had married, both Jersey and Castlereagh held the power to terrorize any debutante's life by refusing to put her name on the list for entry into Almack's hallowed halls.

But once again, Isabel understood Marcus's logic. They couldn't very well leave the ball without thanking their hostess.

She placed her hand on his sleeve, and they wove their way through the crowd. Halfway across the room, they ran into Frederick Gavinport.

"Hawksley! I've been looking for you," Lord Gavinport boomed.

Isabel blinked, and her fingers tightened on Marcus's arm. She was again startled by his short stature, slim build, and cropped black hair, and found it disconcerting that they were almost at eye level.

The man is a murderer-hiring monster, she thought. *I would expect him to be taller . . . larger.*

Gavinport must have liked garlic, for the stench from his pores was overwhelming. He smiled up at Marcus, and eyed him with a calculating expression.

A fleeting image of pretty, young Lady Olivia Gavinport and Donald MacKinnon, her redheaded Scottish lover, flashed through Isabel's mind.

Marcus smiled blandly. "Good evening, Gavinport. Are you certain you've been looking for me and not my brother, Roman?"

"No, no, you, of course," Gavinport insisted. "All *true* art collectors know of each other, unlike the riffraff who are *told* by their art acquisitionists what to buy and who merely believe they are collectors. I've recently added to my collection of sporting artists. I've heard that you possess one of George Stubbs's works, and I've been meaning to ask if you would consider selling."

"Ah, I see. You must be referring to Stubbs's painting, *A Grey Horse*. The artist painted it in 1793, and I went to quite a bit of trouble to acquire the work. It is an important part of my collection. Therefore, I must decline—"

"I fully intend to make a rich offer," Gavinport said, licking his lips.

"Nonetheless, I still decline."

"You should know something about me, Hawksley. When I want something, I go after it no matter the cost."

Marcus's eyes narrowed. "I'm certain you do, but my answer is still the same."

Gavinport laughed bitterly. "All right. Please feel free to call on me when you change your mind." His rapier glance turned to Isabel, and he leered at her. "Wives can be most expensive, and should you ever need the blunt to satisfy the lady, my offer stands for the Stubbs painting." He bowed stiffly at Isabel and walked away.

"Oh, my," Isabel whispered. "What was that about?"

"Don't worry. He does not suspect we were at his town house on Lombard Street. His approach was coincidence."

"How do you know?"

"Dante's body has not yet been found. If it had, Gavinport would not be at the ball, but rather answering questions by the constable. Gavinport would probably claim Dante Black had broken into the town house and that he had no knowledge of Dante's presence. Gavinport would eventually be released, of course, as there is no direct evidence leading him to the murder, and Bow Street is hesitant to detain an influential noble without solid proof."

Isabel bit her lip. "Can we leave now? I feel . . . unwell."

Marcus's gaze snapped to her face. "I'm sorry. I hadn't realized you were ill. We can leave at once."

There was something strangely confounding about the intense look of concern on his face. His attention was focused entirely on her, and she had to remind herself to breathe.

"It's all right," she assured him. "The evening has been more than I am accustomed to."

"I'll have the carriage brought around at once." Marcus motioned at a liveried footman, and the servant snapped to attention.

Moments later, their cloaks were retrieved, and the carriage brought up front.

Waving away the footman, Marcus helped her into the vehicle himself and took the seat across from her. Leaning forward, he took both of her hands in his. "You look pale, my dear. Are you going to faint?"

"I told you before that I have never fainted."

His dark, earnest eyes held hers. "But you said yourself, much has transpired today."

"True. I would have lasted if not for the confrontation with Lord Gavinport. I could not get the notion out of my mind that he murdered a man today, whether by his own hand or by his orders."

Marcus's thumbs began to make circular motions across the backs of her hands. Her skin tingled from the contact, and an invisible warmth rushed through her body, simultaneously enveloping and comforting her.

He shook his head. "This is my fault. You would have been better off if you had refused to act as my alibi weeks ago."

"In case you haven't noticed, I am a strong woman, Marcus. I don't regret my actions, no matter how impulsive they may have seemed to you. What I would not have survived, however, was a life of servitude bound to Lord Walling as his wife."

His dark eyes sharpened and sent a tremor through her. "You are by far the strongest woman I have ever known. I'm quite certain you would have tackled Walling with the same type of fearlessness you have shown today."

She stilled, her heart wildly beating within her breast.

By the time they arrived home, the rain had turned into a full-blown storm. Lightning and thunder crashed outside the town house with enough noise to wake the dead.

Isabel immediately thought of Dante Black.

Kate was waiting to whisk her upstairs into her rooms. The maid helped her out of the violet dress and laid out a nightgown on the coverlet. It was a flimsy, flowing gown, quite ludicrous in Isabel's opinion, but what a newlywed was expected to wear.

At Isabel's questioning look, Kate rushed, "If Mr. Hawksley pays a visit."

Isabel bit her lip to keep from arguing. "In that case, please bring me a large glass of brandy."

Chapter 29

The brandy did not help. Stuck between a nightmare and consciousness, Isabel tossed and turned, but restful sleep eluded her. Images of mutilated bodies, bloodstained floors, and a knife-wielding monster tormented her mind. Rain slashed out of the night to pummel her window. Flashes of lightning streaked the walls in what looked like ghostly paintings and a pair of evil sunken eyes. Perspiration pasted her nightgown to her flesh.

Throwing off her covers, she sat on the edge of the bed, her feet dangling and her chest heaving.

What was the matter with her?

Marcus's words came to her: *You are by far the strongest woman I have ever known.*

She did pride herself on her strength, on never following society's rigid rules even as a debutante. Hadn't she taken matters into her own hands and boldly extricated herself from Lord Walling's clutches? She knew countless other women who had not been as determined and had ended up married to men whom they disliked, detested, or even worse, feared.

But that was not the same as tripping over a man whose

throat had been slashed wide open or brushing up against his killer.

Nothing she had dared in the past had prepared her for such horror.

She punched her pillow in frustration, certain she wasn't going to get a minute's sleep in her state of mind. Pushing her feet into her satin slippers, she pulled on a matching wrapper of the same diaphanous material as her nightgown. She picked up a candle from the nightstand and opened the door.

She crept along the second-floor balcony and down the stairs to the main floor. Other than the rain beating down on the roof and the occasional crack of thunder, the house was quiet. The staff had retired for the night.

A few lamps glowed faintly, and combined with her candle, she headed for her art studio. Halfway down the hall she saw light shining from beneath the library door.

For an instant, she wondered if Marcus was having the same difficulty sleeping, but then she recalled that he worked long and unconventional hours. He had been undisturbed by the confrontation with Lord Gavinport at the Carrington ball, and he had shown notable calm in the carriage ride home. Remarkably, the only concern that had been etched on his handsome face had been for her well-being.

The library was opposite her studio. Not wanting to disturb his work, she slipped inside the studio and quietly shut the door.

The room was located in the rear of the house overlooking a small garden. Heavy drapes were pulled back, uncovering the prized wide windows which would capture the sunlight when she painted. Her candle gave little light, but a half-moon cut a swath through the room and across the hardwood floor.

Isabel leaned against the door, entranced by the power of the moon and the raging storm outside. Two trunks rested in the corner. She flitted to them, her wrapper flowing behind her, and put her candle down on the floor. She lifted the lid of the bigger trunk, and smiled when she spotted a porcelain pan holding over a dozen hard cakes of soluble watercolors.

She sighed, confident coming here was a good choice. She could spend an hour sifting through her trunks, clearing her mind, and then return to her bedchamber and sleep soundly. Thunder and lightning had never scared her, and somehow in this room, *her room,* she now found the violent weather outside oddly comforting.

Perhaps Marcus did as well?

Jenkins had brought in a chair and a throw rug before the fireplace. She pushed the smaller trunk beside the empty hearth, moved her candle close by, and chose to sit on the rug as she pulled out jars and brushes. Ghosts and specters cleared from her mind as she focused on her task. After a half hour, she rose to start on the remaining trunk.

A streak of lightning, followed by thunder and a loud crack, drew her attention. She flew to the window as a giant oak tree sparked and a thick branch crashed to the sodden ground. Her eyes widened at the ferocious power wielded by the storm. She leaned forward and placed a hand over the breath-fogged glass. Sheets of rain pounded the house. The oak sizzled like an angry dragon as the flames were drenched and extinguished.

Lightning struck again, and she blinked as the bright white light pierced her eyes. Outside, the bushes formed huddled shapes in the howling wind, and an odd premonition ran through her. Thunder crashed, and the window panes shook. The shapes outside moved, blending like demons into one dark figure. Her stomach knotted, and her breath stalled in her throat. She ran her hand over the clouded window, clearing the glass, looking closer. A bolt struck the sky. Thunder jolted the floor. Then the figure grew, formed a man, outlined by lightning, standing in the garden, staring in the window, staring at *her*.

Rain plastered ropes of black hair to a skeleton-thin face. Shrunken eyes, evil eyes glared at her . . .

She screamed.

He grinned and raised his hand, aiming a shiny black pistol at her head.

Chapter 30

Marcus burst through the door.

Isabel jumped and turned with a start, her large blue eyes shining wide with terror.

"He's here, Marcus!" she cried out and ran to the door, her sheer wrap flowing behind her like a specter.

Marcus caught her arm or she would have run by him. "Who's here?"

"That man," she stammered. "Dante's murderer . . . he's here . . . outside the window."

She was shaking so badly she could barely stand. Alarm ran through him. "Calm down, Isabel."

She gasped, panting in terror, and made to pull away. "We have to get out of this room. He has a pistol!"

Marcus's gaze snapped to the window. All he could see was a torrent of rain hammering the glass. The weather was miserable, not conducive to a man lurking about.

But still . . .

He pulled her into the hallway, hesitant to release her trembling body.

Footsteps sounded down the hall, and Jenkins turned the corner. A male servant was behind him, carrying a candle. Both wore nightshirts.

"We heard a scream," Jenkins explained.

"Isabel says she saw someone outside in the gardens. A man with a gun."

Jenkins and the servant exchanged a look of alarm.

"I'm going out to look," Marcus said.

Isabel whimpered, and her nails dug into his hand. "No! He could still be out there."

Her face was deathly pale and he feared she would faint, despite all her earlier protestations that she was immune to the condition.

"I want you to wait in the library." He guided her across the hall into his library office and sat her in the oversized leather chair behind his desk. He closed the curtains, blocking the storm from her view. Returning to her side, he coaxed her to meet his gaze. "I must go outside, but I will take precautions. I will return shortly."

She whimpered again, but nodded. He felt impaled by the stark panic in her wild blue eyes. She was completely different from the impetuous, bold Isabel to whom he had grown accustomed. The spurt of anxiety that stabbed through him was as foreign as it was uncomfortable.

He left the room, and Jenkins was waiting for him in the vestibule with his cloak and hat. The butler and other servant were both dressed as well.

Without a word, Jenkins handed Marcus his pistol.

"We go together," Marcus said. "Isabel saw the man outside the window, so we travel from front to back."

Marcus led the group, and in less than a minute after they stepped outside the front door, they were soaked to their skin. Jenkins carried a lantern that sputtered as they walked. Marcus's eyes adjusted to the moonlight, knowing the lantern would provide little light in the storm. He crept around the side of the town house, the weight of the pistol comfortable in his hand. When he came to the garden, he spotted the old oak tree, its thick branch split in half.

No man was hiding out. Whatever footprints he may have left had long been washed away.

Had Isabel imagined the criminal?

She was not the kind of woman prone to hysterics. She had a strong disposition and had proven herself by not fainting, vomiting, or screeching after landing on top of Dante's corpse. Most women of his acquaintance would have been incapacitated after such a gory discovery.

No, if Isabel said she saw the criminal, then he was here.

But why had he shown up? And armed?

Had the murderer learned that they had discovered Dante's body? Did Gavinport suspect they were aware of his involvement and, as a result, had sought to eliminate Isabel or him? Or did the deviant man seek to send a warning to scare them off?

"There's no one here," Marcus shouted to Jenkins to be heard above the storm.

Jenkins nodded, and they made their way back into the house and stripped off their sopping cloaks and boots.

"Secure the house and go to bed," Marcus instructed. "I shall see to Isabel."

He opened the library door to find Isabel in the exact same position he had left her. She sat still as a statue on the chair. Her face was pale, her long, dark hair curling around her shoulders, her hands clutching her thin wrapper tightly about her waist. Sitting behind his massive desk, she looked like a little lost girl waiting to be saved.

A strange wave of possessiveness and protectiveness surged through him.

He went to her side and dropped to his knee. "Isabel, we searched outside and found no evidence of an intruder."

She raised pale blue eyes. "Do you believe that I saw him?"

He didn't hesitate. "Yes. I do. Please tell me exactly what happened."

"I couldn't sleep so I went to my studio. I saw your light

on, but I didn't want to disturb your work. I knew unpacking my art supplies would calm me, and it did, until I looked outside and saw a bolt of lightning strike a tree in the garden. That's when I saw him . . . standing in the rain . . . staring at me." She shivered and rubbed her arms. "He had a gun. He laughed when I screamed and then disappeared in the shadows. I think he sought to frighten me, not kill me."

"Why do you say that?"

"If he wanted to kill me, he could have done so during the half hour I sat blissfully unaware sorting through my trunks."

She was right, but the thought galled him.

He suspected the answer, but he asked anyway. "Why couldn't you sleep tonight?"

"What?"

"You said you couldn't sleep so you came down to your studio. Why couldn't you sleep?"

She bit her bottom lip. "I was having nightmares . . . about Dante."

He cursed softly beneath his breath. "I'm sorry, sweetheart. I want to shield you from everything. Perhaps you should leave now for Paris. I won't have you in danger or tormented on my behalf."

Her head snapped up, and her eyes held a fierce clarity. "No. We had an understanding. We stay together for six months, during which time I help you with your investigation, remember?"

"Yes, I remember."

She reached out and touched his hand. "Will you hold me?"

He stiffened. "Isabel—"

"Just hold me, Marcus. I need . . . I need comfort."

He looked down at her slender hand touching his. "My clothes are soaked. I'll summon your maid."

"No. I need you, not Kate."

The urgency in her voice struck a deep-seated chord in

his chest. That such a beautiful, brave woman should want him to hold and comfort her was incomprehensible. No woman had wanted him, other than for pleasure in the bedroom, for a long, long time.

Oblivious to the sopping condition of his clothes, her hands went about his neck and urged him close. He leaned forward, still on his knees, inhaling her subtle perfume like a dying man sucking in his last breath. His arms rose of their own accord.

Two perfectly full breasts seared his chest through his wet shirt. He stifled a groan and instantly grew rigid. Her diaphanous nightgown failed to offer even the slightest barrier, and it felt like she was naked.

His arms tightened; she slid closer, and the chair creaked at her precarious angle.

His hand rested against the small of her back, the other buried in the silken hair at her nape. He was drowning in lust. It was a wonder his drenched shirt didn't steam against his hot skin. Never before had he desired a woman so vehemently. He fantasized of dragging her off the chair, throwing her on top of his desk, and making passionate love to her.

As her soft curves molded to his hard body, he struggled to remember that she was in shock, that she only sought comfort and reassurance, not a sexual encounter with her new husband. He tried to control his ragged breathing, the hammering of his heart, and reminded himself of their agreement.

Then she buried her face against his throat, brushed her lips against his neck, and whispered, "Please kiss me, Marcus."

He pulled back an inch. "What?"

She dropped from the chair to her knees before him and looked him in the eye. "Kiss me," she urged.

"I don't think that's a good idea."

"I need you to erase the images from my mind."

Her plea was so urgent, his heart briefly sank. "Kissing me will not change what happened today. You seek intimacy because of your fear. You will later regret it when you calm."

She shook her head, her dark tresses tumbling over her shoulders. "I'm only asking for a kiss."

"I know better. It won't help, Isabel."

"Then we have nothing to lose by trying, do we?" She licked her lips, and his heated gaze lowered to her mouth.

"Just one," he ground out. "For comfort."

He brushed her lips once . . . and again . . . then gently covered her mouth. He began to sweat with the effort it took to restrain himself.

Comfort, he thought. *This is only to ease her fears, not devour her. If she knew my thoughts, she would run from the room screaming like a madwoman.*

She sighed and parted her lips, inviting . . . urging him to deepen the kiss. The hunger within him was an all-consuming fire, and every fiber in his body wanted her so badly he could taste it.

Her hands moved to his chest, but instead of pushing him away as he anticipated, she reached for the top button of his shirt. Her deft fingers unfastened three buttons before he realized her intent.

He grasped her hands. "What are you—"

Her brilliant blue eyes clung to his. "Please take off your shirt, Marcus."

A muscle tightened at his jaw. "I'm a man, Isabel. I can only withstand so much."

"I'm not asking you to withstand anything."

"I should leave. You're not thinking straight."

She shook her head. "What happened today opened my eyes. That horrible man . . . that criminal could have killed me, and you know what I most feared when he aimed the pistol at my head? I feared never experiencing intimacy, never becoming a woman, and most importantly, never experiencing *you*. I want to be with *you*, Marcus, no other. Life is too short not to live to its fullest."

He froze and dared not breathe lest the fantasy be broken. She didn't look or sound like a panicked, irrational woman, but one who knew exactly what she desired— which was him . . . she wanted *him* to make love to *her*.

Then miraculously she leaned forward, brushed her lips against his, and his restraint shattered into a million pieces.

He responded with fierce desire, fully claiming her lips, crushing her to him. There was no mistaking his meaning. He kissed her like the starved man he was, like the man he had been ever since she propositioned him in Lord West-ley's room of erotic art.

She reached out to unfasten the next button on his shirt, and this time, he did not stop her. Her fingers skimmed his hot flesh, and he groaned. He had never been so painfully aroused in his life. She came dangerously close to his waistband, and when she grazed his swollen groin in his trousers, he nearly jumped out of his skin.

"Let me," he said, his voice harsh. He pulled off his shirt and tossed it behind him.

Her eyes shone with wonder. "Ever since I was a little girl, I've always wanted to touch you." Her finger traced his pectoral muscle and grazed his nipple. "May I?"

His groan filled the library. "You'll drive me mad."

Her lips curved sensually. "Is there any other way?"

Chapter 31

Isabel's eyes feasted on Marcus's naked torso as she knelt before him. He was heavily muscled and perfectly proportioned. His shoulders were a yard wide and sleek, molded bronze. A light sprinkling of dark hair covered his chest and narrowed down to his waistband where the mysterious part of him had swelled to an alarming proportion. He looked, quite simply, like a flesh-and-blood version of one of the Greek statues at the museum she had always found fascinating.

Tonight, in her most terrifying moments, she had feared never experiencing his touch. When the soulless eyes of the criminal had stared at her through the window, and when he had aimed a gun at her head, the vow of a passionless marriage she had made with Marcus seemed ludicrous, shallow, and meaningless.

Facing her mortality had proved one thing: She refused to go a day longer without knowing Marcus Hawksley as a man.

For what if tomorrow never came—just like it had for Dante Black? Or just as unfathomable, what if Marcus was unexpectedly wounded . . . or killed?

She glanced at Marcus's face. The inky blackness of his

eyes and his firm, sensual features made her breath catch. He was an intense man who she knew would be just as passionate with his lovemaking as he was ambitious with his work. As a child, she was captivated by him; but as a woman, she was enthralled.

She knew little of what transpired between a man and a woman, but her inherent recklessness outweighed her caution, and she wanted to see the rest of him unclothed. He would no doubt be magnificent.

No man of her acquaintance had ever compared with Marcus Hawksley.

At her silence, he chuckled. "If you keep looking at me like that, I won't be able to control myself."

She smiled evocatively, eager for his touch once more. "I wouldn't want you to."

He swept her into his arms, and their lips met over and over as if they were starved for the feel and taste of each other. He exuded a masculinity that jolted her senses, and each time his tongue stroked hers, she became more overwhelmed until she was panting and her nails were digging into his hard biceps.

His hands moved to her shoulders, peeling away her wrapper, and she lowered her arms to help him. The fabric swished, and the flimsy silk skimmed down her arms. Cool air brushed her skin, and she shivered.

He pulled her to him once more, nibbled her ear with his teeth in a way that made her senses whirl. His lips then seared a path down her throat, her shoulder, and the swell of a breast.

She clung to him. "Marcus," she gasped. "That feels so good."

"Yessss," he hissed against the bodice of her nightgown. His hot breath moistened the silk, and she writhed in his arms. She had a fierce need to rid herself of her remaining clothing and craved to feel his mouth on her naked breasts.

Her hands restlessly moved to her nightgown, but he stopped her.

"Easy, sweetheart. Let me."

He held her away from him as he pushed the sleeves down her arms. The silk lowered down her throat and caught on her upthrust breasts. With a mere touch of his finger in her bodice where the gown gaped, the fabric rippled down her hips, exposing her breasts to his hungry gaze.

His eyes glittered with lust, and she reveled at his savage reaction.

"My God," he whispered. "You're so fair."

She watched in fascination as he reached out to gently cup a full breast and brush her hardened nipple with a thumb. A spurt of hungry desire spiraled through her, and her lids slid halfway closed.

At her sigh, he dipped his head to lick a pink nipple, then sucked the whole crown into his hot mouth. Soldering heat rushed in between her thighs. She arched backward, digging her fingers into his hair, drawing him closer. When he turned his attention to her other breast, she moaned, urging him on.

"Damn," Marcus breathed against the side of her breast. "I was going to carry you upstairs to my room, but I can't wait that long. I need to see you, Isabel. All of you."

His large hand went to her hip, and with one smooth motion her nightgown fell to the carpet, revealing her naked body to his hungry gaze.

His pupils dilated and a look of awe crossed his handsome face. "Botticelli's *The Birth of Venus* does not compare."

At the reverence in his tone, her heart leapt in her chest.

He looked around, and roughly pushed the chair she had been sitting on to the side. He laid her down in front of his desk, and the thick carpet tickled her back and buttocks. He lowered himself on his elbows, and she gasped as his bare chest brushed her sensitive breasts.

It was wondrous—flesh against flesh—and passion inched through her veins.

She had a need to kiss him again, so her lips and tongue slid up the column of his throat. She licked him, tasting the rain and the power of the storm on his hot skin.

He groaned and kissed a path down her throat and lavished more attention on her breasts until the world tilted. His hands lowered to her hips and his mouth followed, kissing a path down her belly. His tongue stopped to swirl in her navel, and a fierce need built in her that made her restless for more.

As if sensing her silent plea, he spread her thighs and cupped her sensitive mons. When his finger parted the tight curls between her legs and brushed against her sensitive nub, she arched off the carpet into his hand. He slipped a finger inside, and she felt a honeyed warmth flood her loins. When his finger was slick with her arousal, he stroked in and out of her body, then across her nub until her need grew to a fevered pitch. Her nails raked his muscled back as she soared higher and higher, until waves of ecstasy throbbed through her, and she thought she would die from the pleasure.

Her eyes cracked open, and the faintest thread of moonlight through a crack in the curtains caught a rivulet of sweat on his brow. She became aware of his rigid manhood burning against her thigh. She felt deliciously wanton, sprawled naked beneath him while he still wore his trousers. She knew there was much more to lovemaking and that he had held himself back for her sake. He thought to comfort her . . . to pleasure her . . . even though it meant denying his needs.

But she wanted more, she wanted all of *him*, and she restlessly shifted her hips against his manhood.

His eyes were compelling as he hovered above her. "Isabel, I want more than anything to make love to you, but I shall not take advantage of you. I can still walk away if that is what you want."

"You feel so big."

"Isabel," he groaned. "That won't work to get a man to leave."

"I don't want you to leave. I want to experience everything. I want *you*, Marcus."

His dark gaze was so hungry and full of raw need that a knot rose in her throat.

He stood, and took off his trousers. Leaning back on her elbows, Isabel watched. The crisp hair on his chest narrowed downward, and her eyes widened as his cock jutted from a nest of dark hair. He looked alarmingly large, but with an inherent knowledge as old as Eve, she knew she was woman enough for him.

He came to her then, and his muscled legs pressed against her soft thighs. The hard length of him pulsed against her soft core, and she opened her legs to feel the delicious pressure. His palms cupped her bottom cheeks and raised her until the tip of his cock entered her body. His hardness electrified her, and her arousal grew fierce.

Then slowly, inch by inch, he pressed forward. She thrashed her head from side to side, wanting, needing more until he thrust fully into her satin sheath. She froze at the stab of pain, but then became aware of his luxurious fullness and felt the pulse of his heart within her body.

He began to move slowly at first, then faster, his rock-hard length thrusting in and out of her body. She began to move with him with a desperate urgency of her own, completely abandoning herself to the whirl of sensations flooding her body, and then she cried out as the world exploded and she soared higher and higher to a great, shuddering climax.

Marcus went rigid with her cry and withdrew from her body, his white hot seed scorching her thigh. His breathing was ragged, his heart thundering against hers.

Finally he rolled to the side and made to enfold her in his arms, but his elbow bumped the desk and a cascade of papers flittered about them. They both laughed and looked each other in the eyes.

He kissed her forehead. "I had fantasized of making love to you for weeks now, but never on the floor of my office."

Isabel stretched a hand out and grasped a piece of paper. "I wonder if this will improve your performance."

He cocked a dark eyebrow. "In bed or at the Stock Exchange?"

"Both."

"I was right. You are a saucy piece of baggage, Lady Hawksley."

She reached up to caress his cheek. "Only for you."

His expression grew serious. "Thank you, sweetheart."

"For what?"

"For gifting me with your innocence, your self." He sat up and reached for his shirt. With careful ministrations, he cleaned her thighs.

She yawned, suddenly exhausted. "I don't suppose we can sleep here all night?"

"Jenkins is very discreet, but Mrs. McLaughlin would have my head for debauching my new wife in such a manner."

She picked up her nightgown. "Will you spend the night in my room?"

He eyed her carefully. "Are you afraid of the storm?"

Isabel looked to the window. Even with the curtains drawn, she knew from the soft sound of the rain against the glass that the violence of the storm had passed. "I'm not afraid."

"Isabel, tomorrow morning you may regret what has happened between us."

She clutched her nightgown to her chest and adamantly shook her head. "I won't regret it."

"Are you certain? Lust has a way of robbing one's reason."

She felt an odd hurt at his words. *He said lust, not love!*

But when had she ever sought his love? She had wanted to experience him, not make him fall in love with her. Perhaps it was *he* who regretted what they had shared? A heaviness centered in her chest as she was torn by conflicting emotions.

He was studying her, waiting for her response, and she blurted out the first thing that came to mind. "As I said, I have no regrets as our plans don't have to change."

A brief shadow flickered across his face, but then he nodded and smiled. "Of course not. Shall I help you to your room?"

He assisted her with her nightgown and donned his trousers. He then swept her into his arms and, walking barefoot, silently carried her up the staircase.

Chapter 32

Marcus ran his hand across Isabel's smooth hip and then along her taut stomach. His fingers came to rest beneath the swell of her breasts. His body spooned the back of her naked length, and her head lay on his arm. She was asleep, and in the predawn light of her room, she looked ethereal.

Ebony hair curled around her shoulders, her breasts, and brushed his chest. He blew a silken curl off her shoulder, kissed her warm skin, and listened to her deep breathing. He lay still for a long time afterward, studying her bewitching profile.

He was still reeling from their lovemaking in the library. She hadn't cared about his blackened reputation, his sordid past, but had wanted him for who he was. And she was glorious in her passion. He had once thought Isabel Cameron would be as impulsive and reckless in bed as she was out of it.

He had been right, but there had been so much more . . .

She was giving and generous and had eagerly opened her arms to welcome him in her embrace and gift him with her innocence.

Just like a loving wife . . .

What had happened between them last night had been

miraculous, and he felt more alive than he had in years. Her intelligence and courage . . . her passion for art and for life enraptured him. All the women in his past, including Simone Winston and the doomed Bridget Turner, paled in comparison.

Isabel sighed between parted lips and eased closer to him in her sleep. Pink nipples thrust through her hair, and her luscious bum cheeks pressed against his groin. His body's reaction was instantaneous, but also was his heart's unfamiliar swelling with tenderness and reverence.

After Bridget's duplicity, her suicide, and the destruction of their unborn child, he had never intended to marry or consider a serious future with any woman. Rather he had planned to ruthlessly further his career and obtain whatever expensive art that caught his eye. Then Isabel had come along and asked him to dance at Lady Holloway's ball, a Thomas Gainsborough painting was stolen, and his life as he had meticulously planned it had started to unravel.

He was put in an impossible situation. Now that he had made love to her, his lust hadn't been sated, but had only heightened. Worse was his inexplicable need to keep her beside him, to see her blue eyes widen in wonder whenever she saw a piece of priceless artwork, and to experience her vivacious smile whenever she thought of the spare room in his home that now was her studio.

For a startling instant he wondered if it was love, but then dismissed the thought as fancy. He was too jaded, too cynical, to fall prey to such an unselfish emotion. His feelings for her were nothing more than lust commingled with admiration as he was genuinely fond of her. It made sense, he reasoned, that he was enthralled by her. What breathing man wouldn't stiffen at the notion of the spirited Isabel Cameron in his bed?

Even if she was willing to become his *real* wife in every sense of the word, he was not in a position to offer her what a proper husband should—security and safety. His past had caught up with him once again, and a lord of the realm had attempted to frame Marcus for theft.

As an avid art collector, Lord Gavinport would have known that Marcus sought to acquire Gainsborough's works. When the *Seashore with Fishermen* was up for auction, Gavinport had seized the opportunity to steal the painting and blame another. After all, who would trust the younger son of an earl when it was public knowledge that his own father scorned him?

Isabel's alibi had foiled Gavinport's well-laid plans. The authorities did not suspect Marcus for the crime, yet Marcus would not rest until the man who had attempted to frame him was punished. He had planned on finding the stolen painting, alerting Bow Street, and having Gavinport arrested. But instead of resolving the mystery, Marcus had only succeeded in putting Isabel through horrid experiences.

Neither time had she been secure or safe.

How could he expect Isabel to embark on a future with him when criminals were glaring at her through windows, and he took her to establishments where she stumbled over corpses?

Then there was a promise that stood between them . . . a pact to let her walk away after half a year . . . flee to her aunt and two anticipated lovers.

Damnation.

Isabel's words in the library came back to him: *I have no regrets as our plans don't have to change.*

He had been taken aback, but had been quick to disguise his disappointment. She was right, of course. She had been forthright and honest with her desires, and remaining in London was never in her plans. He had been the one to suggest she immediately leave for Paris. The thought of her having nightmares over Dante's murder or, worse, the thought of her in danger was unconscionable. He'd never forget her fear and panic as she ran from her studio after spotting the derelict outside.

His temper flared at the image. He would find the criminal and tear the bastard apart with his bare hands. He vowed to put an end to the mystery surrounding the Gainsborough theft. He owed it to Isabel just as much as to himself.

Dante Black was already dead. But he would see to it that Gavinport and everyone else responsible would pay.

"You did what?" Charlotte gasped.

Isabel sat across from Charlotte in one of the Bennings' opulent receiving rooms. Isabel looked behind her to make certain the door was shut and no servant had entered with a tea tray.

"I told you, after that horrible criminal appeared, I decided to be with Marcus last night."

Charlotte's blue eyes were as wide as saucers. She ran a nervous hand over her frizzy blond curls. "I don't know what's more shocking. That you tripped over a famous auctioneer's corpse, that a madman tracked you down and aimed a gun at your head, or that you made love to Marcus Hawksley after vowing not to."

"It has been an eventful two days," Isabel said dryly.

"Eventful! Have you gone mad?"

Isabel sighed and shook her head. "Living through such terrifying experiences such as falling on top of Dante Black's corpse and being threatened by the demon that most likely killed him has dramatically changed my beliefs. Life is too precious to waste it wondering 'what if.' Patience has never been one of my virtues, and what if I had been shot last night? I must seize every opportunity."

Charlotte reached out to embrace her. "Oh, Isabel."

A hot ache grew in Isabel's throat, and she bit back unwelcome tears.

Charlotte pulled back to look in her eyes. "Have you spoken with Marcus about what occurred?"

"I never had the chance. I woke up alone. At first I thought I had dreamed the entire experience, but then I turned to the side and saw the indent in the pillow where Marcus had slept. He held me all night and must have left very early. By the time I went down for breakfast, he had already gone to the Stock Exchange, but he left a note for me with Jenkins."

"A note? What did it say?"

"He apologized for leaving early and explained that he had an important client meeting this morning. He requested that I meet him at his office on Threadneedle Street at noon. He wants to take me to luncheon at the Ship and Turtle on Leadenhall Street, which is known for its famous turtle soup. He said many brokers celebrate good fortune there. He also said . . . that he missed me."

Charlotte cocked her head to the side. "Isabel, he is your husband. Have you ever considered that being Marcus Hawksley's wife, his *true* wife, is your calling? After all, you have been infatuated with the man since you were a young girl. Perhaps Paris, Auntie Lil, and art classes are not your destiny."

Isabel felt her world spin. The truth was, since Marcus Hawksley had reentered her life, she had thought less and less of Paris and Auntie Lil. She still loved to paint, but her artistic impulses were commingled with her stirring interest in her new husband. The fact that he was an avid art collector made him a perfect match for her. He understood her passion and respected her aspiring talent by presenting her with her own art studio, something she had desperately wanted, but never been permitted while living under her father's roof.

Still her plans of Paris had been set for as long as she could remember . . .

"Paris is what I have sought for a long time," she mumbled.

Charlotte sighed. "And I have sought to marry for true love for as long as I can remember. My mother, in her own way, has strived for the same thing and is on her fourth marriage to my stepfather, Harold Benning, in her quest to find it. Love is the rarest, most precious gift anyone could wish for. You are lucky enough to have stumbled upon it."

"Lust is not love! Marcus hasn't uttered a word of love in my ear."

Charlotte's eyes were aglow. "But have you allowed him to? You said yourself you told him nothing has to change between you."

"Yes, but still . . ."

"Have you passion?"

The memory sent Isabel's spirits soaring. "Yes, there was passion."

"My mother's most religious acquaintance, Lady Upstance, says a wife's duty is perhaps the most painful, distasteful act she must endure and told her daughter to mentally catalog the pantry while her husband does the deed," Charlotte said.

Isabel's face grew hot. "Catalog the pantry! I couldn't think of anything but him."

Vivid images of their lovemaking burned her mind. For as long as she breathed, she would cherish what had happened on the floor of his library and didn't think she would ever look at a shelf of books the same way again. The problem was she wanted to be with Marcus again. She craved to leisurely explore his powerful body and hungered for the feel of his hands on her sensitive flesh.

Charlotte's lips curled in a devilish grin. "Tell me, Isabel. Tell me everything."

Just then, the door opened and Harold Benning entered pushing a tea tray. A steaming sterling silver teapot and china for two rattled as he came forward.

"Isabel, my dear!" Benning's flabby face spread into a smile. "When I heard you were visiting, I chased the maid away so that I could see you myself. How is your new home as a married lady?"

Isabel stood to greet Harold Benning and tried not to gape at his ostentatious lime green double-breasted jacket with matching shirt and shawl collar. His striped trousers had a thread of the same green color, and his short boots had a three-inch heel. Harold Benning made the famous dandies of the ton, like Beau Brummel, look as masculine as a sweaty boxer at Gentleman Jackson's.

She curtsied, managing at the same time to hide her amusement. "I am faring quite well, Mr. Benning."

He picked up a copy of *The Morning Chronicle* from the tea tray and waved it in the air. "It's plastered all over the papers that the former Bonham's auctioneer, Dante Black, was found murdered on Lombard Street. Wasn't he the auctioneer who had accused Mr. Hawksley of stealing the painting?"

Isabel's hand fluttered to her chest. It was not difficult to look surprised for she truly was taken aback that the body was discovered so soon.

Thankfully, Charlotte had the good sense to look stunned as well.

"I had no idea," Isabel said. "Mr. Black had initially *claimed* Marcus was involved, but he was wrong, of course. I wonder if Marcus knows of his death. Murdered, you say?"

A glint of excitement pierced Harold Benning's eyes. "The details of his death were quite ghastly, and I can only assume the man was immersed in illegal activity. What was most shocking is that the murder occurred on one of Lord

Gavinport's properties. According to the paper, Gavinport claimed the property was vacant and Dante Black had been living there without his consent. Bow Street does not consider Gavinport a suspect." Benning hesitated, then shook his head in utter disbelief. "Lord Gavinport and I go to the same clubs, and I am curious if there is a connection between the two men. Perhaps Mr. Hawksley should further inquire."

A sliver of alarm ran through her at Benning's inquisitiveness. "I will be sure to mention it to him," Isabel said, careful to keep an even tone.

Then Benning shrugged and dropped the newspaper, and his attention flitted back to the tea tray. He poured two cups of tea and handed them to Isabel and Charlotte as if they had been discussing the latest horticulture article rather than a man's murder.

"Did Charlotte remind you of her mother's upcoming surprise birthday ball the first weekend of July? It's not really a surprise since Leticia insists on having a hand in planning the party, but it will be the event of the Season."

"The invitations were delivered weeks ago," Charlotte said, "but I haven't yet had a chance to discuss the details with Isabel."

"I had mentioned it to Marcus, and we are looking forward to attending. Your balls are always spectacular," Isabel said, raising her teacup to her lips.

Harold Benning beamed. "We look forward to seeing the newlyweds together." He kissed Isabel's cheeks with a flourish before leaving the room and shutting the door.

Charlotte set down her teacup. "Did you know Dante Black's murder was in the papers?" she whispered.

Isabel shook her head. "By the time I woke up this morning and made my way downstairs, the newspapers had been long gone. I can only assume Marcus saw the news before he left for the Stock Exchange."

"I'm surprised Benning read the papers. If an article

doesn't have to do with fashion or frivolity, he's usually not interested," Charlotte said sarcastically.

"Perhaps Dante's name caught his eye."

A painful expression crossed Charlotte's face. "Mother thinks he's having an affair."

Isabel was flabbergasted. "With a woman?"

Charlotte grimaced. "Ah, you suspect his tastes run toward the same sex?"

"I'm sorry, Charlotte."

"Don't be. I've wondered for years. I've never uttered a word about it to Mother."

"What makes her think Mr. Benning is having an affair?" Isabel asked.

"He has been absent for longer and longer periods of time. He claims he's at the clubs or at his tailor, but Mother is suspicious."

"What will she do?"

Charlotte shrugged. "Nothing. They both love to entertain on a grand scale and spend exorbitant amounts of money. They will continue doing so while living separate lives. They will be no different from the rest of the married couples of the haut ton."

Isabel's heart lurched. Charlotte was right. True love or at least true passion was rare indeed. Perhaps Marcus was her destiny. Surprisingly, she was considering the notion. Thoughts of Paris did not enter her mind as much as thoughts of Marcus Hawksley.

But while he did not love her, she knew he was in lust with her. After the business with Lord Gavinport was settled, would there be room in his life for her? She was painfully aware that he never wanted to marry. But did he want her to leave? After all, he had suggested she immediately depart for Paris. Or had he been concerned for her safety?

She smiled her secret smile. She never gave up on a

challenge. She was impulsive, reckless to a fault, and stubbornly determined when she truly wanted something. She knew her innocence and her beauty enticed and attracted him.

But the true question was: Could she capture his heart?

Chapter 33

Marcus shook Keith MacKinnon's outstretched hand in the lobby of the Stock Exchange.

"Your decision to buy shares in companies that specialize in gas lighting is a good one," Marcus said. "Baltic companies, whose most important commodity is tallow, have seen a dip in profits, and I anticipate gas lighting to spell doom to the tallow trade in the next few years."

"Aye, Mr. Hawksley. Yer advice hasna led me wrong in the past." Keith MacKinnon rose, leaning heavily on his cane. His red hair was sprinkled with gray, and his shrewd blue eyes shone with an intelligence that accompanied old age.

The tenacious Scot was Marcus's oldest client. He was also one of his wealthiest with substantial landholdings in both Scotland and England. He was as wily with his money as he was with his family.

Marcus recalled when he and Isabel were found hiding in the Gavinports' linen closet. He wondered what the strict Scot would do if he knew his son, Donald MacKinnon, was Lady Olivia Gavinport's lover.

"I'll price the shares today with several jobbers and seal

the bargain with whichever gives me the lowest price," Marcus said.

"I have complete faith in ye, Hawksley."

Marcus waited until Keith MacKinnon departed. He then strode through the lobby, pushed through the swinging doors, and entered the trading floor.

As customary, the arena was thriving. Making his way through groups of brokers and jobbers, he caught pieces of their heated conversations as he walked by. Men waved as he passed, some in greeting, others eager to do business with him or ask his advice. Marcus nodded and acknowledged them all as he walked. He was in his element here, never questioned or criticized, but to the contrary, he was a well-known, highly successful broker whose record stood on its own rather than at the whims of society's arcane rules.

He caught a glimpse of Ralph Hodge arguing with a fellow stockbroker. Hodge's eyes were narrowed, and he angrily waved a paper in his opponent's face. As if sensing he was being scrutinized, Hodge turned his head to glare at Marcus.

Hatred emanated from his green gaze.

He truly despises me, Marcus thought. *Hatred is a powerful motive. I wonder if Isabel's theory that Ralph Hodge sought to have me imprisoned for theft is true.*

Marcus pushed the thought aside. He was convinced Hodge didn't have the knowledge or contacts in the art world. Lord Gavinport was a likelier suspect, especially since Dante Black was murdered on his property.

Dismissing Ralph Hodge, Marcus continued down the elongated hall until he came to the central area where the rostrum was located. Directly above were the gilt dome and the arched glass roof. Sunlight streamed in through the glass, making the temperature around the rostrum several degrees warmer than the rest of the hall.

To the left, a group of jobbers and brokers stood haggling

over share prices. Here, in this vicinity on the floor, the jobbers who specialized in the growing gas and gas lighting technology market gathered. They were oblivious to his presence, and Marcus feigned interest in a clerk up on the rostrum picking up sheets of paper that had fallen from a podium. Marcus focused on their conversations and gathered important information regarding today's prices. When he was satisfied, he turned and approached the group.

Knowing that jobbers earn money for their services by inflating the price they offer the broker, Marcus requested the current prices of three jobbers without revealing whether he was interested in buying or selling. Only when he was satisfied that he had obtained the best price for his client did he agree to a deal. Tomorrow Marcus would send his secretary, James Smith, to verify the agreement at the Exchange Clearing House.

Marcus was about to depart the jobbers' presence when a tap on his shoulder gained his attention. He turned to see a youth, no more than fourteen, with tousled brown hair and a wrinkled jacket gaze up at him. Marcus didn't recognize the boy, and he wondered if he was one of the many underpaid messengers that spent their day rushing to and from jobbers' offices to the Stock Exchange.

"Mr. Hawksley?"

"Yes. What is it?"

The boy handed Marcus an envelope. "This is for you."

Marcus frowned when he noted no return address. "Who is it from?"

The boy shrugged. "The bloke paid me good blunt to deliver it. Said you'd know." He turned and fled into the crowd without a backward glance.

Marcus cursed beneath his breath. He'd had a busy morning and didn't have time for silly distractions. If it was a nasty note from Ralph Hodge, he'd pummel down the bastard's office door.

Marcus strode for the swinging doors, tearing the envelope open as he went. He read the two lines, then froze, oblivious to the racket around him.

You killed what I loved most in this world. Now it is your turn to suffer the same fate.

Christ! They meant Isabel!

Marcus knew deep down in his bones that whoever penned the note was the mastermind behind the theft of the *Seashore with Fishermen* and Dante Black's murder. He also knew that the threat was directed at Isabel.

Icy fear twisted around his heart.

He rushed out of the building, hoping to catch a glimpse of the youth that had delivered the note. But Capel Court was empty save for a few businessmen coming and going.

He pulled out his pocket watch. Eleven forty-five. He had requested for Isabel to meet him at his office at noon to go to luncheon at the Ship and Turtle. Jenkins would have already summoned the carriage, and she would either be on her way or waiting for him in his office.

Sprinting down Threadneedle Street, he pushed his way past a group of businessmen and ignored their rude remarks and stares as he flew by. His heart hammered in his chest; beads of sweat popped on his brow beneath the sizzling summer heat. He reached his office building in record speed and entered the vestibule.

"Has my wife arrived?" he asked the startled doorman.

The man nodded. "The lady is waiting in your office, Mr. Hawskley."

Marcus took the stairs two at a time to the third floor and burst into his office.

"Hello, Marcus."

At the sound of a sultry female voice, he spun around.

His eyes widened in disbelief. "Simone? How did you get in here?"

Simone Winston smiled like a sly cat with a bowl of cream. "Why, Marcus. Did you forget giving me the key?"

He stared at her. She was dressed in a near transparent gown of red tissue with a bodice so low that the tips of her nipples peeped through with each breath she took. Her auburn hair was loose around her shoulders, her slanted eyes lined with black kohl, and her full lips heavily painted. She looked like a concubine, ready, willing, and able to fulfill a man's deepest, darkest fantasy.

A vivid memory of Isabel came to him. Isabel lying naked on the thick Aubusson carpet in his library. Her clear blue eyes compelling and eager for his touch. Her flawless skin, her hair as smooth as midnight, cascading over the curves of her breasts. She was refreshingly honest and innocent, without contrivance, and the complete opposite of the hedonistic woman before him.

He focused again on Simone. His lips twisted in distaste, and he wondered what he had ever seen in her practiced sexuality.

"I thought I made my intentions, or more specifically my lack of intentions, clear the last time we saw each other," he said. "But what I forgot, apparently, was to change the locks."

Her eyes narrowed, and she looked like she wanted to claw his face, but instead she said coyly, "Come now. You can't honestly tell me you are not happy to see me."

Yes, I can. The only woman I want to see is my wife. "I'm very busy today. If there is something you need, please contact my secretary."

He was desperate to locate Isabel to ensure her safety. The mysterious note burned in his pocket, and he needed time to think clearly as to who may have sent it and for what reasons. Simone's unexpected arrival and attempted seduction served only to fuel his anger and frustration.

Simone slithered forward and touched his sleeve. "I doubt very much your secretary could satisfy my needs." Placing her hands on his chest, she slipped them beneath his jacket. "I've been dreaming of you, Marcus. I see your naked body. The muscles on your chest and arms, your long, powerful legs . . . and your commanding cock." Her gaze dropped to his trousers.

He pushed her away. "Stop, Simone. Compose yourself and go home."

Undaunted, she reached up, and with a forefinger, tugged her bodice down. Two huge breasts popped free, her large areolas and their pebble-hard centers painted with rouge. Against the pale flesh of her breasts, her nipples looked like dark chocolate.

"Taste me," she panted. "The rouge is flavored to heighten your arousal." She played with her own nipple, then sucked her finger between blood-red lips. "Delicious."

Disgust roiled within him. "I'm a married man now, or did you forget?"

"Ha! That's precisely why I'm here and just in time from the look of you! Use me, Marcus. Let me be for you what that frigid virgin is not. Use my body to ease you."

He pressed his lips together in anger.

He wanted her gone. Now.

"You need to leave. My wife is expected here any minute."

Simone tossed her hair over her shoulder, her big breasts bobbing with the movement. "Good. Let her see what a lusty fucking looks like!" She threw her arms around his neck and rubbed her naked breasts against him.

He heard the door latch click. Pushing Simone roughly to the side, he looked past her.

What he saw made his heart stall.

Isabel stood frozen in the doorway, astonishment

touching her pale features. Wide blue eyes focused on Simone's bare breasts, then flew to his face.

His first thought was to swing her up in his arms and take her back to the town house, where he could lock her safely inside. His second was that he had an opportunity to protect her by ending whatever small, burgeoning affection she may have for him. It would be a deep cut, like that of a well-honed dagger, and there was the risk that she would be deeply hurt. But Paris would heal her wounds, even if he was left behind with the scars.

In that instant, he knew what he had to do.

Chapter 34

"You're early, Isabel," Marcus drawled.

Shock crossed Isabel's face. "My God, what is going on?"

"I would think it's quite obvious, my dear," he said.

He saw the precise moment that realization dawned on her face, and bitter despair touched her eyes. His firm resolve weakened and threatened to buckle.

No, he thought. *The blasted note was real. I must not capitulate lest she is harmed because of me.*

Simone must have sensed Marcus's change of mood and that he was not going to oust her. Making no effort to cover her exposed breasts, she turned squarely to face Isabel.

Isabel's eyes widened at the woman's rouged nipples.

It was more than Marcus could bear. "You should leave now, Simone."

Simone adjusted her gown and cast Marcus a seductive glance. "Until later, darling," she murmured. She made her way to the door and smirked as she passed Isabel. "I told you that you would not be able to hold his interest."

Isabel stiffened, as if stricken.

Seconds passed as Simone's heeled slippers echoed down the hall.

Isabel turned to leave, her hand reaching for the handle of the door, when Marcus spoke up.

"Wait, Isabel. I apologize for what you witnessed. I had left a note for you to meet me here to take you to luncheon at the Ship and Turtle. Simone's visit was unexpected." Somehow it was important to him that she knew he did not seek Simone out.

Isabel swung around to face him, her eyes blazing. "I'm not a fool, Marcus. The woman was half-naked."

His eyes probed hers, and he braced himself for what he was about to do. "Yes, she was. You and I have been honest with each other, and I believe we should continue on that path. I had mistakenly thought that I had outgrown my roguish behavior, but I'd be lying if I said Simone Winston did not tempt me. I find marriage does not suit me, and as I tried to tell you last night before we made love, I believe it best if you leave immediately for Paris."

From the slight gaping of her mouth, he knew his words wounded her, but she fought valiantly to hide her misery from him.

She has more courage than most men I know.

The urge to fall to his knees and confess the truth was overwhelming. But he must carry on the charade. He had not planned Simone Winston's untimely seduction, but neither had he anticipated a direct threat to Isabel's life.

He needed her safe, far away from him, away from the madman who would kill what he coveted.

She tossed her head, anger and pride coming to her defense. "I told you last night that nothing has to change between us. I knew you had a relationship with Simone Winston before I intruded into your life. I always assumed you would resume those relations after I left for Paris."

"Good. Then we are in agreement?"

A brief stab of hurt flared in her eyes. "As much as I agree with you, I cannot, however, leave immediately as we are invited to Leticia Benning's birthday ball the first weekend in July, and I promised both Charlotte and Mr. Benning that we would attend together. I shall depart as soon as possible afterward. Is that suitable?"

It wasn't, but he was left with no choice. If he appeared too pushy, too anxious, she would sense something was wrong and—knowing her daring nature—refuse to leave. He'd have to ensure her safety at all costs until then.

She stood rigid, staring at him, waiting for his response.

He cleared his throat before answering. "Of course," he said in a coolly impersonal tone, "soon after the ball is suitable."

Her eyes darkened with pain before she turned away. "As I no longer have an appetite for luncheon, I shall hail a hackney."

"No!"

She whirled around at the tone of his voice.

He struggled to compose himself lest he reveal his fear over her well-being. "My phaeton is outside. I shall escort you home."

"That's not necessary. A hackney cab will suit just fine."

"There are few cabs in this part of town, Isabel," he lied. "You will be hard pressed to find one."

When it appeared as if she would still protest, he said, "Surely you do not intend to walk miles in this heat just to avoid me?"

"Fine," she snapped. "I accept your escort." She stormed from his office.

He followed on her heels, her stiff little back marching down the hall.

Chapter 35

Marcus found Roman sipping a brandy and staring out the bay window of Brooks's. Roman looked up as he approached.

"You came," Roman said, cracking a smile.

Marcus pulled out a chair and sat. "I was tempted not to."

Roman nodded as if this made perfect sense. "I thought we could talk . . . as brothers."

Marcus's brows drew together. Their relationship had progressed over the past months, but it wasn't what he would consider *brotherly*. Marcus had been grateful when Roman had helped interrogate Dante Black even though their questioning had been cut short when Isabel had run into the criminal. And they had been civil, near amicable, at Marcus's wedding. But still, the past hovered over them like a dark shroud, dampening their trust for each other.

At Marcus's silence, Roman sighed.

Sitting before the bay window, in the unforgiving light of the afternoon, Roman appeared tired. His eyes were tight with strain, his normally immaculate attire wrinkled as if he had slept in his clothes.

"This is not easy for me, you know," Roman said.

"What do you want, Roman?"

"For us to move forward."

"Are you asking me to forget the past?"

"No, only for you to forgive *me*. I was too quick to judge you back then, and I failed you when you most needed me," Roman said.

Marcus was stunned. When he had received Roman's note asking him to meet at Brooks's, he had been wary. He had never expected this . . . an apology after so many years.

He felt a ripple of concern for Roman and was surprised not to feel the familiar bitterness he had harbored against his kin for so many years. His focus seemed to have shifted—his resentment and hostility subsided—after Isabel had entered his life. His thoughts turned more to her lately than to his past or his grudge against his family.

Marcus looked Roman in the eye. Leaning forward in his chair, in a controlled voice he said, "Bridget was not worth sacrificing our bond as brothers."

And just like that, it was over. The lingering animosity. The distrust. The glowering hatred.

Roman's face lit up, and he gestured to a passing servant. "Two brandies."

The glasses were delivered and the brothers drank together.

"You may have felt forced to leave the family home," Roman said, "but I am the one now tortured by Father on a daily basis."

Marcus found himself grinning. "He's still nagging you to marry?"

"He has actually started bragging about your successful match and brings up the beautiful Lady Isabel every chance he gets."

Marcus burst out laughing. "Ha! That's a change for the old man. You'd best give in and find a wife on your own before he thrusts one upon you."

"I'm considering it. Tell me, is Miss Benning taken?"

"Charlotte Benning? Isabel will be thrilled."

"And how is Isabel faring?"

At the mention of his wife, Marcus stiffened.

"Something's amiss? Tell me. Let me in," Roman urged.

Marcus hesitated as he debated telling Roman the truth. He had become accustomed to keeping his own secrets, solving his own problems, but this was entirely different. Isabel's life was at stake, and he knew deep in his bones that confiding in Roman was the right choice. Two heads were better than one, and surprisingly, he found himself trusting Roman.

"I received a note threatening Isabel's life," Marcus said.

Roman's mouth gaped. "What? From whom?"

"That bastard Gavinport, of course. Who else?"

"You still suspect him behind the art theft?"

"I do. He has gone even further by having Dante Black murdered and now threatening Isabel."

"I heard about Dante," Roman said. "But to threaten your wife?"

Marcus raised his glass and took a deep swallow. "I told Isabel to leave for Paris."

"Why Paris?"

"We had an agreement. Neither of us sought to marry. She seeks to go to Paris to live with her eccentric aunt and further her art studies. I led her to believe that I still lust for my former mistress, and I pushed her to leave sooner than planned."

Roman grimaced. "Surely you do not have to take such drastic measures as to fake affection for another woman and send Isabel away to another country. I see how you look at her, Marcus. A blind man can see. Forget your agreement. Keep her."

Marcus shook his head. "I can't. It's better this way. I

must protect her until I can confront Gavinport and deal with the bastard once and for all."

"Good. I'll help. Tell me when and where."

The words came easier now for Marcus. "According to Investigator Harrison, Gavinport's out of town attending a private art auction at an unknown location. He's to return for Leticia Benning's birthday ball this weekend. It is the soonest I can beat him into a bloody pulp."

"Surely you don't mean a public duel."

Marcus's mouth twisted wryly. "No. Gavinport does not deserve an honorable duel. The Bennings have vast gardens. I plan to get him outside alone."

Roman's eyes flashed like summer lightning. "Isabel is my sister-in-law, Marcus. Count on me to help."

Chapter 36

"Something's amiss," Charlotte said. "His behavior is odd."

Isabel looked up from the canvas before her. She was sketching the outline of Charlotte's face with charcoal, while her friend sat on a stool in the corner of her studio.

"What makes you say that?" Isabel asked. It had been a week since she had walked in on Marcus and Simone Winston, and she had confided only to Charlotte.

"Why would the man invite you to luncheon at the Ship and Turtle and then, at the same time, engage in a tryst with his former mistress?" Charlotte asked.

"Marcus said Simone Winston's visit was unexpected."

Charlotte slid to the edge of her stool. "It makes no sense. You said yourself that his note was affectionate, and that he was looking forward to meeting you."

Isabel gave an impatient shrug. "So? By his own admission his repressed roguish behavior has resurfaced. Whether the man sought out temptation or whether it came to him, it all leads to the same truth. The intimacy we shared meant much less to him than it did for me. I acted the complete fool."

Charlotte pushed stray wisps of hair from her face and

shook her head. "As I am not emotionally involved, I see things in a different light, and I am not convinced. How do you explain his uncharacteristic overprotectiveness lately?"

Isabel gripped the charcoal in her fist. Charlotte was right, Marcus *had* been acting strangely. She had avoided his presence, choosing instead to stay in her studio and work on her projects. It had not been difficult as he spent much of his days at the Stock Exchange or at his office on Threadneedle Street, and when he was at home, he was squirreled away in his library office.

There had been only a few occasions that Isabel had desired to venture out to go shopping or to visit Charlotte, but all had been met with strange reluctance. Isabel had been delighted to learn that Lady Victoria Ravenspear had given birth to a daughter. When Isabel had sought to buy baby gifts, Jenkins had advised that he was under strict orders to have two footmen accompany her. The footmen were unlike any her father had employed in his household. Both men were over six feet in height, heavily muscled, and resembled looming Moors.

Isabel chewed her lower lip. "Marcus's dictates have been ridiculous of late. Perhaps you're right and something is amiss. His affection for Simone Winston would explain why marriage does not suit him, even why he would want me to leave for Paris, but it does not explain his new henchmen."

Charlotte's eyes lit up. "What if he had contact with the criminal that had threatened your life? That would more likely explain the new bodyguards, his concern for your safety, and also why he claims to want you to leave for Paris."

The charcoal fell from Isabel's fingers and skidded across the hardwood floor. She turned to the window, startled by the thoughts that flashed through her mind.

Could Charlotte be right? Dare she hope that something else was behind Marcus's swift change in behavior? Why would he be overly concerned for her safety if he wanted her gone so badly?

Sensing she had found a nerve, Charlotte pressed further. "Ask yourself this: How could he tire of marriage so swiftly when you had only been together for two weeks?"

"Yes. How could he?" Isabel said numbly, her thoughts whirling as she gazed outside.

Charlotte stood. "He has feelings for you, Isabel. I saw the way he looked at you at your wedding. I saw because it is the way I yearn for a man to look at me. Such affection is what my mother has unsuccessfully searched for and still has not found after four husbands, my current stepfather being no exception."

Isabel's eyes snapped to Charlotte's face. "There's only one way to find out if what you suspect is true. I must confront Marcus. If his odd behavior is because he had a run-in with the criminal or with Lord Gavinport, then he owes me the truth."

Charlotte walked around the easel to view Isabel's work. "Marcus is not the only one acting oddly."

"What do you mean?"

"Since when do you draw portraits? I thought you preferred landscapes."

Isabel sighed. "I used to, but after Marcus gave me my own studio, I felt a creative urge to paint a portrait." It remained unspoken that she had desired to paint *his* portrait.

"Which leads me to another point," Charlotte said. "Why would a man who wants you imminently gone to a foreign country give you an art studio in his own house?" She waved to the partially unpacked trunks of art supplies in the corner. "And why in the world would he arrange to have your supplies delivered here?"

Why indeed? Isabel mused. *What was going on?*

To radically alter his behavior, something had occurred in between the time Marcus had left her bed that fateful morning and when she had met him at his office.

Isabel straightened, her ire rising. He was keeping a secret, a critical piece of information from her. They were supposed to be partners, and he was purposely pushing her away, perhaps even using Simone Winston's unexpected visit as a weapon to do so.

Her breath grew ragged, and she fought against the urge to behave rashly. There had been something amiss when Marcus had looked at Simone. Isabel had been too shocked to analyze his response, but thinking back, he had barely spoken to his former mistress, and when he had glanced at Simone, his eyes had been cold, hard . . . aloof.

"From your expression, I take it you are casting off your self-pity and despair and coming to your senses," Charlotte said.

Isabel stooped down and picked up the piece of charcoal. Tossing it in the air, she caught it in a tight fist. "I believe it's time for a confrontation with my *husband*."

Charlotte smiled. "For once I'm glad to see that stubborn glint in your eye. I almost feel bad for Mr. Hawksley. *Almost*."

Chapter 37

Marching across the hall, Isabel barged into Marcus's library office without knocking. He was seated behind his oversized desk, piles of papers on both sides of him. Startled, his head jerked toward the door. When he spotted her, he frowned, his brooding eyes level under drawn brows.

She stalked forward, threw the lump of charcoal at his chest, and hissed, "You're a bloody liar, Marcus Hawksley!"

The coal hit his chest dead center and clattered across the surface of his desk. His eyes widened, and he looked down at a prominent, black smudge across his starched white shirtfront.

He met her glare. "I take it there's a logical explanation for this outburst."

She stomped her foot. "Logical? You want logic when you tire of marriage after two weeks?"

He leaned back in his chair. "Ah, is this about my dissatisfaction with my marital state?"

"No, it's about your swift change in behavior, or more simply put, it's about your deception."

"My deception?"

Walking close, she rested both palms on the surface of

his desk and leaned forward. "You're keeping something from me, and I want to know what it is."

"I heard the front door close minutes ago, and I assume Charlotte Benning has left. Whatever conspiracy you two have conjured up is false, I assure you."

His arrogant tone infuriated her. She came around and sat on the edge of his desk, glaring down at him. "I insist upon the truth. I am not leaving until you confess."

His lips twitched as his gaze dropped from her eyes to her breasts and down to her derriere perched mere inches from his hand. "Do you recall the last time we were in this room together?" he asked, his voice low and smooth.

She blinked at the change in topic. She met his eyes, and the invitation in the smoldering depths was as unmistakable as it was arousing. The pit of her stomach churned, and a now familiar shiver of awareness ran down her spine. Her gaze lowered, and her cheeks grew warm.

Did she remember?

Oh, yes, she did. Only *she* had been seated in his chair, and he had skillfully touched her body and had awakened her womanly passion. The reality of his lovemaking had far surpassed her girlish fantasies.

She raised her chin a notch. "Do not think to distract me from the topic at hand."

He cocked his head to the side. Seconds passed as he seemed to consider her request. "You're right, Isabel. It is unfair of me, and you have proven yourself to be honest and courageous." He opened a slim desk drawer, pulled out a piece of paper, and handed it to her. "I received this on the Exchange floor less than an hour before you came to my office the day we were to go to luncheon."

She took the paper, unfolded it and read it to herself.

You killed what I loved most in this world. Now it is your turn to suffer the same fate.

Lowering the paper to look at him, her brow furrowed. "I don't understand. Who sent you this?"

"It was delivered anonymously by private messenger. I can only assume it was sent by the mastermind who sought to frame me for the art theft, the same man who hired Dante Black and the criminal who threatened you."

She stood and dropped the paper on his desk. "You believe the note refers to me? That I am what you love most in this world and therefore what will be taken from you?" she asked incredulously.

His expression turned grim. "It matters not what I love most in this world. All that matters is what the author of the note believes."

She flinched at the cold honesty behind his statement. *Fool! You know he does not love you!*

Then why was she so devastated to hear it from his lips in such a chilly, efficient manner? His admission affected her more than it should have. Hiding her hurt, she looked him in the eye. "Is the note the reason why your two henchmen have been accompanying me whenever I leave this house?"

"I do not think the threat should be taken lightly. Until you are safely in Paris, I believe the utmost precautions should be taken."

"The note says you killed something he loved most in this world. Whatever did you do to Lord Gavinport?"

Marcus stood, and ran an impatient hand through his hair. "That's just it. I have done nothing to Gavinport."

"Are you certain? The night of Dante Black's death, at the Carrington ball, Lord Gavinport had mentioned a painting he desired."

Marcus nodded. "The George Stubbs painting, *A Grey Horse*, which is currently in my collection. I acquired it from a banker's heir. I never took it from Gavinport. He wasn't even present at the auction. It makes no sense for him to believe I had stolen it from him."

"It is well known that Lord Gavinport is fanatical when it comes to his art collection," she said. "Perhaps he is mentally unbalanced and believes the loss of one painting would make his entire collection, which he loves most in the world, inferior."

"Perhaps," Marcus said, "but we also must consider the possibility that he learned we had broken into his town house and discovered Dante Black's body."

"The news of Dante's murder was in the papers," she pointed out.

"I know. Bow Street does not suspect a connection between Gavinport and Dante Black. But if Gavinport knows we invaded his property, then he must also be aware that we believe there is a connection between the two of them. He may have penned the note to divert us."

"Then we must not allow it to do so," she said matter-of-factly.

Moving swiftly, he cupped her chin and searched her up-turned face. "Not *us*, Isabel. You are to leave for Paris soon after Leticia Benning's birthday ball, remember?"

Startled by his touch, she stepped back and stiffened with challenge. "I am not easily intimidated, Marcus. I want to see this to the end."

"*I* shall confront Gavinport and see it to the end. Afterward, I will gladly send word to you in Paris of the outcome."

"You're being ridiculous," she snapped. "An anonymous note is a weak excuse to change our plans."

"No, I'm not the ridiculous one. I told you before that I long for my days as a bachelor. Even though our marriage cannot easily be annulled or dissolved, I find myself eager to resume my former lifestyle."

She stiffened as though he had struck her. "You mean eager for Simone Winston's attentions." She bit her tongue the moment the bitter words spewed from her mouth, not wanting him to see how much his callous attitude had wounded her.

"I will not dissuade you of your assumptions," he said curtly.

Rage bubbled inside her like a volcano on the verge of erupting. Glowering at him, she set her chin in a stubborn line. "Fine. As Leticia Benning's birthday ball is this weekend, I shall start packing."

She spun on her heel and slammed the door on her way out.

Marcus fell into his chair and exhaled. Her subtle perfume of lilacs lingered in the air. He closed his eyes, recalling her face breathless with fury and her vivid blue eyes blazing with anger. Her nearness had aroused him; her anger had heated his blood.

The volatile combination put his iron will at risk.

For no matter how much she resented him, the memory of their lovemaking in this room remained pure and clear in his mind.

He should not have been surprised by her behavior. Isabel had been intelligent enough to suspect he was hiding something whereas most women would never have picked up on the signs. He had willingly shown her the note, not because he wanted to confide in her, but because he thought that if she knew the truth, she would take precautions for her safety. He should have guessed that Isabel would not back down or be intimidated, but rather, rise to the challenge and thumb her nose at the threat.

She was the most magnificent woman he had ever met.

She believed he harbored feelings for Simone, when it took every ounce of his willpower not to throw Isabel on his desk, pluck the pins from her glorious hair, and kiss her senseless.

It was his cross to bear, his punishment, that Isabel was so close, yet so unattainable. He had seen her disappointment, her hurt, and he had wanted nothing more than to hold her in his arms and whisper erotic words in her ear. If he was truthful with himself, he had no desire to send her away, but would rather keep her with him for the planned six months. Maybe then this hunger and fascination for her would pass.

But it was not to be. For how would he live with himself if she were harmed? If she was injured because of *him*, it would be so much worse than Bridget's ghastly fate.

Bridget had killed herself. But if Isabel was murdered . . .

He would never recover. His soul, black as it was, would be lost. If Isabel leaving for Paris was the price to pay for her safety, then he would force the issue.

The note was real, the threat imminent. He would not rest until he had ruthlessly pursued the man who had tried to frame him and had dared threaten Isabel. It mattered naught that the authorities did not suspect him for the theft of the painting. The mastermind had to be punished, and it had to be by his hand.

He had searched Gavinport's private gallery and his reclusive town house property, but to no avail. His initial plan to search for the painting by clandestine methods was taking too long. Isabel's safety was now in jeopardy, time was of the essence, and Marcus's anger had become a scalding fury. He would confront Lord Gavinport face-to-face and learn the truth by whatever means necessary. And the upcoming Bennings' ball offered the perfect opportunity.

Chapter 38

"May I help you?"

Isabel glanced sideways to see Marcus's outstretched hand. They were outside the town house, on their way to Leticia Benning's birthday ball, and Marcus stood ready to assist her into the carriage. If not for her snug bodice, voluminous skirts, and the delicate train of her gown, she would have snubbed him and climbed into the carriage herself.

Do not give him the satisfaction!

She lifted her chin and placed her gloved hand in his.

The moment they touched, a spark of excitement passed between them. The arrogant devil sensed it, too, for the corner of his mouth pulled into a slight smile as he took the bench across from her.

She lifted the tasseled shade, stared out the window, and tried to shut out any awareness of him. Ever since their confrontation days ago, she had avoided him like the plague. Her feelings were too fragile, too confused to tolerate being in close proximity to him. For despite his change in behavior and his desire to send her packing, she was by no means blind to his attraction.

"You look lovely this evening, Isabel. Your emerald

gown was an excellent choice. The color suits your fair complexion and dark hair."

She turned to face him, and the smoldering flame she saw in his eyes startled her.

"There's no need for false flattery," she said, her voice sounding harsh to her own ears. "Jenkins has already inquired into passage on ships to France. I'm certain Auntie Lil will be thrilled, and—knowing her—she will immediately arrange for art lessons with a renowned French master."

"I've always believed you have promising talent, and I would be happy to pay for your lessons. Please have your aunt send me the bills."

She shifted in her seat, uncomfortable with his praise and kindness. He was much easier to dislike when he insisted upon his dissatisfaction with their marital state than when flattery and generosity spilled from his mouth. Tonight, he seemed like his old self . . . the Marcus she had come to admire, the man to whom she had willingly given her innocence.

Of course he's being kind, he knows I'm leaving!

The carriage began to move through the city's cobbled streets. His knee brushed her skirts, and she became increasingly aware of him. She could smell the faint scent of his shaving soap—sandalwood and cloves—and she studied him beneath lowered lashes.

He looked startlingly handsome in formal evening attire. His white shirt contrasted with his bronzed face and throat. Dark breeches clad his long legs, and his tailored jacket accentuated his muscular form. Must he be the most virile and arresting man she had ever known?

They finally arrived at the Bennings' mansion in Grosvenor Square. Following the crowd inside, Isabel and Marcus glimpsed the two gargantuan Chinese statues just outside the entrance to the ballroom.

"I see Ming and Chang are still in the house," Marcus drawled.

Isabel shrugged. "Charlotte hates them, but Mr. Benning insists Chinese décor is all the rage and that the two emperors bring good luck."

One corner of Marcus's mouth twitched upward. "Some foolish people believe whatever their decorators tell them."

Isabel felt a ripple of mirth, but struggled to mask her amusement. She refused to fall prey to his charm tonight.

They reached the top of the stairs, waiting for their turn to enter the grand ballroom. She leaned toward him and whispered, "We must act as if we are enjoying ourselves for Charlotte's sake. She is devastated that I am leaving so soon."

"I do not have to fake my enjoyment. I've always found your company fascinating."

She whirled to face him a second before a liveried footman formally announced them.

"Mr. and Mrs. Marcus Hawksley."

"Smile, Isabel," Marcus said, his hand resting on the small of her back. "You look as if you just sucked on a lemon."

You rogue! As if your flattering words would not confuse me.

They floated through the crowd together, her gloved hand resting on his sleeve, a smile plastered on her face.

The Benning family stood to the side, greeting their guests. For once, Leticia Benning's peacock gown and towering hairstyle—complete with bobbing peacock feathers—outdid her husband's attire. Harold Benning's pale blue eyes were glassy, and he held a near-empty glass of burgundy. He blotted at beads of perspiration on his forehead with an embroidered scrap of lace that matched the drooping lace at his shirt cuffs.

Charlotte stood beside her mother and stepfather and

was dressed in an elegant sky blue gown, which accented her eyes. Her fair hair was curled around her delicate face in a soft, flattering arrangement. Although her family loved attention and excess, Charlotte clearly preferred a less brazen style.

Marcus and Isabel came forward. Isabel hugged Leticia Benning and wished her a happy birthday. Marcus bowed and gallantly kissed the older woman's hand.

"Why, Marcus," Leticia drawled, "I'm so happy you came to my party."

"I wouldn't miss your birthday, Mrs. Benning."

"It's Leticia for you, darling. There is no reason for formality between us."

Isabel did not miss the lusty look Leticia gave Marcus. Since walking into the ballroom, she was uncomfortably aware of the many feminine stares he received. As a bachelor with a roguish reputation, Marcus had been eyed as a sensually dangerous man. It seemed his marital status to the daughter of an earl had not deterred the lascivious women of the ton, but had only served to make him more attractive in their eyes. The thought occurred to her that he would be free to seek out whichever lady he chose after she was gone.

She mentally shook herself, angry at her wayward thoughts. Paris was what she had dreamt of for years. Marcus's insistence that she leave, no matter the reason, served her plans perfectly.

Harold Benning, seemingly oblivious to his wife's wanton looks, slapped Marcus on the back in greeting. "Good to see you, Hawksley. I take it marriage suits you?"

Marcus grinned. "Isabel is all a man could wish for in a wife."

Benning laughed, swaying on his buckled pumps, and Isabel wondered how long the intoxicated dandy would last on his feet.

Charlotte took advantage of her parents' distraction and drew Isabel aside. They wandered through the crowd, smiling and nodding at acquaintances, until Charlotte pulled Isabel behind a potted bamboo plant.

"Are you certain Marcus still wants you to leave?" Charlotte whispered.

"Yes. He has not said otherwise, and I think it is for the best."

"I still do not believe he harbors any feelings for Simone Winston. Mother's friends have said the woman is now involved with Lord Tenning."

Isabel's heart skipped a beat as an unbidden thrill coursed through her. If what Charlotte said was true—and Isabel had no reason to doubt her sources—then Marcus was not interested in Simone Winston. Marcus was too possessive to tolerate his mistress taking another lover.

A sudden doubt nagged her. "Perhaps there is another woman Marcus is interested in," Isabel said.

"I have heard nothing to suggest so."

"Marcus is a private man, Charlotte. How would your mother or her friends learn of it?"

"Marcus may not whisper a word, but the women always do," Charlotte said. "I spoke with Mother, and Marcus has not been seen with or approached any other female since your betrothal."

If it was not another woman, then was the blasted note the sole reason Marcus wanted her off to Paris? Could it be that the stubborn man was trying to protect her, rather than revert to his bachelorhood?

Charlotte reached out to squeeze her hand. "Mother has agreed to send me to Paris when the Season is over. She's aware that I have had interested suitors each year—this Season it is the assertive Mr. Peter Andrews—but all have failed to stir my heart. Thankfully, Mother will not force me to marry without love. I believe she does not want me to end up like her, and since there are no prospects for a love match in England, she hopes to find me one in France. She also wants to find herself a Parisian lover. She is quite certain my stepfather is having an affair, and she refuses to be outdone."

"Are all men so hedonistic? I'm sorry for your mother, but I am relieved you will be visiting me in Paris. We will have such fun." Isabel's voice sounded dull to her own ears.

The dining room opened, and Marcus appeared by her side to escort her inside. As she sat next to him, she was keenly aware of the warmth emanating from his body.

Dozens of footmen brought forth savory dishes certain to appeal to every discernable palate. Copying the Regent's own French chef, an elaborate sugar sculpture of a Chinese maiden served as a stunning centerpiece. The Bennings had clearly spared no expense tonight. Yet Isabel had no appetite for the sumptuous food; rather, the man beside her captivated her attention.

Marcus was maddeningly attentive, quick to wave to a footman to refill her wineglass as soon as she took the last sip. He smiled, laughed, and made sure to include her in whatever conversation he was having with the guests around him. Confusion flooded through her, and she wildly wondered at his game.

Biting her lip, her gaze traveled down the table to search for Charlotte.

She spotted her friend seated beside Marcus's brother, Roman. To Isabel's surprise, the couple were amicably conversing. She watched as Roman laughed heartily, leaned to the side, and brushed Charlotte's sleeve with his arm. Charlotte in turn giggled and gazed up at him adoringly.

Isabel's eyes widened at the exchange.

"You see it, too," Marcus whispered in her ear.

A shiver passed down Isabel's spine as his lips came close. "Although I had tried to introduce them before at our wedding breakfast, I never really thought they would be so . . . agreeable."

"Attraction between a man and a woman cannot be predicted. It is animalistic in nature and does not follow the rules of logic."

She raised her gaze to his. His eyes were filled with a curious deep longing. Her heart lurched, enthralled by what she saw.

He's right. Logic has nothing to do with it!

"What shall we do?" She referred to Charlotte and Roman, but as the words left her lips, she realized they could just as easily refer to their own relationship.

He did not miss her meaning. "When the attraction is that strong, there is little the couple can do to refrain."

"Then they must exercise all caution. Especially if one of them is irrational."

His mouth twitched with amusement. "I take it you mean the woman, since the female of the species is known for thinking with her heart instead of her brain."

In a flash, she stabbed his hand with her fork, then returned it to her plate.

He stiffened, no one around them the wiser, and grinned. "Animalistic, indeed!"

A loud laugh farther down the table diverted their attention to where Lord Frederick Gavinport sat next to his beautiful young wife, Olivia.

Gavinport was engaged in a heated discussion with Horatio Ponsby, a decorated Royal Naval Captain, seated directly across from him. Olivia sat unmoving, her face devoid of animation, looking exceedingly bored. Even seated, she was a full six inches taller than her elder husband.

Marcus's eyes narrowed, and his expression hardened. Hatred emanated from him in waves, and he looked like a man who would call out across the table and challenge his nemesis to a duel.

Alarm erupted within her. "Whatever are you planning?"

His hard stare never left Gavinport's face. "It no longer concerns you, Isabel."

Gone was the flirtatious, attentive husband of the evening. In his place returned the coldhearted man who wanted no part of her or their marriage.

A determined avenger.

"Please do not do anything tonight, Marcus. Not here," she implored.

"Don't fret, Isabel. I promise not to cause a scene."

Chapter 39

The rest of the meal progressed painfully slowly. When the last course was consumed, Isabel rose with relief and left the dining room without a word to Marcus.

The tension had taken its toll, and her temples began to throb. Fearing the beginnings of a headache, she sought the solace of the cool evening air. She headed for the nearest open French doors and escaped the crush of heavily perfumed bodies.

The terrace was blessedly empty. She leaned on the railing as a refreshing breeze soothed her heated skin. Muted strains from the orchestra spilled through the doors. A full silver moon hung low in the sky, a giant gleaming orb. Glancing below at the meticulously manicured gardens and maze, she could see the blazing torches from the Chinese pagoda, and the distant iron-and-glass horticultural conservatory.

Seeking further escape, she went down the stairs and stepped into the gardens. The sound of running water drew her, and she strolled toward a pond filled with tiny, colorful fish. Several minutes passed as she watched exotic blue, yellow, and orange fish dart beneath the smooth rocks that lined the bottom of the pond. Only after the threatening knot in her temples eased did she turn to go back inside.

The sounds of voices made her stop midstride.

The last thing she wanted was to come face-to-face with a pair of clandestine lovers. They would undoubtedly enter the maze for privacy. Skirting the maze, she followed a stone path that wound through the rest of the gardens. When the couple was well hidden in the shrubbery of the maze, she could backtrack and return to the ballroom.

She came to a bench sheltered behind an ancient oak and sat. The soles of her satin slippers were not made for extensive walking outdoors, and the stones bit into her now tender feet. Taking off a slipper, she rubbed her arch.

Low voices came from the shadows. She raised her head, surprised that the pair had followed her down the stone path rather than enter the secluded maze. She put her slipper back on, stood, and looked beyond the oak tree.

The faint silhouettes of two figures appeared. Not a male and female, but two men.

"I expected my blunt, yer lordship. When ye didn't pay, I 'ad no choice but to track ye down 'ere."

At the sound of the distinctive, raspy voice and gutter accent, shivers of alarm raced down her spine.

It was the demon of her nightmares.

The killer. The man who had threatened her not once, but twice. First when she had come face-to-face with the skeleton-thin criminal at the moment Marcus and Roman were interrogating Dante, and then when he had stalked her outside the window of her studio and aimed a pistol at her head.

And he was here. In the Bennings' gardens.

She strained to make out the second man, but the towering trees blocked the moon's light. Pressing the front of her body flush against the thick trunk, she winced as the rough bark bit into the soft flesh above her bodice. She put the discomfort from her mind and listened to their conversation.

"How dare you confront me here, Robby Bones."

"If ye'd paid, I wouldn't 'ave 'ad to."

"You'll get your money when you finish the job."

"It'll cost ye, yer lordship. Ye still owe me fer dealin' with Dante."

"Do not speak to me with such insolence, Bones. I never wanted Dante killed. He's no use to me dead."

"I 'ad no choice. 'E refused to move the painting like ye wanted. 'E could've gone to the constable."

"Finish with Hawksley and they're be extra in it for you."

The criminal's name was Robby Bones. An apt name for his emaciated appearance. The second man gave the orders, most likely the mastermind that Marcus insisted existed. Her eyes strained to see who it was, but she could only make out shadows. She dare not venture closer for fear of discovery.

One thing was certain. Whoever "his lordship" was, he was not Lord Gavinport. This man was taller, not as lanky nor as thin as Bones, but larger nonetheless. Gavinport's distinctive short stature was not present.

The question was: Who was he?

Something about him was vaguely familiar, but she could not place it. She struggled with a nagging unease, and she knew deep in her gut that she had met his lordship before.

A squirrel jumped from a higher branch to one just above her head. The movement startled her, and she gasped.

"What was that?" Bones hissed.

"Go find out. I must return before I'm seen."

Mercy! Heavy footsteps came her way, and she darted from behind the oak to a dense hedge of bushes off the stone path. Crouching low, she wedged her body between the hedges. She was thankful she had chosen the emerald gown for it blended with the shrubbery and helped conceal her in the shadows.

Booted feet crunched on stone, coming closer.

Her heart pounded, and panic rioted within her. What had started out as a walk for solitude and respite had turned into a remarkably foolish decision. Her thoughts spun wildly, and she realized with dismay that no one knew of her whereabouts.

Marcus, I need you! her inner voice cried out.

The distinctive scrape of a knife leaving its scabbard rent the air.

"Come out. I won't 'arm ye," Bones rasped.

Sheer black fright swept through her. She knew with pulse-pounding certainty that if Robby Bones recognized her, he would kill her. If she stayed where she was, he would eventually stumble across her. But if she tried to run, dressed as she was with voluminous skirts and satin slippers, he would easily catch her. She wouldn't even make it far enough to scream for anyone to hear.

She scanned the area, frantic for an alternative. Lanterns from the horticultural conservatory bobbed in the distance. If she could get inside, lock herself in, maybe she could buy herself time.

She crawled from beneath the bushes, branches scraping her face and arms and bramble snagging her skirts. Sweat trickled between her breasts as she made her way toward the distinctive shape of the iron-and-glass conservatory.

The sounds of footsteps came closer. "Come out . . . come out wherever ye are," Bones taunted.

She was running out of time. She looked up, gauging the distance to the conservatory.

If she sprinted, she could make it . . .

Grasping her skirts in one hand, she leapt to her feet and dashed for the entrance.

Please God, let the door be unlocked!

Bones immediately spotted her. "Stop, bitch!" His boots crashed through the shrubbery in pursuit.

Isabel's blood pounded in her ears, and her breaths came in great gasps. Her chest felt as if it would burst in her tight bodice.

She reached the glass door and turned the handle.

Locked.

She pumped the handle furiously before giving up and scrambling around the side of the conservatory, overcome with panic. Out of time.

She thought of Dante Black.

Her throat would be slashed, her bloody body left behind for the gardener to stumble over.

Then she saw it. A sliver of moonlight reflected off a gardener's shovel, leaning against the glass structure. She picked up the shovel and raised it above her head. Her arms trembled from its weight, but the blood rushed to her limbs just as Robby Bones reached the front of the conservatory.

She turned the corner, swinging the iron shovel with all her might, and struck the side of his head with a deafening crack.

He screamed and fell to his knees, clutching his head.

She fled, running like a madwoman toward the stone path that led back to the ballroom.

Low tree branches and shrubs tore at her skirts and bare arms, but she did not slow. The foliage was dense; the moon shifted behind a cloud and failed to illuminate a clear path. She spotted the distant lights from the Chinese pagoda, and sprinted in their direction until she ran into a solid, impregnable wall.

She fell, landing on her backside with jarring force, the wind knocked from her chest.

"Isabel!"

Marcus fell to his knees beside her. "My God! Are you hurt?"

She rose on her arms, never more relieved to see anyone in her life.

He was not alone. Roman knelt beside them, his face etched with worry. "What happened?"

Marcus cradled her in his arms. She clutched his shirt-front, desperate to inhale his comforting scent.

He pulled back, his eyes missing no detail of her disheveled hair, the abrasions on her face, chest, and arms. He swore beneath his breath.

Large hands cupped her face, his gaze intense. "Tell me what happened."

She touched his hands, wanting him to embrace her once again. "The criminal . . . Robby Bones is his name . . . met with another man deep in the gardens. I went for a walk . . . must have wandered too far . . . I tried to hide but Bones saw me . . . I hit him in the head with a shovel and ran into you."

Marcus gently shook her. "Where? Where did you leave him?"

She shivered, unnerved by his intensity. "By the conservatory."

Marcus stood. "Stay with her, Roman," he demanded. He reached into his jacket and pulled out a pistol.

Her eyes widened. "Marcus, no!" she shouted, but he was already gone, running in the direction of the conservatory.

Struggling to rise, she looked to Roman. "It's not safe! Bones is a hardened criminal, the assassin who murdered Dante Black. He has a knife!" Fear for Marcus knotted inside her, and she fought to maintain her fragile control.

Roman's green gaze glittered in the moonlight as he helped her to her feet. "Don't worry. Marcus can take care of himself."

She clutched his arm. "Go after your brother, Roman. Please."

"Marcus would have my head if I left you. Besides, he is a crack shot, and Robby Bones is a wounded criminal, thanks to you. You are a courageous woman, Isabel. No wonder my brother is so enamored."

She ignored his remark. "Why were you with Marcus? Why was he armed?"

"Marcus had asked me to help him."

"Why? I thought you two had differences."

Roman smiled. "We have a past, but we have been working on making amends. Marcus planned on confronting Frederick Gavinport tonight in the gardens."

"Gavinport! But the man I saw tonight with Bones was definitely not Lord Gavinport."

Footsteps drew their attention. Marcus's familiar frame came into view.

Isabel flew to his side and clutched his sleeve. "Thank God!"

Marcus scowled and took her hand in his. "The bastard was standing, cradling his head, when I approached. You must have hit him hard," he said, eyeing Isabel. "He ran off when he spotted me. I chased him all the way to the end of the Bennings' property, to the side road, where he jumped into a waiting hack and disappeared." His grip on her fingers tightened. "Are you certain you are unhurt?"

"I'm shaken up, but fine."

His gaze raked her form. "Do you want to go back inside?"

She looked down at her torn jade dress and muddy hem, noting the scrapes on her chest and deeper cuts on her hands and arms. She became aware of the stinging as if seeing the injuries firsthand brought on the pain. Her once white satin slippers were ruined. Her elegant hairstyle had come loose, and her hair curled around her face in frizzy disarray from the July humidity.

"No," she whispered. "I cannot return to the ballroom looking as I do. It would ruin Leticia Benning's party to learn that a criminal had assaulted one of her guests. I have no desire to be gawked at either."

Roman spoke up. "I shall go inside and have Marcus's carriage brought around to the side road. You will have to wait in the gardens as it will take some time. Will you be all right?"

Marcus nodded. "We shall stay deep in the gardens. If by chance we are seen, no one will think twice about a newly married couple seeking privacy. How will you get home?"

"I can return to the party on foot and claim my own carriage," Roman said.

"Charlotte will inquire about my whereabouts," Isabel said. "You will have to tell her the truth. She will be alarmed, but please assure her that I am unharmed and that I shall speak with her tomorrow."

Roman's tense expression relaxed into a leisurely grin. "It shall be my pleasure to discreetly speak with Charlotte Benning."

A faint smile touched Isabel's lips. "Perhaps my friend has a reason to stay in England after all."

Chapter 40

Roman spotted Charlotte Benning speaking with a young man in the corner of the ballroom. Not for the first time, he wondered why she was a fourth-year debutante and had not yet married. It could not be for lack of suitors for she was a beautiful woman. Over dinner, he had discovered that she possessed a charming wit and intelligence as well. The combination was a pleasantly rare surprise.

He had always preferred brunettes, but Charlotte Benning's halo of golden curls and flawless complexion captivated his attention.

He knew the eager-looking buck by her side. Peter Andrews—the son and heir of a wealthy industrialist. Roman watched as Andrews smiled and boldly raised Charlotte's hand to his lips.

A ripple of annoyance passed through Roman, and he raised a finger to loosen his suddenly constricting silk cravat. He straightened, headed straight for the pair, and firmly tapped Andrews twice on the shoulder.

"Pardon my interruption, but I must have a word with Miss Benning," Roman said.

Charlotte raised startled blue eyes. "My lord. May I introduce—"

"Mr. Andrews and I are already acquainted," Roman said.

At his sharp tone, her lips parted in surprise. "Oh, I see."

"A word alone, please?"

She turned to Peter Andrews with an apologetic expression. The man eyed Roman warily before walking away.

Charlotte looked up at Roman, her brows furrowed in confusion. "What—"

"It's about Isabel," Roman said.

A shadow of alarm touched her heart-shaped face. "Isabel? Is she all right?"

"She is now, but I'd much rather speak in private."

"Yes, of course. Follow me."

She led him toward the dining room, and for a brief moment, he thought she was going inside, but then she turned a sharp left and proceeded down a long hallway. She came to the first door and stopped. Opening the door, she motioned for him to enter. He strode inside a well-appointed library.

She entered and shut the door behind her. "My stepfather's private library. He rarely uses it, and we will not be disturbed here. Now please tell me what is so urgent."

Her perfume wafted to him—a subtle scent of delicate roses—and he struggled with the urge to reach out and touch her, but time was ticking. Marcus and Isabel needed him. He breathed deeply and chose his words with care.

"Isabel was attacked in the gardens tonight by the criminal that had previously threatened her, the same man responsible for Dante Black's murder. She fought the blackguard off and is safe with Marcus in the gardens as we speak," he said.

Her jaw slackened in shock. "Dear Lord! I shall go to her at once."

He stepped close and shook his head. "No, you cannot. As I said, she is with Marcus and is fine."

"Fine!" she cried out, her disbelief resounding in her tone. "Your brother got her into this mess. I hardly think she is *fine*."

Clutching her skirts, she turned to leave.

Roman reached out to grasp her wrist.

She glared sideways at him. "What are you doing? Release me at once!"

"Only if you promise to be a good girl and stay at the ball and act as if nothing untoward has occurred. It would be best if you advise anyone that asks that Isabel had a headache and Marcus took her home early."

She tugged on her arm, her blue eyes spitting fire. "A *good girl*! How dare you, sir!"

He immediately realized he had made a grave mistake and instead of ensuring her cooperation, he had unwittingly angered her. As the heir to an earldom, he was accustomed to people unquestioningly following his orders, and the combination of the urgent situation and his attraction to the woman before him had made his task that much more difficult.

Frustration roiled inside him, and he blurted out the only thing that came to mind. "You must trust me."

"Trust you?" she asked incredulously. "I hardly know you, and you are asking me to ignore my best friend after she was nearly killed in my family's gardens. I must see her."

Acting on impulse, he pulled her into his arms and kissed her. She stiffened in shock and made a protesting mewling sound. Fists pounded on his chest, and she pushed back, freeing her mouth.

"Are you crazy?" she gasped.

He tightened his hold. "I assure you that Isabel is unharmed and safe. She asked me to find you and requested that you stay at the ball. Those are her wishes, not mine. She will see you first thing tomorrow."

He knew the moment his words pierced through her

frantic haze to rush to her friend's side. Her tense features slightly relaxed, her shoulders eased a fraction of an inch downward, and she stilled in his arms. Yet he sensed her remaining reluctance to obey.

She opened her mouth to protest, and he dipped his head, touching his mouth to hers. Moving his head back and forth, he brushed her lips with his. "I've wanted to taste you all through dinner," he murmured huskily. "And here . . . now . . . I finally have you alone. Do you feel the spark between us?"

Her eyes widened at his bold words, but she did not pull away.

This time, when he claimed her mouth, her lips parted on a sigh. He deepened the kiss, and slowly, ever so slowly, he felt a tiny fissure of excitement course through her stiff body. He was conscious of her fists unfurling and her palms sliding around his neck. Her full lips softened and her fingers delved in his hair.

She kissed him back, and he thrilled at the response.

His body's reaction was swift and fierce, and he felt an overwhelming need to pick her up and lay her on the nearby settee. But then the mantle clock reached midnight and chimed noisily, reverberating throughout the room. A rush of cold reason quenched his haze of lust like a bucket of ice water.

Marcus needed him.

This time he would not fail his brother.

Roman pulled back and gazed into her eyes. Confusion and passion had turned them a deeper shade of blue. Her full lower lip was glistening like a ripe strawberry, and he fought the maddening urge to suck it into his mouth.

"Trust me and stay at the ball," he said, his voice hoarse. Exhaling slowly, he lowered his arms, kissed her forehead, then turned and strode from the room.

Chapter 41

After Roman returned to the ballroom, Marcus took Isabel's arm and led her down the stone path, deeper into the gardens.

"It will be a while before Roman can meet us," Marcus said. "The conservatory offers privacy, and is a good place to rest. Will you feel comfortable there?"

She knew he was asking whether she would feel uneasy waiting in the conservatory after her confrontation with Robby Bones outside its glass doors.

She looked up into Marcus's strong, chiseled profile. With him by her side, she knew she would feel safe. "The conservatory would be fine, but it is locked."

He grinned mischievously. "Have you forgotten my talents, my dear?"

She laughed for the first time that evening. "Who would have thought? The son of an earl who can pick locks."

"One of many secrets I have managed to keep from my disapproving father."

They reached the horticultural conservatory. Lying at the foot of the door was the shovel she had used on Bones. Fresh blood stained the gardener's tool and what looked like a clump of stringy, black hair was caught on its sharp edge.

Isabel trembled as a fresh wave of fear impaled her.

If the shovel had not been there . . . if Bones had used his knife on her . . .

Kicking the shovel aside, Marcus reached into his jacket and pulled out his lock picks. He made quick work of the lock, pushed the glass door open, and ushered her inside.

Humid warmth enveloped her. The full moon cut a path of light through the glass walls. The space was crowded down its center with three long worktables, holding gardening tools, sacks of potting soil, and pots in every size imaginable. The scent of flowers, plants, and moist soil hung in the air like heady perfume.

She walked to a bench where a tray of small green clippings ready for planting had been placed, probably in a hurry by one of the gardeners. Pushing the tray to the side, she sat on the bench.

Marcus slipped his lock picks inside his jacket, then closed and secured the door. Walking to her side, he sat beside her. His hands enveloped hers.

"You're shaking, Isabel," he said.

"I'm sorry. It's just the thought of what that ghastly man could have done . . ."

"Shh." His expression darkened with an unreadable emotion. He stood and pulled her into his arms. "You're safe now. I swear to do everything in my power to keep you so from now on."

For many minutes he simply held her. His embrace offered comfort and solace, both of which she needed after her traumatic ordeal. She dropped her chin on his chest with a soft sigh. She listened to the strong beating of his heart and inhaled his clean and manly scent.

He kissed the top of her head, his lips lingering. She inhaled sharply, and raised her eyes to glimpse his face. His eyes, shining like black satin in the pale light of the moon, brimmed with unmistakable need.

Firm lips brushed hers. She hesitated, fighting her own battle of personal restraint. But before she could gather the strength to push him away, his arms tightened about her, and his mouth covered hers hungrily.

She stiffened. She had decided never to give herself completely to him again. She had gone down that path, no matter how passionate or physically satisfying it had been, and afterward he had told her that he wanted her off to Paris. But that thought barely crossed her mind before his tongue swept past the barrier of her teeth and stroked her own, sending liquid tremors down her limbs. She was astonished at the spark of excitement, and she knew she could not deny herself his touch tonight.

His kiss was raw and savage . . . an affirmation of life . . . and after her harrowing escape from certain death, a temptation that she could not resist.

Her arms wound around his neck, her fingers threading through his dark hair. He grunted when she tugged on his hair and pulled him closer. Silk sizzled against broadcloth where their bodies touched. His mouth turned savage, and she knew the frantic need that pulsed through her seized him as well.

"Oh, Marcus," she sighed against his lips.

His head lowered, and he nipped the pulsing hollow at her throat. Heat spiraled low in her belly, and she clutched his shoulders. His lips traveled above the low-cut bodice of her gown, and he tenderly kissed the abrasions on her sensitive skin. She arched her spine toward the silken heat of his mouth, feeling both cherished and desperately aroused at the same time. The combination was volatile and the perfect outlet following the aftermath of her near-death experience. The passion that threatened to consume her would temporarily blot out the tormenting image of Robby Bones from her mind.

Marcus's fingers splayed on her rib cage and his mouth hovered over her breast, his hot breath making her nipples ache.

"You'll drive me mad," she whispered.

He raised his head. A sliver of moonlight partly illuminated his expression. Fierce desire lit his glittering dark eyes.

Her heart pounded an erratic rhythm. He was so compelling, his magnetism so potent, that her breath caught.

"*Isabel*, it is you who has driven me to the edge of madness. You have robbed me of all reason."

A buried longing pierced her. *He desperately desires me. Perhaps he will come to want me to stay.*

He slowly reached behind her, his fingers deftly working the tiny row of buttons down her back.

"I have to see you by moonlight."

She did not consider arguing. The gown loosed, and he pushed the sleeves down, careful of the scrapes on her arms. He made quick work of her thin chemise all the while kissing her eyelids, her lips, her throat.

The gown and chemise bunched around her waist, baring her breasts to his heated gaze. He sucked the crown of a breast into his mouth, and she thought she would die from the pleasure. Her nipples hardened like diamonds, and liquid heat burst between her thighs. She clutched his shoulders, and then slipped her hands beneath his jacket, kneading the powerful muscles beneath, frantic to feel his naked skin against her sensitive breasts.

The humid air seemed to burst into flame, like a blazing furnace.

He suddenly swooped her into his arms and turned to one of the long worktables. With an outstretched hand, he pushed pots, flowers, and plants aside and set her on the edge of the table. A bag of soil fell to the floor and ripped open. A peat pot with colorful flowers rolled across the table, tottered on the edge, until it fell to the floor with a loud thud.

She cared naught and felt no shame, her need for this man was so great.

Lying back on the table, with her legs dangling off the edge, he came over her. He kissed her mouth and her breasts, and the bulge in his trousers pressed against the sensitive V between her legs.

His hand reached beneath her skirts, his palm sliding up her silk stocking. His fingers grazed the apex between her thighs and she cried out. He rolled down a stocking, and she kicked off her slippers to aid him. She arched as her need clawed at her, and sighed when he reached for and peeled her other stocking down her leg. The temperature and humidity in the room grew, and a bead of sweat glistened between her breasts.

He made quick work of her drawers and they, too, joined her stockings on the floor.

She felt an overwhelming need to touch him as he was touching her. Sitting up, she pushed his jacket off his shoulders and nearly dragged his shirt from his waistband. He, too, was overheated for the shirt felt damp beneath her hands. He helped her, almost popping his shirt buttons off in his haste to disrobe. In his urgency, he bumped against another pot, and it slid across the table, spilling potting soil as it went.

The sweat-slicked muscles of his chest gleamed in the moonlight. She touched him everywhere, her hands caressing his heated skin, her nails leaving marks in her urgency.

The bulge in his trousers seemed enormous, but instead of a virgin's fear, she felt a thrill that she could arouse this fascinating male to such an extent. She made to reach for the top button on his trousers when he stopped her.

Her eyes flew to his face. His look was so sensual, it took her breath away.

"Let me love you like I've craved," he said hoarsely.

He kissed her, pressing her back until she lay on the table.

She was aware of her bodice pushed to her waist, sprawled on the worktable, legs dangling. She should be mortified, yet all she could think of was her voracious need for this man.

He tugged the hem of her gown up until it bunched around her waist. She gasped in surprise when her naked buttocks came in contact with the wooden table.

His head lowered, and he blew his hot breath on her sensitive mons. Firm hands separated her thighs, and she experienced an instant's panic. Then all thought and reason dissolved as he made love to her with his mouth. He plundered, he sucked, he laved, and when his tongue stroked across her highly sensitive bud, she felt as if her body was on fire. It was sinful, erotic, lustful . . . and looking up at the stars through the glass roof, it was otherworldly.

She banged her elbow against a sack of soil when she gripped his sweat-glistened shoulders. As her pleasure built, she arched restlessly beneath him, reaching for the pinnacle, hurtling herself above and beyond, until she climaxed in a shuddering explosion.

Panting through slightly parted lips, she opened her eyelids a crack. Marcus loomed above her, his expression one of enthrallment and ferocious lust.

"You're beautiful in your passion," he said in a husky voice.

She reached for him. "Make love to me, Marcus."

He needed no further encouragement. Reaching down to free himself from his trousers, he cupped her buttocks and plunged inside her honeyed sheath.

She was slick with need, and her body encased him like

a wet glove. He stilled and groaned from the pure pleasure of it before he began to move. Squeezing her legs about him, she urged him to quicken his pace.

The table shook with each thrust within her welcoming body. More gardening tools and plants crashed to the floor. Sweat glistened on his chest. None of it mattered, but the man who made love to her. She felt her body build to another climax, and looking up at the fierce desire etched on his face, she knew she loved him.

"I love you," she whispered.

He thrust once more and they climaxed together.

He stayed within her as they both gasped for breath. Finally, he pulled back and adjusted his trousers. He reached for his jacket on the floor and pulled out a handkerchief. Wiping her thighs, he helped her sit up and straightened her gown.

"Are you all right?" he asked.

"Yes, just overly warm."

"I had not meant to be so rough."

He made no mention of her admission of love, and she wondered if he had heard her during their passionate lovemaking. A sense of despair swept over her.

What if he had heard her, but did not feel the same?

She looked up at him, and a flicker of emotion crossed his face before he hid it with a smile.

What was he feeling? Regret? Awkwardness?

"As much as I'd like to stay and hold you, we need to leave and head for the side road," Marcus said. "Roman should be waiting by the time we get there."

"Yes, of course." She made to smooth the wrinkles from her skirts, then laughed at the ridiculousness of the task.

"What is it?"

"My gown, my shoes, my hair . . . I don't think I've ever been in such dishabille."

He gave her a grin that sent her pulses racing. "You've never looked lovelier."

Her breath caught in her throat. Afraid to speak, lest she again declare her love for him, she turned sideways and glanced at the worktable. Pots and soil were scattered over its rough-hewn surface.

"The Bennings' gardner will surely complain tomorrow morning," she said.

"No doubt. But it's probably not the first time this conservatory was used for illicit purposes during one of their parties."

Isabel looked at him in surprise. "Do you really think so?"

"I've learned throughout the years that the members of the ton may require strict manners, but they also have the loosest morals."

She flinched. "I suppose that includes us."

He took her hand in his and reverently kissed her palm. His steady gaze searched her eyes. "No, Isabel. You are my wife. We made love, we did not have salacious relations. There is a difference."

Her heart pounded in her chest. *Tell me you love me, and I'll forget all about Paris.*

She was shocked at her own thoughts. When had she begun to care for him so much?

Uncomfortable with her feelings, she said, "Let us be on our way, Marcus." She made to pull away, but his grasp tightened.

"Isabel, I . . . I would very much like for you to stay in London . . . perhaps I was wrong to insist you leave for Paris so suddenly."

She froze. Despite her fear, she felt a hot and awful joy. Was he asking her to stay forever? Or until the six months they had initially agreed to?

She wanted to ask him to elaborate, but for the first time in her life, she was at a loss for words. Her own mind swirled with confusion. To stay with him forever meant abandoning her dreams of Paris. The thought did not scare her as it once had, but was she ready to do so without Marcus's love?

For he had not said he loved her.

She struggled to find her voice. "Marcus, I—"

"Hush," he said, placing a finger over her lips. "You have been through much tonight, and I surprised you. I want to give you time to think."

I would not need time if you told me you loved me!

She stayed silent as they left the conservatory and headed away from the mansion. The woods became thick, and several times Marcus had to hold back tree branches for her to pass. The moon did little to illuminate their way, and Isabel was glad Marcus seemed to know where they were headed.

After walking for fifteen minutes, exhaustion set in, and Isabel's feet began to throb. The stress of the evening had finally caught up to her. Her muscles protested from the strain of running from Robby Bones, and her back ached between her shoulder blades from lifting the heavy shovel to defend herself. Despite her determination to keep up with Marcus, she slowed her pace and rubbed her eyes.

"Isabel?" Marcus asked, his face etched with concern.

"I fear the evening has taken its toll."

Marcus swung her up in his arms. When she made to protest, he cut her off. "We're almost there. I don't want you to pass out."

"I told you many times before, I never faint."

He ignored her and continued onward. Despite her complaint, she was glad for the comfort of his solid chest and muscular arms. The heat from his body seeped into hers, and she rested her head against his shoulder.

Marcus's black-lacquered carriage came into view.

Roman stood beside the horses speaking with the driver. When he spotted Marcus carrying Isabel, he rushed over.

"How is Isabel?" Roman asked.

"She's exhausted," Marcus said.

Isabel scowled. "I'm fine, Roman. Marcus insisted on carrying me."

Roman grinned. "No doubt. Since I trust you are in good hands, I shall head back to the ball. I will stop by tomorrow morning to see you, Marcus." Roman turned to leave.

"Roman, wait," Marcus called out.

Roman stopped and looked back at his brother.

"Thank you," Marcus said.

Roman nodded, then disappeared into the woods.

The driver opened the door to the coach and Marcus placed Isabel on the seat. Moments later, the vehicle jolted forward, and then swayed on the bumpy side road.

Isabel sighed and rested her head on the padded leather bench. "I was pleasantly surprised to learn you and Roman were working together again."

"We were going to go after Gavinport tonight to obtain his confession, learn the location of the Gainsborough painting as well as the hiding place of his criminal lackey, Robby Bones. When Roman visits me tomorrow, we will finish what we had intended."

Isabel was roused from her exhaustion as if a jolt of lightning had struck her. She jerked forward. "But Lord Gavinport is innocent! I had meant to mention it to you after Roman told me what you two had planned tonight, but in my fear for your safety when you had pursued Robby Bones, I had forgotten."

"What are you talking about?"

"When I was in the gardens, I overheard Robby Bones speaking with someone he called his lordship. I don't know who Bones was talking to, but I *know* he was the mastermind and he *wasn't* Lord Gavinport."

Marcus's expression hardened. "Then we are back to the beginning. The only way to learn the truth is to find and interrogate Robby Bones."

Her eyes widened. "No! The man is a cold-blooded murderer, Marcus! He confessed to killing Dante Black."

A swift shadow of anger swept across his face. "It is of no consequence. It's time to end this once and for all."

Fear threaded in her belly for she knew Marcus was bent on seeking and destroying his enemy, no matter the cost.

Chapter 42

Early the next morning, Marcus hastily descended the stairs and headed straight for the kitchen. He found Mrs. McLaughlin and Kate sitting at the servants' table eating biscuits and sipping tea. They both rose, eyes wide in surprise, when he burst inside.

"Is something amiss, Mr. Hawksley?" Mrs. McLaughlin asked.

Marcus knew both women were clearly taken aback by the unusual appearance of the master of the house in the servants' domain.

"Please sit, Mrs. McLaughlin. Nothing is amiss. I was merely concerned that Mrs. Hawksley is not yet awake. Is she unwell?"

Kate spoke up. "She is not sick, Mr. Hawksley, but tired after last night. I thought it wise if I did not rouse her."

Marcus nodded. He knew Kate as well as Mrs. McLaughlin wanted to know why the mistress of the house arrived home from last night's ball looking a fright, but both servants held their tongues. He suspected they would question Isabel when she woke.

He departed and sought the solace of his library. He attempted to work and picked up *The Times* which Jenkins had placed on his desk, but his eyes refused to study the fine lines of stock figures listed in the morning's newspaper. His mind kept returning to Isabel and the prior night.

When Isabel had run into him in the gardens with terror, stark and vivid, glittering in her eyes, he had experienced a riveting fear. If not for her quick thinking and her guts in striking Bones with the shovel, she would have been killed. The panic and ensuing rage that had rushed through him was shocking. Blood lust had seized control of his brain, and he had fervently anticipated tearing Robby Bones apart limb by limb.

Afterward—when he was finally alone with Isabel in the conservatory—he had fallen upon her like a man starved for her flesh. Her passionate response, heightened by her sense of survival, had thrilled him. Then, with her body writhing beneath his on the verge of a fiery climax, she had cried out that she loved him. His heart had lurched at her admission, and unbelievably his desire mounted higher, like the hottest fire, clouding his brain, and he exploded within her. The thought of withdrawing from her body, as he had the first time they made love, never entered his mind.

Dear Lord, she had said she loved him. It had been torture to pretend he hadn't heard her. The sudden and extreme changes in his emotions made him wonder if he loved her, but his brain rebelled against his heart.

Bloody hell, he could not love her! It was obsession, not love, he rationalized. She was a beautiful female who responded to his touch like hay to fire. She was a passionate challenge, hard for a flesh-and-blood man to resist. A sensual glance from her eyes could make his body temperature soar and his blood surge through his veins. He had wanted to keep her with him, if only to satisfy this voracious need, and in a selfish moment of weakness after their lovemaking, he had asked her to stay in London. He had promised to do everything in his power to keep her safe, and he had felt confident in his ability last night.

He had been certain that with Roman's aid he could obtain Gavinport's confession, find the painting, and learn the location of Robby Bones. With Bones and Gavinport either incarcerated or dead by his own hand, he thought to end it once and for all. There would no longer be a threat to Isabel's life, and she could remain in London as originally planned. Surely this madness that robbed him of reason where she was concerned would be sated in six months' time.

And then she had told him Gavinport was not the villain, and Marcus's plans came crashing down around him.

He cursed beneath his breath. The threat to her life, that damnable note, came back to him in a rush of anger and helpless frustration.

A soft knock on the door disturbed his thoughts.

"Enter," he said.

The door opened and Isabel came into the room. She looked lovely and very young in a pale yellow dress with modest neckline. Her thick dark hair was tied behind her back with a matching ribbon.

Clear blue eyes ringed with thick black lashes regarded him. "Kate told me you had asked for me."

He rose and walked behind his desk to her side. "I was concerned. How do you feel?"

She smiled up at him, and his heart squeezed uncomfortably. "I feel tired."

He reached out to trace the scrapes above her bodice. "Are you in pain?"

"No," she sighed.

Taking her arm, he led her to an armchair by the fireplace and took a seat across from her. "Isabel, I was thinking about what you told me in the coach on the ride home last night."

"About Gavinport not being the culprit we had suspected?"

"Yes. When we had discovered Dante Black's body in Lord Gavinport's town house, I had been wholly convinced he was the mastermind. But if Gavinport is not involved, then it must have been a coincidence that Dante Black was killed in his town house."

Isabel stared at him, baffled. "What do you mean a coincidence?"

"We know two things: that Gavinport had utilized Dante Black's services in the past, and that Gavinport is a great collector of Thomas Gainsborough's works. What if Dante knew Gavinport owned the town house on Lombard Street, and Dante truly was hiding out there without Gavinport's knowledge?"

"Is that likely?"

"I did not think so at first," he said. "There was no evidence of forced entry. The lock on the front door was not tampered with, and when I returned that night, I checked all the windows. They were secure. However, Dante could have had a key. Lady Ravenspear said Gavinport may have stored art there. If Dante had sold Gavinport anything after his marriage to Olivia and after he owned the town house, Dante would have been given a key to deliver the merchandise."

"But if this theory is true, then why was Dante murdered there?" she asked.

"Robby Bones could have followed Dante, learned where he was hiding, and then killed him," Marcus said.

She shivered. "I still don't understand the senselessness of Dante's murder."

"Maybe Dante outlived his usefulness after the Gainsborough painting was stolen or after he unsuccessfully accused me of the larceny. Or perhaps Dante refused to carry out a new order and threatened to expose the truth," Marcus said.

"Yes, I remember now," Isabel said. "When I overheard them, his lordship had said he never wanted Dante killed, but Robby Bones protested that Dante refused to cooperate by moving the Gainsborough painting. Bones was convinced Dante planned to go to the constable so he murdered him."

A thought struck her, and she sat forward in her chair. "Perhaps Robby Bones was smart enough to know that we would be sidetracked into believing Lord Gavinport was involved if Dante's body was discovered on Gavinport's property."

"Either way, things have changed," Marcus said. "There has to be another involved, someone in the *beau monde* with money and motive. A rancid street criminal like Robby Bones could not plot and carry out such involved crimes on his own."

"What do we do now?" she asked.

Marcus glanced at the mantel clock. "I expect Roman any minute. Now that we know Robby Bones's name, we can track him down. With enough coercion or money, we can learn the identity of his employer."

Isabel rose. "I need to eat something so I can be ready."

Marcus stood and took her arm. "Wait, Isabel. I realize I asked you to stay last night after we made love, but that was before I had learned what you discovered."

She stiffened beneath his hand. "What do you mean?"

"You should not cancel your travel plans."

Her face drained of all color. "You can't be serious."

"I'm as serious as the continued threat to your safety."

She snatched her arm from his grasp. "As I recall, the so-called threat existed last night when you asked me to remain in London."

"That was different. I thought I knew who was responsible for the note, and I had planned on taking care of him. Now that I know that Gavinport is no longer the suspect, the warning must still be heeded. Don't you see, I cannot adequately protect you if I don't know who is trying to harm you?"

Her lips thinned with irritation. "All I see is that I am a fool. You tell me to leave, and then in the next breath, you ask me to stay, only to demand I not cancel my travel plans a few hours later. Worse yet, you dangle your mistress before me, claim you miss bachelorhood, and then make love to me."

Marcus ran his fingers through his hair and let out a burst of air. She was right. He had done all those things, but what he was hesitant to tell her was that he cared nothing for Simone or his bachelorhood, only her. If she believed him a total cad, then she would leave as planned and be safe.

She met his eyes. "I told you I loved you," she whispered.

He looked away, unable to meet her steady gaze. "And I have come to care for you greatly, Isabel. That's why I offer you my protection."

She looked crestfallen. "You think I seek your protection? I never intended on falling in love with you, Marcus. It was the opposite of what I had planned. It just . . . happened."

He swallowed the lump in his throat, and struggled with the foreign words buried deep within his heart. "Isabel, I—"

A man clearing his throat drew his attention. Jenkins stood in the doorway, Roman by his side. The library door had been left ajar, and from their stark expressions, it was clear that they had heard what was said.

"What is it?" Marcus snapped.

Roman strode forward, hat in hand, and sympathetically stole a glimpse at Isabel. She flushed and turned to leave, but Roman stopped her with a raised hand.

"I have news the two of you should hear," Roman said. "Bow Street received an anonymous note as to the whereabouts of the stolen Gainsborough painting. When they arrived at the premises, there was an altercation with Robby Bones. The constable beat and killed Bones and took possession of the painting."

"Where?" Marcus demanded.

A dilapidated studio in the artists' district. Our investigator, Mr. Harrison, said the studio is now abandoned, but information leading us to Bones's employer may have been left behind."

Marcus turned to Roman. "Let's go. Now."

Isabel whirled toward him. "I'm going with you."

Marcus opened his mouth to protest, but Roman spoke up first. "She has a right to know, Marcus. She has been involved from the beginning, and it is her well-being that is threatened by the anonymous missive you received."

Marcus's flat, unspeaking eyes held hers, prolonging the moment, until he curtly nodded at her. "Since I don't trust you will stay put in this house, Isabel, I believe you will be safer with us."

Isabel raised her chin, meeting his dark gaze straight on. "Good—as I've decided to no longer listen to you."

Chapter 43

The art studio was located inside a run-down building on the outskirts of Shoreditch. Weeds grew in abundance around its crumbling foundation, and rusted iron bars covered its windows. As they entered the building and stepped inside the small vestibule, the shabby interior was no better. Garbage and cigar stubs littered the area and the walls were painted an uncomely green.

Isabel's stomach churned as the stench of cheap tobacco, rotting refuse, and oil paint assailed her nostrils. She had heard of such dilapidated studios where the poor, struggling artists of London awaited recognition and fortune that almost never befell them. Her experiences were limited to exhibitions and sales at the dazzling Royal Academy of Arts—far from such squalid desperation.

"Robby Bones was hiding on the second floor," Roman said, breaking the tense silence.

Marcus turned to her. "Stay behind us, Isabel."

She nodded and followed Marcus as they climbed up a rickety wooden flight of stairs. As she reached the top step, the wood splintered beneath her foot and a loud crack rent the air.

She gasped, hands flailing for the banister. Marcus spun around, grasped her arm, and hauled her up to the landing.

"I'm fine," she rushed to assure him before he could ask.

His mouth was tight and grim as he glanced down. The splintered step was still intact, but clearly posed a hazard for the next user. "These steps are a death trap. Bones probably knew which rotting one to avoid."

She swallowed, her throat dry as old, parched paper. "Let's keep going."

The trio continued down the hall until they came to the first of three doors.

"Harrison said the other two studios in the building are abandoned," Roman explained. "Bones was found in the first one. The lock was broken by the constable."

Marcus reached for the door handle, and when it opened easily, he stepped inside. Roman followed next, and only when she heard them say it was empty and safe was she permitted to enter the studio.

The pungent smell of paint and turpentine that immediately engulfed her was almost overwhelming, and she coughed. She scanned the studio, her eyes widening at the sight.

Roman whistled between his teeth. "Bones must have put up a good fight."

Paints in different hues were splattered across the wood floor and walls in what looked like a gruesome display of violence and mayhem. Bottles with their caps missing, dirty rags, sponges, shattered glass jars, and brushes were scattered everywhere. The wooden shelves were bare except for heavier cans of turpentine, which were knocked over. One of the shelves had tipped on its side and rested against a splintered easel. Ripped canvases were torn off the far wall, and paper littered the floor.

"If Bones was this violent, then no wonder the constable had to kill," Isabel whispered.

"The bastard got exactly what he deserved," Marcus said coldly.

Heavy footsteps sounded down the hall, and Benjamin Harrison appeared in the doorway. "Bludgeoned to death by Bow Street's finest, so I'm told," he said as he walked forward, kicking an empty can out of his path.

Isabel recalled previously meeting the investigator in Marcus's home. The straight slash of his bushy eyebrows over intense brown eyes reinforced her earlier impression that he was a shrewdly observant man.

Benjamin Harrison inclined his head in her direction. "Good morning, Mrs. Hawksley."

She smiled. "I suppose one could call it that."

Harrison leaned against a worktable and crossed his arms over his barrel-shaped chest. "I've been through here and couldn't find much to reveal who Robby Bones was working for. The lease is in the name of H. Turner, which tells me nothing as it is a very common surname. The owner of the building never met the tenant face-to-face, and he never cared to as the rent money was always timely delivered by Bones."

"What about the stolen painting?" Marcus asked.

"It was found in the rear of the studio, wrapped in plain brown paper. I suspect Bones had planned on moving it and soon," Harrison said.

"Where is it now?" Marcus asked.

"It went back to its rightful owner, Lord Westley's heir, who had originally planned to auction it off at the estate sale when it was stolen. I've heard it has already been sold to an affluent collector."

"Not Lord Yarmouth on behalf of the Regent?" Marcus asked.

Harrison looked up from beneath craggy brows. "Why? Were you interested, Mr. Hawksley?"

Marcus laughed. "No. That painting has brought me

nothing but trouble. I can only imagine the bad luck I would have if it were hanging over the mantel in my home."

Isabel experienced an odd twinge of disappointment at Marcus's words. He failed to mention that if it wasn't for the theft of the painting, they would never have married.

But he doesn't want you, her inner voice taunted. *Why act surprised?*

Isabel turned away from the men, and wandered the perimeter of the room. She paid careful attention to where she walked, lifting her skirts and stepping over paint and shards of glass as she went. She reached the back of the room, where a pool of red paint caught her eye. The same color was also splattered on the wall. She bent over to get a better look, and then backed up a step as she realized it was not paint, but blood.

"Was Bones killed here?" she asked over her shoulder.

The men approached. Harrison squatted down and touched the red substance. Rubbing his forefinger and thumb together, he said, "Definitely blood."

At the investigator's proclamation, her hand fluttered to her chest.

Marcus's eyes were drawn to the movement, and he touched her sleeve. "Do you want to leave, Isabel? I do not wish you to relive Dante Black's death."

She shook her head. "No. This is different. I'm glad Bones is dead. To be honest, I had hoped I'd killed him with the shovel."

Marcus raised an eyebrow, and a slight curve touched his mouth.

She ignored him and walked away, continuing her perusal of the room. She took a deep breath, hoping to calm the throbbing tension in her body that gnawed away at her confidence. Despite her best efforts to appear brave, the specters of Dante Black's death did loom in the recesses of her mind. But her pride and stubbornness remained, and she refused to reveal her vulnerability to Marcus—not after his cold treatment of her earlier in his library office.

She had said she loved him, not once, but twice. There had been a tangible bond between them during their heated lovemaking in the conservatory. His eyes had darkened with fierce desire and something more—an intense, almost desperate *need*. She hadn't imagined his powerful, potent response.

Yet today he had rejected her. He had told her to be gone, and he now clearly wanted nothing to do with their marriage or with anything they had shared. Her emotions were like a whirlwind inside her head. One moment sorrow would choke her, and the next wild rage would rip through her. Both extremes left her shaken and unable to think clearly.

For all their intimacy and shared confidences, Marcus Hawksley was an enigma, more a mystery to her than ever before.

She pinched the bridge of her nose with her thumb and forefinger and forced herself to concentrate on the scene before her. Her eyes focused, and were drawn to the art materials haphazardly scattered across the floor. She roamed about, pushing brushes and bottles aside with the tip of her shoe, and then bit her lip as a nagging suspicion solidified in her mind.

When she'd finished and returned to the spot where she had started, she raised her head. "Whoever lived here was not an artist himself," she said.

All three men turned to look at her.

"How can you tell?" Roman asked.

"The oil paint is old. The cakes of watercolor are crumbled from age. The brushes are splintered and dried out, their bristles missing. The canvases are old as well; not an ounce of fresh paint is on them."

Harrison's brows drew downward. "What about the paint spilled on the floor? It wasn't dried out."

"No. But I suspect it was left behind when the previous tenant leased the studio," Isabel said. "This building is in the artists' district. I assume it has been occupied by many faceless artists over the past decade. I have heard of landlords forcibly removing prior tenants without notice and then turning around and renting whatever supplies the poor artist had to the next available tenant. That is what must have happened here. Whoever the tenant was, when he leased this studio, the painting supplies were included in the lease."

"She's right," Marcus said. "I should have seen the signs myself."

"If he was not an artist, then why rent a studio? There are plenty of moth-eaten apartments for rent in London," Roman said.

Marcus spoke up. "It would be easier to carry stolen artwork here, wrapped in inconspicuous brown paper, without raising the curiosity of the neighbors. Plus no one would question the comings and goings of a well-known art auctioneer such as Dante Black. Those interested in buying a stolen painting could view the work here without raising suspicion as well."

"Your theory makes sense," Harrison said.

"There's something else," Marcus said. He walked to where a newspaper was thrown on the floor and picked it up. The front page was splattered with paint, but the name was legible. "What poor artist would bother to read *The Morning Chronicle*? I check this paper for stock prices, and as far as I'm aware, not one column is dedicated to the arts. Whoever H. Turner is, I believe he is the mastermind and is a member of the upper class."

"He most likely used a fake name on the lease," Harrison said.

"Could it be your nemesis at the Stock Exchange, Ralph Hodge? He would read *The Morning Chronicle*."

Marcus shrugged. "I still don't believe so, but I am going to confront him nonetheless. He has no connections to the art world and wouldn't recognize a valuable piece of artwork if it landed on top of him, but hatred is a powerful motivator."

"Who else would have reason to hate you so?" Roman asked.

A muscle flicked at Marcus's jaw. "I have asked myself that question a thousand times. I have professional adversaries at the Stock Exchange, but none that I can think of who would despise me to such an extent as to attempt to implicate me in a theft or to threaten to kill 'what I love most.'"

"Who gave Bow Street the tip that Robby Bones was here?" Isabel asked.

"No one knows," Harrison said. "Bow Street received an anonymous note."

"It was the mastermind," Marcus said. "He wanted Bones killed. Isabel had overheard them arguing over Dante Black's death. He probably resented Bones taking matters into his own hands and wanted him dead. He must have known Bones would not have surrendered to the constable, but would die fighting."

"Then we have nothing to worry about regarding my safety," Isabel said. "With Robby Bones dead, there is no one left to harm me. I doubt the villain would risk getting caught."

Marcus's eyes bored into her. "You're wrong, my dear. He can just as easily hire another vicious street criminal to carry out the deed. I suspect he has already done so."

A terrible tenseness enveloped her body. She wanted to argue with him, but his logic, no matter how brutally honest, made sense.

Harrison stroked his jaw. "I suggest questioning the neighbors in the adjacent buildings and across the street. Someone must have seen something that may aid us in identifying the tenant."

Marcus nodded. "Offer them a monetary reward for information. Money always loosens the tongue."

"I'll start right away," Harrison said, tipping his hat on his way out the studio. "I'll be in touch with any information I learn."

They left soon after Benjamin Harrison. Roman's crested carriage and prime team of horseflesh awaited outside. Next to the run-down buildings, the resplendent conveyance gleamed like gold beside rust.

Marcus assisted Isabel inside and sat beside her while Roman took the seat across from her. In the small confines of the carriage beside the long-limbed, muscular brothers, Isabel felt small and feminine.

She glanced at Roman beneath lowered lashes. The elder Hawksley was extremely handsome with chiseled features, green eyes, and a swath of jet hair that she suspected he styled to look as if it fell casually on his forehead. As the heir to an earldom, he had acquired a polished veneer that drew the female eye.

But it had always been—and remained to this day—Marcus Hawksley who captivated her. There was a firm strength, a coiled power, within him that came from ignoring society's dictates and carving his own way to success that she found irresistible.

Isabel pulled her drifting thoughts together and lifted the tasseled shade to look out the window. There was no sense brooding over Marcus; he had made his intentions clear.

Fool! she thought. *If only it was that simple.*

The bitter truth was she knew cleansing him from her mind and heart would be a slow, painful task.

The carriage turned onto St. James's Street and came to a stop outside of the town house.

"Let me know what Harrison discovers. I'll either be at home or at White's," Roman said.

Marcus nodded and jumped out of the coach. He held out his hand for Isabel.

She placed her gloved hand into his, stepped down, and followed him up the porch stairs. Marcus held the front door open, and Isabel swept inside the vestibule.

"Marcus!"

At the sound of the familiar female voice, both Isabel and Marcus turned their heads.

Simone Winston stood in the doorway of the parlor, obviously waiting for their return. When she spotted Marcus, her lips parted and she rushed forward. Her enormous breasts threatened to pop out of her daringly low-cut bodice as she ran, and her azure gown strained against her shapely hips.

"Marcus, darling," Simone breathed as she reached his side. She touched his sleeve and the gluttonous gleam in her eyes was blatantly sensual. "I have information I must share with you regarding the whereabouts of the painting you were accused of stealing."

Isabel stiffened as a stab of jealousy pierced her like a sharp blade. She boldly faced her nemesis. "Ms. Winston, we have already heard about the recovery of the painting. It is regrettable that you have wasted your time in coming today," Isabel said, her voice dripping with sarcasm.

Simone arched a brow. "Nonsense. I'm sure Marcus wants to know all of the details that I have heard." She tilted her head and gave Marcus a flirtatious smile. "Isn't that so, Marcus?"

Marcus drew his lips in thoughtfully. "She may have useful information." He motioned for Simone to follow him into the library, and without a backward glance, he shut the door behind them.

Isabel stood stunned as anguish seared her heart.

I cannot believe he has the audacity to shut himself in a room with his former mistress in our own home!

She stared unblinking at the closed library door until she heard the tap of footsteps on the marble floor, and she became aware of Mrs. McLaughlin standing beside her.

"I'm terribly sorry, Mrs. Hawksley. I never would have allowed that woman to cross the threshold, but one of the new maids had allowed her entrance," Mrs. McLaughlin said, wringing her plump hands in agitation.

Isabel's thoughts were jagged and painful as she looked at the housekeeper. "Never mind, Mrs. McLaughlin. Clearly, my husband is not disturbed by Ms. Winston's presence."

The look of pity in the housekeeper's gaze made tears well within Isabel's eyes. Biting her lip to keep from crying, she fled up the stairs.

Chapter 44

Isabel pushed a hand-knit shawl into one of three overstuffed portmanteaus on the floor of her bedroom. "I'm finished with him. Paris cannot come fast enough."

"Oh, Isabel," Charlotte said, sitting forward on the bed as Isabel rushed about gathering clothing and personal items. "I am going to miss you terribly."

"You shall have to visit as planned." Isabel bent over to pick up a pair of silk stockings and tossed them on the bed. Her movements were jerky, her mood sour. Try as she might, she could not erase the image of Marcus escorting a smug Simone Winston into his library office yesterday afternoon. She'd spent most of last night packing her belongings and cursing herself for acting the fool.

How could I have allowed myself to fall in love with him!

Charlotte interrupted her thoughts. "I'm afraid I gave you false advice."

Isabel stopped in midstride, holding a fistful of bonnets and a pair of drawers, and looked at Charlotte. "Whatever do you mean?"

"About Marcus . . . about the Hawksley men. I all but told you Marcus was trustworthy and good and was worth fighting for, but I was horribly wrong."

"About Marcus or Roman?"

Charlotte flushed miserably. "Both, I suppose."

"I thought you were getting along quite nicely with Roman. From what I saw in the dining room at your mother's birthday ball, you were conversing in an overly familiar fashion."

"I was wrong to do so," Charlotte snapped. "Roman Hawksley turned out to be arrogant, overbearing, and ridiculously stubborn."

Isabel laughed. "He sounds exactly like his brother."

Charlotte sighed and slid off the bed. "When Roman told me that you had been attacked in our gardens by that wretched criminal during the ball, I realized I had led you astray. Your first instinct to go to Paris was correct. Marcus has inadvertently put you in great danger. He has offered you nothing in return for your heart, especially after your one night of passionate lovemaking."

It was Isabel's turn to color hotly. Dropping the bonnets and drawers on top of the rising pile of clothing in a portmanteau, she said, "We spent more than one passionate night together."

"What? When?"

"The night of the ball, after I hit Robby Bones over the head with the shovel and fled."

"Right after? Where, for goodness' sake?"

"In your father's prized horticultural conservatory."

Charlotte's mouth floundered open and closed, and then she burst out laughing. "I have lived vicariously through your impulsive behavior for so long, I've decided that I must finally experience some wicked adventures for myself."

Isabel reached out and clutched at Charlotte's hand. "You must never utter a word to your stepfather."

Charlotte hastily drew her hand from Isabel's grasp and shrugged. "You needn't worry about that. He has all but left us. He has indulged himself in an entirely new wardrobe, probably to impress his next mistress and rarely comes home."

"Must all men be so selfish?" Isabel said tersely.

"I've come to that conclusion."

Isabel hesitated, then smiled mischievously. "Marcus said Roman has asked about you."

Charlotte froze, a flustered expression crossing her face. "Truly?"

Isabel started to answer when a knock on the door interrupted her.

"Yes," Isabel called out.

Jenkins opened the door. Dismay crossed his gaze as he took in the overstuffed trunks. "Lord Roman Hawksley is waiting downstairs in the receiving room, Mrs. Hawksley."

Isabel's thoughts scampered vaguely around. "I'm sure Marcus will be pleased."

"He has asked for you, Mrs. Hawksley, and is aware that Marcus had left earlier for his office on Threadneedle Street," Jenkins said.

"I see," she said, even though she was confused by Roman's arrival. "Please tell him I will be down shortly."

Charlotte rushed to the door, stumbling over a pair of Isabel's shoes in her haste. "Oh, I have to leave!"

"No, stay! We have seen so little of each other lately," Isabel protested.

"No. I'm not dressed properly and my hair," Charlotte sputtered, patting her abundance of blond curls. "Perhaps if I rush out, he won't see me in such a state." She left the bedroom and walked briskly down the hall.

Isabel rushed to keep apace. "But you look beautiful."

"You don't understand. Roman and I haven't exactly been civil," Charlotte huffed as she sped for the stairs.

"What happened between you two?"

Charlotte ignored her and began to descend the staircase with Isabel on her heels.

Halfway down, Charlotte came to an abrupt stop; Isabel nearly crashed into her friend's back.

"Charlotte, what are you—"

"Hello, Miss Benning."

At the sound of the deep, masculine voice, Isabel peered around Charlotte and spotted Roman. He stood at the bottom of the stairs, looking up. His heated gaze was riveted on Charlotte's face.

Charlotte stood still as a statue, her slender frame trembling.

Isabel nudged her friend in the shoulder, and Charlotte finally came to life. "You have nerve, my lord," she burst out.

Roman merely grinned, flashing straight white teeth. "So I have been told."

"I was just leaving," Charlotte said.

He waited until they reached the bottom of the stairs, then raised Charlotte's hand to his lips. She snatched her hand back and glared at him.

He chuckled, his green eyes bright. "I did not know that you would be here, Charlotte, but I am thrilled to see you again. You look even lovelier than the last time I saw you at your mother's ball."

Charlotte inhaled sharply at Roman's flattering words, and a faintly eager look lit her blue eyes. Something intense flared between the pair.

"May I call on you in the future then?" A confident smile curled the edges of Roman's mouth, a hint of masculine arrogance about him.

Charlotte stiffened as if coming to her senses. "Do not trouble yourself, my lord."

"Roman," he corrected.

"Do not trouble yourself, *Roman*."

Roman grinned again as Charlotte whirled to leave, his eyes riveted upon her with unmasked interest. She marched outside without a backward glance as Jenkins held open the door.

Isabel looked away, feeling the suffocating sensation of loneliness well within her breast. Despite their strange twist in behavior, especially Charlotte's uncharacteristic coldness and rigid propriety, they were clearly drawn to each other, a perfect match. Isabel was certain that whatever battle of wills they were currently fighting, the startling sparks of attraction between them would overcome. They did not have myriad complications which would prevent them from being together. Roman did not punish himself for a bitter past, a madman was not trying to put him in prison for theft, nor was a killer stalking Charlotte. Theirs *should* be a simple romance without entanglements, murder, or heartbreak.

Roman turned his attention to Isabel as if nothing untoward had just occurred. "I was hoping to speak with you, Isabel."

"I don't know what has occurred between you two, but I don't think Charlotte will ever be the same. I hope your intentions toward my friend are honorable," Isabel said with cool authority.

He offered her a forgiving smile. "I like Charlotte very much, and I insist on choosing my own wife."

"Ah, pressure from your father?"

Roman winked. "I'm starved. Have you eaten luncheon?"

Isabel eyed him suspiciously. "I see you are avoiding my question, but I will allow it this time. Luncheon sounds fine."

He followed her into the dining room and politely held out a chair for her before taking one himself.

She snapped open a crisp white napkin, placed it on her lap, and then looked at him. "I cannot imagine you came all this way just to socialize and eat luncheon with your sister-in-law. Why are you really here?"

"To speak about Marcus."

She straightened, instantly on guard. "There is nothing to speak about. He has made his wishes perfectly clear to me."

"You love him?"

Her breath caught. The thought to lie crossed her mind, but when her lips parted, the painful truth burst forth. "Yes, but it makes no difference."

"You still intend to leave for Paris then?"

Her lips puckered with annoyance. "Despite what you may think of me, I am not a complete idiot. Marcus wants me gone. The sooner the better."

"He loves you more than any woman he has ever known, but he is too frightened to acknowledge his feelings."

"That's ridiculous," she said in a choked voice.

At that moment, a maid entered carrying two plates of mutton stew and biscuits. She placed the plates before them, then departed as quietly as she had come.

"Isabel, there are things about Marcus's past that you do not know," Roman said. "Things that have carved his character and have made it difficult for him to accept the notion of unconditional love."

Isabel twisted the napkin in her lap. "I'm aware he was spurned by a woman in his youth, but I find it hard to believe that something so inconsequential that occurred years ago could affect his behavior toward me now."

Roman leaned forward, his green eyes sharp and assessing. "You're wrong. It was not inconsequential, at least not to him. There are also other factors that have made Marcus the man he is today. His behavior is a lifetime in the making."

"Then tell me," she said, her voice full of entreaty.

"From the moment Marcus was born, he had a rough

path to travel. Our father—the mighty Earl of Ardmore—is a hard man, and he disliked Marcus on sight. He had the heir to the earldom already and treated Marcus harshly. Our mother tried to defend him, but she had been a meek, quiet woman who was dominated by our father, and she died when we were children."

"The earl's attitude toward Marcus makes no sense. What about the old adage of 'an heir and a spare'?" Isabel asked.

Roman's lips twitched with distaste. "Nothing about our father makes much sense. He is an arrogant man who was born into wealth and luxury and truly believes he is entitled to everything he has inherited and that God would not dare strike down his only heir."

Isabel vividly recalled her wedding night when Randall Hawksley, the Earl of Ardmore, and her own father had surprised them by arriving at their door for dinner. The animosity that oozed between father and son had been shocking.

"For his entire lifetime our father told Marcus he was the worthless younger son," Roman said. "We were close brothers as children, but when I left for school, Marcus remained behind and soon he began to believe our father's ranting. It became a self-fulfilling prophecy, and as he grew older, he started drinking, gambling, and womanizing. Then he met Bridget, the pretty, flirtatious daughter of a wealthy merchant whose family did not socialize with the *beau monde*. I still do not know who seduced whom, and I warned Marcus to end the liaison, but he refused to listen. Then Bridget became pregnant, and Marcus came to me for advice. I told him he had a financial responsibility to care for the girl and unborn babe. But unbeknownst to me, Marcus decided to marry Bridget. He thought to fix all the wrongs done to him by our father and treat his child with the kind of unconditional love he had never received."

"Did they marry?"

"They decided to elope," Roman said, "but when Marcus showed up at their arranged meeting place, Bridget never appeared. He went to her house and banged on the door, and when no one answered, he went inside and found Bridget hanging from the rafters. She was still alive when he cut her down, but he was not able to save her, and she died in his arms. With her last breath she told him she would rather be dead than marry and birth the child of a penniless younger son. You see, she was not acquainted with the titled members of the ton and had mistakenly thought Marcus was the heir to the earldom. She had deviously contrived the pregnancy with the hopes of trapping him into marriage. Too late she had learned that she was enceinte with the wrong brother's child, and her condition had enraged her father. When I learned of her death, I'm ashamed to say I blamed Marcus, and we had a terrible fight. I was angry that he did not listen to me, that he did not end the affair as I had advised. Worse, I did not believe his story—that Bridget could be so cunning and naïve at the same time—or that he did indeed plan to marry her. I thought he had abandoned Bridget. I could not understand why a pregnant woman, a commoner at that, would commit suicide when she was offered marriage. I was terribly wrong," Roman said, his voice cracking.

Isabel felt tears well in her eyes as she pictured a younger, vulnerable Marcus finding Bridget. The woman's ultimate betrayal must have reinforced his father's cruel opinions regarding his worth.

She leaned forward in her chair. "It wasn't your fault, Roman."

Roman's eyes looked bleak. "I failed my only brother when he needed me most. He sees love as a weapon to be wielded against the weak, just as our cold-hearted father used it against him as a child, and as Bridget used it against him as a young man."

"You made a mistake, but you are his brother, and he has forgiven you," she said.

Roman nodded. "It has taken years to rebuild our relationship. After Bridget's death, Marcus drank himself senseless for weeks. But then he snubbed our father and society altogether by entering trade as a stockbroker. He immersed himself in work and, against all odds, climbed his way to enormous success and financial stability. He started acquiring expensive art, and I have often heard him say that 'money and art don't betray you; only people do.' Until you came along, he was a recluse and valued only his business reputation. He cared naught what the judgmental society ladies or the mamas of the ton thought of him."

"He must have loved Bridget a great deal," Isabel whispered.

"He cared for Bridget, but he did not love her. Her betrayal and malicious cunning destroyed whatever fondness he had held for her. He grieved more for the death of his unborn child."

A disturbing thought pierced her mind, and she bit her lip. "He must think me just as manipulative as Bridget. I sought to use him for his tainted social reputation to avoid an unwanted betrothal. Because of my reckless and thoughtless behavior, Marcus was forced to marry me."

Roman's tight expression relaxed into a smile as he looked at her. "I know all about that. Marcus may have initially been angry with you, but no longer. Nothing in his past compares to what he now feels for you."

Isabel shook her head. "You're mistaken. I told Marcus I loved him. I would be willing to give up Paris and art studies if he would just ask. Instead, he has told me repeatedly to leave."

"That's because he is deathly afraid to love, to open his

heart to someone only to have her ripped from his life. When he received the threat to your life, he was reminded of Bridget's death, only it would have been far worse. Bridget died by her own selfish hand, but if you were hurt, it would be because of a madman seeking vengeance against him. In Marcus's mind, he would be as responsible as the killer. He could never live with himself if you were taken from him. Don't you see, he loves you, but he is stubbornly refusing to acknowledge his feelings for fear of losing you."

Isabel shook her head. "I want to believe you, but I find it difficult. What about Simone Winston?"

Roman's brow furrowed. "His former mistress? Simone means nothing to him."

"When we returned to the house yesterday, she was waiting for him. She said she had information about the recovered painting. He took her into his library office. Alone."

"Then he wanted to find out if she knew anything that would lead him to the mastermind," Roman said.

"That is what he said, but—"

"Marcus is obsessed with determining the true villain's identity. He is compelled to follow every lead—leave no stone unturned—even if that means interrogating Simone. He will not rest until he has destroyed the man responsible for the mysterious note."

"But the note never mentioned my name; it only threatened what Marcus loves most," Isabel argued.

"Exactly. That's why he wants you safely ensconced in Paris. But I believe we can keep you well guarded until the true identity of the mastermind is determined. You must convince him to acknowledge his feelings."

She laughed. "Your brother is too headstrong to persuade when his mind is set."

"You alone have the power. I've told you everything so that you understand him and do not give up on him and leave for Paris. Your love can heal his bruised soul. You are what he needs, not work or expensive art."

She placed her fork down. She'd suddenly lost her appetite for the food before her. Could she do it? Unpack her bags and risk her bruised pride and try to reach Marcus once again? Attempt to heal his wounds and make him acknowledge his feelings for her?

She rose and placed her napkin beside her full plate. "Thank you, Roman, for everything."

He stood, an expectant expression on his handsome face. "Will you stay then?"

"I need time to think." She made to leave, and then stopped and turned to face him. "One more question. Whatever happened to Bridget's family?"

Roman shrugged. "Bridget Turner's father was a well-to-do merchant who was too busy to pay her much attention, and her mother was deceased. Her elder brother, whom we never met, was in the army stationed in France."

Something about Roman's story disturbed her, and she fuddled with myriad confused emotions before a thought clicked in her mind.

She anxiously looked up at Roman. "Turner, did you say?"

Chapter 45

Marcus arrived at his office on Threadneedle Street by eight-thirty that morning. He sat behind his desk, surrounded by stacks of correspondence and company stock reports, and waited with his door wide open. He occasionally glanced at the papers, but he had no interest in the columns of figures.

His eyes returned to the brass name plate which identified Ralph Hodge's office directly across the hall. A ray of sunlight from the window behind him reflected off the brass as if to mock him.

Marcus's mouth thinned with displeasure. He disliked waiting for anyone, especially the sly, traitorous Hodge. But Marcus knew the wily stockbroker was due shortly at his office.

He was rewarded fifteen minutes later when the sounds of footsteps echoed down the hall. Marcus shot up, closed his door halfway, and hid behind it.

Keys jangled, then came the distinct sound of a bolt sliding from its lock and a door opening.

Marcus rushed out and roughly grabbed Ralph Hodge by the M-cut collar of his tailored jacket. Marcus pushed the smaller man inside his office, slammed him against the wall, and kicked the door shut.

Ralph Hodge's eyes bulged in his face. "Hawksley, what the hell—"

"Shut up, Hodge." Wrapping his hand around the broker's throat, he squeezed. "I want the truth," Marcus growled.

Ralph helplessly pulled at Marcus's hand. "I don't . . . know what . . . you're talking about," he wheezed.

Marcus eased up on his grip. "I'm talking about Isabel."

"Your wife? I never touched her!"

"I never thought you did. But did you threaten her?"

"Threaten her? No, I merely suggested a liaison should she tire of you."

Marcus released him. "Not bloody likely, you fool."

Ralph Hodge massaged his throat and stepped away. "You're crazy, Hawksley."

"What do you know about Thomas Gainsborough?"

"Is he one of your clients?" Ralph asked warily. "I swear I never approached him."

Marcus laughed despite himself. "I find your ignorance of the art world reassuring." When a look of utter confusion passed over Hodge's face, Marcus asked, "Did you hire anyone to frame me for the theft of a piece of artwork?"

"No, but the idea has merit."

"You would love to see me ruined, wouldn't you?"

Ralph shot him a withering glance. "I won't deny that I dislike you. Our past is less than amicable, but I would never threaten your wife, and I had nothing to do with any painting."

Marcus nodded. Despite his aversion toward Ralph Hodge, he sensed the stockbroker was telling the truth. Marcus had never believed Hodge was the mastermind even given the animosity and rivalry between them. Ralph was unethical, arrogant, and ruthlessly ambitious, but he was not a murderer, and he lacked the knowledge and finances to contrive and carry out such an intricate plot.

The sound of booted feet outside Hodge's door drew their attention.

A persistent rapping followed.

"Open it," Marcus instructed.

Hodge straightened his jacket and stepped to the door. He opened it, and a man dressed in a crisp uniform complete with red jacket, black trousers, and a high hat with a matching red hat band stood expectantly. His distinct uniform marked him as a courier, and the service that employed him often delivered packages to stockbrokers and jobbers that occupied the offices in the building.

"Good morning, sir," the man said to Ralph. "I have a delivery for the businessman across the hall." He looked down at a paper in his hand. "A Mr. Marcus Hawksley. Would you be so kind as to accept the package on his behalf?"

Marcus stepped forward. "There's no need for that. I'm Marcus Hawksley."

The courier's eyes lit up. "Very good, sir." He turned around to retrieve a sizable package over three feet high and four feet long wrapped in brown paper, and rested it against the door. "Pleasure to be of service, sir," the courier said before turning to leave Hodge's office.

Marcus's brows drew downward as he stared at the package. *It can't be!*

In two strides he reached the package and tore it open. His eyes widened as heart-thudding recognition struck him. Through the roaring din in his skull, he murmured out loud, "It's the *Seashore with Fishermen*."

Never could he have fathomed that the stolen painting would be delivered to his doorstep. He reached out to touch it just to be sure it was real. The critics had been correct. The coastal scene, showing three fishermen sitting in a boat with a fourth pushing the boat into the surf, was so lifelike that you could almost feel the wind and the spray of the ocean waves on your face. Three other fishermen handled a net in the surf as they struggled against strong winds and pounding waves.

"Is that the artwork you almost strangled me for stealing?" Ralph asked behind his shoulder.

Marcus ignored him and scanned the brown wrapping for a return address. He found nothing, but a white slip of paper stuck in the lower left corner of the frame caught his eye. He plucked it from the frame and unfolded it.

I had mistakenly believed Gainsborough's art was what you most loved. But now the time is here to take what you truly cannot live without.

Fear spurted through him, and his heart thundered in his chest. Dashing to the door, he turned to Hodge. "Keep that safe," Marcus said, pointing to the painting. "The Regent wants it."

He then ran down the hall, holding raw emotion in check, and prayed he was not too late.

"It's a coincidence," Roman said, stepping away from the dining room table to approach Isabel.

"How can you be certain? Do you believe the surname 'Turner' too common as Investigator Harrison had suggested?" Isabel asked.

"No."

"Then why?" she asked. "It's logical that Bridget Turner's brother thinks he has motive for his sister's death."

"It cannot be the same man," Roman insisted. "Bridget Turner's brother died in the army while stationed in France."

"How do you know?"

"The body was never sent back to England, but we had heard he had contracted consumption and had expired from the disease. We never had reason to question otherwise," Roman said.

"I see. That would explain why Marcus never made the connection when Harrison had said the studio's lease was in the name of H. Turner."

Jenkins interrupted them by clearing his throat and entering the dining room. He was trailed by a servant she did not recognize. The middle-aged man was squat with small black eyes and a bulbous nose. Drops of perspiration clung to his damp forehead, and he was out of breath as if he had run a great distance.

"This is Horatio Kulzer, Charlotte Benning's footman," Jenkins said. "He has pressing news."

Kulzer spoke up. "Pardon the interruption, Mrs. Hawksley. After leavin' yer home, Miss Benning 'ad wanted a ride in Hyde Park. All was fine till 'alfway through the park Miss Benning fell ill. She's there now with her coachman and told me to rush 'ere. I ran the entire way. She's askin' fer ye, Mrs. Hawksley."

Isabel paled at the news. "Do you know what is ailing her?"

"No, Mrs. Hawksley. Only that she's lyin' down inside the coach and insisted that I fetch ye right away."

"I shall come at once," Isabel said, rushing from the dining room.

Roman and Jenkins followed. "I shall accompany you," Roman said.

Kulzer eyed him. "Miss Benning asked only fer Mrs. Hawksley, my lord."

Roman's eyes narrowed. "I'm going with Isabel. We can take my carriage."

A muscle quivered at Kulzer's jaw before he nodded deferentially. "As ye wish, my lord."

Chapter 46

They piled into Roman's carriage and were fast on their way. As Horatio Kulzer instructed, they followed along the Serpentine River. It was a pleasant July afternoon, and Hyde Park's well-traveled track was littered with carriages and phaetons of high society.

They did not stop here, however, and continued onward until they left the familiar cobblestone path. Thicker foliage, low tree branches, and bushes brushed the sides of the swaying carriage as they passed.

"Why would Charlotte's coachman bring her here?" Roman asked.

"She wanted a private spot to rest," Kulzer explained.

The Bennings' crested coach came into view, and they stopped beside it.

Roman leaned forward, peering out the window, concern etched across his features. "I don't see the coachman."

Kulzer opened the door and jumped down. "Maybe 'e stepped away fer a moment."

Wasting no time, Roman and Isabel followed the footman and ran to the coach.

Isabel rapped on the door. "Charlotte! It's Isabel. Are you ill?"

Kulzer opened the door, lowered the step, and motioned for Isabel to enter. Roman made to join her, but Kulzer put out a hand to stop him. "Mayhap ye should let the lady enter first to see to Miss Benning." Lowering his voice an octave, he murmured, "She asked specifically fer her."

Roman stiffened, but he nodded and stepped aside.

Isabel entered the coach, and Kulzer closed the door behind her.

Blackness enveloped her. The dark shades were drawn and the gas lamps unlit. Her eyes struggled to adjust. An odd smell lingered in the coach, nothing like Charlotte's familiar perfume.

"Charlotte?"

A deep chuckle reverberated inside the coach. Isabel reached for the shade, but a strong hand grasped her wrist.

"Let me, my dear," said an eerily familiar voice.

The shade opposite the side she had entered snapped open, and Isabel squinted against the now bright light.

"Mr. Benning!" she gasped. "Whatever are you doing here? Where is Charlotte?"

"My stepdaughter is at home, of course."

She stared at Harold Benning in confusion. "Is this some kind of jest?"

He regarded her with impassive coldness for a moment before his lips twisted into a cynical smile. "This is no joke, my dear."

She found him vaguely disturbing, and her pulse began to beat erratically. As her eyes nervously darted over him, she noted his stiff posture and his uncharacteristic clothing. Gone was the flamboyant, effeminate attire. He was wearing a severe-cut navy coat and fawn breeches. Sturdy Hessians encased his feet rather than high-heeled buckled shoes. His eyes no longer held the glassy gleam of alcoholic overindulgence, but were pale blue and sharp. His speech wasn't slurred or high-pitched, but a deeper timbre.

A primitive warning sounded in her brain.

She reached for the door handle. "I must tell Roman that Charlotte is fine and at home. He's right outside."

A glimmer of amusement passed over Benning's face. "Please do." He reached across her to open the door.

She gasped at the sight that met her eyes. Roman was on his knees, hands tied behind his back; Horatio Kulzer held a gun to his head. Roman's driver lay unconscious beside them, blood tricking down his hairline onto his cheek.

Roman met her wide eyes. "Isabel—"

Kulzer cut Roman off with a hard kick to his side, and Roman grunted.

Isabel screamed and made to leap from the coach, but she was jerked back by a vicious grip on her arm.

Roman struggled to rise. "Don't touch her!" he bellowed.

Horatio Kulzer pressed down on Roman's shoulder with a meaty hand. "Unless ye want to see the lady shot, ye better stay put."

Benning sneered and increased his grip on Isabel's arm. "I take it Hawksley was easy enough to subdue?" he asked Kulzer.

"Aye. The lovesick fool was so concerned with the 'appenin's inside the coach that I 'ad no problem takin' care of 'im and 'is driver." Horatio Kulzer broke into a satanic smile, revealing two missing front teeth.

Isabel was immediately reminded of Robby Bones.

She twisted to glare at Harold Benning. "Dear God, what have you done!"

"Only what justice has demanded for years."

The shock of discovery hit her full force. "*You* are the mastermind! I recognize you now. You were the one speaking with Robby Bones in the gardens at Leticia Benning's birthday ball. It was you all along!"

"You always were quite clever, Isabel," Benning drawled.

"You are H. Turner . . . Harold Turner," she sputtered. "You were Bridget Turner's brother."

"We thought you were dead," Roman ground out.

Harold Benning's eyes hardened like glacial ice. "Your bastard brother killed me the same day he murdered my sister."

"He didn't murder her. She took her own life," Isabel protested in a choked voice.

"She was forced to do so," Benning snapped, "the moment she discovered she was carrying Marcus Hawksley's bastard child. I adored my sister, and we had grand plans for her future. Our father was a merchant, but Bridget deserved better than to be the wife of a mere tradesman. She was worthy to be one of the titled nobility. We plotted as children for her to accomplish such a goal. Years later when I was stationed in France, she wrote to say she had bagged an heir to an earldom. The pregnancy was but a hook to lure him into a bigger trap. But Marcus Hawksley misled Bridget into thinking he was the heir. You see, for all her flirtatious knowledge and conquests of the opposite sex, she was raised as a simple merchant's daughter in the middle class, and she was never exposed to the faces behind the complex social rankings of the *beau monde*. When I wrote back to tell her that Marcus was the younger son, I reassured her that the brat in her belly could have been dealt with. But somehow our father had learned of her condition before she could seek out the abortionist, and he planned to oust her from the family home without a farthing. Bridget was forced to take drastic measures and end her own life."

"That's insane! How can you blame Marcus when Bridget intentionally tried to trap him?" Isabel asked.

"He was a rogue, a womanizer, and a liar. He would have said anything to bed a woman."

"That's a lie," Roman said. "Marcus never misled her.

You said yourself she had never been exposed to the members of the ton. As brothers we look alike; it was she who assumed Marcus was the older son. He planned to do right by Bridget and the child by *marrying* her," Roman said.

"She did not want a younger son; his lies forced her to hang herself. He took my Bridget from me!" Spittle flew from Benning's lips and sprayed Isabel's face.

She recoiled at the insanity that shone bright and clear in his eyes. Her stomach churned at the realization that Harold Benning's feelings for his sister had extended well beyond brotherly love.

"I have spent years traveling throughout the continent and perfecting my plans," Benning said. "I have re-created myself time and again until I became the perfect stylish, wastrel—Mr. Harold Benning—the fop who blended in with every other useless dandy. I returned to England and married the perfect companion, the vain, but deeply insecure Leticia Benning, a pathetic woman who desperately needs affirmation that true love exists in this cruel world."

Isabel blinked, stunned at the hatred that dripped like acid from his voice. "Have you no conscience?"

Benning's burning gaze bore into her. "My conscience was crushed the day my sister was taken from me. Now I shall return the favor and take something from Marcus Hawksley. I had initially planned to have the Thomas Gainsborough painting he coveted stolen and his freedom taken from him when he was arrested and incarcerated for the theft. But you, my dear, interfered. I was furious at first, but then I saw the way he looked at you and knew he had fallen in love, and my prior dismay turned into instant bliss." He hesitated, a haughty smirk crossing his face. "I thoroughly enjoyed taunting him with my menacing notes. I even arranged to have the elusive painting delivered to his office today. I only regret not being able to see his reaction when he recognizes it."

Isabel's jaw dropped a notch at his crazed words. Her eyes scanned the interior of the coach and the woods beyond for a way to escape, but he must have sensed her desperation for his grip on her arm tightened.

"I admit I regret it was you he fell in love with, Isabel," he continued. "I was always fond of you, and it is a shame you must die. But you must hang from a rafter for the murder scene to be accurately re-created, and Marcus Hawksley must be the one to find you," Benning said, his tone coolly impersonal as if he were discussing the weather.

"You'll never get away with this," Roman hissed. "Marcus will kill you."

"I don't believe so. He has failed to identify me so far, and by the time he discovers the truth, I shall be long gone from London." Benning cocked his head to the side and studied Roman. "Your arrival was not part of my plans, my lord, but nonetheless, you shall serve a good purpose. When you rouse, kindly tell your brother he can cut his wife down from a rafter in the art studio where I took care of Robby Bones."

Roman's struggles increased. "Don't do this, Benning."

"What do you mean 'when he rouses'?" Isabel asked.

Just then, Horatio Kulzer raised the butt of his pistol and slammed it into Roman's temple.

Isabel screamed as Roman crumpled to the ground. "You killed him!"

Benning gave an impatient shrug. "Neither Roman nor his driver are dead, my dear. Only knocked unconscious. They should wake in an hour or so with a nasty headache and a large lump on their skulls. Just in time to fetch your dastardly husband."

She flew at him, taking him by surprise. She clawed at his fingers that held her arm, then raked her nails down his face and kicked his shins with the pointed toes of her pumps. He grunted in pain and released her arm.

She immediately pulled his hair and tried to slam his head against the side of the coach.

Horatio Kulzer came to Benning's aid, and it took both men to overpower her. She cursed and bucked as Benning restrained her, and Kulzer tied her hands and feet and stuffed a dirty rag in her mouth.

Kulzer left the coach, and she was forced to sit across from Harold Benning. He wiped his damp brow with a handkerchief, his expression holding a note of mockery as he glared at her.

She heard the squeak of springs as Kulzer climbed into the driver's seat, and then the coach jerked forward.

Chapter 47

Marcus burst through the door of the town house like a tornado. "Where's Isabel?" he asked a startled Jenkins and Mrs. McLaughlin.

The two servants exchanged a look of alarm before Jenkins stepped forward. "She went with Lord Ardmore."

"My father?"

"No, sir. Your brother."

"Roman was here?"

"Yes, sir."

"Where did they go?"

"Lady Charlotte fell ill inside her coach during an outing at Hyde Park. Her servant came to fetch Isabel. Your brother accompanied her," Jenkins said.

Marcus listened with bewilderment. "That's odd."

Mrs. McLaughlin twisted her starched apron with callused hands. "I thought the same as well when Jenkins told me what had occurred."

"How long have they been gone?" Marcus asked.

Jenkins glanced at the long-case clock in the corner. "Over a half hour, sir."

Just then, the front door opened and Roman stumbled inside. The right side of his face was bloody, his jacket torn, and his fawn-colored trousers covered with dirt and grass stains.

"Christ, Roman!" Marcus shouted. "What happened? And where's Isabel?"

Roman leaned heavily against the wall, his face ashen. His breathing was labored and his brows drawn together as if the effort of standing caused him great pain.

Marcus strode to his side, but Roman waved him off with a trembling hand. "Isabel is in great danger," Roman gasped. "We have to get to the art studio where Robby Bones was murdered. My carriage is outside."

Fear spurted through Marcus. *I'm too late! The madman has her!*

His gaze snapped to Jenkins. "Help me with Roman. We have little time."

Both Marcus and Jenkins held Roman's arms and helped him back into his carriage. Marcus's eyes widened at the sight of Roman's unconscious driver sprawled across the seat, a splotch of fresh blood staining the leather beside the man's head.

"I drove," Roman said before Marcus could ask. "We were both pistol whipped."

A thousand questions flew through Marcus's mind, but he bit his tongue. Time was critical, each second could be the difference between life and death; they had to get to Isabel.

Marcus gave Jenkins a sideways glance. "Let's get the driver inside. See that a doctor comes to the house to care for him and inform Investigator Harrison of our destination. He'll know who to contact at Bow Street."

Roman's man was carried into the house, and Jenkins instructed one of the footmen to hop into the driver's seat. Marcus retrieved his pistol from his desk drawer before jumping back into the carriage.

He sat opposite Roman as they sped through the London

streets. The wheels hit a rut in the road, and Roman groaned, holding his head in his hands, a bloody handkerchief pressed to an oozing egg-sized knot above his temple.

"Tell me what happened," Marcus said.

Roman raised his head. "Harold Benning is the mastermind. He is Bridget Turner's brother, and he seeks vengeance for his sister's suicide."

Shock flew through Marcus. "I thought Bridget's brother was dead."

"So did I. But he faked his death and changed his identity. The man is insane and has focused all of his efforts on you and is intent on hurting you by killing Isabel."

Marcus closed his eyes as despair rushed through him.

"He concocted a story about Charlotte's well-being to lure us into an isolated area of the park," Roman said. "His new henchman knocked both me and my driver unconscious. When I roused, Benning was gone. He took Isabel with him. I believe I awakened faster than he had anticipated, but I pray that we are not too late."

Marcus's eyes met Roman's. "Too late for what? What is he planning?"

"To hang her from a rafter just as Bridget died. He wants you to be the one to find Isabel as you did Bridget."

Panic like he'd never known before welled in Marcus's throat. If Harold Benning was truly the mastermind, Bridget's insane brother returned from the grave after all these years, then his deep-seated hatred must have festered like pestilence. He would be merciless when it came to Isabel. Her cries would fall on deaf ears.

Fear and despair clawed at his innards. He thought of the last time he had privately spoken with Isabel in his library office, the morning after they had made love in the Bennings' conservatory. He had been cold and businesslike as if he were conversing with one of his clients in the lobby of the Stock Exchange. She had told him she loved him, and he had asked her to leave. Worse still, he had led her to believe he had feelings for Simone Winston.

He recalled Isabel's pain-stricken face as he had escorted Simone into his library office. He had only sought to determine whether Simone had useful information, but he could have interrogated her in front of Isabel. Instead, his calloused actions reinforced Isabel's false belief that he had feelings for his former mistress.

How could he have acted like such a fool?

He could no longer deny the truth. He loved Isabel. His obsession to keep her safe and protect her had nothing to do with honor or repayment of a debt for her alibi, but had everything to do with love. He had stubbornly refused to acknowledge his feelings and reciprocate her heartfelt words simply out of fear.

Since his father's emotional abandonment and Bridget's perfidy, he had thought of love as a weapon to be used against the weak and vulnerable. He had immersed himself in his work and had surrounded himself with outrageously expensive artwork. He had sworn never to love or need another's love again, and had believed money and art could fill any emotional void.

Then Isabel had burst into his life and added splashes of bright color with which no masterpiece he had ever set eyes upon could compare. He had been instantly enraptured and had fallen helplessly in love with her. Her beauty had initially attracted him, but it was her bold impulsiveness, her artistic creativeness, and most refreshingly, her complete disregard of society's cruel opinions that had captured his heart. The undeniable truth was that he needed her love to heal his bruised soul. Instead, he had put her in grave danger and failed to protect her as he had promised.

"What are your plans?" Roman interrupted Marcus's thoughts.

"How well armed are they?"

"I do not think Benning has a weapon, but his new henchman, Horatio Kulzer, is armed and is an experienced criminal."

Marcus's mouth twisted into a threat. "Then I must kill him first."

Roman dropped the handkerchief on the seat and glared at him. "I plan on being of use, Marcus. I'm not dead, you know."

"Good. I'll need all the help I can get."

Roman reached over to touch his hand. "Have faith, brother. You will yet be able to tell her that you love her."

Chapter 48

The muscles in Isabel's back were screaming in protest by the time Harold Benning's carriage arrived at the run-down art studio. The ropes Horatio Kulzer had used to bind her limbs were unbearably tight, and she had strained and pulled against them to no avail. Her throat was dry and sore from the filthy rag he had stuffed in her mouth, and she breathed in quick, shallow gasps.

The carriage finally stopped, and Benning leaned his fleshy face to within an inch of hers. His breath smelled of onions and tobacco and she recoiled, pressing her head against the padded bench.

"I'm going to untie you and remove the gag so that we may enter the building without attracting unwanted attention from the neighbors. My man has a weapon. He is a nasty type of criminal, much like Robby Bones, with whom I understand you were well acquainted, and he will not hesitate to hurt you. Do you understand?"

Fresh fear threaded low in her belly; she nodded yes.

The carriage swayed as Kulzer jumped down from his perch, and the door was opened. Shielded by the door, he pulled out a wicked-looking six-inch blade hidden in his jacket. With two quick downward slashes, he cut the ropes binding her hands and feet.

She immediately yanked the dirty rag from her mouth, coughed, and swallowed twice.

Kulzer laughed. "I don't suspect a lady like ye 'as ever been bound and gagged before. What a waste."

She shot him a nasty glare as she flexed her numb fingers, trying to get the blood to circulate. She would love nothing more than to punch the odious man in the face.

He must have caught her meaning for his eyes narrowed. "Don't even think about doin' something rash. I 'ave no qualms about usin' my knife, lady or no."

"She's been warned, Kulzer," Benning said curtly. "Let's get inside."

Isabel was dragged from the carriage and escorted between Benning and Kulzer. Her eyes darted nervously from side to side, but she saw no one. It seemed the occupants of the shabby neighborhood were all inside, probably hard at work painting to earn a living like most starving artists. She thought of screaming for help, but she had no doubt that Kulzer would use his knife to silence her. Such a man would know precisely where to stab a woman to ensure her silence without killing her.

No, it was in her interest to stay alive as long as possible. There was a chance—however small—that Roman would rouse himself and seek aid.

They entered the shabby vestibule of the building. It appeared untouched since the last time she had been here, only the putrid stench of the garbage that littered the small space had intensified.

With Kulzer's viselike grip on her arm, Isabel was pulled up the steps leading to the second floor. The wood creaked beneath their combined weight, and as they came close to the landing, her eyes darted to the corner of the top step.

The splintered wood remained.

Her thoughts whirled to that moment she had nearly fallen through the rotten step. If not for Marcus's quick reflexes, she would have been seriously injured.

An idea sprang to mind, and she pretended to stumble, leaning heavily on Kulzer in an effort to push him toward the treacherous trap. But at the last moment, he jerked her upright and stepped safely to the second floor.

Harold Benning followed suit.

Her heart plummeted at their good fortune, and she was dragged like a rag doll down the hall to the first door.

Benning pulled out a set of keys. "I doubt I'll need these as the constable broke the lock three days ago, and the landlord is too cheap to make any repairs without securing a new tenant."

He turned the handle and the door opened. She was thrust inside.

The scene that met her eyes was strikingly similar as before. Evidence of the fight between Robby Bones and the constables remained—the paint-splattered floor, the scattered art supplies, the tipped bookcase, and the splintered easel. A broom and mop leaning against a corner caught her eye, along with an empty bucket nearby. It appeared that the landlord had brought cleaning supplies here, but had not made any effort to use them.

"Get to the back," Kulzer ordered, pushing her.

She headed for the rear of the room, and as she neared the back wall, Kulzer gave a rough shove. She lurched forward, stumbling over a can of turpentine and falling on all fours. Rising up on her knees, she instantly recognized the dried circle of blood staining the floor.

Robby Bones's blood.

Dear Lord, flashes of Dante Black's murder scene seared her mind.

Only Dante's blood was fresh. Robby Bones's was days old.

She skirted to the side and made to rise, but Kulzer pressed down on her shoulder.

"Sit," he demanded, "or I'll be forced to bind and gag ye again. And don't bother screamin'. The other studios are abandoned."

She huddled with her back to the wall, wrapped her arms around her knees, and looked away from where Bones had bled out. Her eyes followed Benning as he went to a supply closet, opened the door, and retrieved a rope. With sure, practiced movements he tied a noose and threw the opposite end over a rafter in the center of the room.

Grasping both ends, he leaned on it, testing its strength.

Her stomach knotted, and she began to tremble. The sight of the noose threatened to shatter her fragile control, and she began to pray that Roman had revived.

Please God, let Roman wake and alert Marcus or the constable.

But would Marcus himself come for her?

Yes, he would. Not because he loved her, but because he had sworn to protect her. He was a man of honor who took his promises and his duty seriously.

She forced herself to take deep breaths. She must not allow panic to overtake her senses and steal her logic. She could not rely on others to arrive in time, but had to use her wits to survive Benning's murderous plans.

Turning to Horatio Kulzer, she glared up at him with burning, reproachful eyes. "You're nothing more than his lordship's newest hired lackey. He'll use you to do his dirty work, and when you finish his task, he'll not pay you. When you complain, he'll deal with you, just like your predecessor Robby Bones." She pointed to the old pool of blood on the wooden floor beside her. "This is where

Bones bled out, killed by Bow Street after his lordship turned him in. I suspect you'll be next."

Harold Benning strode forward and slapped her. Her head snapped back from the unexpected blow and pain seared her jaw. "Shut yer bloody hole."

Horatio Kulzer's eyes narrowed at Benning's display of temper and uncharacteristic gutter talk. "I'm no fool. I don't doubt what she says about old Bones. I want my money up front."

Benning's nostrils flared. "You'll get your blunt after the chit hangs just like we agreed."

"I don't think so," Kulzer said, his voice hardening ruthlessly. "I want it now."

The two men began to argue heatedly, circling each other with menacing expressions.

Isabel took advantage, frantically scanning the cluttered floor for anything that could serve as a weapon. She spotted a shattered glass jar that had been used to hold a cluster of brushes, and she crawled forward until it was within her reach. Most of the brushes were old, their bristles missing, their long, wooden handles splintered. She chose the two largest, one with horsehair bristles, the other with Asiatic. The brushes were intact, but she easily snapped them in half, using her skirts to muffle the sounds while Benning and Kulzer shouted. The ends were jagged, precisely what she wanted.

She looked up at the men, her eyes narrowing on the squat but wiry Kulzer. She knew from firsthand experience of the hardened criminal's strength and speed. Even though Benning could easily overpower her, his paunchy stomach and lavish lifestyle of overindulgence had made him slow.

No, it was Kulzer she had to wound first, and her strikes must be deadly enough to kill or—at the very least—disable him. She was out of time; her survival was in her own hands . . .

The argument came to a sudden stop when Benning relented and, with disgust written on his face, pulled out a wad of banknotes from his inside jacket pocket and threw them down before Kulzer on a scarred worktable. She suspected it was the money Benning had planned to utilize to flee the country rather than pay his immoral associate.

"I held up my end of the bargain," Benning spat. "Now see to the girl. *Exactly* as I described."

Kulzer reached for the money and tucked it into his coat, the pistol he carried visible as he did so. He then turned to her. His pupils dilated as he approached; anticipation and arousal were clearly written on his pinched face.

With startling clarity, she realized he enjoyed killing and received pleasure from the violent act. Her heartbeat throbbed in her ears, and she clutched the makeshift stakes behind her back so tightly her fingers ached.

He reached for her, and she flew at him, stabbing him in the left eye and the side of his neck with all her might.

His bloodcurdling scream pierced her skull like a shot. He went wild, thrashing about like a wounded animal. He knocked a jar off a bookshelf behind her head, and it smashed at her feet in a shower of jagged glass.

She darted around him and ran to the door, ignoring the pain as shards of glass cut through the soft leather soles of her shoes. She heard Benning's shouts and saw the blur of his navy jacket as he ran after her in hot pursuit.

She sprinted down the hall and headed for the stairs. She recalled the dilapidated top step and jumped past it, landing on the next step. She was near the bottom when the entire staircase shook, and a deafening crack rent the air. Glancing sideways, she saw Benning's flailing arms as the faulty top step crumbled beneath his weight.

She reached the ground level and looked back to see a gruesome sight. Harold Benning's legs had fallen through, his chest impaled by a monstrous splintered plank. His head lolled to the side, his eyes wide open, the blue irises sightless in death.

She froze, panic welling in her throat.

Just then, Horatio Kulzer turned the corner, his pistol raised in his hand, aimed at her. Blood streamed down the side of his neck where he had pulled out her makeshift weapon, but the stake in his eye remained.

She screamed as a shot rang out. But instead of the anticipated pain of a bullet ripping through her body, Kulzer collapsed to the ground.

"Isabel!"

She whirled around to see Marcus behind her, a pistol in his hand. His eyes glowed with a savage inner fire, brimming with purpose and urgency.

She flew into his arms, and the world tilted on its axis and spun into darkness.

Chapter 49

"I thought you never fainted, sweetheart."

Isabel lay in drowsy warmth as the masculine voice washed over her.

"Please wake, my love."

The murmured words echoed in her mind, and she knew she must be dreaming. For it was Marcus's voice, filled with reverence and love. She snuggled deeper into the soft bed she lay upon, further beneath a downy coverlet, perfectly content for the dream to continue.

"Isabel."

She wrinkled her nose as her subconscious thoughts surfaced. She fought waking, not wanting the Marcus of her dream to vanish or to face reality. Something ugly had happened. She could not recall exactly what, but she knew it was a cataclysmic event that she did not want to face.

A soft caress cupped her cheek.

She sighed and opened her eyes. Marcus sat in a chair beside her. His handsome face was a mask of concern, his square jaw tense. His curly, jet hair was unruly as if he had run his fingers through it repeatedly in agitation. His dark, earnest eyes brimmed with disquiet as he gazed upon her.

A brief glance at her surroundings told her she was in her bedroom at the town house on St. James's Street.

"You fainted," he said.

She blinked and focused her gaze. "I never faint."

His tight expression relaxed into a smile. "I have been worried sick. You haven't stirred for two hours."

She sat up, and a cold shiver spread over her as memories of recent events rushed back to her in an avalanche. She remembered everything . . .

The studio. The noose. Harold Benning and Horatio Kulzer.

Her feet felt strange, and she flexed them beneath the covers. There was a dull pain, and she realized they were tightly bandaged.

"We had to remove shards of glass. Do they hurt?" he asked, deeply concerned.

"Not badly." She glanced down at her hands folded in her lap, and whispered. "You came for me."

"I was not soon enough. My God, Isabel, please forgive me."

She met his eyes. "You shot Horatio Kulzer and saved me. You more than fulfilled your duty."

He looked aghast. "My duty? Is that why you think I came?"

"You had said—"

"Forget what I said. I've been a fool."

Her heart lurched at the eager look in his eyes. Dare she hope . . .

He cradled her hands in his. "I refuse to allow one more moment to pass without confessing the truth. I love you, Isabel."

"But Simone . . ."

"I swear to you I have no feelings for Simone Winston or any other woman. The moment you crossed the Holloways' ballroom and boldly asked me to dance, I began to fall under your spell."

Tears welled in her eyes. "Then why did you ask me to leave?"

"I used the threat to your life as an excuse to bury my feelings, and I foolishly focused on vengeance against an unknown enemy. But the truth was I feared to love, to open my heart. When I had learned you were abducted, I nearly lost my mind and the truth in my heart became clear. You are a rare treasure, the only woman who has truly loved me despite my past and has given me hope for the future."

Raising her hands, he placed a heated kiss on each palm. "I want you as my *real* wife, Isabel. I *need* you."

Crying out with joy, she embraced him, and his arms immediately tightened around her. "I have waited forever to hear you speak those words, Marcus. I have adored you since childhood, and when I believed you did not want me, my heart was shattered."

He kissed her eyes, the tip of her nose, and then her lips. His kiss lingered, savoring the moment like velvet warmth against her lips.

Pulling back, he looked in her eyes. "My heart's desire is for you to stay with me forever. But I'll not force you to give up your lifelong dream of studying art in Paris."

"Oh, Marcus. Paris stopped being my dream the night we made love in your library."

"I have many contacts in the art world. I shall arrange to have the best watercolor instructor at the Royal Academy tutor you himself. I would never discourage you from pursuing your artistic endeavors," he vowed.

She thought of her father, Lord Walling, and her past suitors. All had frowned upon a woman studying anything other than how to be a proper wife and hostess. She had known all along that Marcus Hawksley had always been special, and her heart raced at his thoughtfulness.

Her lips trembled with the need to smile. "I'm certain that Roman will be pleased if I stay in London."

"Roman?"

"Yes. If I were to leave, Charlotte would follow and your brother would be quite upset."

He grinned. "He does fancy her."

"He'll have to woo her. From what I witnessed, she'll not make it easy," she said.

"Roman likes a challenge."

A troubling thought occurred to her. "What will we tell Charlotte about her stepfather?"

"A constable from Bow Street, accompanied by Investigator Harrison, has notified Charlotte and Leticia Benning of Harold Benning's demise. They were told it was an accident," he said.

"An accident?"

Marcus nodded. "Bow Street concluded that Benning was acquiring art in the artists' district and fell through a faulty step. Investigator Harrison did not enlighten them as to Benning's shady background. Instead, Harrison moved Horatio Kulzer's body to the back alley, where the constable found the corpse. Kulzer was a well-known thug wanted for numerous crimes, and the authorities assumed he was killed in a separate incident."

"I have my doubts that Charlotte will believe such a tale about her stepfather, and as my best friend, I feel compelled to tell her the truth. But does Leticia believe the story?" she asked.

"From what I was told, both women thought Harold Benning was having an affair and that he planned on leaving them. Neither shed a tear when they were told of his death."

He studied her thoughtfully for a moment, his eyes bathing her in admiration. "Isabel, do you feel confident about giving up Paris?"

"Marcus Hawksley, you *are* a fool." Rising on her knees, she reached for the top button of his shirt. "Who needs Paris when I have the perfect male model before me begging to be painted?"

He laughed and caught her roaming hands in his. "Be certain, my temptress. Once you commit to me, I shall never let you go."

She shot him a saucy look. "Certain about not going to Paris or about painting you?"

"Both."

"Auntie Lil will survive without me. Perhaps we can visit her one day. As for you," she drawled as she unbuttoned more of his shirt, "it will take me years of practice to capture you just right."

AUTHOR'S NOTE

Thomas Gainsborough was a British painter who was born in 1727 in the village of Sudbury, in Suffolk County. He was known as a portrait painter, and during the height of his career, he was commissioned by important politicians, nobility, and royalty alike to paint their portraits. One of his most famous is *The Blue Boy*. Even though he was renowned for his portraits, Gainsborough's true love was to paint landscapes of simple country life and of the peasants who lived on the land. In 1781, he exhibited a set of coastal scenes. One of those paintings was the *Seashore with Fishermen*, also known as the *Seashore with Fisherman and Boat Setting Out*, which is mentioned in this book. Of course, the painting was never stolen, and I used literary license when I wove the theft of the painting into my book. Gainsborough died in 1788 in London of cancer.

I have also mentioned other famous artists and their works, all of whom I greatly admire and have included in my story. I hope you enjoy reading my book as much as I have enjoyed writing it.